Intro

Milly Johnson
North of England correspondent

The *L* monster I cannot control. Think a Pit Bull on a piece of cotton. But one I love dearly. I only ever use it in my novels when it has a purpose, not gratuitously which is why if it isn't warranted, I can't put it in. But people, apparently, look forward to it so much that I've had reviews that have said, 'I considered taking a star off because there was no *Daily Trumpet* in this book'. Gulp. They didn't, but – see what I mean. The lunatic is taking over the asylum.

In case you were wondering, the idea for it came from the *K----- News*, a newspaper I used to read every Friday when I lived near Keighley (whoops – spilled-secret alert). I went out with a cricketer and every Friday in the King's Arms in Haworth, the team would gather and read out the reportage of the previous week's match hoping for a mention of their sporty acumen. But more often than not, they got something wrong. A Frank became a Fred, someone's twenty-three-year old age was inflated to eighty-three and I noticed that over time they were looking out for the bloops more than they were the flattery. This lodged in my brain for twenty years, until it was needed. Until I wrote *The Teashop on the Corner* and needed a device to carry information. And the *Daily Trumpet* was born and I only ever intended to use it for one book. But we all have those best intentions... And I needed its services again. And again. Not just for bloops but, in *The Queen of Wishful Thinking*, for what a sympathetic editor might do who had a duty to report a story but who also had a heart. I do have a column in our local rag *The Barnsley Chronicle* and the editor there is a good bloke and has helped me so much with newspaper background. It's a privately owned paper, like the *Trumpet*, but there the similarities end. Sir Basil Stamper is not based on anyone, he was formed in my imagination. The *Chron* is run properly, not as a lucrative joke.

In *My One True North* I ended up bringing in the *Daily Trumpet* offices and more interaction with the long-suffering editor Alan Robertson. And by the time *The Happiest Ever After* came out South Yorkshire's favourite newspaper was covering the whole of Yorkshire. A few books down the line and they'll be national, international, interplanetary. I only wish I were as successful.

I had stores of bloops waiting to be utilised, so when people said 'You should write a book of them' I thought, that might be quite a good idea.

It was my pal and fellow novelist Jill Mansell's idea to get people to cough up to be mentioned in a *Daily Trumpet* entry for charity (yorkshirecatrescue.org in case you were wondering). I couldn't believe how

Jill Mansell.

many people queued up to be humiliated. The coffers of the charity are fuller by a few grand thanks to Jill's idea. Please feel free to visit their website and their online shop. There are so many cats out there needing help and any contribution, donation etc you can spare is most gratefully received and NOT spent on swanky office furniture or fat cat salaries (excuse the pun). I got my first cat from them nearly forty years ago to keep the dog company when they were just a one-man band as Haworth Cat Rescue and they've grown and fattened out over the years, though haven't we all.

So here we are with a dedicated book of gaffes and all the people who kindly bought entries for themselves, relatives, in someone's memory get a big thank you in the back. Both the charity and myself are very grateful.

And finally, a word of advice: it might be a bit much to read it all in one fell swoop, like over-stuffing yourself with Black Forest Gateau. So leave the book in the loo and dip into it when you are in for a long sit, to pass some time. As well as whatever else you are in there to pass.

And feel free to leave a nice review on Amazon (short as you like) for this little charity book, they really do help with things.

Don't be a tw*t who leaves a one-star review because you've had a bad day. The Karma fairy is watching and you might miss out on a lottery win.

Thank you for buying. That's a kind thing to do because we need more of that in this weird, scary world of today. Never mistake the gentleness of kindness for a lesser quality.

Hope you enjoy, folks!

Lilly Johnson x

Here is the News...

HELMSEY CHURCH was packed to the gills for the Easter service last weekend where the fripperies of Easter were very much celebrated. The ladies of the parish wore their best homemade bonnets, children brought their toy rabbits with them to place around the altar, then the Reverend Paul Bennett laid an egg in the middle of them.

A WOMAN who has lived in her house for forty years has made ten separate complaints about the amount of dog muck on her local street without success and says she is worried that the families likely to be guilty are too rough for the council to deal with. Frances Copeland of School Street, Guiseley, who does not wish to be identified, told the *Trumpet* that 'Enough is enough and it has to stop.' Mrs Copeland has supplied her name and address to the *Trumpet* but we choose to respect her anonymity.

Mrs Copeland fingers recent suspect.

Party for One of World's Longest Married Couple

A SURPRISE party is planned for married couple John and Christine Lockwood of Beck Hole, Cayton Bay. Jane and Chris are celebrating their Oak anniversary – 80 glorious years. The party will be held in the back room of their local pub The Furry Ear. The *Trumpet* offers Mr and Mrs Lickwood huge commiserations for being married to each other for so long.

WIFE TELLS MAN TO GET HIS CHOPPER OUT

RALEIGH enthusiast Wayne Harwell has been told by his wife Ramona that she is sick of the sight of his chopper in the house. 'There were only 750 of the special editions made and it is too valuable to keep in a garage,' Wayne told the *Trumpet*. 'So do I keep my old bike or the Chopper? It should be an easy decision to make but it really isn't.'

CENTENARIAN HAS CAKE MADE BY BAKE OFF WINNER

CENTURION Julia Casker had a special gift from one of the contestants on her favourite programme. Hugh Martin, winner of last year's Back Off competition sent Julia a giant two-foot square cake with her full-length photo printed on the top icing to share with her family at the party they had arranged for her. Mrs Caesar told the *Trumpet*, 'It was a beautiful cake, my favourite flavour vanilla sponge, jam and cream.' Her son David said, 'We ate the lot apart from a bit in the middle because no one felt comfortable eating mum's crotch'. Julius also got a card from King Charles II.

RENOWNED LECTURER ON VE DAY AT BULMER VILLAGE HALL

Norbert 'Nobby' Clifford delivered a lecture to a packed Bulmer Village Hall on VD day about his childhood memories of the 1940s, in particular when he was ejaculated during the war. Rather than paint a dismal picture, Nobby said that these days were among the happiest of his life. He recalled being spirited away from the city to the countryside where he saw ghosts, pigs and sheep for the first time and which gave him such a love of farms that he became a farmer himself. When Nobby retired, he set up the Young Farters charity to encourage young people to follow a similar career path and a raffle on the night raised £643 for it.

Archive photo of newly emasculated children in Devon.

9

SPORTY ALAN HAS CHANGE OF CAREER IN KOREA

MALTON sportsman Alan Saunders from Malton will soon be exchanging his former life of an endurance runner to be a runner in the production crew of South Korean hit programme Squid Game. Once upon a time Alana, who has been sporty since a young age, ran marathons and played racket games and is an accomplished squash player, so he's going to find a total change of pace going forward when he swaps Malton for Seoul. Alas for Alan, there are only high-speed trains in the country which will scupper his downtime pursuit of getting steamed on old locomotives.

ANYONE WANT FLOORING?

A DECKING firm in Northallerton has been inundated with requests to commit violence after their sales advert appeared in the *Daily Trumpet*. MD Andrew Fay of Fay's Flooring told us, 'When we put in our ad: If you know anyone that needs decking, give us a call and we'll sort them out, we was referring to wooden decking not a thumping. We aren't hitmen. However, three of those initial enquiries have converted to sales so we are hoping a nice new garden feature will take the edge off their anger.'

THREE STRIKES AND OUT FOR JOKER GROOM

NEWLYWED BRIDE Sharon Pickersgill left her new husband Christopher less than a day after her nuptials when his latest 'joke' went terribly wrong. 'I was all set for a honeymoon in New York,' Sharon told the *Trumpet*. 'And instead the b***tard took me to Newark. He thought it would be funny.' It was not the first time practical joker Chris had played this trick. 'We were going to celebrate our engagement in Turkey, but he'd got us a hotel in Torquay. It rained for the full week and I didn't get to wear one of my bikinis. And for my twenty-fifth birthday I thought he was taking me to Boston, Massachusetts, not effing Boston Lincolnshire. It was crap. I said if he ever did anything like this again, that would be it. And he did. So he can f*** off to f***ing Nottinghamshire by his f***ing self,' said an irate Sharon, who the *Trumpet* believes is now drowning her sorrows on a last-minute booking with her sisters in Ronda, Spain – not Rhondda in Wales.

GREAT BIG FAT LOSER BARBARA – AND IT'S ALL DOWN TO BOOZE

BARBARA SMITH from Pudsey is seven stone lighter this year than she was at the same time last year and it's all down to alcohol. 'I owe my new body to the gin,' she said proudly to us. In the past Barbara had tried calorie-counting and various fad diets but says only with that has she had any success. 'I am happy to talk to anyone who wishes to follow my regime who hasn't been able to shift the flab any other way as I know what it's like,' offered Barbara.

An old gin palace

New Shop on the High Street and the Owner Promises an Opening Like no Other

A WARM WELCOME IS extended to all for the opening of Maria York's new shop on Wetherby High Street this Saturday. There will be cake and balloons for children, and for the grown-ups there will be boobs as far as the eye can see. There will be a celebrity cutting the ribbon in the shape of influencer Katie Price, who has been Mrs Norks friend since school.

VISITING CELEB COMES TO CLEETHORPES

GLAMOROUS celebrity personality Carol Kingsford came to Cleethorpes last week to open up a new children's centre bringing her own children Pan, Demented, Collapso and Herpes with her. Ms Kingsford has Grease down one side of her hence why her children are all named after classical deities.

MORLEY WOMAN GIVES BIRTH ON 21ST BIRTHDAY

MORLEY WOMAN Kelly Methley didn't know she was having a baby until her labour pains started as she was doing the Lambada on the dance floor, celebrating her 21st birthday with friends and family. Kelly gave birth to a whopping nine pounds four-ounce daughter, Krystal. Father Barry who took Kelly to hospital in his meat delivery van had to be treated for shock when he arrived in A & E. 'To be honest, our Kelly is such a big unit that it was no wonder none of us noticed including her. We just thought she'd been caning the chips recently,' said the proud grandfather.

CHARITY LUNCH GOES DOWN A BOMB

THE LORD LOW SHERIFF hosted a magnificent feast in aid of charity last Friday in Ripon for the Duck and Duchess of Highfield in the form of a 'grazing table' buffet. The fare was supplied by Dronfield's Butchers. Dronfield's were keen to parade their veterinarian offering and this was an ideal opportunity to showcase their plant-based sausage rolls and pasties to the Duke and Duckling who have been virgins since the turn of the century. Proceeds from the evening went to aid the explosion of landmines.

AN ART DECO ball that was held in Furlongs Hotel last week in Hatfield, Doncaster to raise funds to buy disadvantaged kids raised £10.50. The mayor Simon Jones dressed as a spiv and his wife, councillor Angela Jones, went as a slapper, a persona to which seemed born said their fellow guests.

LOVE RAT STEALS PENSIONER'S SAVINGS

MAVIS Dingle from Goldthorpe has lost a chunk of her life savings after almost marrying a man she met on holiday. Mavis, 87, told the *Trumpet*, 'I met Tony on a beautiful Mediterranean beach and he had all the gab. He told me I looked no older than thirty and he was so tall and good-looking, even though I wouldn't normally have found someone so much younger appealing, I was putty in his hands. I thought he loved me for me,' said Mavis tearfully, clutching a photo of Tony, 22, who she would have married next month had she not been contacted by another of Tony's conquests who warned her off. 'Tony said that he didn't like slim young women but someone natural and older and he had a thing for white bubble perms. I handed over two thousand pounds so he could put a deposit on a house for us.' Mavis told us that equated to her paying a gigolo twenty pounds for every time they had sex in the two-week courtship period they were together.

13

For the whole of August, Leeds Museum of Art has an exhibition by artist Dick Van Dyke.

Tickets are free to see it.

SUTTON-in-Craven millionaire Andrew Peters-Jones knows what he is talking about where money is concerned because his father and grandfather were a pair of bankers. 'My father Rathbone, who was a wizard on the stocks and shares markets, initiated me into his world when I was a little boy and taught me the most important word in his world: Incest. He taught me what to do and where to put my moolah for optimum effect as his father had taught him.' But when asked by the *Trumpet* to elaborate on the secrets of his father's dealings, Andrew tapped his nose and said with a wry smile, 'We keep that sort of info firmly in the family.'

MOTHER AND DAUGHTER IN BATTLE FOR CUP

Mother and daughter bakers Iris and Deborah Heeley are in direct competition with each other in this year's Hemsworth Cakey-Bakey, an annual event where the winner walks off with five hundred pounds and a rose bowl. Iris is entering her famous Iris's Lemon Dribble cake, named after herself. And Deborah is entering her much-acclaimed Fat Nasty Slob Cake, named after her husband.

A HONLEY man Stanley Albert Godwin Pertwee has been arrested for ten thousand indecent images on his computer. On pages 4,5,6,7 our reporter Dan Jones has more.

Dianne Invites Everyone to View her Bra and Pants

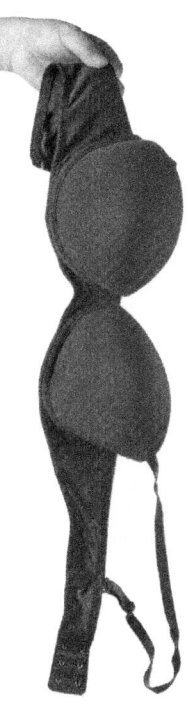

Dianne Brassiere doing what she does best.

A new shop will be coming to Earby town centre next week in the shape of a lingerie shop "Di's Brassiere" and, by coincidence, owned by a woman whose name was made for such a business.

It has been a long-time dream of Dianne Brazier to own her own establishment. As she told the *Trumpet*, 'I just want to see lots of people queuing at my drawers ready to have a good time. I'll be looking after all my punters and there will be plenty of fun and laughter as soon as they're inside them.'

There will be a special offer on the first day for new punters and with every giant pizza you get two pants of lager. Her drawers open 12pm Saturday and will stay open until midnight.

MURDER
COMES TO CUSWORTH

LOCAL SCRIPTWRITER Donald Christie has penned a play in the style of his heroine Agatha Christie (no relation) and tickets are now on sale for its five-night run. Donald told the *Trumpet* that he is very proud of 'the twist' and no one will guess whodunnit.

Prop as used by ex-Sooty Show actress, Caroline Bickerstaffe.

Local actors will be starring in the roles including ex-Casualty extra Peter Leonard, who will be playing the victim Midge Owen and Caroline Bickerstaffe, who has appeared on the Sooty Show, Emmerdale and Doctors will be playing Lady Olga, the murderer.

Sally Wows WI with her Tales of Mr Kipling

HISTORIAN Mrs Sally Furness held the ladies of Birdwell Ladies Croup in the palm of her hands with a talk about Mr Kipling and his cakes last week. Who knew that Mr Kipling found his inspiration for his Battenburg Slices, Apple Pies and French Fondant Fancies in the jungle? Sally got a standing ovation for riveting everyone and there was were many questions put to her for more info over the post-talk tea and buns.

COOKERY COURSE — MASSIVE TURNOUT FOR WRONG REASON

Janice Jones pictured in her cocaine class

AN UNFORTUNATE printing error helped to 'break the internet' when Janine Jones advertised her cookery class. 'I knew something had gone wrong because I thought I'd struggle to fill the fifteen places but the spaces were filled in minutes and there was a waiting list of over seventy-five' said Janine. 'The autocorrect had altered Cooking with Janine to Cocaine with Janine. I think a lot of people were disappointed but only two left early, the rest were sent home with a lovely homemade lasagne and space cakes for dessert.'

When beauty therapist Hannah McDonald introduced a new service to her body spa she didn't expect to have to set on extra staff to deal with the increase in trade. All because she had the 'novel' idea of encouraging men to read more love stories by giving them a free romantic tome when they booked a speciality 'Happy Ending' massage treatment. 'Reading is great for mental health and here at our centre we treat the mind as well as the body which is why I thought it would be a good idea to guarantee our gentlemen a happy ending as a finale to their session. There has been a fantastic response to my advert. I can't believe how popular it has been. It seems to have worked for everyone as my staff are declaring record tips for delivering the extras and my gents have all left the building with a smile on their face as well as a book in their hand.'

FIRE PUTS PAID TO AUTHOR'S FLAMING BOOK SIGNING

DUE TO a fire in the High Street Bookshop local author RW Cobley has had to cancel his book launch set for Thursday. Anyone now wanting a singed copy of his 'The Up and Downside of Flame', a factual book about the up and downside of fame, will have to get them online from his website.

REVEREND ROB DREW AND VICKY DREW

HORNSEA REVEREND Rob Drew and his good lady wife Vicky put on a wonderful spread for the visiting Bishop of Skipton at a private gathering last week. Rob said it was a delight to host him and members of the orgy were glad that he could stay and join them for a *post coitum* glass of Vicky's home-made wine. Vicky, a talented amateur chef, served up a menu of prawn cocktails, Toad in the Hole followed by Vicky's speciality stocky toffee pudding.

VISITING WWII GUEST SPEAKER AT WOMEN'S FEDERATION ANNUAL LUNCH

Bob Hoskins pictured with her World War II chair
from the second world war.

There was a rousing reception for WWII veteran Bren Hosking visiting from the Women's Institute Wiltshire Federation last week in the grand hall of York University. Bren brought with her a chair from the war which was a precious momento of those years. As well as an inspirational talk by Ben, the women were treated to a meal of pea soap, roast chicken, apple crumble and then coffee with pinafores.

FISHMONGER Deirdre Calloway is retiring from her stall on Knaresborough market and going to live in Cornwall where she spent her youth. 'I used to go and catch crabs from Cornish fishermen,' she told the *Trumpet* gleefully. 'Those where the days'. Her son Trevor will be taking over the business when his mother finishes her last shit at Christmas.

||||||||||||||||||||||||||||||||||||||||||||||||||||||||||||||||||||||||||||||||||||||||||||||||

NEW BUSINESS FOR CHILDREN HITTING QUEENSBURY

CARA CRONK has been in the baby business since the 1970s and she's not stopping yet. As a self-proclaimed dyed-in-the-wool Death Mother Cara told the *Trumpet* she hanged her first baby when she was only eleven – her little sister. 'I never looked back after that,' she said. 'I knew I'd found my happy place in life.' She has self-financed her car crash of a business as the bank weren't keen to take a risk but she's raking in the cash as, she says, so many tired parents need her services these days. 'I can do this job in my sleep. It's like money for old rope.'

||||||||||||||||||||||||||||||||||||||||||||||||||||||||||||||||||||||||||||||||||||||||||||||||

Schoolchildren at Millhouse Green Primary welcomed 103 year old Lucy Welbeck to talk to her about life many years ago. Lucy entertained them with stories about her family, including her dad 'Jammy Jones' so-called because he was renowned for being lucky. 'My

School photo taken at Millhouse over 100 years ago. Sadly, Lucy was absent due to a dose of mumps at time. The son of the rag and bone man is 3rd from the left on the front row.

father was very famous in these parts for being lucky in love, lucky at cards, lucky with the horses, lucky with everything,' Lucy told a delighted young crowd. 'Alas I never met him as he died at twenty-three after being knocked down by a rag-and-bone man's horse just before I was born.'

**What a big load of bull!
Violent Terrible in Angler's field.**

NOLAN SISTER'S TERRY-BULL CHANGE OF LIFE

EX-NOLAN SISTER Angela Nolan has left behind a life touring and mixing with celebs for a calmer existence on the farm. Angela now tinkers with her tractor, mucks out the chickens and cows from whom she collects eggs and hangs out, not with famous stars like Robbie Williams and the Pet Shop Boys as she once did, but with her prize-winning bull Terrible. 'He's a very big boy and gores me all the time when I'm in his field,' Angela tells the *Trumpet*. A big change to acclimatise to indeed, Angela!

FASHION SHOW FOR LARGER LADIES

CHRISTA PEAKE of Christa's Gowns is having a fashion show on Thursday night at 7pm in the upper room of The Three Lumps in Goldthorpe for ladies with fuller figures. Attendees will be treated to models strutting down a catwalk showing off bridal wear, cruise attire and fux fur coats, as Christa is a supporter of PETA. 'The quality of fake furs these days is so good that no one needs to kill a dead animal to wear the real stuff,' Christa told the *Trumpet*. Tickets are £5 and include a glass of fizz upon arrival, nibbles and quality smack.

NEIGHBOUR'S PLUMS ALWAYS MAKE GLAD GLAD

Gladys 'Glad' Penn from Haxby romped home with the Jam Maker of the Year title for her damson preserve at the village fair and she couldn't be gladder about it. The secret of her success, she says, is putting her next-door-neighbour's plums in the mix. 'Sam's damsons are famous in the village,' said Gladys. 'I don't know what his secret is because no other gardener I know has such big, juicy plums. Though, he does say he talks to them while stroking them and I know he does because I've seen him do that through the fence when he thinks no one is looking.' Gladys won £100 and a trophy and says she is splitting the prize money with Samson next door.

Gladys cups her neighbour's plums.

NEW MUM'S GROUP TO START IN JACQUI'S CAFÉ

Jocky Wilson with one of her Tits and Bums ladies.

CAFÉ OWNER Jacqui Watson will be holding weekly Tits and Bums meetings in her JW's tearoom in Mexborough starting this Friday 11am. Jaqcqui said, 'It's a way of bringing people together with shared interests' she said and hopes it will be resounding success.

SHARON LOOKS FORWARD TO ANOTHER SUCCESSFUL MEET UP AND 'MINGLE'

THERE will be yet another social gathering at the Three Swans on Pond Lane, Pontefract this Friday at 6pm. Event organiser Sharon Maw was delighted with the turnout for the last one. 'It was a great success although that was probably because the *Trumpet* printed that it was 'a meet up and minge' event. We aren't complaining because most of the people who turned up stayed anyway and our charity raffle raised over £900'.

PAT'S ST PAT'S SHOW IS A SELL OUT

SEASONED singer and raconteur Pat Harris's new show was a near sell out within days of the tickets going on sale. Pat told the *Trumpet* that she has been a successful staple on the club circuit for many years and owes her career longevity to daily training, cold showers, raw eggs and vigorous sex. Said Pat 'It has become a standard joke that people in our profession shouldn't have intimate relations before our main event, but I find rogering my partner makes the blood flow to where it needs to.' Pat will be appearing at Pocklington Theatre on St Patrick's Day with a specially curated pick of gaelic and Irish classics.

A MATCH MADE IN HEAVEN

Husband and wife Boris Canford and his wife Maisie make the perfect duo as he is an award-winning gardener and she has won prizes for her pickles and chutneys. So many in fact, they've had to buy a new shelf for their trophies. 'Boris grows the produce, brings it into the kitchen and leaves me to it,' said Maisie. 'I've been tickling his onions since before we were married. In fact I think it was my skills in that department that persuaded him to propose.' Boris could only agree, but conceded he thought he had the better half of the deal.

MARY IS BIG DOWN UNDER

HUDDERSFIELD author Mary Aberline is enjoying UK success with her first book Toothy the Loan Shark a children's book, but even bigger success in her homeland of Australia, where she has sold twenty copies. 'I never thought I'd be this successful,' said Mary. 'It's made me want to start on the next one. Sharks are obviously the way to go.'

Loyal dog poised to be entered into the competition.

AT THE ILKLEY summer dog show, breeding expert Joseph Grinter will once again be hoping his three working spaniels repeat their previous successes. 'I've been entering my dogs for a decade and apart from one year they've always come first,' said Mr Grunter. 'And for anyone who says it's cruel, it's not. They love it as much as I do.'

The Grotto is Finally open for Children

THE MEN'S underwear department at Sloan's department store, Fox Valley has been transformed into a grotty for Christmas and is finally open following a leak in the ceiling. Satan will be there waiting to find out from the children what they want for Christmas from Saturday 3rd December 9am-5pm.

Santa's getting ready. It's hoped thatt his special Christmas package will also encourage more mums to come.

CAROL'S LOOKING FOR LOCAL SWINGERS FOR CHRISTMAS FUN

RETIRED professional singer Carol Dyke is hoping to round up a bunch of amateur swingers for fun Christmas evenings. Says Carol, 87, 'I should be past it at my age but the urge always comes upon me around September and I just want to get a group of like-minded people together to perform. We've done it every Christmas and we go down well. I always say that we touch people in places they didn't know they could be touched. So here we are once more. Even if you don't think you're very good at it, do try and come. We'll be at St Basil the Blessed, Heckmondwike 7-8pm every Friday from now until Christmas. We will be visiting lots of care homes in December and asking the guests if they'd like to join in with us.'

MAYOR MEETS MAIR AND HAS A MARE OF A DAY

PLUCKY pensioner Mair Howe met local Mayor Dr Tim Watt on Tuesday to be presented with the Freedom of the Town award after bravely tackling a shoplifter in her knitting shop, but the medal had the wrong spelling on it and Mary had an allergic reaction to the prawn cocktail sandwiches which had been put out on the buffet. Luckily Dr Who was once a GP and knew what to do. The council are making sure that Mrs Where has her proper day soon and it isn't a mair next time.

FOLLOWING the phenomenenmal success of the Horsham Theatre Group's Christmas panto – Beauty and the Breast, director Billy Whittle is intending to bring three more popular musicals to the town next year starting with Ryvita, the story of the life of Eva Peroni.

CRICKET UMPIRE IS TOUCHED BY MANY PEOPLE

ON Friday in Park Lane Social Club, over a hundred sports lovers turned out to say a fond farewell to retiring umpire Billy Buttle. Billy had been an emperor for over fifty years but decided to call it a day after his recent lip replacement operation. A three-course dinner was followed by friends and family ascending the stage to deliver their testicles which moved Mr Buttle to tears.

50+ and out! Billy was bowled over by all the generous massages.

Jump Woman's Leap Day Surprise Ends In Skip

A WOMAN from Jump proposed to her boyfriend at a football match never expecting that at the same time as she produced the ring, he confessed he had been seeing another woman.

Sharon Hopwood had arranged for the words 'Will You Marry Me Lee Price' to appear on a massive screen at half-time but just before they did, he turned to Sharon and said that he had been seeing another woman and was moving into her house which is also in Hop. A tearful Sharon said that she had been waiting months for jump year to come so she could propose, as tradition allows, on Feb 29th, Leap Day.

'I never suspected a thing,' she said. 'He met her while he was bouncing on the doors of a nightclub and she lives around the corner from me so I'll see them all the time. The crowd cheered when the words came up and I had to leave really quickly because I was so embarrassed. I threw the ring in a skip on the way home.'

Leap Price was unavailable for comment.

BILLY'S FINALLY FINISHED WITH HIS LOLLIPOP

LOLLIPOP LADY Billy Longcar of Higham is handing over his lollipop to a suckcessor after shoving it up children for forty years. Billy has worked at various schools in Barnsley but most recently at Lock Street Primary.

Headmaster Veruca Salt from the school said that everyone loves Willy Longcar and it has been a privilege to know him. A gloop of schoolchildren presented Mr Wonka with a leather rucksack as he intends to do a lot of biting in his retirement.

JEANETTE GASCOYNE

JEANETTE Gascoyne needs no introduction to those into ball sports. Who can forget when Vinnie Jones grabbed the famous Gascoyne groin or them getting a yellow card and crying in the semi-final against Germany. What a sight it still is watching Gascoyne dribbling on the TV. It is therefore tragic that Gascoyne is so drawn to the demon drink.

DEPUTY Council Leader of Bridlington, Tommy Hurd said that, during the pandemic period, he never once missed crapping loudly on his doorstep for doctors and nurses. 'All the street was out doing the same,' said Mr Turd. 'It was important we conveyed what we thought about the NHS.'

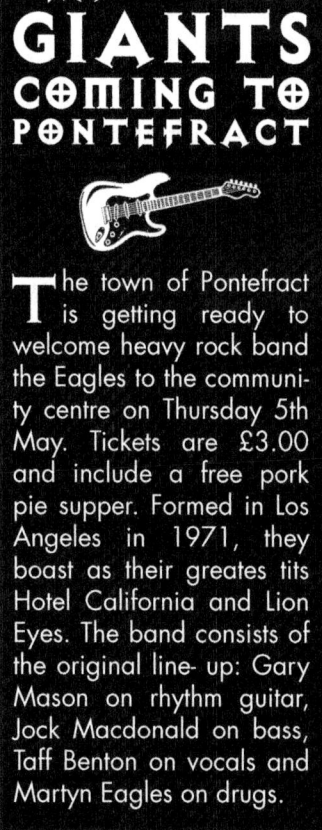

The town of Pontefract is getting ready to welcome heavy rock band the Eagles to the community centre on Thursday 5th May. Tickets are £3.00 and include a free pork pie supper. Formed in Los Angeles in 1971, they boast as their greates tits Hotel California and Lion Eyes. The band consists of the original line-up: Gary Mason on rhythm guitar, Jock Macdonald on bass, Taff Benton on vocals and Martyn Eagles on drugs.

SOME APOLOGIES

WE DO sincerely apologise to Mrs Rose Darrowby, winner of the East Yorkshire Gardening competition, for printing that when she proudly showed off her brazilian to the judges, she knew that's what had swung it for her to get first place. This should have read that she showed off her pavilion. The judges all agreed that Mrs Darrowby's cute brazilian was a truly magnificent thing, and the perfect size to display in a back garden in Bridlington.

PLEASE NOTE that in the up and coming Amateur Operatics programme, Jennifer Williams will be playing Tosca, not Tosser as we mistakenly wrote in the arts supplement at the weekend.

APOLOGY — BERYL RIGBY IS NOT AN NYMPHOMANIAC

THE *Trumpet* wholeheartedly says sorry to Beryl Rigby for referring to her as a nymphomaniac last week. The story was about Beryl embracing the technological world of the internet and running classes for silver and golden surfers. We should have said she was a kleptomanic and apologise most profusely for the maligning.

IN MONDAY'S Focus on Politics pull-out, we reported that idle Councillor Sandra Wagstaffe was admitted to hospital suffering from an embarrassing case of A cups after they had drawn unnecessary attention in a planning meeting, despite her doing her best to cover them up. This should have read that she had an embarrassing case of hiccups.

LESLEY BOOTH AND TRACY BURDETT

WE APOLOGISE to Lesley Booth and Tracey Burdett for an article about the opening of their new craft shop which we inaccurately described as a crap shop. 'Tracey and I have been pals for many years and there is nothing we wanted less than to open up a shop together catering for dedicated crafters,' said Tracey when our reporter visited to check out thes wanky new store. Lesley said, 'Lesley and I are booth passionate about artisan goods and wanted to give our customers a one-slop shop for everything they might need for their hobbies'. Boooth and Burnett is situated on Denby Dale High Street and is open Tues-Shat 9am-25pm.

CLARE JARVIS

APOLOGIES to Ms Clare Jarvis who did not, as reported, win a talent competition with a Maradona impersonation but as Madonna. She wowed the crowd at Bradfield central hall last week singing like a virgin, Ray of Light and Beautiful Strangler.

Like a Virgin: despite being in her late 60s, the real Madonna shows that she still has that unique style that catapulted her to fame.

WE inadvertently reported that treasurer to the Normanton council Keith Shuttleworth had a self-defecating sense of humour when we meant that his humour was self-deprecating. We apologise to Mr Shittleworth for this error.

IN our Feature on Farming last month, we referred to Trevor Potten from Sneaton as an horrible farmer. We meant that he was an arable farmer and apologise for any confusion. We hope that dinner for two in his local hostelry on us will smooth out any bad feeling between Mr Rotten and ourselves.

PLEASE NOTE that Selby florist Mrs Susan Pierrepont did not work in an escort agency before she bought her shop but in an estate agency. We have made a small contribution to her affiliated charity SLAG (Selby Teenage Action Group) which supports the youth in her hometown.

WE HEARTILY apologise for an item reported on last week about Northallerton vicar Darryl Booth and his wife Mrs Booth's afternoon tea to celebrate the King's birthday. This was wrongly advertised as a Vicar and Tarts event and not Vicar and Cake. We apologise to those who had turned up in fancy dress interpreting our words as a dress code.

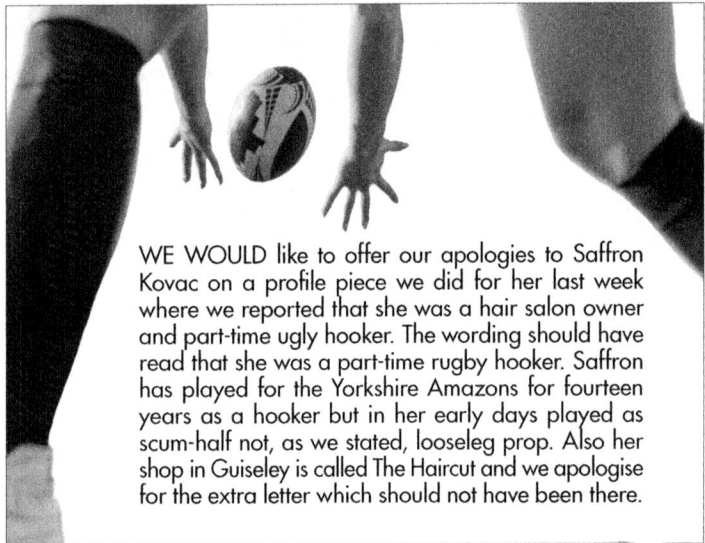

WE WOULD like to offer our apologies to Saffron Kovac on a profile piece we did for her last week where we reported that she was a hair salon owner and part-time ugly hooker. The wording should have read that she was a part-time rugby hooker. Saffron has played for the Yorkshire Amazons for fourteen years as a hooker but in her early days played as scum-half not, as we stated, looseleg prop. Also her shop in Guiseley is called The Haircut and we apologise for the extra letter which should not have been there.

PLEASE do note that an advert advertising Michelle Pierce's aromatherapy business had unfortunate wording. Michelle can travel to your home to restore you with her essential oils and not restore one with her essential holes. We apologise for any confusion.

WE OFFER our sincerest apology to ex-lollipop Mr Willy Longcar after an article appeared about him last week. Billy intends to do a lot of biking in his retirement and not biting. We also apologise to the headmaster of Lick Street Primary who is called Victor Holt and not Veruca Salt.

*T*HE TRUMPET apologises to amateur magician Damian Linekin of Hickleton after saying that new medication finally helped to get rid of the lemons in his head. We did of course mean, demons. Domaine is now firmly on the road to recovery after a bad case of citrus following his girlfriend leaving him for footballer Gary Lineker who plays in goal for Fruits of the Forest.

Mr. Linkedin presumably now only finds rabbits in his hat, not lemons.

Food Glorious Food

A *Daily Trumpet* lifestyle special

PLEASE NOTE, last Friday's recipe for summer fruit salad should have read, add 200g of lychees and not leeches as was printed.

OAP SPECIAL of July on the Ship and Shovell pub menu is pan-fried carp and not pan-fried crap.

IT'S ALL Greek to Me Geek Restaurant in Horsforth will be having a £12 speciality menu this weekend to celebrate owner Eros's Mouskuri's 50th birthday. Price includes his famous Greek mess and a glass of house wine. Bring this article along for a £2 discount.

LAST FRIDAY'S recipe for spicy bean starter should have said 1/2 oz of chilli flakes and not 12 oz.

THE BLACK Monk in Orton will now be serving bad lunches from 12-3pm. Dinners will be served as usual in the restaurant from 7pm.

PLEASE NOTE that the new ice-cream parlour on Scarborough front is called Gelato and not Gestapo as advertised last week.

THE SOUP we featured on Saturday is not called Leeky Pee soup but Cream of Leak and Pee soup.

THURSDAY DINNER special at the White Lion pub, Staithes: £30 for starter, main, choice from the sweat trolley, coffee and mince to follow.

OAP SPECIAL of August on the Shit and Shovel pub menu is poached pollock and chips and not poached pillock and chips.

THE FOCUS on Mexico recipes what appeared in last weekend's supplement, should have stated: Spicy Fajitas and not Spicy Vajinas. We apologise for any mex up.

O'BURGER in Saltaire introduces our new XL Breakfast Bap. Toasted muffin, egg, hash brown, streaky bacon and TWO sausage panties.

PLEASE NOTE next week we will be publishing a selection of healthy curd dishes for dinners and not healthy turd dishes.

CONFUSION RESULTED from a recipe we printed last week for carb-free crab cakes as it was entitled crab-free carb cakes. The cakes were free of crabs for a Keto-friendly low-crab diet and not free of crabs, of course. We apologise for any cronfusion.

PLEASE NOTE the Victoria Sponge recipe from last week should have said bake for 45 minutes and not 45 hours.

OAP SPECIAL of September on the Ship and Hovel pub menu is John Dory and not John Wilkinson, who is the landlord.

THE RECIPE for eggnog in the Christmas Treat special should have read add a hearty splash of advocaat for a seasonal twist and not avocado.

IN LAST week's top cooking tip: to avoid your eyes running while chopping onions, dip briefly in boiling water – we did of course mean dip the onions in the water and not your eyeballs.

ALL ARE welcome to Reverend Jonas Penn's Vicar's Tea Party, St Mary's church, Ripon. Entrance is free but the ladies of the parish have been busy baking and cakes and scones will be available in exchange for a small feel.

OAP SPECIAL of October on the Skip and Shovell pub menu is a phall fish curry and not a foul fish curry.

LIL'S CAFÉ in Holmfirth is offering a free Caesar salad with every quiche and chips and not a free caesarean as was printed last week. We apologise for the error.

PLEASE NOTE that the low-fat chip recipe in Tuesday's newspaper should have said best cooked in an air-fryer and not best cooked with a hair-dryer.

WE APOLOGISE to Mrs Nora Cryer of Hemsworth for reporting that she had killed her husband, which came as a shock to her spouse who had merely ate a homemade Death by Chocolate birthday cake made for him by her.

APOLOGIES TO Mr Eros Moussaka for miswording that appeared in a recent advert. There will be a £12 speciality menu tomorrow at his It's All Geek to Me restaurant. Price includes his famous Greek meze and a glass of house wine. Bring this article along for a £20 discount.

LOCAL PRIZE-WINNING butchers Terry Stamp and Son are holding a tasting evening at 6pm this Friday. Terry recently won the prestigious Pastry King award at a swanky ceremony in London for his famous steak and kidney pee poe.

PLEASE NOTE that the vegetarian option for the Castleford Tigers annual dinner will be mushroom curry cooked with cauliflower rice and not cauliflower ear.

A HUMOUR error occurred last week in advertising the new menu for Luigi's café in Scarborough. Fellatio Alfredo will not be on the menu, but Fettucine Alfredo will. Café owner Luigi told the *Trumpet* that his bookings had never been as full but now the error has been discovered, there would probably be a few cancellations.

PLEASE NOTE that the Black Monk in Orton will be serving bar lunches and not bad lunches from 12-3pm. Sinners will be served as normal in the restaurant from 7pm.

A COUPLE of errors occurred when advertising the Thursday night special menu for the new Fhucket Thai restaurant in Sandal. It should have said Tom Yum soup and not Tom Thumb. And the Bad Prick Sod curry comes with sticky rice and not stinky rice, as advertised. There will be a free welcoming drunk for early bird diners.

SUNDAE GIRL CHANGE OF OPENING HOURS

OWING TO a complaint about their opening hours, Julie Munday's new ice cream parlour Sundae Girl situated in the market in Brough will now not be open on Sundays. This means that 'Sundae Sunday' when her world-famous sundaes are on a special offer, will now be held on Saturdaes instead. And as Halloween this year is on a Friday, the Wednesday Addams party for girls under 10, will be on Thursday 30th October as there is a private party booked for Friday the 31st. Ms Tuesday told the *Trumpet*, 'It's been a pain having to alter everything thanks to some horrible **** complaining and I hope that no one minds that our Sunday Sundays are now on a Wednesday. Now we have spoke to you, we hope that will be the end of any confusion.'

Wednesday's Sunday.

THE SUNDAY QUIZ – WRONG ANSWERS RECTIFIED

IN THE bible, the wife of Noah was *Naamah* and not *Joan of Ark*

P. J. Proby's most famous hit was *Somewhere* and not *Smack My Bitch Up* which was of course the Prodigy

THE LORD of the Rings was written by *J. R. R. Tolkien* and not *J. R. Hartley*

THE CLUEDO character with a military rank is *Colonel Mustard* and not *Colonel Sanders*

THE NAME of the dish with muffins topped with ham, poached egg and hollandaise sauce is *Eggs Benedict* and not *Benedict Cumberbund*

THE GLEN known as the Rhinestone Cowboy was *Glen Campbell* and not *Glen Fiddich*

THE CHEF known for his Reggae Reggae sauce is *Levi Roots* and not *Levi Jeans*

THE FIRST man to walk on the moon was *Neil Armstrong* not *Louis Armstrong*

THE MOST common blood type is *O* and not *red*

THE LATIN name for the kneecap is the *patella* and not the *paella*

JOAN CRAWFORD and Bette Davis were the two stars of *Whatever Happened to Baby Jane* not *Whatever Happened to the Likely Lads*

THE FILM inspired by Johannes Vermeer's famous painting is *Girl with the Pearl Earring* and not *Girl with the Pearl Necklace*

THE ACTOR playing the role of Rose in Titanic was *Kate Winslet* and not *Ray Winston*

THE ANTI-HERO of Wuthering Heights is *Heathcliff* and not *Cliff Richard*

THE SECOND man on the moon was *Buzz Aldrin* and not *Buzz Lightyear*

VITO CORLEONE in the Godfather was played by *Marlon Brando* and not *Marlon Dingle*

HENRY VIII'S first wife was *Catherine of Argos* not *Catherine the Dragon*

THE BRITISH store famous for its fat-pack furniture, which closed in 2008, is *MFI* and not *MI5*

THE FIRST name of the composer Liszt was *Franz* and not *Schindler*

IT WAS *Randy Crawford* who sang Rainy Night in Georgia and not *Randy Warhol*

DR BRUCE Banner's alter ego is the *Hulk*, not *Hulk Hogan*

THE CAPITAL of Venezuela is *Caracas* and not *Crackers*

THE LARGE area of woodland in Gloucestershire is the *Forest of Dean* and not the *Forest of Gump*

THE PAINTER of the Mona Lisa was *Leonardo da Vinci* and not *Leonardo DiCaprio*

CLAUSTROPHOBIA IS the *fear of small spaces* and not the *fear of Father Christmas*

THE CAPITAL of Australia is *Canberra* and not *Cranberry*

GEORGE ORWELL'S real name was *Eric Blair* and not *Lionel Blair*

CLASSIFIEDS

Tel: 01228

TOMORROW'S SALES TODAY: *NOW*

RS:

0pm

SALES

MORBIDITY SCOOTER. Suitable for very old person or large immobile one who can't walk far.

BRIDAL GOWN, size 16, never been worn. Also groom's three-piece suit. Slight blood stain on neck and missing buttons on shirt.

CONDESCENDING tumble drier. Sort of reliable.

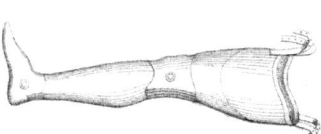

WOODEN LEG (left), tan colour, foot to knee, big toe chipped off. Would suit someone five foot five who has been in the sun.

RED VULVA 1980 (W reg). Been round the block a bit but still in good working order and can go like the clappers when it has to. Roomy interior, one lady owner from new. Test ride recommended.

SMART WHITE LADIES trouser suit size 14. Brown stain on back of trousers and down left leg. Should come out with Vanish.

37

FORTY PACKS of vintage 1970 After Eights. Unopened. In mint condition.

INFLATABLE BOAT. Good as new apart from one slight puncture underneath.

GARAGEFUL OF QUALITY tools, Bosch, DeWalt, Makita, Black and Decker, everything £1. Open house this Saturday 9am start. Everything must be sold before Tuesday when husband gets back from Tenerife with slag girlfriend pretending he's been on a building course in Glasgow.

MINI CLUBMAN

RED with one black replacement passenger door. Dent to front bumper, light to heavy scuffing on back bumper. Front alloy wheel damaged. Slight chip to front windscreen. Bent windscreen wiper. Broken electric window switch. One careful lady owner from new.

GOLDMAN ANTIQUES
For all things old and quirky

SPECIAL CLEARANCE offer on religious dick pics which came from the recently closed St Anne's convent.

SUPPLY OF STUFFED boys for large boisterous puppy to play with as he goes through them quick. Don't mind if they're a bit mucky, he'll destroy them quickly and we need a limitless supply.

GOOD HOME needed for ex-polite dog. Can be trusted with old people (he'll do anything if you feed him pigs liver, toddlers and even tiny babies). Present name: Maniac.

LOST & FOUND

LOST: Large oval locket, full-colour painted front of Marie Antoinette in Barnsley market ladies toilet.

WANTED

HOUSE TO RENT. Dore, Sheffield area for family of six. Must have large garden and either indoor or outdoor poo.

TRANSLATING work for very good translator. I speak many language and fluently write. Rates reasonable priced. You contact me for initial responsing and then we takes it from there. Very come recommended by many.

EDUCATION

STEER CLEAR DRIVING SCHOOL

WANT TO LEARN to drive quickly?

Then come and enrol on one of our crash courses.

Ring Gerald Nutter on 01924 745

SITUATIONS VACANT

BUSY DOCTOR'S SURGERY seeking locust to help with workload Oct-March.

DO YOU have an eye for detail? Is your grammar and punctuation up to scratch? Do you pride yourself in crossing your 'T's and dotting your 'T's? Then apply to be our new proof-reader.

WANTED – reliable cleaner who isn't too bulky to bend and do skirting boards and doesn't pretend to do the bedrooms while she's actually sat on her arse on my bed texting. Also doesn't go half an hour early and says 'I'm done' when paid to do two hours and there are fingermarks all around the light switches which she must have been blind to miss. No time wasters please, I've had enough of those to last a lifetime.

NEEDED accounts manager. Must be over 25 with at least 30 years experience.

ARE YOU a go-getter, hard worker, not a clock-watcher, skilled in sales and admin and accounts and management and meeting the public to be integral member of a team in it for the long haul. Must have degree, preferably Masters. Come join us and we will value you! Terms: Minimum wage, zero contract.

WIDOW CLEANER seeks assistant as too much work on for one man. Cloths, buckets etc provided. Must commit to being thorough.

BIRTHS

SAILOR Tom and Ann. Announcing the birth of a daughter **Popeye The** on November 11th at Leeds General Infirmary, 6lbs 12oz.

ANNOUNCING THE birth of a daughter to Dalton actress Charlene Williams and her husband Charlene. **Elizabeth Mary**, born by caesarean selection on 8th May, at Leeds General Infirmary 8 stone and 14 pounds. Mother and baby doing well.

IN MEMORIAM

GREEN, Alfred
It's so lovely here without you, Alf.
From your loving wife Betty.

RICHARDS, Barry
For a dear Dad - the deadest man who ever lived.
From your loving children, Martin, Pam and Sophia.

FORTESCUE, Neville
We have shared so many pears together. It will be hard to go on without you but I'm just glad you are no longer insane.
Your loving wife, Elsie.

BIRK, John
We will miss you at the George and Dragon making us all laugh with your tail and fanny stories. Hope they enjoy them up in heaven, mate.
Bill, Brian, Paul, Steve and Dino..

WHITEHEAD, Blanche
The funeral of Blanche will take place on Thursday 5th May at 10.30am. Mourners are asked if they would wear something shite, or cream to bring a little light to the sad proceedings.

STELLEN, Wayne
Sadly passed on Friday 14th, surrounded by loved ones at home. Hopefully reunited with your beloved old dogs wife Mabel and sister Alice.

MURPHY, Sandra
Dried peacefully on Saturday 12th. Funnel at St Jude's church, Ripon, Thurs 31st at 4000 pm. Only family blowers, donations accepted in the loo for the charity Yorkshire Canal Volunteers.

CLAYTON, Pat
Many words could describe you, but the most important one,
Is what you've been and what you'll stay, forever always – *Bum.*
Laughter Elaine, sons Ian, Kelvin (and granddaughter Dotty).

UNWIN, Brian
Announcing the sad passing of Brian of B. Unwin's Fish and Chip emporium in Batterley on Tuesday 4th. Rest in peace.

HUDD, Hudd
Darling Dickie, the glove of my life. Gone but I will never forget you.
Your loving wife, Oliver.

CROPPER, Vic
Reporting the sad loss of Vic Cropper of Vic Cropper's Bread Factory in Richmond. Friends are invited to gather by the fireside of the Miller's Arms in Scotton on Tues 12th, 11am, where we will toast him before the funeral.

ARMSTONG, Stanley
Just made it to your 100th birthday, Stan. It's been a pleasure to know you.
From your old crew – the Worksop cooperative Hairy Ladies.

HENDERSON, Colic
Colin – my soul mate, life will never be the same again. My hearth is broken.
Your grieving partner Nags and Milo the dog.

HUNTER-NESBITT, Jonah Moan
Announcing the sad passing of Joan, my awful wedded wife, my one and only, until we are once more united.
Your devoted husband Ken.

OLDFIELD, Marvin Stanley Norman
Missing you more than worms can say.
Your loving wife, Vera.

SMITH, Alas
Always remembered, never forgotten.
From all the family.

STALIN, Joseph
Passed peacefully in Autumn House Care Home, Birstall. Funeral mass, St Michael and all Angles Thursday 14th May, 11am.

COOKRIDGE., Helen
Loving wife to Gerald, beloved mum to Norma, precious naan to Curry. RIP.

41

JENKINS, Harry
Always thought of, always pissed. *Your loving husband, Maureen.*

REID, John
In loving mammory of a dear aunt who passed over aged 2. A good innings, but always too soon.

DAILY TRUMPET ♥ MEET-UPS ♥

STEVEN (54) Fisherman, good catch, WLTM solemate for romantic evenings and fin dining. Not fussy lookswise as personality of more importance. Must be 5ft 8 – 5ft 9 1/2 , aged 17-22, blonde hair to at least shoulder length, no tattoos, minimum body hair, no fatties but big boobs essential.

GERALD (55) Likes baked potatoes, reading the newspaper, word searches, solitaire, having a bath. WLTM similar go-getting dynamic woman for energetic fun times.

PIERS (44) Seeks lady to be by my side, who craves my company, who would enjoy spending her mealtimes with me, wants to cuddle up on the sofa, long walks together in the countryside. Not fussy about looks but needy types should not apply.

DAVID (42) Genital giant, more Goliath than David, seeks woman for relaxing in front of a log fire in the evenings and long wanks in the countryside in the daytime.

MIKE (53) Recently lost wife in a dark place and needs another woman to drown. With love and affection.

LIAM (32) Shy bi foodie nerd. Looking for someone who enjoys epicurean delights. Ideal partner would be someone who shares a love of good wine and experimental home cocking.

WINO (42) Enjoys nothing better than sitting in a summer garden with a semi on and a good woman. Are you that woman?

ERNEST (85) Life in the old dog yet. WLTM stunning young lady aged 20-29 for fun and frolics. Must like cleaning and cooking and laundry. No hair and false teeth but I own my bungalow. No tattoos or piercings please. Will need to show birth certificate to prove you are in your 20s.

RICHARD (40) Pluses: kind, smiley, caring, handy around the house, keen gardener, fun, rich deep voice, plenty of own teeth and hair. Minuses: I look like Fred West. Can wear mask if it's a problem.

JONATHAN (63) Love-starved, used to half measures, looking for any hole. Some fulfilling relationship. Me: kind and tactile, you: nice lady.

IAN (45) Modern, metrosexual masseur with own successful business looking for modern woman who likes to clean and have a meal waiting for her man when he comes home from work. In return I will give sensual back and foot sausages.

PHIL (60) Me: gent, refined, suave, cultured. You: not droopy breasts but nice big ar*e and definitely not a bitch like my ex-wife. Let's hook up soon.

BILL (61) Me Tarzan looking for you Cheetah for fun in the jungle. I have a loin cloth waiting for you.

RICHIE (45) King looking for his Queer. Likes a wide range of exotic and gastronomic experiences so don't apply if you are a pussy eater. Enjoys walking, talking, cinema.

JAMES (699) Country Gentleman, enjoys all the cuunty pursuits like shooting, fishing, fine wines.

PAUL (42) Looking for female to share mellow times, constipation over a glass of wine and lazy Sunday mornings.

SANDY (47) pale and interesting minger. Would like to meet fellow ginger for fiery fun.

JOSH (32) It's a long shot and I'll come straight out with it but looking for nice but ugly woman as I have a premature ejaculation problem and I think her lack of looks might help. On the upside, I am kind and generous and considerate.

ARTY (58) Old-Fashioned Tom Collins looking for a Cosmopolitan Shirley Temple/Porn Star for a Slow Comfortable Screw Against the Wall, or even Sex on the Beach. I go down easily, do you?

SUZY (60) Recently widowed, own house, own car. Likes TV and days out. WLTM good honest man looking for love and infection.

BRENDA (89) looking for sugar daddy to treat her to gifts and day traps.

MO (59) likes eating out people, watching, walking on sunset beaches, swimming, cruises, boat trips.

MARGARET (37) Looking to feel a special spank that has been missing with other men. Can you supply? Willing to drop everything for you if you turn out to be my ideal right-hand man.

JANICE (45) World-weary, looking for someone like me: genuine, unmaterialistic, kind, what-you-see-is-what-you-get. Prefer millionaire.

KATHERINE (39) Nice legs, shame about the face type. Easy to please, likes everything, staying in, going out, drinking, eating pets children and old people.

MORAG (35) How would you like a nice warm slot to put all your filth in? I'm waiting for you.

HARRIET (45) Dumped, sad, fed up, WLTM man who appreciates a good home-cooked lamb/beef/chicken Sunday roast (so only teat eaters apply please – no veggies).

SYLVIA (50) Me: gorgeous, tall, blonde, hourglass 40-288-38 figure, modest. You: tall, dark, handsome, kind and scaring prince. I'm waiting for you to harm me.

MAURA (62) Looking for nice man to shave the best things that life has to offer because we are hair today and gone tomorrow. I promise I won't disappoint.

MARIAN (62) Sick of men giving me sh*t. Seeking generous manure man.

JULIE (48) Good-looker, good-cooker, good-fucriend to all. Never had a boyfriend. Want to be my fist?

TERESA (62) Met Mr Always Right, met Mr Right Arsehole, married Mr Right Wanker, just want to meet Mr Right. Is that you?

JOAN (54) Seeks big, strong, neanderthal type no one under 6ft 5 need apply. Living not too far away from me must be hirsute around the Wetwang area.

SUE (53) It's my philosophy that a strangler is just a lover you haven't met yet. Let's make contact. Please be manly with big hands.

WANTED
AMENDMENTS

GOOD HOME needed for ex-police dog. Can be trusted with old people (he'll do anything if you feed him pigs live), toddlers and even tiny babies. Present name: Mac.

BIRTHS
AMENDMENTS

TAILOR Tom and Ann. Announcing the birth of a daughter **Poppy Thea** on November 11th at Leeds General Infirmary, 6lbs 12oz.

IN MEMORIAM
AMENDMENTS

REID, John
In loving memory of a dear uncle who passed over aged 1002. A good innings but never too soon.

RICHARDS, Barry
For a dead Dad – the deadest man who never lived.
From your loving children, Fartin, Pam and Sophia

ARMSTRONG, Stanley
Just made it to your 100th birthday, Stan. It's been a pleasure to know you.
From your old crew - the Workshy Co-operative Dairy Ladies.

BIRK, John
We will miss you at the George and Dragon making us all laugh with your tales and funny stories. Hope they enjoy them up in heaven, mate.
Bill, Brian, Paul, Steve and Dildo

CLAYTON, Pat
Many words could describe you, but the most important one,
Is what you've been and what you'll stay, forever always – *Mum.*
Daughter Elaine, sons Ian, Kelvin (and granddaughter Botty).

HUDD, Richard
Darling Dickie, the love of my life.
Gone but I will forget you.
Your loving wife, Olivia.

HENDERSON, Colin
Colin - my foul mate, life will never be the same again. My heart is broken.
Your grieving partner Mags and Lilo the dog.

MURPHY, Sandra
Died peacefully on Saturday 12th. Funeral at St Jude's church, Ripon, Thurs 311st at 4 pm. Only family flowers, donations accepted in lieu for the charity Yorkshire anal Volunteers.

SMITH, Alan
Always forgotten, never remembered.
From all the family.

COOKRIDGE, Helen
Loving wife to Gerald, beloved mum to Korma, precious nan to Carrie. RIP.

STARLING, Joseph
Passed peacefully in Autumn House Care Home, Birstall. Funeral mess, St Michael and all Angels, Thursday 14th May, 11am.

MUNTER-NESBITT, Moaner
Announcing the sad passing of Joan, my lawful wedded wife, my bone and only, until we are once more untied.
Your devoted husband Ken.

FORTESCUE, Neville
We have shared so many years together. It will be hard to go on without you but I'm just glad you are no longer in pain. Your living wife, Elsie.

UNWIN, Brian
Announcing the sad passing of Brian of B. Unwin's Fish and Chip emporium in Batley on Tuesday 4th. Rest in peas.

MAURA (62) Looking for nice man to share the best things that life has to offer because we are hairy today and gone tomorrow. I promise I won't disappoint.

BILL (61) Me Tarzan looking for You Jane for fun in the jungle. I have a loin waiting for you.

JONATHAN (63) Love-starved, used to half measures, looking for any wholesome fulfilling relationship. Me: kind and tactile, you: nice laddie.

DINO (42) Enjoys nothing better than sitting in a summer garden with a semillon and a good woman. Are you that woman?

BRENDA (19) looking for sugar daddy to treat her to gifts and gay tips.

MORAG (35) How would you like a nice warm Scot to put all your faith in? I'm waiting for you.

the
DAILY
TRUMPET
Apologises...

...to butcher Jimmy Brian butchers for misreporting that he sells eff all of quality in his unit at his Sheffield farm shop. This, of course, should have read offal of quality.

...Rupert Jones who we said had been an inferior decorator for forty-three years. We meant, interior decorator.

...to Martin Walker for referring to him as a much-heralded masturbator of forty years, and not master baker as what he is. Mr Wanker's factory MW Bakery started in the humble beginnings of a back kitchen in Oxenhope and grew to such a size there was no bigger in bred than he was. We wish Martin a long and happy retirement.

...to Sir Tarquin Gibbons-Smith recently describing him as a polygamist instead of a philanthropist. Sir Tarquin would like to point out that his wife Lady Janet is still one too many.

...Mrs Susan Britain of Honley after writing in our Neighbourhood Witch report that she had complained to the council numerous times about her permanently clogged up back passage. We were, of course, referring to the passage at the back of her house in Long Green Lane and not her colon.

...to Maggie Jones for an unfortunate spello in last week's Focus on Health feature in which we relayed that she holds twice-weekly Keep Fat Classes. This should have read Keep Flat Classes. We apologise for the error.

...to local 'twitcher' Rita Best for a recent article by our roving reporter Pete Brownlee who wrote that it was a delight to be invited to see Rita's great tits in her garden. We did, of course, mean the pair of birds nesting in a box and not Mrs Bust's personal attributes.

...Mr Jeffrey Dunn who we described as being a former fairyman. This should have read that he was a former hairyman.

...Sandra Stanley who we said had a severe reaction to having buttocks injected into her face. We meant that she had a severe reaction to injected Botox.

...Fergal Mason who we said did the Great North Run in record time despite the several craps he had halfway round. We did of course mean cramps.

... East Yorkshire police after they were called to Sublime Journey massage parlour last week after a customer collapsed. We meant foul play was suspected and not foreplay as was written.

...Rodney Harden who is Mayor-Elect of Driffield and not Mayor-Erect. Mr Hardon will become the fully-fledged Mayor after all the local erections are finished in May.

...West Yorkshire police for an error that appeared in last Thursday's Focus on Crime. Chief Inspector Kevin Utley actually said that 'youth offenders would be castigated', not castrated as was mistakenly worded.

...Lord Haversham of Cubley who we said held an annual peasant shoot of pleasants on his land every year. This should have read, pleasant shoot of pissants.

...Les Sumpson of Les for Bargains who had on special offer last week in his shop four-ply tissues and not foreskin tissues as we mistakenly advertised.

...Raymond and Martin, Opticians Ltd who have opened their new specs shop in Brighouse and not sex shop as we wrongly said.

...Father Joseph Sligo who last week entertained children with a puppet show of the Parable of the Lost Sheep and not the Silence of the Lambs as we reported.

...Mr Fred Woodward of Lavender House estate near Leyburn as we reported that a dispute had erupted into violence when he put weed killer on Mrs Lydia Lambert's labia after it spilled into his garden. We did, of course, mean lobelia and are sorry for embarrassment caused to Mrs Labia.

...Bob Wisbech, whom we mistakenly referred to as a long-time marsupial on the car racing circuit and not a marshal as would have been correct.

...Paul Delaney of the Slattercove Theatre Group who we reported was playing Long Dong Silver in the production of Treasure Island. Mr Delaney is actually playing Long John Sliver. Tickets are available from Slattercove cox office which is open 4-7pm.

...to Donna Babbage for inadvertently referring to her as Donna Kebab in last weekend's feature on South Yorkshire takeaways. Her establishment Cabbages has had a substantial refurbishment and will be once again open for business on Thursday 12th April.

...Barbara Montgomery for saying that she was AC/DC when we did mean she was a fan of AC/DC, a band from Australia.

....Tony Appleton who received a Pride of Settle award for being cricket umpire of the year and not cricket vampire as reported.

...Mrs Mabel Attercliffe for writing that she gave Reverend Wilton of St Nicholas Church, Dore one of her famous quickies when he fell ill in the hope it would revive him. We did of course mean kisses.

...to Paul Brian of Mirfield after unfortunate wording appeared under a photo of him last week with his dog. It should have read: Pictured, Paul Brian with his Shih Tzu and not, Paul Brian with his shit suit. We do apologise profusely and have made a substantial donation to a charity of Mr Brain's choice.

...to Jim's Electrical Store, Skipton for mistaken wording saying that he had George Formby grills at half-price until the end of the month. We did of course mean Joe Frazier grills.

...Ms Lesley Lewis after we referred to her as Lennox Lewis in our Focus on Dinnerladies special last weekend. We would like to point out that Lesley has never been a heavyweight world champion nor has she ever knocked out Mike Tyson.

...Drama teacher Ms Regina Small after an article appeared in which we named her as Vagina Small. We have made a substantial contribution to Ms Small's theatre group 'Down There for Dancing' that encourages improvisation and hole play for females.

....Julie Smith of Shelley, who is a now retired horse-riding trainer with the police and is not a retired police horse as we wrote. We did not in any way mean to insinuate that she looked like a horse. We have donated to Julie's chosen charity for retired horses, 'Old Nags' as Julie is a proud Old Nag. Founder member.

... Simon Hill of Hillsborough. Last week we referred to him as the town Sumo champion. This should have read Sudoku chimp. We are sorry for any distress caused to Simon who has won many awards for his pizzle skills.

...Baroness Fenella Oberman who we mistakenly said married a man who had been raised by wolves in the Highlands. This should have read that he was raised in Wolverhampton in the Midlands.

...Pat Morrison who we erroneously described as a world-famous psycho when she is actually a renowed psychic. Due to unforeseen circumstances, Pat's show on 3rd in Scunthorpe Civic Theatre as had to be cancelled.

...Marjory Powell, after an unfortunate spelling mistake gave her childhood memories of living on a naval base in her childhood an unwanted slant. We did of course mean that there was a surfeit of seamen everywhere she looked and not semen.

...Amelia Marie Potts who we said had a new tattoo for her 4th birthday from her grandparents. This should have said that she had a new tutu. The legal age for tattoos in the UK is 8.

...Fred Fawkes who is the lead bassist in the Uckerby band and not lead racist as was wrote last week in our Focus on Fckuerby.

...New bride Hazel Frisbee and groom Danny Frisbee for our reportage of their wedding in which we said that the male groomsmen all wore pink roses in their bottomholes and not buttonholes.

... Dame Shirley Dyson-Fforbes, whom we mistakenly referred to as the French Lieutenant's woman and not the Lord Lieutenant of South Yorkshire. Dame Shirley is a great supporter of youth charities and so we have made a donation to Dame Shirley's chosen charity: Mouth Support in Yorkshire.

...Michaela Bentine, who retires this week as a dental nurse and not a rental nurse as published. Ms Dentine has worked for The Smile Mental Practice for thirty years and is looking forward to a long and happy retirement.

...to amateur chef Janie Dodson after we said that her winning dish in the finals of an amateur chef competition was Salmon Rushdie when in fact it was Salmon en Croute.

POLICEMAN SMELLS CRACK IN PUBLIC TOILET

FISH SHOP OWNER BATTERED LOVE RIVAL

WOMAN SQUATS FOR A MONTH IN PUBLIC TOILET

Vagrant toilets yesterday

BODY WITH NO HEAD FOUND IN TOPLESS BAR

STUDENTS BAKE AND SERVE PENSIONERS

STOLEN HANDBAG FOUND BY LAMPPOST

PERFUMIER KATH WINS TOP AWARD FOR HER SMELL OF WHORES

Beautiful Whores and the delicate aroma of freshly-trimmed bush inspire award-winning oralfactory delight.

DISCHARGE LOUNGE IS MESSIEST PLACE IN HOSPITAL

PEOPLE WITH STAMMERS PEOPLE WITH STAMMERS LIKELY TO BE RIDICULED SAYS PPPPPOLL

CHILDREN SHOULD BE BELTED IN BUSES, SAYS SAFETY CHIEF

MAN KILLED TO DEATH

FAMOUS MEMORY MAN CANNOT REMEMBER HOW MUCH WORK HE DOES FOR CASH IN HAND

Rothwell Woman Has to Sit on Chair for 3 Months Because Sofa Hasn't Arrived

Roswell: woman vents her anger in front of the chair she's occupied for months.

OWLS SMASH BLADES 1-1

OUT OF DATE SANDWICH SOLD TO NINETY-YEAR-OLD WOMAN

MAN FATALLY WOUNDED MAKES RECOVERY

ACTOR FAILS AUDITION FOR PART PLAYING A BAD ACTOR

COFFEE IS FOR MUGS SAYS OWNER OF TEA COMPANY

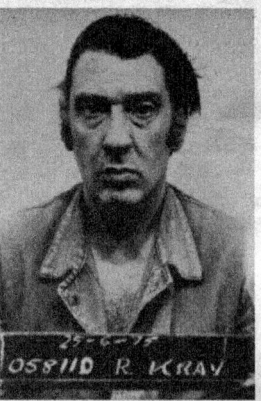

Example of historic mug, shot in the mid-1900s.

CHURCH FROM A DISTANCE LOOKS LIKE ALAN CARR

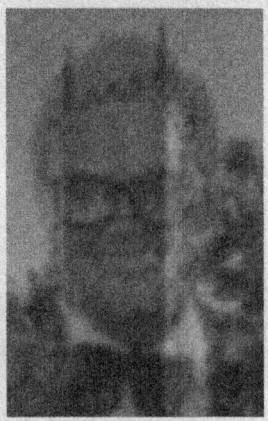

If the onlooker squints, the likeness becomes quite apparent.

KEN GIVING FREE LESSONS ON HOW TO GROOM KIDS BIG AND SMALL – ALL WELCOME

pg 352

RIDER TOSSED OFF HORSE IN CHARITY RIDE

The horse involved was an American Curly, a breed famous for it sperm-like mane.

FUN HAD AT PARTY

BAKE OFF JUDGE DOESN'T LIKE PARKIN

FORMER PAGE THREE MODEL'S BRA SHOP GOES BUST

CHIEF SITTING BULL VOWS TO ACT ON COWBOY BUILDERS

KEIGHLEY WOMAN MARRIES WIND TURBINE

Girl Guide Leader Arrested for Filling Brownies With Marijuana

UF.O

WAS ONLY A BIG FLAT CLOUD

ILKLEY 35 STONE MAN FORCED TO BUY 2 SEATS ON PLANE FINDS THEY ARE ROWS APART

A lunchtime spread normally requires 2 chairs - *next to each other.*

SUSPICIOUS BAG BLOWN UP BY POLICE OUTSIDE CHARITY SHOP WAS BAG OF DONATED PANTS

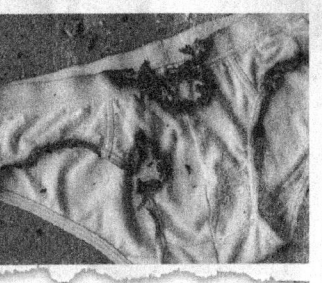

UMBRELLA REFUSES TO OPEN FOR EMMERDALE ACTRESS

ROWING TEAM FINED FOR COX BEING TOO SMALL

GET UP AND GO CLUB CLOSES AFTER NO ONE TURNED UP TO MEETINGS

HEALTH FOOD SHOP CLOSES DUE TO ILL-HEALTH

FRIGHTENING NOISE HEARD IN PARK TURNS OUT TO BE NOTHING

Breathing Linked to Long Life

DANGEROUS PSYCHOPATH REPORTED ON TRANS PENNINE TRAIL

GOLFERS AT CLUB WARNED ONLY TO PLAY WITH THEIR OWN BALLS

Whilst working on their stroke, members have been asked to keep to their own balls.

STARVATION CAN LEAD TO EARLY DEATH

URINE SMELL IN OFFICE LINKED TO DISGRUNTED WORKER PEEING IN COFFEE MACHINE

HOMELESS MAN WHO STOLE CAR BATTERY WILL BE CHARGED

DROWNING OF HUSBAND RUINS WOMAN'S HOLIDAY

LUKE LITTLER'S LOOKALIKE LOOKS NOTHING LIKE HIM

'NO TWO WEE S ARE THE SAME IN THIS JOB', SAYS SEWER WORKER

DEAD BODIES FOUND IN GRAVEYARD

HOSPITAL PATIENT WAS ALIVE HOURS BEFORE DEATH

MARITAL BREAK UPS LINKED TO DIVORCE

FATAL ACCIDENT AT HEALTH AND SAFETY CONFERENCE

DRUGS MAKE PEOPLE XXY!FSAE* ?UUUUUU

SURVEY FINDS PEOPLE ARE FED UP OF SURVEYS

ACTOR NEARLY GOT A DOG FROM LOCAL DOG'S HOME

VIAGRA CAN MAKE THINGS EVEN HARDER THE BEDROOM

61

MAYOR'S SON NOT BOTHERED ABOUT LEARNING TO DRIVE

WOMAN DIES AFTER BEING GIVEN MIRACLE CURE

MYSTERY SPADE FOUND ON FARM

PEOPLE WHO PUT CREAM ON SCONES FIRST MORE LIKELY TO ARGUE

COME TO NEW BARNSLEY BOHO BAR — FREE SPIRITS!

SOME MORE APOLOGIES

WE UNFORTUNATELY reported that Stewart Milsom of Mirfield bred Yorkshire terrists for over thirty years before retiring. We did of course mean Yorkshire Terriers. We have made a donation to Yorkshire Terrists Rescue in his name as due recompense.

SANDY SHORT

Last week we mistakenly reported that leading chantreuse Sandie Shaw made a surprise appearance at the Crown and Anchor karaoke in Barnsley. This should have read Sandy Short from Full Sutton prison. Sandy sang Muppet on a String so well she received a standing ovulation from the crowd and walked off with first prize of a meat parcel.

WE ISSUE our sincerest apologies to Manita: Human Cannonball of Starr's Famous Circus, after referencing him as Maneater, Human Cannibal in error. We stress that Mr Manita is a vegetarian and has never eaten anyone. The circus will be situated on the flaying field in Sowerby Bridge for the whole of June.

PAULINE WEBBER

WE EXTEND our apologise to Pauline Webber after reporting that she appeared on the Readers' Wives page of a top-shelf magazine. In reality, Pauline appeared in the magazine Breeders' Lives which is a magazine devoted to the breeding of chickens. The magazine can be bought in larger stores on lower shelves. We apologise to Pauline who recently won a top breeding award for her Naked Neck. *Chick pic below.*

MR COLIN BADGERY

Colin Budgie pictured with his friend Stella's Seagull

WE WOULD like to apologise to Mr Colin Badgery of Thirsk Falconry Centre for the misrpint which appeared in last Friday's edition. We mistakenly relayed that after a thrilling flying display of eagles outside Thirst town hall, Mr Badger then gave an entertaining talk about his bowels and why they are mainly active at night. We did of course mean his owls.

DEBRA GRAHAM

APOLOGIES to Debra Graham who we mistakenly referred to last week as a Rogue model. This should have read that Debra is a Vague model. Soup model Graham has appeared on the front cover of many glossy magazines, been the face of perfume house Creed for sixty years and bases her image on fellow model Stirling Moss.

PLEASE NOTE that the Wednesday morning film next Thursday at the Pateley Bridge Odeon is Pumping Iron and not Humping Irene.

TANIA ABBOTT

Apologies to Mrs Tania Abbott who we reported was playing a courgette in the Pickering local amateur dramatic production of Les Miserables. This should have read Cosette. The production has been put on to raise money for a local cat charity Le Cat that Shat on the Mat.

GENEROUS Whitby gardener John Sutcliffe died last Thursday 'the way he would have liked to have gone' said his widow, Mabel, as he keeled over while weeing in his garden. Neighbour Marjorie Bright said that John was a proper fairy. Who would sort out everyone's dandelions for them and want nothing more as payment than a cup of tea and a piscuit. 'We will all miss conversing with him as he was doing what he did best, splashing his poison on the weeds, watering the lawn and always with a smile on his face,' she said. 'He was such lovely, entertaining company.'

RODNEY BICKERSTAFFE

WE DO APOLOGISE TO Councillor Rod Bickerstaffe for an error in reporting his health condition. When we wrote that Mr Bickerstaffe did not partake of the afternoon tea at Mirfield Old People's Home because he is pathetic, we meant diabetic.

JESS SHORT

Jed Short with one of the bandanas discarded at the end of her polenta class

WE WRONGLY wrote in our 'Focus on Health' that Jess Short holds Pirates classes every Saturday morning in Clayton Village Hall. This should have read Pilates classes. Jess said that it was highly amusing how many grown men turned up last week with eye patches and toy parrots on their shoulders wearing bananas and she had to send them home disappointed.

PLEASE note that there was a misspelt headline yesterday which caused confusion. It should have read **POLICE CHIEF SITTINGBOURNE VOWS TO ACT ON COWBOY BUILDERS** and not **CHIEF SITTING BULL**. Newly instated West Yorkshire Police Superintendent Leslie Sittingbourne is determined to protect people in the county from the misery caused by Teepee Wigfield Construction, a family firm of cowboy builders responsible for fleecing pensioners all over the north of England.

PLEASE NOTE that Leader of the Hull council Mr Trevor Sinclair-Phillips has had to cancel his engagements because he is in laid up in hospital with an enlarged prostate and not an enlarged prostitute.

HEDGEHOG EXPERT SARAH TO GIVE TALK TO ROTARIANS

PLEASE NOTE that the speaker for the Rotund club's annual conference in June will not be the poet laureate Simon Armitage as advertised but Sarah Armitage. Sarah is an expert in financial matters and will be doing a talk about hedgehogs with Q and A to follow. We apologise for the mix up.

IIIIIIIIIIIIIIIIIIIIIIIIIIIIIIIIIIIIIIIIIIIIIII

TIMOTHY BRIERLAND KFC

PROFUSE apologies to KC Timothy Brierland who is a leading criminal barrister and not, nor has he ever been, a barista serving coffees as we mistakenly reported. Also, he trained at Bucks University and not Starbucks as also erroneously stated.

IIIIIIIIIIIIIIIIIIIIIIIIIIIIIIIIIIIIIIIIIIIIIII

WE EXTEND our apologies to Dr Marian Lebowski, chief clinician who works in the sexual health clinic in Middlesbrough and not in the sex industry as reported in our last weekend issue. Luckily Dr Lebowski saw the fanny side of our error and has accepted Sunday lunch for four at her local hostelry by way of consolation.

WE FALSELY stated that householder Barry Rogers gave sneak thief Jordan Jepworth a good licking when he found him ferreting in his cupboards. This should have read dicking. 'He wasn't going to nick my valuables without a fight,' said the plucky pensioner.

APOLOGIES TO Professor Sheridan Smith-Cowell for an error that appeared in a story recently where we erroneously referred to him as Deputy Vice-Chancellor and Pervert of Muncaster University. We did of course mean Provost which is a chief academic orifice.

DEIRDRE CALLOWAY

WE DRAW your attention to a story about fishmonger Deirdre Calloway who we mistakenly relayed caught crabs from Cornish fishermen in her youth. This should have read that Cornish fishermen gave her crabs. Teenager Deirdre was too young to travel with them on their boats so they sorted her out at the quayside. We do hope this amendment clarifies the situation and wish her well when she finishes her last shaft at Christmas on her stall.

ROSIE FERGUSON

WE ARE SORRY for any embarrassment caused to Rosie Ferguson of Rosie's Pub, Doncaster after reporting that she would be telling cock tales at her open mike night on 1st of next month. This should have

A nice pair: Rosie shows off her big soft baps

said selling cocktails. There will be a special offer of buy-one-get-none-free on the evening and ticket-holders will be treated to her famous baps free of charge. Tickets can be obtained from Rosie's Pube from Monday onwards.

IN OUR recent Focus on Malton we apologise to the mayor for reporting that his wife the mayoress had a particularly horrible anus in 2025. This should have read that she had an annus horribilis.

A Dore man was admitted to hospital with ten creme eggs stuck up his rectum that he said he had put there for 'safekeeping away from the wife's greedy mitts'. Hospital surgeon Dr Ben Wallender said that sadly it is not an arsolated occurrence. 'We've had people with phones, marbles, Ken dolls and Barbers, once even a blender.' Dr Bellender said that he does not not recommend the practice of bumhole and bellend insertions.

CAROL RUDD

PLEASE NOTE that Carol Rudd will be doing nails for £10 on Saturday mornings at her Wakefield salon Carol's Testicles during November and not doing males. We apologise for any confusion.

STEVE AND JULIE HOUGHTON

PLEASE NOTE that the visiting dignitaries Mayor Steve Houghton and Lady Mayoress Julie Houghton from Kingswinford did not enjoy a dessert of banana spliffs made by local schoolchildren at Morley town hall, but banana splits. We apologise profusely for the error. The Mayor and Mayoress were also treated to a visit to the Golden Hours local retirement home where the inmates entertained them with a display of the splits which the visitors deemed very autistic.

DO NOTE that Professor Marvin Spark is doing a talk entitled The Evolution of Man from Australopithecus to Homo sapiens and not to Homo sexual as printed.

PLEASE NOTE that in our TV weekend timetable, the film Pale Rider features Clint Eastwood as a lone horseman and not Vivienne Westwood as stated.

Vivienne Eastwood.

A LINE of waiting punters almost a quarter of a mile long was outside Marlene's Ice Cream Parlour in Scarborough last weekend after a *Daily Trumpet* article in which we mistakenly reported that they was giving free sixty-nines every Saturday in June for anyone who could prove they were a Red Light worker. This should have read ninety-nines. And also they were giving the free cones to Blue Light workers, not Red Light ones. We also extend our apologies to the traffic police who had to disperse the crowds.

There was a slight mistake in Saturday's interview with Dewsbury-born actor Finley Goddard in which we reported he had a walk-on part in the Sopranos playing a lobster. This should have read mobster.

EMILY WRIGHT

EMILY WRIGHT CATERING from Haxey served up a fine serving when serving guests at the Mayor Making ceremony in Doncaster last week. Emily's staff circulated expertly serving champagne and a can of peas and then there was a magnificent bucket full of food to follow. Guests said that the food was in line with the new mayor who is an acquired taste.

PLEASE note that the lecture in Cleckheaton village hall on Thursday is entitled The sinking of the Lusitania and not the Genitalia which is not a ship.

THERE WAS an error in Friday's issue when we reported that in Penny's Mansion of Beauty she was offering a brand-new treatment of demonic possession. This should have read colonic irritation.

WE APOLOGISE to Russian expert Dr Mikhail Spivak for wrong information about his up and coming presentation of the country's history in Otley college. The talk will be on scientist Ivan Pavlov and not ballerina Anna Pavlova. Dr Spivak will deliver a fascinating talk about the genius who discovered by ringing a bell, he could make his dogs salivate for meringues. There will be a second part of the talk the month after in which Dr Spock will deliver a talk about Fabergé eggs and why they smell of Brut. We apologise for any confusion.

AN UNFORTUNATE front-page headline caused embarrassment to Mrs Shirley Stagg last week. *Local Tart Wins National Award* referred to the lemon tart that Mrs Slagg submitted in a *Homebaking Monthly* competition and not to Mrs Stagg herself. The prize-winning tart comes from Boston Spa and was described by the judges as 'naughtily fruity, exciting on the tongue and best enjoyed with a generous covering of squirty cream'.

PLEASE NOTE that visiting art critic Denzil Creighton's talk in village hall is on the subject of Whistler's Mother and not Hitler's Mother as previously advertised.

EVEN MORE APOLOGIES!

PLEASE note that the firm of cowboy builders which Big Chief Sittingbourne vowed to act on is called T.P. Wigfield Construction and not, Teepee Wigfield Construction. Police Superintendent Sittingbull has since reported that several arrests have already been made following nightly raids and four members of the Wigwam family remain in custody.

LEADER OF THE COUNCIL WALTER WILKIE

THE *TRUMPET* apologies profusely to the MD of Yorkshire Toys International Mr Len Walters for a profile piece that was featured in July. When questioned about what he considered the most important thing in life, Mr Walters actually said, happiness, and not a penis as we reported he did. We hope lunch for two at a local pub of his choice will more than make up for it.

IN A recent issue we reported that Halifax-born Paul Crabtree was working as a Death Row welcome host. This should have read Heathrow.

WE RECENTLY ran an advert offering Jason Momoa's services for £20 per hour. This should have read Jason the Mower. Jason's services are limited to cutting grass around his local area of Silsden as he is seventy-nine and told our reporter that he wishes he could still do half the things he has been asked to do since the advert and his telephone number appeared in the *Trumpet*.

PLEASE NOTE that keen gardener Elsie May will be exhibiting her exotic plants at the Farsley show and not her exotic pants as we wrote last week.

WE RECENTLY ran a story about Martin Shawbsy visiting from Mars to talk to schoolchildren about how the galaxy and the milky way came into being. We in no way meant to infer that Mr Shawsby was an alien. He is an ex-manager of the chocolate firm Mars and his talk was about the invention of various familiar bars we have come to love. According to the headteacher, the children were more delighted to be dragged into the assembly hall to hear all about chocolate and taste the free samples on offer than to be bored rigid from a talk about planets.

AT THE Huddersfield flower show, John Thompson won best in class for his Krinkled White peonies and not crinkled white penis as stated. We apologise to John Thomas for any embarrassment caused.

IN A RECENT feature about Yorkshire women during the war, we inadvertently reported that Irene Burke worked as a mermaid in Filey. We did of course mean milkmaid.

JACQUI WATSON

WE APOLOGISE to café owner Jacqqui Watson for copy recently published. Jaqcqcuqui will be holding weekly Tots and Buns meetings in her tearoom in Mexborough and not Tits and Bums as we mistakenly wrote. Jaqcqui said, 'It's a way of bringing mothers of small children together to have tea and eat some cake and just talk,' said Jacququcqi. 'Alas the last group had to be abandoned as there were too many single men with no kids who turned up so I'm hoping now everything is sorted it will be great,' said Jacqcuqucquqquuui.

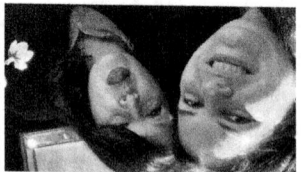

Ms Wilson pictured with friend who will be bringing her two small tits to the sessions.

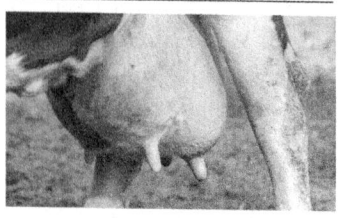

||||||||||||||||||||||||||||||||||||||||||||||||||||||||||||||||

APOLOGIES to Dr Bunty and Bruce Carruthers who recently visited Leeds zoo to give a fascinating lecture on tropical birds. We reported that Dr Bunty had a special affinity with the giant Hyacinth Macaws whereas Dr Bruce preferred a small cock or two. This should have read cockatoo. We apologise for any unintended sexual reference. We have made a donation to their bird rescue charity in Dr Bruce's name by way of apology (more info on www.bigbirdsandsmall.co.ck)

WE WOULD like to apologise for misleading wording that appeared recently under a photo taken at the the Yorkshire Pedigree Dog event in Sheffield. When we put Mrs Delia Temple and her prize-winning puppies we did of course mean her two Chihuahuahuas Scamp and Rascal and not Mrs Temple's breasts. We apologise profusely to Mrs Temple and her breasts for any embarrassment caused.

APOLOGY TO BEST IN BREED WINNER

WE WOULD like to apologise for wording that appeared recently under a photo featuring Mrs Edna Holthorpe at the Yorkshire Pedigree Cat Event in Pannal. It should have red that she was pictured with her best inbred seal point cat Ling An Zhou and not her Siamese twins Lynn and Sue.

RE OUR FOCUS ON BEAUTY issue in May. Kerry's Spa had a weekly special offer of twenty per cent for Indian Heads only. We did not mean to insinuate that only customers with an Indian Head got a special offer. The money off offer was for the Indian Head treatment which consists of a pampering of the back, neck, shoulders, scalp and face. This week Kerry is offering twenty per cent off a back, smack and crack massage.

||||||||||||||||||||||||||||||||||||||||||||||||||||||||||||||||

MR NORMAN JOHN BARKER

WE ARE very sorry for an unfortunate error pertaining to the above late gentleman Mr Norma Jean Baker in his obituary. Mr Barker was shot in the Balkans in 1913 and not in the bollocks as what was written. The *Trumpet* has made a substantial donation in the name of Ms Baker by way of fit recompense and we apologise to his family sincerely.

THE FAMILY of nonagenarian Terry Tatchell would like us to point out that in his early days he was a professionally trained bugler and not a burglar as stated.

PLEASE NOTE that the fundraising evening in St Mark's church last week was to raise money for an emergency defibrillator outside the ladies' club and not an emergency vibrator.

AFTER UNFORTUNATE wording appeared under a photograph of her in last Tuesday's edition. We erroneously referred to Candy Brown as being the owner of Candy's, the infamous chain of sweat shops. This should have said she was the owner of the famous chain of sweet shops. Andy has asked us to point out that she has never employed cheap labour in her sweat shops, on the contrary always pays less than the minimum wage, especially where young student weekend workers are concerned. She has generously accepted a contribution towards her favoured charity.

WE WOULD like to apologise to Miss Lesley Pott for referring to her as a lavatory assistant and not a laboratory assistant. We are sorry for any distress and we are happy to announce that Piss Pott has accepted lunch for two at her local hostelry by way of due recompense.

BISHOP STEVEN HINCH AND MS KATIE COMPTON

WE APOLOGISE for careless wording that appeared under an photograph about the Great Yorkshire Show last week. The headline, Katie Compton and her Stinking Bishop did refer to the cheese she was holding and not her partner Bishop Steven Hinch who appeared on the photo with her. Ms Compton's Stinking Bishop has won many prizes and it is made on her family farm in the West Midlands. She was currently crowned Arsonist Cheesemaker of the Year by the Cheese Marketing board.

WE WOULD like to apologise to travel-mad local lady Anne Bickerstaffe after we mistakenly wrote that she goes bananas every Christmas. This should have read that she goes to the Bahamas every Christmas. We are sorry for any distress inflicted.

PLEASE NOTE leading gemstone expert Carl Rothschild will be doing a talk entitled The Complete Guide to Opal and not The Complete Guide to Oral as denoted on last weekend's event page. Carl told the *Trumpet*, 'All the tickets sold out in thirty minutes and as there's a no refund policy, people might as well come along and learn something.'

LYNNE HOWELL

WE ARE so very sorry for a piece what appeared on Saturday about Lynne Howell who we said was the first person in the 1980s to set up a brothel in Pudsey to service those in need. This should have read, soup kitchen. Lynne made sure that her home-made broth was packed with nutrients for the streetwalkers to fortify them against the cold and received an STD from Queen Elizabeth in 2015. We apologise for any embarrassment caused and hope that Len will be happy with a meal for two at her local pub The Horse and Tart by way of recompense.

PLEASE NOTE that Bradford-born Rav Dhani is a coin artist at London's Royal Mint and not a con artist as we mistakenly referred to him. Mr Dhani was responsible for the stunning updated portrait of Britannia for a special coinage edition and not a portrait of Burke and Hare as reported previously. They have not, and probably never will, feature on a coin of the realm.

PLEASE note that Tessa Smart was the winner of the Ladies Menston Cycle race and not the Ladies Menstrual Cycle race as mentioned last week.

OUR SINCEREST apologies to Sheila Delaney who we wrongly described as a geriatric nit nurse last week. This should have read, geriatric unit nurse.

THE SUNDAY QUIZ – FURTHER RECTIFICATIONS

MICKEY MOUSE was originally called *Mortimer Mouse* and not *Bob Mortimer*

THE REAL name of songstress Tina Turner was *Rita Mae Bullock* and not *Jerry Lee Lewis*

THE SCIENTIFIC theory that explains the origins of the universe is the *Big Bang Theory* and not *Chitty Chitty Bang Bang*

GLOSSOPHOBIA is the fear of *public speaking* and not *paint*

THE CHARACTER in Cinderella who is Prince Charming's servant is *Dandini* and not *Dandruff*

THE ACTRESS famous for appearing in Rosemary's Baby and marrying Frank Sinatra is *Mia Farrow* and not *Mo Farah*

THE INVENTOR of the television is *John Logie Baird* and not *Yogi Bear*

A TOTAL mix up last week when we asked who wrote and sang *I Love My Cat* and we gave the answer *Dog Stevens*. The song was *I Love My Dog* by *Rat Stevens*

WHO FAMOUSLY crossed the Alps with elephants on the way to war with the Romans was *Hannibal* and not the *Von Trapp family*

THE ANIMAL-PRINT-WEARING barmaid in Coronation Street was *Bet Lynch* and not *Bet Fred*

THE GREAT Mongol ruler who conquered an empire stretching from Asia to Europe was *Genghis Khan* and not *Chaka Khan*

THE POTATO named after a royal member is *King Edward* and not *Prince Albert Bartlett*

NB: WE mistakenly referred to the actor Benedict Cumberland as Benedict Cumberbund in a quiz answer amendment. We do apologise for any confusion

WE HAVE made a substantial donation to a charity of Mr Cornelius Slater-Jubb for an unfortunate error made in a recent issue of the Daily *Trumpet* in which we referred to him as a merchant wanker of thirty years and not banker. Mr Jubb would also like it pointed out though he remains a Chartered bonker, he actually retired from wanking three years ago.

THE TRUMPET would like to draw your attention to a headline in *The Trumpet* recently referring to Eric Grimshaw where we wrote: Rider Tossed off Horse in Charity Ride. Driving instructor Eric would like us to point out that he was in fact tossed off by his horse. We apologise for any misrepresentation of what happened.

THE ENTREPRENEUR known for his leadership of Tesla and Space X is *Elon Musk* and not *Eton Mess*

THE CHILLY-SOUNDING character played by Kit Harington in Game of Thrones is *Jon Snow* and not *Vanilla Ice*

THE LAST of the James Bond films is *No Time to Die* and not *No Sleep Till Brooklyn*

THE BIGGEST snake in the world is an *Anaconda* and not *Anna Karenina*

THE NATIONAL dish of China is *Peking Duck* and not *Willow Pattern*

THE ALTERNATIVE name for the large red Christmas houseplant is a *Poinsettia* and not a *Pointer Sister*

THE FIRST cloned sheep was named after *Dolly Parton* and not *Larry Lamb*

THE VELOCIPEDE was a nineteeth-century prototype of a *bicycle* and not a *dinosaur*

THE ROMAN goddess of health is *Salus* and not *Bupa*

THE FACE that was said to have launched a thousand ships was *Helen of Troy* and not *Jane of McDonald*

THE AUTHOR of The Grapes of Wrath is *John Steinbeck* not *Jeremy Vine*

THE YOUNGEST member of a famous pop group who had a hit with Long Haired Lover from Liverpool was *Jimmy Osmond* and not *Richard Osman*

INSULIN IS commonly used to treat *diabetes* and not *diarrhoea*

THE QUEEN who famously said 'Let them eat cake' was *Marie Antoinette* and not *Mary Berry*

PLEASE NOTE that Dame Catherine Temple's third talk at Halifax Town Hall on Saturday is: Part Three: My Olympic Phase and not, as was printed, Part Three: My Ozempic Face. Dame Catherine wishes it to be pointed out that her face is totally natural and not the result of any medical intervention with fat jabs.

THE TRUMPET apologises to Damian Limekin of Hickleton for a catalogue of wrong information that appeared on Friday in the *Trumpet*. Mr Ramekin is a professional musician and not a amateur magician and had been suffering from a bad case of tristesse after his girlfriend left him for Garry Tinker, second-reserve goalie for Nottingham Forest and not Gary Lineker as reported. We had a young reporter who has since left for incommpitence is our only excuse. We apologise holeheartedly to Demon and wish him all the best for his recovery.

Fiona Tomkinson

WE ARE very sorry to Fiona Tompinkson for wrong wording that appeared in a piece about her award-winning homegrown cherries. The judges said that they were firm and ripe and not firm and tripe, as we reported. Mrs Tonkimson also won second prize in the homegroin gooseberries secretion and got a special raspberry for her giant raspberries.

OUR APOLOGIES to Mr Nigel Prentiss after we wrongly reported when his business collapsed the stress made him go gay overnight. This should have read that it made him go grey overnight.

JENNIFER CURTIS
IN A recent article we referred to Jennie Curtis as one of the world's most renowned jugglers when this should have read jewellers. Our sincerest apologies to Ms Circus.

SIR KEITH FFORDE
PLEASE NOTE that Sir Keith will be giving a lecture about Mount Kilimanjaro and not Mounjaro about of which he has no experience.

APOLOGIES FOR THE APOLOGIES

WE DO sincerely apologise to Huddersfield author Mary Aberline for the embarrassing headline that appeared last week in conjunction with the story about her book featuring Toothy the shark. The title of the book should have been, Toothy the Lemon Shark and not Toothy the Loan Shark. She is now working on a sequel, Alki the Hammered Shark.

Melon shark.
Apologies for the confusion.

WE ERRONEOUSLY described Mr Jeffrey Dunn recently as a former hairyman. We meant dairyman.

APOLOGIES TO Professor Simon Smythe-Cowell for the error we made with his name in a recent story. Professor Smith-Smythe is Provost and Deputy Chancellor of Vice at Muncaster University.

ONCE AGAIN we extend our apologies to Driving instructor Mr Eric Grimshaw for unfortunate wording about his charity ride and horse. He has never tossed off a horse, nor been tossed off by one. He did, however, fall from his horse during the ride and yet still managed to finish the gruelling ten-mile course on foot raising over £2000 for pensioners with severely bruised legs covered in cow pats. Mr Grimshaw has graciously accepted our apology with good humour.

FOR THE whole of August, Leeds Museum of Art has an exhibition by artist David Icke and not Dick Van Dyke as previously printed. Tickets are free to see it.

● ● ● ● ● ● ● ● ● ● ●

WE ARE SORRY to the Tadcaster Players for miswording what appeared last week to advertise their forthcoming Commedia dell'arse production. Sally Padgett is playing Columbine, not Columbo. Patrick Watkins is playing Pedro not Pierrot and Philip Rivers is playing Punch and not Paunch. We do apologise for the catalogue of errors.

It is our sincere regret that we falsely published that married couple Colleen and Terry Carter of Huddersfield came to dogging in the park at a mature age. We did of course mean they came to jogging in their years of maturity. Our profuse apologies to Collie and Terrier for the discomfiture we caused.

WE MISTAKENLY printed an advert for Goldman Antiques (all things old and quirky). The special clearance offer was on religious diptychs which came from the recently closed St Anne's convent, not dick pics as written.

WE FALSELY stated that householder Barry Rogers gave sneak thief Jordan Jepworth a good dicking when he found him ferreting in his cupboards. This should have read kicking. 'He wasn't going to lick my valuables without a fight,' said the plucky pensioner.

APOLOGIES FOR THE APOLOGIES FOR THE APOLOGIES

FOR THE whole of August, Leeds Museum o fArt has an exhibition by artist Jon Bon Jovi and not David Icke or Dick Van Dyke as previously printed. Tickets are free to see it.

WE DO sincerely apologise to Huddersfield author Mary Aberline for the misinformation about her new children's book which will not be called Alki the Hammered Shark but Alfie the Hammerhead Shark who was named after her late father and we have been asked to point out that he was neither an alki nor a hammerhead shark.

APOLOGIES AD INFINITUM

Trans Pennine Trail

We apologise for causing alarm with a mistaken headline last week when we reported there was a dangerous psychopath on the Trans Pennine Trail. This should have read, dangerous cycle path. The heritage society have now sorted it.

BARBARA ISN'T A GREAT BIG FAT USER THANKS TO GIN

WE HEARTILY apologise to Barbara Smith from Pudsey who we said lost all her weight from gin. Our reporter had misheard and Barbara lost it in the gym. Since our feature, Barbara had many calls asking for advice but Barbara told us they put down their phones as soon as she says it was the gym and not the gin that was responsible.

Please note that a lack of punctuation in a headline last week gave it an unsavoury slant. Ken Midler is giving free lessons on how to groom horses and ponies and kids big and small are all welcome. We did not mean to insinuate that he was giving lessons on how to groom children. The lessons are free and will take place at his stables situated at Kiddy Fiddler's Farm in Follifoot.

FOR THE whole of August, Leeds Museum of Ars has an exhibition by artist Jan van Eyck and not Jon Bon Jovi, David Icke or Dick Van Dyke as previously printed. Tickets are free to see it.

IN A PIECE written about Raleigh enthusiast Wayne Harwell last week, the wording that should have appeared under the picture of him and his wife and his chopper was 'Wayne, his wife and his Chopper' and not 'Wayne, his old bike and his Chopper'. We in no way intended to insinuate that Ramona Harwell was the old bike.

THERE WAS an inaccurate heading to a story last week for which we apologise. Perfumier Kath McQueen won a top industry award for her Scent of Hawes not Smell of Whores as we reported. The judges said, 'It evoked the verdant countryside of Hawes', which is a market town in Wensleydale, an area famous for its cheese. Kath described her award-winner as 'Fondly reminiscent of my home' with top notes of Vetiver, middle notes of freshly-cut grass and base notes of cheddar'. Kath's fragrance will be manufactured by top perfume house Lee Van Cleef and Sharples for release early next year.

FASHION SHOW FOR LAGER LADIES

Please note that the Christa's Goons fashion show is in the Three Lamps pub in Goldthorpe and not as we mistakenly advertised on Tuesday. Tickets can be brought online from the shop in person or from Christ's website. They cost £5 and include a glass of jizz upon arrival, nibbles and quality snakes.

MR AND MRS JOHN AND CHRISTINE LOCKWOOD

THE TRUMPET is very sorry that we spoilt the surprise of the surprise party by printing it in the newspaper that the family of John and Christian Cockwood were having a surprise party for them in their local pub the Furrier - not the Furry Ear as we relayed. Also they have not been married for 80 years, which would be impossible as they are only in their 70s. They are celebrating their anniversary in their favourite ways, Christine with alcohol and John gambling.

PLEASE NOTE there was an error in reporting the concert which will take place in Pontefract community centre on Thurs 5th May. It will be not be the American giants of rock band the Eagles performing but the Beagles from Goodwick in Pembrokeshire. Also Martyn Eagles is on drugs and not on drums as previously stated.

BREN HOSKING – AN APOLOGY

Bren Hosking is a chair of the WI in Wiltshire.

APOLOGIES TO Bren Hosking for us getting totally the wrong end of the stick last week in our reportage of her visit from Wiltshire. Bren is the acting chair of their WI and has nothing to do with WWII as she wasn't even born during the war. We also have no idea why our reporter got her title of chair mixed up with the real chair what she was pictured with which is not a momento from the war but a modern one what belongs to the university and is which Ms Haskell sat on to do her business. Also after a three-course meal, coffee was served with petit fours and not pinafores as wrongly reported. Bern's visit was very well received by the ladies and a receptacle visit to Wiltshire is planned for later in the year.

CAROL RUDD

Please note that Carol Rudd's Wakefield business is called Carol's Cuticles and not Carol's Testicles as we wrote in a previous issue. Apologies to Carlo who has asked us also to mention that you will have to bonk well in advance if you want her to do you.

Ms Carol Kingsford

WE DO offer our regret to celibate personality Ms Carol Cleethorpes for misinformation last week regarding her children's names which we mistakenly gave as Pan, Dementia, Calypso and Herpes. This should have read Ian, Demeter, Caliper and Hermes. Carol also asked us to point out that we also misreported about her heritage, as she has no Greek in her, rather her four fathers came over from Ireland during the potato famine. We also feel duty bound to point out that Ian is not named after a Greek God.

WE APOLOGISE yet again to the Tadcaster Players for miswording their forthcoming Commedia dell'arte production. Patrick Watkins is playing Poirot not Pedro and they wish us to further point out that Gary Kimble will be playing Harlequin and not Harry Kane. We do apologise for the litany of errors.

|||||||||||||||||||||||||||||||||||||||||

SALLY FURNESS

WE DO apologise for the wrong details in reporting a story about a talk given by historian Sally Furness to Birdwell Ladies Group last week. She did a talk about Ruddyhard Kipling, author of the Jingle Bells and other famous stories featuring characters such as the man-cub Mogwai and Blue the bear. In fact, Mr Kipling is nothing to do with Mr Kipling. The post-talk buffet however did feature many of Mr Kipling's cakes as supplied by Malcolm's Misshaped Cakes in Birdwell market. On offer were a selection of Cherry Bakewells, Viennesse Worlds, Angel Slices and Fondle Fancies.

|||||||||||||||||||||||||||||||||||||||||

ALAN SAUNDERS

WE RECENTLY ran an story that Malton sportsman Alan Saunders from Malton was joining the production crew responsible for Squid Game in North Korea. This was untrue. Alan will be part of a squad of squash players who will be attending the Asian Games in Soeul. Alan has no interest in being any sort of runner other than the sort of runner who runs on running tracks. Until recently Adam also run marathons and ran endurance running all over the world. Alan, who has been spotty since a young age, is an accomplished squid squasher and was the Yorkshire under-21s squat champion in his younger days when he was under 21. We mistakenly gave the information that Alan enjoyed getting steamed on old locomotives. This should have read that Alan enjoys travelling on steam trains while getting steamed.

IRIS AND DEBORAH HEEELY

Apologies to mother and daughter bikers Idris and Deborah Heeley who are in direct competition with each other in the Hemsworth Cocky-Bakey competition, as we reported last week. There were a number of errors in our reported piece. Firstly, Irish is entering her Lemon Drizzle cake and not Melon Dribble. And Debenhams is entering her Fat Tasty Slab Cake and not a Fat Nasty Knob Cake. Also it is not named after her husband and we have no excuse why that was written. We apologise on all counts and hope that our contribution to a charity of Irisssss's's and Debrabrah's choice will make up for our error.

THERE WAS an error in Thursday's issue in an pology to Penny's Mansion of Beauty. She is offering a brand-new treatment of colonic interrogation and not irrigation as reported.

DEBRA GRAHAM

OUR PROFUSE apologies to Debra Graham for a litany of mix-ups in a recent article. Debra is a supermodel and not a soup model. She has been the face of perfume house Creep for six years, not sixty as published and bases her image on fellow model Kate Moss and not Stirling. Debra is currently appearing in a poster ad campaign for raw eggs.

JEANETTE GASCOYNE

WE DO apologise to the above lady for an article last week that somehow got smashed with footballer 'Gazza' Gascoigne's profile piece. Jeanette's profile will be in our Saturday supplement. By firm contrast, Janice is a church warden whose favourite things are knitting with chunky wools and cats and old people. She is not into anything involving balls.

CARA CRONK

IN AN article about Cara Kronk's child-minding business we inadvertently referred to it as a car crash of a business when we meant her business is called Cara's Crèche. We also called her a Death Mother instead of a died-in-the-wool Earth Mother. Also Cara changed her first baby when she was eleven, not hanged her little sister. We have made a financial settlement to Ms Crank in the hope that it will alleviate the loss of the clients to her business and we further hope this apology will rectify any damage to her child-binding service.

MRS MABEL ATTERCLIFFE AND REVEREND WILSON

Please note that Mrs Maple Attercliffe gave the Reverend Wilson of St Knickerless Church, Sheffield one of her famous quiches not kisses, nor quickies, to revive him when he fell ill recently. We do apologise wholeheartedly for the double error.

DIANNE'S BRAZIER

THE DAIRY Trumpet apologies most profusely for an article that we ran last month about Dianne's bra. Ms Brazier is opening up a new bar and restaurant on Saturday called "Di's Brasserie" and not a fingerie shop as we inadvertently advertised. Ms Brassiere told us that she cannot wait to see lots of people queueing at her doors ready to have a good time and not queueing at her drawers. We do apologise for any wrong wording that put a seedy take on the article.

Ms Brazier sampling some of her wears.

MAIR HOWE – TAKE TWO

WE DO apologise to Mrs Hair How for an unfortunate series of errors that occurred in our paper reporting on her day at the town hall where a day that should have been special turned out to be the sort of nightmayor one where her head swelled to twice the large size it usually is. The Mare – Dr Dim Witt, made sure that the second attempt at giving Mair her medal for bravery went this time without a hitch. There was no shellfish on the buffet and the medal had Marie's name spelt correctly. Mrs Who said that she had had a lovely day with Dr No and that it was well worth waiting for, and that she would weir her medal with pride.

Apologies to Barbara Montgomery for last week saying she was a fan of AC/DC when we should have stated in fact that she had OCD and doesn't like any sort of heavy cock music.

LYNNE HOWELL

Once again we do need to apologise to Lynne Howell for misinformation that appeared in a piece about her last week and hereto rectify. Lynne set up a soup kitchen to service street dwellers in the 1880s and received an MBE from Queer Elizabeth for her outstanding services to the community. We have made sure that she will be looked after in the Horse and Cart pud in Pubsey when she goes for her dinner there on us.

PLEASE NOTE that a recent featured photograph of Mr Colleen Badgery of Thirsk Falconry Centre had the wrong wording underneath it. The bird he was featured with was a Steller's Sea Eagle. He has no friends He has no friends named Stella.

Stella: not a seagull.

SARAH ARMITAGE

Please note that the speaker for the Rotary (NOT Rotund) club's annual conference will be financial sexpert Sarah Armitage who will be doing a talk about hedge funds, followed by a C and A. She will not be talking about hedgehogs as we previously reported.

REVEREND ROB DREW AND VICKY DREW

There were red faces at the *Trumpet* this week when we reported the visit of the Bishop of Skipton to Hornys to see Reverend Rob Drew and his wife Rocky. It should have read that members of his clergy were glad he could stay and join them for a *post cenam* glass of Vicky's home-made wine. Vicky served up porn cocktails, Toad in the Hole followed by Sticky Vicky's tacky toffee pudding. We have made a substantial donation to the Drews' chosen charity: Euthanasia - For Teenagers, a movement set up especially to deal with that age group.

TANIA ABBOTT

Apologies to Mrs Tania Abbott after the article we stated last week in which we said that she was raising money for the Le Cat that Shat on the Mat charity. This should of read, Le Chat on the Mat charity. Tania is playing the character of Miserable Les at the local theatre, one of the principal roles, and will donate her actor's fee towards cat welfare.

COUNCILLOR ANGELA JONES

Our apologies to Councillor Angela Jones after we described her as dressing like a slapper at the Art Deco ball held in order to raise funds to be used to buy equipment to disadvantage kids. This should have read she was dressed as a flapper. The ball raised £10,500, which everyone agreed was a wonderful amount to buy children some things with what they are in need of.

Apology – Beryl Rigby is Neither a Nymphomaniac nor a Kleptomaniac

THE *TRUMPET* apologises once again to Beryl Rugby for referring to her as a kleptomaniac in an article that apologised for calling her a nymphomaniac. The word we should have used was technomaniac. Beryl took it in good humour as she told the *Trumpet* that she was eighty-eight and her days of being oversexed and stealing things were well and truly over. She has accepted lunch for two at her local Hungry Horse by way of apology.

PLEASE NOTE that we described Councillor Sandra Wagstaffe in a recent article as idle. This should have read, Idle Councillor Sandra Wagstaffe, as in pertaining to the village of Idle in Bradford. There are three idle councillors there and Ms Wagstaffe has been one the longest serving, inactive since 2016. We do apologise for any distress caused and hope that Ms Wagstiffe will enjoy the voucher we have given her for dinner for two at the new restaurant set up in the idle local peoples Community Centre.

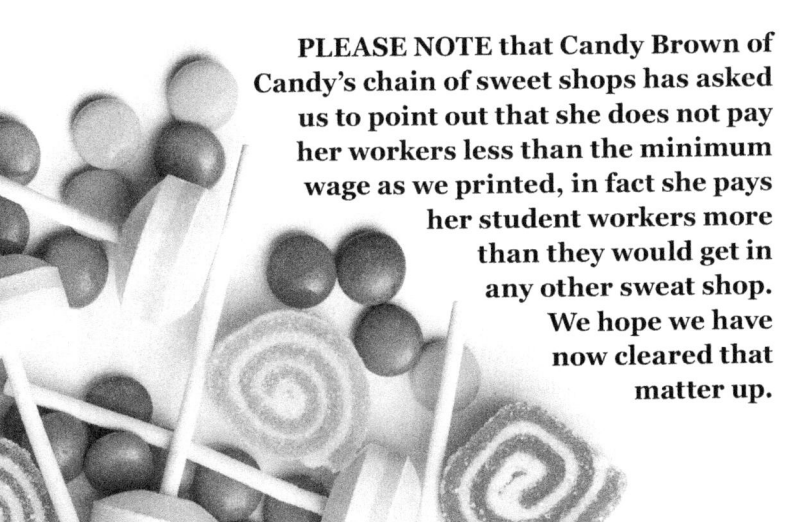

PLEASE NOTE that Candy Brown of Candy's chain of sweet shops has asked us to point out that she does not pay her workers less than the minimum wage as we printed, in fact she pays her student workers more than they would get in any other sweat shop. We hope we have now cleared that matter up.

ANGELA NOLAN

WE DO apologise to Angela Nolan for an item that appeared in our Change of Career supplement last weekend. Angela was not in the Nolan Sisters band, as reported, and as such never met Robbie Williams or any member of Take That. She

Angela (left) is not a Nolan Sitter.

previously worked in pet shop which was owned by local businessman William Roberts. Also we apologise to Terry the bull who we much maligned by saying his name was Terrible and mistakenly saying he gores Angela regularly, when in fact he guards her when she is in his field. We do wholeheartedly apologise to Angela and Jerry and hope that a voucher to the Arthur and Miller Steakhouse for a three-course dinner for two is of due recompense for any offence caused.

ANDREW PETERS-JONES

THERE WAS a very unfortunate spelling mistake in a feature about the Peters-Jones family last week. Andrew Peters-Jones's late father Rathbone Zeta-Jones gave him advice to invest and not as we misreported. Mr Peters-Jones senior was famous for his banking acumen in the 1960s and earned the family fortune investing in blue movies for export. We apologise to the family wholeheartedly.

CAROL DYKE

WE ARE grateful to retired professional club singer Mrs Carol Dyke of Heckmondwike for accepting lunch at her local pub the Mucky Dick as an apology for an article in which we stated that she was currently on the search for fellow local swingers for alternative fun in the church. This should have read that Carol was currently on the search for fellow dykes.

JANINE JONES

WE DO apologise to Janine Jones for an article featuring her Cooking with Janine class. Jolene has asked us to point out that her enlistees were sent home with lasagne and spice cakes and not space cakes. Next week, Janice will be cooking hash as a main and caraway weed cake for dessert.

RIGHT: A chilled Janine preparing to get baked.

APOLOGIES TO Kerry's Spa for miswording in Saturday's issue. Kerry is offering twenty per cent off a back, suck and crack wax and not a back, sick and cock massage.

EMILY WRIGHT

We do apologise to Emily Wright of Emily Wright Catering for wrong wording that appeared in last week's *Trumpet*. Her staff served champagne and canapes not a can of peas, and she put on a magnificent buffet of food, not a bucket of it. Also apologies to the mayor. We did mean that guests reported that Emily's food was in line with the new mayor who had acquired a taste for fine food, meaning that it was all good stuff. We in no way intended to imply he was a bit unlikeable.

SANDY SHORT

LAST MONTH we ran a story about Sandy Short who wowed the crowds in a Barnsley pub by singing Puppy on a String and winning the first prize of the meat parcel. We do need to clarify that Randy is from Sutton Coldfield and not Full Sutton Prison as stated and are sorry for any embarrassment caused.

PAT HARRIS

PROFUSE APOLOGIES to singer Fat Harris for an article that appeared about her in January. Unfortunately the story was smashed up with that of local boxer Patrick 'Bomber' Harris and his training routine. (Ms) Pat Harris owes her career longevity to drinking lots of spring water, plenty of rest, proper warm-ups before her events and avoiding too much caffeine and alcohol. She will be appearing at Picklington Theatre on St Patriot's Day to sing a specially curated pock of garlic and Irish classics.

THE DUKE AND DUTCHESS OF LOWFIELD AND THE LORD HIGH SHERIFF

WE APOLOGISE for insensitive wording on the title of the piece about the do hosted by the Lord High Sheriff last week about it going down a bomb, which should never have happened. The piece should have been titled, 'Charity Lunch goes down a Treat'. Also the Duke and Duchess are not virgins but vagrants. They have a strictly no animal products policy, including eggs and milk which they have not even dressed in since 1995. We have made a substantial gift to the Lardmine Aid charity in their names.

MICHAELA BENTINE retired last week from her profession as a dental nurse working at the Slime Dental Practice and is not a mental nurse. We apologise for any miswording that occurred in previous posts. We wish her a long and gappy retirement.

JESS SHORT

IN OUR apology to Jess Short last week, we inadvertently wrote that men had turned up to her Pilots class wearing bananas. This course of should have read, bonanzas.

Jess demonstrating that bandanas are clearly not items of headwear.

AN AMENDMENT to Chez Sharon's pensioner's special offer running through November which should have read: To celebrate our new shop on Clarnon Street, Rotherham, there will be a special offer for over-65s. Perm, clit and blow dry for only £300. Booking essential.

MARIA YORK

WE APOLOGISE for the misinformation in last week's *Trumpet* in which we gave out some misinformation. A rogue spelling inferred that Mrs York's bookshop on Wetherby High Street would be full of boobs and not books. And opening the store was not leading glamour model Katie Price but Katie Prince a leading influencer who has over two hundred followers on Instagram.

Thankfully Mrs York was delighted by the amount of people who turned up to help christen the store, so many in fact that she ran out of wine and nipples and had to send out for more. 'I sold more boobs in a day that I usually sell in a month' said a delighted Maria. 'And Katie has got a hundred more followers for her Instagram page so all turned out well in the end.'

Bishop Steven Hinch And Ms Katie Compton – A Further Apology

THE DAILY TRUMPET would like to further apologise to cheesemaker Katie Compton who was crowned Artisan Cheesemaker of the Year, not Arsonist, by the Cheese Marketing board for her Stinking Bishop, which is nothing to do with her partner Bishop Steven Hinch who does not smell of cheese or otherwise and by all accounts is a man of fragrance. Bishop Lunch and Ms Compton have generously agreed to accept hinch for two at the County Girl pub, which is local to the bishop's dialysis in the West Midlands by way of our deep regret for the quality of our reportage.

STEVE AND JULIE HOUGHTON

WE APOLOGISE to Mayor Steve Houghton and his Mare Julie Houghton for an error that appeared in our paper last week in which we mistakenly reported that they were treated to the sight of local inmates from a retirement home doing the splits. They are not inmates but residents and they did not do the splits but showed them a display of the mats they had been making which the Houghtons found very artistic. We also wholeheartedly apologise wholeheartedly to the old people in the Golden Showers retirement home for any discomfiture that we may have caused.

APOLOGIES ARE OWED TO DONNA BABBAGE

WE INADVERTENTLY referred to Donor's newly refurnished takeaway as Cabbages and not Baggages as would have been correct. Mrs Cabbage has a special offer on kebabs until the end of the month where buyers can purchase two kebabs and chips for the price of three.

EVEN MORE APOLOGIES FOR MORE APOLOGIES

DEBRA GRAHAM

APOLOGIES to supermodel Debra Graham for a mistake appearing in Wednesday's apology to her. Debra is currently appearing in a poster ad campaign for Rolex and not raw eggs.

Please note that Ken Fidler is giving lessons to children on how to groom horses at his home K D Midler's Farm in Follifoot with brushes and not for sexual purposes. We apologise profusely for any distress caused to Kev and his horses.

THE PETER-JONES FAMILY

WE EXTEND our greatest apologies to the Peters-Jones family last week for a correction what appeared for the original article. Mr Peters-Jones senior earned his fortune by investing in the mineral Blue John for export and not blue movies. We apologise to Andrew Peter-Jones and to the memory of his late father Catherine and have donated a substantial sum to the charity set up in his name: The Rathboner Trust.

REVEREND ROB DREW AND VICKY DREW

PLEASE NOTE the charity the Reverend Drew and his wife Vicky support is not Euthanasia - For Teenagers, but Youth in Asia - For Teenagers.

BERYL RIGBY

Once again we issue an apology to Beryl Rigby for wrong information in our last article about her. Beryl has never been oversexed or a shoplifter, not even in her youth. She was a dinnerlady for forty years and is well known locally for being a regular goer at her local church. Our thanks to Beryl for finding the funny side of our error.

SALLY FURNESS

We mistakenly said in our article about historian Sally Furnace's talk featuring Mr Kipling that he wrote Jingle Bells and not the Jungle Book. We have made a small contribution to a charity of Silly's choice for our misreporting. She as chosen for the funds to go to the Birdwell Library to purchase some books wrote by the late, great Mr Rodney Kipling.

KATH MCQUEEN

WE ARE SORRY for inaccurate information about Perfumier Kath McQueen's perfume which won a top industry award for her. Her successful scent Smell of Hawes has base notes of cedar and not cheddar. Kath's fragrance will be manufactured by top perfume house Van Morrison & Arpels for release early next year.

AN APOLOGY to ex-professional swinger Mrs Carol Dick of Heckmondwike who is lunching, on us, at her local the Mucky Fuck and not the Mucky Dyke as recently stated. As a reminder, any one who likes to sing and wants to join Carol's Carol Singers, please meet Carol and her grope at St Brian the Blessed church, Heckmondwike every Friday 8-7pm. We profusely apologise for any embarrassment caused to Carol and to the Mucky landlord.

MRS RAMONA HARWELL

In an article that appeared last week about her husband's chopper, we meant to say that Mr Harwell was considering whether to get rid of his old bike or the Chopper and not, as stated, keep the old bike his wife.

MR AND MRS JOHN AND CHRISTINE LOCKWOOD

WE OFFER our extended apologies to Mr and Mrs Woodcock for getting some details wrong in coverage about their anniversary which is only 55 years and not 800. Christine enjoys the odd cocktail and we in no way meant to insinuate that she has a problem with drink and John only has the occasional bet on the horses every day and is not a serial gambler. Also we should have offered our huge congratulations and not commiserations as we mistakenly printed. We do hope that Sunday lunch for four at their local pub the Farrier and not the Farrier as we printed will hope to amend some of the damage.

WE APOLOGISE to Russian expert Dr Mikhail Spivak for wrong information about a talk he will be doing in Otley college. Dr Sputnik will be discussing the genius of Carl Fabergé in July but we have no explanation why it was wrote that they smell of Brut as that reporter has left but we would presume that the Fabergé name was merely borrowed to imply quality. Fabergé eggs can go for millions and Brut is still available and can be bought for £7.80 which would be a clue this would be correct. But, the *Trumpet* says... go to the lecture and find out!

LEFT: Fabergé Egg = £1m+ at auction
RIGHT: Brut Deoderant = £1.67 at Boots

Thank you to the following contributors for their generous sponsorships for the charity. I do hope you enjoy being STARS. It's always lovely to see your name in a book, even this one where one is ritually humiliated. I am indebted to you for seeing the fun side and may Karma bring you lovely things for doing this very nice and kind job to help a little cat charity.

Oh and if you are reading this and thinking 'Ooh I wish I'd got my act together and got an entry in this superb book' then I have a limited number of slots for the reprint. You can write to me on www.millyjohnson.co.uk/contact/ and we can get that in place.

Thank you to this lovely lot...

Lesley Armitage for Sarah Armitage

Nikki Badgery for Colin Badgery at Thirsk Falconry Centre (my Happy Place) www.falconrycentre.co.uk

Darryl Booth for Lesley Booth and Tracy Burdett

Victoria Collins for Mair Howe

Katie Compton for herself and Steve Hinch

Pam Cummings for Rosie Ferguson

Vicky Drew for herself and Rob Drew, Julie and Steve Houghton

Martyn Eagles

Andrew Fay

Andrew Furness for Sally Furness

Ruth Haigh for John and Christine Lockwood

Deborah and Iris Heeley

Bren Hosking and the Wiltshire Federation of WIs

Lynne Howell

Victoria Joffe for Debra Graham

Eleanor Jones for Janine Jones

Sharon Maw

Angela Nolan both for herself and for Jeanette Gascoyne

Gill Partington for Tania Abbott

Amanda Prados for Carol Irene Kingsford

Deborah Saunders for Alan Saunders

Rob Short for Jess Short and Sandy Short

Jacqui Watson

Tracy Wright for Emily Wright

Dianne Walker/Brazier

ABOUT THE AUTHOR

Milly Johnson is a *Sunday Times* Top Two (ahem!) bestselling novelist born and bred in Barnsley, South Yorkshire. She is also a poet, professional joke-writer, after-dinner speaker, stage performer and columnist. But not with the *Daily Trumpet*. Her books have been translated into many languages and have sold in their millions around the world.

You can read more about her on her website www.millyjohnson.co.uk. Do sign up for the monthly newsletter featured on there to hear even more, be in the birthday draw and maybe win stuff because she does do a good parcel of goodies.

If you are reading this in the USA (howdy!) then Milly has a dedicated US website www.milly-johnson.com

Her social handles are here, do give her a follow – even if it's just out of sympathy.

TikTok: @millyjohnsonauthor

Facebook: @millyjohnsonauthor

Insta: @themillyjohnson

Twitter/X: @millyjohnson

Substack: @millyjohnson

Photo credits

Japan's
Big
Bang

Japan's Big Bang

The Deregulation and
Revitalization of
the Japanese Economy

Declan Hayes

TUTTLE PUBLISHING
Boston • Rutland, Vermont • Tokyo

First published in 2000 by Tuttle Publishing, an imprint of Periplus Editions (HK) Ltd,
with editorial offices at 153 Milk Street, Boston, Massachusetts 02109.

Library of Congress Cataloging-in-Publication Data in Process

ISBN: 0-8048-3227-7

Distributed by

USA
Tuttle Publishing
Distribution Center
Airport Industrial Park
364 Innovation Drive
North Clarendon, VT 05759-9436
Tel: (802) 773-8930
Tel: (800) 526-2778

CANADA
Raincoast Books
8680 Cambie Street
Vancouver, British Columbia
V6P 6M9
Tel: (604) 323-7100
Fax: (604) 323-2600

JAPAN
Tuttle Shuppan
RK Building, 2nd Floor
2-13-10 Shimo-Meguro, Meguro-Ku
Tokyo 153 0064
Tel: (03) 5437-0171
Fax: (03) 5437-0755

SOUTHEAST ASIA
Berkeley Books Pte Ltd
5 Little Road #08-01
Singapore 536983
Tel: (65) 280-1330
Fax: (65) 280-6290

First edition
06 05 04 03 02 01 00   10 9 8 7 6 5 4 3 2 1

Printed in The United States of America

To the two women in my life, Michiyo and my mother.

TABLE OF CONTENTS

Japan Inc.

"The buck stops here." [1]

"In Japan, the buck keeps circulating."[2]

Although Japan has proved remarkably adept at earning the bucks, she has proved incredibly clumsy at handling them. Much of the wealth she earned during the 1970s and 1980s has been frittered away in the 1990s. No one has accepted responsibility for this; they have instead preferred to pass the metaphorical buck. The Big Bang is an attempt by the Japanese to stop the hemorrhage of their hard-earned dollars. Part of this rejuvenating process involves making the buck stop. It means making incompetents suffer the consequences of their mistakes. It means stopping Japan's financial institutions using dishonest accounting practices to hide their losses. It means owning up to past mistakes. It means the total transformation of Japan's corporate culture. It means the abandonment of old and obsolete ways and the wholehearted adoption of new and modern ways of handling both money and responsibility. It means what it says. It means a Big Bang, a total transformation of the way Japan works.

Japan, which seemed till very recently to be on the road to world economic supremacy, has allowed her domestic economy to put herself and the entire world economy in jeopardy. Although Japan excels at producing cars, cameras, electrical goods and other largely export-oriented products, her sheltered sector remains bloated and grossly inefficient. Her hard-earned bucks have had to support a veritable army of overprotected laggards. The construction industry exemplifies. A massive 550,000 construction firms employ a 7,000,000-strong army. One in ten of Japan's total workforce is, in other words, tied up in construction. Construction, though grossly overmanned, is thus a key industry: it commands electoral and, therefore, political sway. As chapter two will explain, property's central use as collateral in Japanese financial dealings has allowed it to play a key role in fomenting Japan's current economic chaos. It has been an underlying brake on Japanese economic activity for the whole of the last decade.

Japan's construction industry is not unique in this most unique of countries. Japan's traditional distribution system is also notoriously inefficient. Some 230,000 primary wholesalers deal with secondary wholesalers who in turn deal with a host of subwholesalers, large retail stores, and innumerable small shops and stores countrywide. Given this phalanx of grocers' assistants, labor productivity is, to put it mildly, low and retail prices are, without overstating the point, absurdly high. Watermelons can cost up to $100³ each and grapes come individually gift-wrapped.

The grapes, like the rice, more often than not come from Japan's grossly inefficient agricultural sector, which commands even greater political power and influence than their fellow Luddites in the distribution and construction sectors. Although attempts are being made to reform there, too, their political clout and the willingness of the urban Japanese to buy—and adulate—their rice and other over-priced products will make agricultural reform all the slower to achieve.

These are all gigantic hurdles that Japan's Big Bang must overcome if Japan is to have a viable future. Although these issues are discussed sporadically throughout this book, the underlying point to grasp now is that Japan's psychological inertia is its biggest impediment. Generations of Japanologists have convinced the Japanese public and outsiders that the normal rules of commerce do not apply, that Japan is unique.

At their most extreme, these people have claimed—and many have believed—that Japanese intestines are markedly different from those of other peoples, that the Japanese mind is wired differently, that Japanese baseball is different from the American brand that spawned it, and, equally ludicrously, that Japanese snow is qualitatively different from the snow that falls elsewhere on planet Earth.

These differences have been used to bolster trade restrictions. Because the Japanese game was qualitatively different, baseball bats could not be imported from the United States. Because the snow was different, only skis made in Japan could cope with its unique properties. Because the intestines were different, foreign beers were taboo: the Japanese could drink only locally made beers which took such singularities into account.

These unique traits acted as effective barriers to trade until very recently. And, although these large, and largely reactionary, lobbies can still muster considerable political clout, the winds of change are blowing in with increasing force from abroad. Traditional distribution chains are being increasingly bypassed as Japan responds to consumer pressures and restructures. Direct importing is increasing and firms, both local and foreign, are erecting modern shopping malls: Japan currently has only six super malls of over 80,000 square meters, compared with almost 700 in the United States, a disparity up with which the long-exploited Japanese consumer will no longer put. Indeed, because these large malls cannot be dependent upon Japanese hobby-farmers and their tiny rice paddies and cabbage patches, change here is impacting itself further down the supply line. A major shakeout of these overprotected sectors is, however slowly, beginning to bite.

Examples abound. The Osaka-based trading firm Itochu is using technology from the American drugstore Walgreens to open 1,000 pharmacies by 2002: bad news for the little pharmacies that dot metropolitan Tokyo but further potentially good news for the over-exploited Japanese consumer.

Elsewhere in the distribution sector, British Petroleum has entered the gas station business, in direct competition with 13 other oil companies. Restructuring will, at the very least, prune the current 60,000 stations to a more rational figure of 25,000 or less. When the dust settles, the survivors will resemble their equivalents elsewhere. Nippon Oil, for example, has agreed to allow McDonald's to build 5,000 restaurants in Nisseki service stations. This should give Nippon Oil and BP, with their considerable expertise, dominant market share. McDonald's should, meanwhile, raise the collective cholesterol levels of the Japanese a few more notches. By further changing Japan's urban landscape, these distributional changes should usher in even more profound societal ones.

Though change is in the air, it is happening on the ground too, in particular in infrastructure and information technology. Japan has efficient, if grossly overpriced, transport and telecommunication systems. She has the highest mobile phone penetration rate in the world—over 33% of the entire population are hooked up. Though telephone usage, rental, and installation fees are expensive by global standards, regulations are being relaxed in both broadcasting and communications, and foreign concerns are gaining greater access to this huge, if somewhat idiosyncratic, market. Still, although partial deregulation has seen new domestic and foreign entrants flood into the mobile and international call markets, Nippon Telegraph and Telephone Company (NTT), which previously had a monopoly, continues to dominate large sections of the market. The market, like so many other Japanese ones, remains deliberately tilted in favor of the home team.

These currents of change are noteworthy in other key areas as well. Tokyo's Narita International Airport, for example, ranks 25th in the world, having over 25 million passengers annually and growing at 5% per annum. It is also Asia's busiest cargo port. Tokyo's domestic airport, Haneda, ranks sixth in the world, with 46.6 million passengers and a 2% annual growth rate. Of Japan's other airports, Kansai International Airport, serving Osaka, is worth especial mention. With 19 million passengers a year and growing at over 14% per annum, it is the world's 42nd busiest airport. A technological wonder, built on a man-made island, it is Japan's first 24-hour-a-day airport.

Japan's unique mix of modernity and obsolescence manifests itself here as well. Although Japan's airports are world-class, her ubiquitous regulations ensure that domestic air fares are among the most expensive in the world, and that, as a consequence, tourism and other potential revenue earners remain underdeveloped. Japan's quaint ownership structures further impede progress. Thus, for example, plans for the much-needed massive expansion of Narita are being impeded by a small number of existing landowners: a scenario that replicates itself thousands of times over in metropolitan Japan.

Most importantly, it reverberates through the finance industry. This uniquely Japanese quirk of insisting on a stifling consensus before moving even an inch forward will be a refrain resonating throughout this book. Japan, the world's second largest economy, finds key development projects stymied by minnow property holders and other vested interests. Japan, to take another example, has over 1,000 seaports, of which 20 are internationally important and a further 13 are of major import. Gross overmanning make these Japanese ports twice as expensive and 30% slower to use than their American counterparts. These feather-bedding practices replicate themselves throughout corporate Japan; they epitomize Japan's sheltered sector and are central to explaining her current malaise.

Her bureaucrats, as chapter three will explain, have been charged with making Toyota, Sony, and Honda international models of probity and efficiency, while simultaneously lumbering them with systems which were models of improbity and gross inefficiency. Under their tutelage, her cost-cutting car, camera, and camcorder manufacturers, in earning Japan her much-needed dollars, propelled Japan Inc. forward. Simultaneously, her banks, builders, grocers, farmers, and general factotums kept her firmly entrenched in outmoded practices. These dichotomous forces made Japan the most misunderstood and misrepresented nation on earth. The vested interests of Japan's bloated protected sector, channeled through Japan's policymakers and opinion formers, created the whole mess the Big Bang is now trying to rectify.

Japan is, paradoxically, both a developed and underdeveloped economy. Public transportation in Japan and especially in metropolitan Tokyo is clean, efficient, safe, and among the best in the world. It is being improved at considerable cost, with several hitherto unconnected or poorly serviced areas being linked to the main hubs. This will facilitate Japan's legions of workers getting to their workplaces, where the makers of cameras, cars, and camcorders will continue to keep Japan Inc. afloat and where their compatriots in the sheltered sector will continue to keep Japan's bottom line in the red. The Big Bang, if it is to succeed on both the economic and political fronts, must accommodate these contradictions.

The truth is that, though Japan's infrastructure has been modernized, most of her economy underperforms. Her hotel and tourism sectors, for example, remain underdeveloped. Japan, in fact, runs a net deficit in international tourism with departures outnumbering arrivals by nearly 4 to 1. Inward visitor expenditure in 1996 was around $3 billion, helped in large part by the weakening yen. If tourism and leisure are to play major roles in Japan's economic future, radical and fundamental changes are needed at all levels to redress current imbalances.

Though noting the scale of change needed, this book will concentrate on the core of the problem, Japan's financial sector. Because the problems, as later chapters will explain, run deep, their resolution will not be easy. One of the main reasons that this is so is because Japan is, paradoxically, a lopsided economy. Although it is a seemingly modern economy, it is carrying gross inefficiencies the British and Americans weeded out decades ago. Its governing mandarin class, epitomized in the much-maligned Ministry of Finance (MOF), is trying to weld Anglo-American global governance standards onto an unwelcoming host, which has traditionally surpassed global benchmark standards in producing cars, cameras, and camcorders but which has failed dismally to meet them in finance, construction, tourism, and agriculture. Starkly put, powerful, well-entrenched, and long-established forces want to impede change. They want to keep Japan lopsided.

These forces ensure that Japan has a lopsided workforce to go with its lopsided economy of a highly efficient export sector and a grossly inefficient sheltered sector. However, the chill winds of market forces are coming to bear here as well, and changes in long-established customs and practices are beginning to take effect. Redundancies, outsourcing, and accountability are becoming increasingly important benchmarks in corporate Japan.

Attitudes are changing in response to these forces. Though not devotees of machismo, Japanese corporate man traditionally believed that a (respectable) woman's place, if not at home, was as a low-paid, low-bowing, tea-pouring "office lady." These days, corporate man has to think of his own place as well as that of the down-

trodden members of the second sex. Labor market fluidity, accentuated by the bursting of the bubble economy, has eroded his system
of lifetime employment, one of the cornerstones of Japanese industrial policy. Although lifetime employment was largely a feature of
the larger companies and had no bearing on the working lives of
over 70% of Japan's workforce, even the myth is now dissipating.
Downsizing and its concomitant financial and societal problems are
becoming a sad reality for a growing number of deflated Japanese
"salarymen."[4]

These downsizings with their attendant traumas are occurring in
a country that rebuilt its ravished economy on the basis of harmo-
nious industrial relations, predicated on all working for a common
and greater good. Now, many of these workers are redundant to the
common good of Japan Inc.

Japan, having reached the status of the world's second largest
economy, has now presumably reached that common and greater
good, for which the postwar generation sacrificed so much. The
returns from that greater good have not been equitably redistributed. At the top end, hordes of politicians, bureaucrats, and bankers
recently have been embroiled in a series of financial scandals which
are, however belatedly, shattering the illusion that Japan was, somehow, ethically unique in business affairs. At the bottom end, hordes
of salarymen are being thrown onto the unemployment and home-
less human scrapheaps. In the middle, the hard-pressed middle-class
scrimp to fund their children's education and their own pensions: all
this in a land that has lived beyond its means. It is a land in crisis.

Government debt is now bigger than the nation's gross domestic product (GDP), and personal debt is double the size of Japan's
GDP. Japan, on paper at least, remains the world's second largest
economy. The country's GDP of $4.4 trillion represents an approx-
imate income of $35,000 per capita. With gross national savings
equal to 30% of GDP, the nation accounts for one-third of global
savings.

Although these and similar Japanese economic figures can
sound dauntingly impressive, Japan has been in an unofficial recession since her bubble economy burst in 1991. In accordance with
Japan's uniquely lethargic etiquette, the recession was only belated-

ly acknowledged in 1998, seven years after it first bit. Japan is a country where lengthy policy-recognition and policy-implementation time-lags are the norm. Buddha-like bureaucrats in the MOF give the aura of thinking in decades, if not in millennia. Unlike those in the more ruthlessly pragmatic West, Japan's much-needed reforms must, they say, be arrived at by achieving group consensus, if not group nirvana which, more often than not, slides into group inertia and group apathy.

The MOF's search for the holy grail of an all-inclusive consensus means that the metaphorical buck gets continually shuffled about as no one will take responsibility for Japan's many failures. Japan's banking crisis, discussed at length in chapters two and four, is now in its second decade. With such an utter disregard for trying proactive solutions, it is no wonder that Japanese corporate life breeds such gross inefficiencies.

Japan, a nation in economic crisis, is not panicking. Farmers, construction workers, grocers' assistants, and small plot-holders must all be taken onboard the convoy of Japan Inc., which more resembles John Lennon's anarchic Yellow Submarine rather than the invincible flotilla it was portrayed as in the 1980s.

This, to repeat, is a country that does not panic. This is the country that it took two nuclear hits to defeat and that even contemplated fighting on for victory after the United States obliterated both Nagasaki and Hiroshima. This is the land of Zen, where decisions and consensus are arrived at by means tortuously, laboriously time-consuming to all but the most unworldly, mildest-mannered Zen devotee.

Japan, the land of Zen, is also the land of yen. The yen's importance in international trading has been in secular decline since 1991, and interest rates remain very low. Long-term funds continue to be available at less than 2.5% per annum and short-term rates remain stable at around 1.6%. Thus, even though the zeal for consensus remains, the zest to grow has been stifled. Despite rock-bottom interest rates, banks will not lend and businesses cannot borrow. Although, being Japan, no one is panicking, stagflation and paralysis reign supreme nonetheless.

The Tokyo stock market, the Nikkei Stock Average, has also

been in secular decline from when the bubble burst. This secular fall has been accentuated by unprecedented difficulties in Japan's financial services sector, which have muffled the zest to grow. This paralysis in the financial sector and the attempts of Japan's mandarin class to kick-start this corpse into life are the main focus of this book.

While all of the subsequent chapters discuss these matters in greater detail, chapter three focuses on the role of the MOF and makes plain that its mandarins have a daunting task. Domestically, Japan's deposit-taking financial institutions are carrying a staggering $250 billion of nonperforming loans[5]. Most are technically bankrupt. Compounding the problem, Japan's banks have $150 billion exposure to financially troubled Asian markets. By this reckoning, Japan is a financial ambulance case. By this reckoning, Japan should be panicking.

Because the Japanese banking system is currently the biggest threat there is to world stability, the rest of the world is concerned. That said, because Japan has the world's largest pool of capital, European and American financial companies are frenetically preparing for the rapid expansion of their Japanese operations. Liberalized access is creating opportunities for funds management, complex financial instruments, and property restructuring, opportunities at which the foreigners excel and the Japanese and their obsolete practices have not yet mastered. Japan, believed to be on the way to global financial hegemony in the 1980s, is reckoned to be the last major finance opportunity of the twentieth century. Japan Inc. has been transformed from the financial vultures of the 1980s to the vulture meat of the late 1990s. The Americans and Europeans are here for the last big financial windfall of the twentieth century and the first of the next century. They are here to feast on the carcass of Japan Inc.

Their arrival has brought twitches of life into the stagflated corpse of Japan Inc. Though Japan is moving at glacier-like speed to take the hand of opportunity that the foreigners represent, marriages between Japanese companies and overseas companies are proceeding at a comparative gallop. Sumitomo Trust and Banking Company and Citibank are now betrothed; the Nippon Credit Bank and Bankers Trust have joined hands; Nikko Securities and Smith

Barney are arm-in-arm; Nippon Life Insurance and Putnam Investments are planning to build their future together; so too are Chiyoda Life Insurance and Indosuez Asset Management.

It is, in other words, a happy-mating time in Japan, where marriages are very expensive and very ceremonial. In the secular world, families often hire private detectives to check out the other family to the marriage for traces of low-caste, Korean blood or other perceived impurities that might lessen the value of their newly acquired stock. Clearly, by traditional Japanese standards, these courtesans are not kosher: they are not sons of the soil; they are gaijin, foreigners, and therefore, to say the least, suspect.

They have been portrayed as inheritors to Commodore Perry's black boats, the American flotilla, which forced Japan, by gunboat diplomacy, to enter the world of modern international trade. Like Perry's cutthroats, they are seen as the threat that they are. Not only are they busily and brashly grabbing market share but they are doing it in their own way, thereby irrevocably transforming Japanese corporate culture in the process.

Given the foreigners' ways of doing things, the Japanese are, in fact, not at all sure that these marriages will be blissful. Because the Europeans and Americans are now more powerful financially, they will be able to dictate the pace of change. Corporate Japan, drunk on its own mystique, does not like change: especially when impertinent foreigners, disrespectful of the Japanese way of doing things, set the pace.

Further, despite the wedding bells chiming throughout corporate Japan, some of the foreigners seem decidedly coy. Citibank's Japanese subsidiary seems to have no time for frivolous romance. It is busily expanding its domestic branch network and workforce in an effort to lure cash-rich individual investors from its Japanese competitors, who are so preoccupied with their massive bad debts and consequent restructuring that they have not gone a-courting. Not that Citibank seems to care. With its 19 branches in Japan's biggest cities, it has, thanks to its 24-hour automated teller machines and its high-yielding foreign-currency deposits, become a major presence in Japan's financial markets. Like so many other foreign financial houses, it is nibbling itself out a greater and more viable market share.

American Express is in no rush to the altar either. It intends to provide financial advisory services to its Japanese cardholders through its wholly owned subsidiary, American Express Financial Advisors, which manages about $202 billion in assets for some 2 million clients in the United States. It hopes to exploit both its expertise and the market power its volume gives it to recruit clients from among its 1.1 million cardholders in Japan. The new subsidiary is capitalized at ¥150 million and plans to start operating as soon as it receives a discretionary account management license from the MOF.

The foreign suitors do, however, seem to have imbibed some of the Japanese ways. They have sent their own spies to check out the other family, to wit, corporate Japan. As subsequent chapters explain, they are demanding greater degrees of efficiency and transparency from Japan's unwieldy financial system which, broadly speaking, consists of 225 brokerages with 110,000 employees and assets of $640 billion; 70 insurance companies with over 200,000 full-time and 420,000 part-time employees and assets of $2 trillion; and 150 banks with 442,000 employees and assets of US $7.6 trillion. The foreigners are not dumb: they know that the dowry is potentially huge. But they want to decimate the numbers of guests to the party. The West's global standard yardsticks demand massive rationalizations. And more redundancies.

Japan's unique feather-bedding system has no place in today's global village. If Japan Inc. wishes to be co-opted into World Inc., it must obey its rules. It must, in other words, agree to massive redundancies, rationalizations, and the other euphemisms for sackings Western workers learned to dread. These are not words Japan Inc. wishes to hear.

There are, in other words, party-poopers on the domestic side of things. Chief of these is the Japanese government, which wants to protect the nonperforming Japanese sectors. It wants Western investment banks in Tokyo to contribute money to a fund that would protect depositors when Japanese brokers fail. The collapse of brokers such as Echigo, Ogawa, Sanyo, and Muruso emptied their depositors' insurance scheme of the ¥38 billion it had put aside for such contingencies. The new gaijin-tax plans, which have been drawn up by the Japan Securities Dealers Association and their MOF overseers, have been triggered by a growing liquidity crisis in Japan's brokerage houses. The foreigners believe it is an unjustified attempt to foist part of the cost of reforming Japan's brokerage industry onto their innocent shoulders. The MOF, on the other hand, quite reasonably argues that such a down payment is merely an acknowledgment of the inroads those modern-day black ships have made in looting Japan's vast crocks of gold.

Although, like all marriage partners, they are already quibbling over the finances, the gaijin are unlikely to sue for an early divorce. They are making big money. Goldman Sachs has some $6 billion under management in Japanese mutual funds targeted to local investors—a business it didn't even enter until June 1996; this has catapulted them to ninth position in Japan. Commerz Securities, the brokerage arm of the German banking conglomerate, bought a seat on the Tokyo Stock Exchange (TSE) in early 1997. Crucially, the TSE decreed that Commerz did not have to be physically present but could conduct its affairs through electronic screens at a lower cost than their Japanese competitors; Commerz is thus sitting pretty, waiting for the windfall the inevitable upswing in the TSE will bring them. Merrill Lynch launched a commercial paper program in March 1998 to raise up to $1 billion, making it the first non-Japanese company to tap the fast-growing yen-denominated commercial paper (CP) market. The transaction is expected to boost the yen CP market, which is worth over ¥30,000 billion. Deutsche Morgan Grenfell has tripled its Tokyo staff since 1997 from 160 to 500; the major Wall Street houses are increasing Japan-based personnel at 10% to 15% a year. They are reaping a bonanza.

They are not the only ones. In recent months, Citicorp, Swiss Banking Corp., and Bankers Trust have all announced significant tie-ups with Japanese concerns. Societe General Asset Management, the fund management division of the French bank, bought an 85% stake in Yamaichi Capital Management, one of Japan's largest fund management companies with some $20 billion under management. Other overseas concerns are assessing other sections of Yamaichi for takeover.

Yamaichi, alas, has proved a fickle suitor for some. UBS, for example, incurred considerable losses on the derivatives markets in part due to the collapse of Yamaichi, Japan's fourth largest brokerage house until it went belly-up. UBS was particularly exposed to the Yamaichi-affiliated Fuji Bank, whose shares were suspended from trading for three days in January 1998. When UBS tried to cut its losses by selling Fuji Bank shares, their sell-off just made the index plummet and compounded their losses. They tried to sell futures positions to hedge themselves. But the Nikkei index and their shareholdings became increasingly uncorrelated to each other. This compounded their losses. Still, UBS are deep-pocketed adults, so not too many tears should be shed for them.

Yamaichi, by contrast, has caused many tears to be shed. Its bankruptcy, the biggest ever in Japanese corporate history, has been surpassed by even more massive failures since. Fuji Bank, its would-be rescuer, now finds itself in danger of collapse. Uncertainty and the fear of failure stalk the hitherto perfectly predictable world of Japan Inc.

Although these calamities and their consequent upheavals are detailed in subsequent chapters, the reader should be aware that massive change, epitomized in the tie-ups with foreign outfits, are proceeding at almost breakneck speed in Tokyo. Though not all of them are made in heaven, these marriages of convenience and sheer necessity continue. Many Japanese financial institutions (JFIs), desperately short of expertise, are joining with, colluding with, or forming loose or tight alliances with foreigners. Bankers Trust and Nippon Credit Bank in securitization, Nikko Securities and Smith Barney in wrap accounts, and Goldman Sachs and Yasuda Trust in property are but a small cross-sample of this tide which Japanese cynics snidely call the Wimbledon scenario. They point out that, though the British host the world's premier tennis competition, a Briton never figures in the finals. Extending their analogy, they point out that since the British Big Bang, a host of venerable British financial houses have been gobbled up by foreign concerns. They fail to point out that in the aggregate, the British have done well out of their Big Bang, and that if Japan's Big Bang is successful, so too, in the aggregate, will Japan be.

The Wimbledon metaphor, in fact, misses the essence of the British Big Bang, which, after all, is the prototype for the Japanese model. The British knew that their old boys' clubs and other outmoded practices were costing them money. They bit the bullet, pensioned off or sacked their redundant staff, hollowed out their industry, amended their laws, and got back to business with, let it be said, a resounding bang. Lloyd's and other groups who stuck to outmoded modalities paid the price and were let pay the price of failure. The City in London moved on without them.

Japan Inc. is moving on as well. Though Japan seems quiet on the surface, massive shakeouts are happening beneath the bow. Japanese banks cut off credit lines to 12,048 companies during 1997. Credit suspensions to construction companies, wholesalers, and retailers increased particularly dramatically. The value of bankruptcies topped $100 billion, up 75% on 1996. Even solvent firms are finding it difficult to get loans, such is the scale of change.

The old days of being a part of the cozy flotilla of Japan Inc. are gone. The Tokyo Chamber of Commerce is planning to start a market for mergers and acquisitions (M&A) in a bid to help the growing number of failed and abandoned Japanese companies find buyers. The Chamber's M&A market aims to act as a matchmaker between the increasing number of small and medium-sized companies hoping to sell their businesses and financial institutions specializing in M&A activities. The Osaka Chamber of Commerce set up a similar market in April 1997. Corporate Japan is, however belatedly, adopting this important cornerstone of Western commerce.

This, in itself, is a profound change. Because their society considered being acquired a shameful admission of failure, Japanese companies have traditionally lacked a secondary market. As a result, broadcasting a decision to sell one's company would result in their banks cutting their credit rating, their business partners stopping dealing with them, and their employees fearing for their job security. In other words, neither hostile takeovers, nor the financially disciplined culture such takeovers breed has ever been a part of corporate Japan—even though they have been one of the key components in making Anglo-American market standards the world's norm. Implanting such an alien corporate culture into the main body of Japanese corporate life will require a seismic shift in attitudes. It will require managers taking responsibility for their mistakes and living with the consequences of their mistakes. It will involve a change as fundamental as Perry's black boats wrought.

That fundamental change is now happening. Times are, however slowly, changing. In 1995 and 1996, 1,190 cases were reported of mergers and acquisitions involving Japanese companies, valued at ¥2,476 billion. Though currently moving at glacier-like speed on the surface, the tempo could pick up somewhat. This impending deregulation of the Japanese financial market is expected to be a catalyst for the deregulation of other under-performing sectors in the economy.

Foreign banks, investment banks, and insurance and mutual fund companies stand to massively benefit from this transition. Foreign direct investment in real estate, banking, insurance, and other services has risen from $1.7 million to $6 billion in 1998. The foreigners, despite being of lesser blood, might end up being the prize catch themselves. They will certainly transform the way business is conducted. In Japan, banks oversee a business from inception to dissolution. The banks have, in fact, been central to Japanese business, to a degree almost unimaginable in the West. The banking sector has traditionally been the source of both short- and long-term financing, and there has been relatively little emphasis on raising finance through the issue of shares or bonds compared with other developed capital markets. This, one of Japan's most damaging financial idiosyncrasies, is, with the arrival of gung-ho foreigners, being irrevocably changed. As this changes, so also does Japan's postwar financial corporate culture.

Cuckolded by the MOF mandarins, Japan's banking institutions grew at incredible rates. By the mid 1980s, they ranked among the world's largest by market share and by capitalization until recent scandals, coupled with the Nikkei's free-fall and the collapse of Tokyo property prices, shook them to their foundations. Regarded as world-conquering financial samurai a decade ago, they are now being targeted as easy meat by their leaner—and meaner—Western counterparts.

So bad is the dilemma that Japan's banks are even abandoning some of their best customers in their scramble to survive. They are the antithesis of good business practices, never mind good banking. Their demise had proved beneficial to their foreign competition. Whether they are concentrating on nibbling into niche markets like Lloyd's is doing or whether they are more ambitious like Merrill Lynch, collectively they are capturing huge chunks of the Japanese market. In the process, they are creating the Big Bang.

The Westerners have poured into Tokyo in recent years to avail themselves of the opportunities deregulation and a discredited, disorganized, and dysfunctional domestic financial Japanese sector has bequeathed them. There are over 90 foreign banks operating at various levels in Tokyo, while many others retain representative offices.

As noted earlier, the Japanese media have painted these foreigners as the predatory descendants of Perry's buccaneers. Like the American Commodore Perry and his crew, these foreigners are not coming to Japan solely for altruistic reasons. They see the inefficiencies of the Japanese system and they are here to milk them. They see the banking, securities, and general financial services industry as being the vehicles with most promise for them. Thus, although foreign financial institutions are much more pronounced than hitherto in Tokyo, the number of foreign corporations listed on the TSE is down from the 125 at the start of the 1990s to less than 40 today due to the high cost of listing and low trading volumes of recent years. Because Japan's structural inefficiencies debilitate the use of the TSE as a fund-raising forum, the foreigners are bypassing it in favor of greener and more lucrative pastures.

The Big Bang may, in time, change this scenario. The TSE handles the majority of share trading volume with a smaller volume being conducted on the Osaka exchange. If it can reform itself and become as efficient and transparent as London, it might conceivably emulate London and capture significant off-shore business.

The British Big Bang is, after all, the prototype for the Japanese one, and the City in London has shown by example what the rewards of successful transformation in business culture are. The TSE is aware of the possibilities and, in glacier-like gear, is instituting change. In 1996, the TSE introduced less stringent criteria for companies seeking to list on the second board. In addition, it became easier to have subsidiaries of parent companies and foreign companies listed. In July 1997, options trading in individual shares was introduced.

All of this gives the semblance of moving toward a sophisticated, modern stock exchange meeting modern global governance and operating standards such as pertains in London or New York. The host of reforms already implemented show that this is not just the normal Japanese savoir-faire of time-buying, cosmetic window-dressing. This time, real change is happening.

This time, the changes are actually being implemented. Listing requirements have been simplified. Professional fund managers are being allowed to manage publicly sponsored pension funds. Leasing companies and nonbank loan companies can now issue debentures and commercial paper. Regulations governing the size and frequency of privately placed corporate bond offers have been abolished, and eligibility standards for the issuance of corporate bonds have been eased.

Because these reform are enabling eligible companies to obtain cheaper finance than bank borrowings, the opportunities for investment bankers and others who broker such deals are increasing almost exponentially: Tokyo, as previously mentioned, is a latter-day, high-tech Klondike. It is a gold mine for those firms, local and foreign, that can nurse Japan Inc. into the modern financial world. Thus, the interest of the foreigners and the concerns of losing market share-and profit-of the JFIs.

The whole deregulation packages set in train by former Prime Minister Hashimoto could, in fact, trigger a galaxy of new freedoms and opportunities in a financial Big Bang that will bring almost unprecedented opportunities for the fit and concomitant dangers for the unfit.

According to the schedule he set, restrictions on foreign exchange trading were lifted in 1998; the removal of the ban on derivatives trading is due to follow suit; banks are being permitted to sell investment trusts, and their subsidiaries are being allowed to underwrite a wider range of bonds; and brokers can deal in unlisted stocks and offer asset management accounts. Banks are being allowed to use holding companies and to trade over-the-counter derivatives; off-exchange trading of listed securities and the use of asset-backed securities is being permitted; the licensing of securities companies is being liberalized; and foreign currency trading is being opened to any individual or institution. The bank monopoly on foreign exchange trading has been abolished, and companies trading overseas can now shop around or deal direct for their foreign exchange requirements. Brokerage commissions are being deregulated, the issuing of bonds and commercial paper by nonbank financial institutions is being allowed, and, crucially, international standards to auditing are in the pipeline

Early 2000 is to see the completion of the review of the taxation system; the introduction of real-time gross settlement into the money market; banks will be able to trade equities through subsidiaries and brokers will be allowed to manage pensions through subsidiaries. By early 2001, banks will be permitted to enter the insurance market and vice versa; and cross-marketing in different financial sectors by insurance companies and other institutions will be allowed.

This is, by any yardstick, an ambitious project Mr. Hashimoto has set corporate Japan. To take but one example for the moment. Under a review of the Foreign Exchange Law approved in May 1997 and effective from April 1998, not only are companies and individuals able to handle foreign exchange transactions without government authorization, but they can deposit funds freely into overseas accounts. Prior to this amendment, individuals required approval from the MOF for sums in excess of ¥2 million and corporations needed approval for overseas investment, via a cumbersome process taking many weeks. If freely allowed, this alone is a massive change. When all the other reforms are included, they amount to an almost epoch-making metamorphosis for Japan, which has traditionally been opposed to any noncosmetic changes to its structure.

Although this book is devoted to exploring these proposals at greater length, the sheer scope of the proposed changes cannot be overemphasized. Both the size and nature of the changes underline the revolutionary nature of the Big Bang. It will mean the MOF's abandoning its former policies of informal control and building, almost ab nihilo, a codified body of rules to allow the deregulated goals of free, fair, and open markets to be reached. It is an awesome task.

It is also a difficult project to cover in one tome. Although asset-backed securities and other high-risk financial instruments are touched on in chapter two, implementing these changes and introducing such an array of new and exotic products will demand a massive and unprecedented shake-up in Japan's legal and governance systems. Because it was welded onto a welcoming host, Britain's Big Bang, by contrast was more of a whimper. Hashimoto's proposals, then, by any yardstick, are a proposal for a colossal big bang, which, even if it won't rock the universe, will radically transform Japan. Hashimoto, in effect, intended to scuttle Japan Inc.'s archaic fleet and replace it with a modern, state-of-the-art financial industry. These changes are, in essence, as fundamental as those of the Meiji Restoration or the MacArthur years. They tackle the root causes of Japan's malaise.

Before we consider Mr. Hashimoto's Big Bang proposals in detail, we must first examine Japanese corporate society. Properly speaking, we should follow the well-worn path of Japanologists of yesteryear and go back into the mists of time to more thoroughly understand, appreciate, and get ourselves lost in the myths of Japanese snow, Japanese intestines, and Japanese business practices. For our purposes, a brief postwar overview that throws some glimmers of light on Japan, past, present, and future, will instead suffice.

Japan, during the postwar Occupation years, was a ravished, demoralized, impecunious society. Her once-glorious navy rusted at the bottom of the Pacific Ocean, her once-glorious cities had been fire-bombed and leveled with atomic weapons, her once-glorious troops scavenged on her city streets, her once-glorious emperor-god had declared himself to be mortal, and her once-despised conquerors were dismantling her corporate fabric and superimposing their will and order on her body politic.

This was not to be the Meiji Restoration Mark II. This was the cold reality of utter defeat and the disadvantages of unconditional surrender. It was from these almost insurmountable disadvantages that Japan, under the guidance of her bureaucrats, had to rebuild, if not rearm. Both money and the capacity to generate wealth were almost nonexistent. Careful and prudent rationing of very scarce financial resources, coupled with an almost national iron discipline, were imperative if Japan was not to become a perpetual basket-case of demobbed shoeshine boys. Japan had to pull itself back up by its bootstraps.

Japan's postwar financial markets had therefore, by American or European standards, to adopt a very rigid and very segmented structure, where finance and finance franchises were rationed out in the national interest. Financial markets could not be independent: they had to be a redistribution mechanism for Japan's policymakers, providing low-cost finance to the nascent Japanese companies, which would, in time, become her exporters and financial saviors. In the apocalyptic conditions they faced, cooperation, bordering on downright collusion, had to be the norm between policymakers and the companies they regulated.

Japan's postwar banking system, therefore, followed a compartmentalized model. The primary categories of banks—ordinary banks, long-term credit banks, trust banks, and mutual banks—were each assigned a specific role with regard to obtaining and lending funds. It was, as has been said, a system designed to promote economic recovery after the war by channeling scarce capital resources to carefully selected ends. With this in mind, Japan also separated the banking and securities businesses along American lines.

Japan Inc. had to sail in tight formation. Given her formidable constraints, there could be no room for needless squandering of resources or unnecessary overlapping of functions. Japan's mandarins had set their sights on the promised land of economic-led recovery, and all the ships in the national convoy, with the MOF as the authoritarian admiral of the fleet, had to sail in that same direction.

By contrast to this rigid system of directional control, regulatory intervention in banking operations was relatively flexible and the banks were allowed to pursue efficient banking practices within the parameters of the overall guidelines. Although the banks and the other core financial institutions were segmented by MOF decree into a number of well-defined roles, they were protected by the very powerful and most intrusive MOF, who virtually guaranteed them both their clientele and their considerable profit margins as long as they complied with national socioeconomic objectives, as stipulated and interpreted by the Ministry. Ultimately, it was a cash-cow franchise where profits were free and easy—but only so long as the national guidelines of the MOF were met.

The MOF had bigger fish to fry. Because the principal aim of Japanese policy in the postwar era had been rapid economic development, securing a plentiful and cheap supply of long-term capital for Japanese business was essential to national recovery. Japan's savings rate of 17% of disposable income, the highest savings rate in the world, guaranteed the supply of low-cost funds, which the national consensus allowed to be funneled into subsidizing the vital export-focused growth sectors.

This was the pattern from 1945 up to 1995. The Japanese people saved for a myriad of reasons, they deposited their funds into low-yielding accounts, and those funds, under MOF guidance, were channeled, in accordance with national objectives, into a variety of JFIs. Because these JFIs got this money at preferential rates, they could lend it at preferential rates as well. Japanese companies, funded by subsidized capital, could capture overseas market share. Having captured market share, they could then turn that market power into profit.

These, then, were the building blocks of recovery: cheap, MOF-regulated finance, tough quality control, and capture of market share through the "better and cheaper" motto that Japan was to make her own over the following decades.

The Japanese set about this singular task almost single-mindedly. When de Gaulle met the Japanese prime minister, he complained that he had not met a real statesman (like his eminent and illustrious self) but a mere transistor salesman. De Gaulle was mistaken. Japan was cash-strapped and so the prime minister was doing the most important job he could do for Japan: flogging transistor radios to whoever would buy them. The Japanese exporters of these low-cost, high-quality Sony transistor radios, compact Minolta cameras, and low-cc Honda motorbikes could use their government-guaranteed low-cost finance to augment their other advantages-a disciplined and motivated workforce, well drilled in quality control and other cost-cutting and quality-enhancing devices-to make Japan, if not the powerhouse of the world, at least exporter to the world. The United States, as policeman to the Free World, was, in the earlier postwar decades, happy to see its main Asian ally and chief prop against Chinese communist expansionism in Asia, prosper. By the time of the Korean War, Japan Inc., with the MOF at the helm, had turned the corner. Recovery was assured.

Japan regenerated itself in relative isolation from the rest of the world. Protected by the U.S. 7th Fleet, she rigidly controlled access to foreign sources of capital. Capital had to be raised in Japan and monitored by the MOF, so that the national policy of postwar recovery could be met. The myth of a Japan unique in virtue, in diligence, in its snow, in its baseball, in its intestines, had to be nurtured to protect domestic markets and regain lost ground abroad.

The MOF, with its eyes on national recovery, had to reengineer Japanese society to meet the singular national objective of economic recovery. The Japanese were encouraged, if not coerced, into being compulsive savers. There were considerable fiscal and institutional incentives for high savings, especially through bank deposits and postal savings; consumer credit and home mortgage loans were severely curtailed; welfare programs, where they existed, remained grossly underdeveloped. The returns on savings were pitifully small. The low returns were compensated for by making the capital totally and utterly safe: an important consideration when we consider that Japan's unconditional surrender in 1945 had pauperized her people, who had been forced to buy government bonds to fund Imperial Japan's Manchurian and other adventures. For Japan, unlike Britain, Australia, and other combatants, war's end was not to bring relief in the form of the welfare state or any such thing. It was work as usual and keep saving for the inevitably many rainy days that inevitably lay ahead.

Pensions, schooling, housing—all had to be provided for out of one's own pocket, out of one's savings. The Japanese had no choice, but to save, save, save. They became the almost pathologically busiest beavers the world had ever seen. Abroad, the Japanese became synonymous with working and with saving.

The capital thus wrested from this diligent, pliable, and compliant workforce was strategically allocated in accordance with national industrial priorities. There was a strong emphasis on manufacturing and public utilities industries. Smokestack, export-oriented steel industries and similar sunrise industries got priority. Costly, infrastructural development was, if not put on the longest of long fingers, generally totally ignored. Not only were paved roads a comparative rarity until the 1964 Olympics, but Tokyo, the organizational heart of Japan, still remains as ill-prepared and under-insured as Kobe was for the massive earthquake—The Big One—that is overdue to devastate it. Export-led growth was to be the nation's salvation and preoccupation: there was no finance left to fritter away funding against such contingencies. It was myths and gambles such as these that allowed Japan to rebuild

In typical fashion, the Japanese authorities had said that all of Japan was prepared for whatever contingencies the elements might throw at her. Kobe proved that this was not the case. Roads and buildings that the authorities said were earthquake-proof tumbled down, killing thousands. Fires spread unchecked. International relief efforts were spurned. Domestically, only the Yamaguchi-gumi, Japan's biggest organized crime gang, could organize a coordinated relief effort. The authorities had other, "more important" things to do than to worry about the mayhem their empty promises and corrupt building practices had caused.

The authorities' singular pursuit of national recovery had blinded them to the risks inherent in such myopic strategy. The authorities and the agents they worked through had, in trying to resuscitate the nation, lost sight of her people. None were as blind as the JFIs.

The public financial institutions played an unabashed role in dividing up the financial cake. Japan's postal savings system, aided by substantial tax aids, became the world's largest personal savings system; it supplemented, supplanted, and competed with private financial institutions to wrest the nest eggs from the legions of workers who were too busy reconstructing Japan to question why their returns were so paltry. Their low-cost source of finance allowed other government-sponsored institutions to extend long-term lending facilities to specified groups to build up long-term competitive advantage. Under MOF stewardship, Japan was to quickly transform itself from the transistor radio makers de Gaulle

despised to the competitors in cracking the fifth-generation computer de Gaulle's successors envied. This was a remarkable achievement, a new way which seemed to not only turn the Western ideal
about the sanctity of the market on its head but to surpass the
Westerners in their own marketplaces as well.

MOF-directed finance was at the core of this achievement.
Capital allocation between the competing industrial sectors was
organized through the banking system. The armies of small savers
got a derisory choice of products to pick from; the lack of competition from Japan's underdeveloped money and bond markets made
Japanese banks the biggest in the world on paper by assets and
deposits. Because the Japanese stock market was not geared for
finance raising, the banks had a virtual monopoly in supplying
Japanese industries with funds.

Like the Kobe response or like the national objective of economic recovery, these policies had their own built-in contradictions.
The economic collapse of the 1990s would magnify these contradictions. On the one side would stand Japan Inc, totally discredited.
On the other would stand the Japanese people, totally disillusioned
with the keepers of the national purse.

During Japan's recovery, her banks, the repository of Japan's
low-yielding savings, became, by far, the main source of capital formation in Japan and, ultimately, in the world. They worked in close
collaboration with their corporate clients for the long-term common
aim of allowing them to exploit the cheapest and, ultimately, the
largest capital mine in the world. Because Japan's financial institutions were a vital cog in promoting industry, their interests were
given regulatory precedence over those of their consumers and
small depositors. Japan's financial institutions, in other words, benefited from their considerable shackles. Both Japan's media and public supported this cross-subsidization in the national interest of
export-led postwar recovery. JFIs were given a privileged place in
Japanese life: an almost overprotected domestic base, with hefty
built-in profits and a client base of diligent, one could almost say
compulsive, savers, who were prepared to accept minuscule returns
on their very considerable savings for the common good of Japan
Inc.

This was the logical consequence of the only rational policy open to the MOF after the War. They took this option and worked wonders with it over the next 40 years. The country's national consensus and cooperation helped make the Japanese financial services industry the world's largest and, in the 1980s, the most feared and commented upon. No longer would the Japanese prime minister be despised as a hawker of cheap transistor radios. Now, he was Tojo reincarnated, determined, with his millions of workaholic fellow-citizens, on world domination. It was, to read the plethora of learned books on the subject, as if the Japanese had found the elixir of economic life: their trade balances, savings rates, living standards, stock markets, property prices, and life expectancies were all headed upwards, in seemingly unstoppable, perpetual motion.

Although, on the surface, this seemed to be the case, the Japanese had not been so lucky. Japan's rise to glory had necessarily been accompanied with a series of risks, most of which had surfaced only during the golden bubble years of the 1980s when, like all bad news, they were ignored, until they resurfaced in more recent years in starker form. It is, in fact, the downside to the bubble years that is fueling the march toward deregulation and the Big Bang.

Like any singular strategy, Japan's convoy system contained the seeds of its own destruction. Because these financial institutions were so tightly controlled, self-correcting market signals were blurred and distorted. Because savings from the household to the industrial sector were funneled through a relatively small number of financial institutions whose activities were tightly regulated and controlled by the MOF and the Bank of Japan, complacency, corrupt practices, and widespread systematic abuses all took hold. Although this tight ordering and even tighter control allowed the national interest goals of export-led recovery and growth to be met with maximum strategic impact, the massive price Japan had to pay for ignoring global market standards became apparent only after the bubble burst. The Big Bang is, in part, an effort by the MOF to clean up this unholy mess.

Although the MOF, in control of this economic tiger, was able to impose a low interest rate policy with tight controls on all interest rates and terms of new issues of bonds, not all Japanese benefited to the same extent. The MOF-brokered availability of low-interest loans allowed Japan Inc. to develop her successful better-and-cheaper policy, and the small savers, whose sacrifices made the strategy viable, got scant regard in the scheme of things. Control, authority, and rewards all radiated from the MOF outward.

Beneath the veneer of success this singular policy presented, a myriad of dangers lurked, unseen and uncorrected. As befitted such a conservative, quasi-feudal setup, bricks-and-mortar collateral was required for all borrowings. This was to have unexpected negative consequences when the bubble burst. Although specifically dealt with in chapter two, the consequences of this overdependence on bricks-and-mortar collateral is also a central refrain resonating throughout this book.

So also is the organization of Japanese society. Thus organized into a disciplined, single-purposed convoy were the Japanese able to follow a classic neomercantalist strategy to world commerce and trade. From postwar devastation Japan had, under the guidance of her mandarins, resuscitated herself to conquer foreign markets and take her place as the second largest economy in the world. This was a remarkable achievement which, as chapter seven explains, was copied, warts and all, by the Asian tigers.

Central to Japan Inc.'s strategy of domestic recovery and, later, world preeminence was the *keiretsu* system of interlocking relationships between companies and financial institutions. Keiretsu, *kigyo shudan*, and *kigyo* group are interchangeable terms to mean both horizontally connected groups and vertically integrated groups in Japan. The keiretsu were the postwar reincarnation of the prewar *zaibatsu*, whose slogan Sangyo Hokoku, "Promote Industry to Serve the Country," lived on, in spirit if not in name, through them.

Convoy-fashion, banks were at the center of these alliances that sailed, in predatory fashion, through commercial Japan and thence to the world outside. Intragroup stability was reinforced by cross-ownership of stocks. Members of the keiretsu were interlocked in sickness and in health. Though this was a fortuitous system in postwar recovery, it proved obsolete in the post-bubble years.

The major ten zaibatsu of Mitsui, Mitsubishi, Sumitomo,

Yasuda, Nissan, Asano, Furukawa, Okura, Nakajima, and Nomura virtually controlled the Japanese economy up to 1945. Their structural organization was hierarchical: the holding companies and/or the zaibatsu family held the shares of all the companies belonging to it and exercised centralized vertical control. Under the paternalistic command of the holding company and/or the zaibatsu family, banks belonging to the hierarchy controlled the financial aspects of its operation and trading companies dominated the distribution of goods.

In their efforts to emasculate Japan, the American Occupation forces dismantled the major zaibatsu and split them into smaller, weaker, and more disjointed ones. Banks, however, were exempted and, once the American yoke loosened, former relationships were quickly reestablished, often with the exempted banks forming the nucleus. The zaibatsu were metamorphosed as keiretsu. Because MacArthur's purges left the MOF virtually unscathed, they emerged to take up the helm at Japan Inc.

Bowed but unbeaten, the convoy of Japan Inc. set sail again. The present Mitsubishi, Mitsui, and Sumitomo Groups are historical extensions of the prewar zaibatsu. The Fuyo Group succeeded, in large part, the Yasuda zaibatsu and centered around Fuji Bank, whose subsequent demise is discussed in chapters three and eight. The DKB and Sanwa Groups comprised the major clients of the leading city banks, and their latter-day problems are also discussed in subsequent chapters.

Still, for over 40 years, this convoy seemed invincible. Spearheaded by financial institutions, especially the city banks through loans to the keiretsu's affiliated companies and clients, these keiretsu groups consolidated their power over the following decades. The Mitsubishi, Mitsui, Sumitomo, Fuyo, DKB, Sanwa, and IBJ Groups typified the horizontally connected keiretsu that involved themselves over a wide spectrum of industries. Vertically integrated groups clustered around their parent companies such as the Toyota Group, the Matsushita Group, or the Sony Group, the emphasis normally being the parent companies' core industries.

The six major vertical industrial groups of Mitsubishi, Mitsui, Sumitomo, Fuyo, DKB, and Sanwa are characterized by each company within a particular group holding very substantial blocks of shares in the other companies within the same group. For example, in the Mitsubishi Group, interests in Mitsubishi Corporation, one of the largest general trading firms, are held by the leading group companies such as the Mitsubishi Bank, Tokio Marine and Fire Insurance, and Mitsubishi Heavy Industries. In turn, Mitsubishi Corporation owns some interest in those three firms. The same relation exists between the remaining Mitsubishi Group companies. The objective of this exercise was to protect each group company from outside control or takeover threats, thereby maintaining one another's status through interdependence and, as already stated, this objective was easily achieved for the best part of 40 years.

Presidential councils further reinforced these interlocking industrial groups. In a presidential council, all member presidents take part in discussions as equal partners. The presidential councils allow a forum for friendship and coordinated tactics to be developed. Theoretically, it provides cohesion, while allowing a large degree of autonomy. Group cohesiveness, built with capital cross-commitments and augmented by presidential councils, is further enhanced by sending staff members into key positions in affiliated companies. Retired government officials are also retained to maintain close contact between the keiretsu and the regulatory authorities. Thus, by these interlinking pieces, is Japan Inc.'s tight convoy formation arrived at.

Although this convoy system worked well in the postwar years, its sell-by date has now passed. One of the main reasons for this is because the aforesaid retired government officials have a lot to answer for: their ineptitude, complacency, and sheer selfishness is, in fact, a refrain that will resonate not only through the following chapters but through corporate Japan as well until meritocracy replaces its current plutocracy and mediocrity. Japan's Big Bang, if it is to be as successful as the British prototype, will have to hollow out Tokyo's rotten wood as assiduously and as ruthlessly as the British dispensed with theirs.

Japan's interwoven organizational structure will complicate such a task. There are even more webs reinforcing Japan Inc. The six major industrial groups and the Tokai Group have general trading firms along with the city banks at the center to further reinforce their unified, corporate approach. Originating as the trading arms for industrial groups between Japan and overseas and as whole-salers/distributors within Japan, they have more latterly been focusing on promoting new businesses both at home and abroad, and also extending financial assistance in the form of business credits, loans, and payment guarantees to their subsidiaries and customers in order to expand their businesses.

General trading firms also act as coordinators for exporting entire plants, setting up subsidiaries and joint ventures overseas; they have, capitalizing on their global information/marketing networks, significantly increased their involvement in offshore transactions. From the establishment of joint ventures to the construction of oil plants, general trading firms often organize, for a common purpose, a group of participants, some of which originate from its own group and others from rival groups. Trading firms actively promote new businesses through mergers and acquisitions, which have been almost always friendly in corporate Japan. They are aware that the Big Bang should cause these activities to significantly grow. They intend to be, as ever, there to facilitate corporate Japan.

Outwardly at least, they recognize they must transform themselves to continue. The Tomen trading group, for example, intends to quickly turn itself from a sprawling and inefficient conglomerate, trading in all types of unconnected goods and services, into a tightly focused group, structured along Anglo-American profit-maximizing lines. Tomen now wishes to abandon its consensus-based, bottom-up Japanese style of management and replace it with a system modeled on creating long-term shareholder value. They want to obey both the spirit and the letter of the Big Bang.

Tomen is the 17th largest company in Japan and 40th largest in the world by sales volume. With 400 subsidiaries in more than 60 countries, it has sales of over $40 billion per annum. Clearly, if size were enough, Tomen could metamorphose itself overnight. Because Western accounting and governance standards and structures take longer to put in place, Tomen, like the rest of Japan, might not find the transformation as short or as painless as they would like to imagine. Indeed, as the evidence of this book shows, there is much hollowing out to be done yet.

Of the other keiretsu, the IBJ Group has a unique, interesting, and important structure. The Industrial Bank of Japan was established to assist Japan's financial rehabilitation after the war. The bank acts as the main financier for more than 100 large companies listed on the stock exchange. It is the flagship of the Japanese financial service industry. Like the smaller ships in the convoy, recent scandals have sullied her sails and, limpet-like, they dampen her enthusiasm for expansion. Its demise shows how deeply the surgeon's knife will have to cut to save Japan Inc.

That said, the keiretsu system has, up to now at least, been beneficial for all parties to the convoy. It has allowed them to gain world preeminence in their chosen fields. The United States, however, regards keiretsu as nontariff barriers, inimical to the brand of free trade they espouse and as quasi-cartels, engaging in collusive practices, including price rigging and market rigging, which have effectively frozen out foreign companies, especially those of the United States. The Americans wants to scuttle the keiretsu. They particularly want to obliterate the *dango* price-rigging system, where Japanese conglomerates would meet to devise common marketing and pricing strategies.

The dango system is, like sumo, uniquely Japanese. Large players tussle about Japan's small domestic market. There are only enough of these Japanese conglomerates large and fit enough to compete and, like sumo wrestlers, they all have to be walking giants to figure at all. Their rigidly rigged system kept the little guy in his place and helped Japan compete on almost equal terms with the West. It was, after all, these zaibatsu that stopped Perry from turning Japan into a den of opium-smoking coolies. American objections notwithstanding, the Japanese are well aware of the debt they owe these industrial monsters and the mandarins who guided them.

Keidanren, Keizai Doyukai, Nikkeiren, and Nihon Shoko Kaigisho are the four major business associations in Japan which further go to complete the interwoven mosaic of Japan Inc. The Keidanren is the headquarters of the *zaikai*, the business world. The Keizai Doykai, the Japan Association of Corporate Executives, was set up in 1946 to aid postwar reconstruction. The Nikkeiren (Nihon

Keieisha Dantai Renmei, or Japan Federation of Employers' Association) was set up in 1948 by employers anxious to have stable labor-management relations to facilitate postwar reconstruction. The Nihon Shoko Kaigisho, the Japan Chamber of Commerce and Industry, integrates approximately 500 chambers into one nation-wide voice modeled, one could say, on the zaibatsu's prewar motto of serving the country by building up industry.

Japan Inc. has worked well in serving and resuscitating Japan. Whether we look at banking, beverages, food, iron and steel, non-ferrous metals, automobiles, chemicals and pharmaceuticals, pulp and paper, or fibers and textiles, Japanese companies are among the largest, often the largest, in the world. Japan, then, resembles an economy, whether developed or underdeveloped, where a handful of affiliated, interconnected companies tower over the rest. It is, alas, this overconcentration that precipitated and accentuated the bubble and subsequent recession.

The Big Bang is, in part, a backward-looking attempt to put the bubble behind them and, in equal measure, a forward-looking plan to remain competitive. This book therefore must simultaneously look backward and forward to see why the Big Bang is happening and where the Big Bang should bring Japan.

The MOF must also look in both directions. It must look forward to see these reforms through and backward to take the knives out of its back. Though currently being harassed by opportunistic politicians, goaded by public contempt, and prodded by a tottering banking system, Japan's Finance Ministry has proposed these top-to-bottom reforms to bring long-overdue competition to Japan's banking, securities, and insurance industries. Under the Bigu Ban (Big Bang) reforms, protective walls between Japan's various financial sectors are being removed; prices, commissions, and product offerings are being decontrolled; and consumers are to be given more choices in investment services. Market forces will, by all accounts, rule.

These reforms mean the destruction of Japan's postwar convoy system and the adoption not only of the rhetoric but also of the free-market methodology epitomized by Margaret Thatcher's Britain. If both the spirit and the letter of the reforms are adhered to, it will be one of the most momentous changes of this century.

The three key words used in the official government statement to describe the Big Bang reforms are "free," "fair," and "global." The reforms aspire toward a free market where the market mechanism prevails in determining market entry, product design, and product pricing. The reforms aspire toward a fair, transparent, and credible market, codified in a body of rules that, inter alia, protect investors' interests. The reforms aspire toward a global market, meeting global needs and global legislative, accounting, and governance standards. Rule-bound Japan has a long way to go to reach this particular freewheeling economic nirvana.

In plainer English, Japan wants its financial system to be more modern, more efficient, and more accountable to its stakeholders. They will have to pay a heavy price for these changes.

Definitionally, the Big Bang implies a reversal from Japan's conventional philosophy of consensual change. No longer will hobby farmers, tiny plot-holders, and a hundred-dozen divisions of under-employed construction workers and grocer assistants hold the country to ransom. Sweeping measures are to be carried out in a single explosion suggestive of the big bang hypothesized as having created the universe. The Ministry of Finance, which will continue to be the top authority in public finance and fiscal policy, is overseeing the changes, even though one key Big Bang objective is to moderate its pervasive control over Japan's financial markets.

The MOF mandarins have to accommodate the changes a resurgent America is imposing on them. Foreign rating agencies, foreign investors, and foreign advisors are now an integral part of the Japanese market. They are exerting their own pressure for the reform of Japan's purposely vague and traditionally opaque methods of governance into one that conforms to Anglo-American concepts of global governance. They want the Big Bang to concentrate on altering the Japanese business mind-set, which obscures accountability and personal responsibility. Their power means that their views must be taken into account.

No matter which philosophy prevails, this is an epoch-making change, reminiscent of Commodore Perry's adventurers or the Meiji Restoration. Just as the Japanese learned from Europe at that time, so also are today's Japanese elite copying a more recent European model. This time, the Japanese prototype is the British Big Bang, the biggest deregulation of the London stock market in modern times, which took place in October 1986 when industry rationalization and the introduction of screen-based computer trading revamped the industry and allowed London to regain the market-share out-moded practices had lost it. In 1985, before the implementation of the Big Bang, the London stock exchange's turnover was only one-thirteenth of New York's, and only one-fifth of Tokyo's. Now, London is once again preeminent in world financial affairs. The LSE's launch of the computerized Crest share settlement system on Monday, October 20, 1997, was the start of a switch from a quote-driven system of trading to an order-driven system, the objective being to replace paper in the share-settlement process with more cost-efficient automated screen-based trading. This second wave will guarantee London's pivotal role in the world's financial markets long into the next century.

London's Big Bang has been an unqualified success. It was, in essence, an assertion that competition should rule; that the cozy car-tels and old boys' clubs that had previously dominated the City had no future in the modern world; that barriers to entry should be removed; and that modern techniques should be embraced.

The British can claim, with considerably more authority than the Japanese, that their culture is unique. Whatever about their cul-ture, their international experience is certainly unmatched by any other nation. Their Big Bang is, in true British tradition, a unique prototype for any nation to aspire to.

The Wimbledon scenario notwithstanding, it has certainly been good for Britain. London's reforms raised the industry from 13.6% of Britain's GDP in 1985 to 17.2% in 1990. London has become an increasingly important international financial center for cross-bor-der stock transactions. Further, with their advanced transaction expertise and product innovation, London has become the epicen-ter of European investment banking. The LSE's merger with its Frankfurt counterpart and developments in the euro-market should guarantee London's preeminence well into the next century.

The British Big Bang has been successful both as an expression of Britain's provincialism and of her pragmatic internationalism. Britain has benefited from a significant influx of foreign-owned capital, foreign ideas, and new techniques. The Eurobond business, the international swaps and derivatives business, and international equity trading are typical of London's many internationally focused successes. London's insistence on enforcing stringent disclosure and transparency standards to increase market efficiency and market confidence in the fairness of the system has, clearly, brought tangible benefits to London in particular and Britain in general.

Britain has, of course, an almost unique legal infrastructure and system which has helped her Big Bang immensely. Japan, traditionally opaque, xenophobic, and rule-ridden, has considerably deeper and more entrenched hurdles to overcome, if it wishes to emulate London's resurgence as one of the major centers of international finance. Britain and Japan have taken different evolutionary paths. Whereas Japan has been traditionally inward-looking, Britain has had her empire and the whole legal infrastructure that has supported her preeminence since Elizabethan times.

Even setting aside these differences, Japan is trying to implement her Big Bang as the country grapples with her worst postwar recession. Plummeting asset prices have compounded the probability of success by wiping out a decade of wealth creation. Several leading banks are technically insolvent, and abysmal investment returns in a savings-rich country have badly eroded the public's support for a financial industry they now regard as inefficient, corrupt, cosseted, and uncompetitive. Now, with revelations that securities firms improperly compensated their bigger clients—at the expense of their smaller clients—for losses and that all of the bigger ones colluded with the Japanese mafia, the yakuza, to manipulate the market, the entire structure of the Japanese capital market is under severe scrutiny. This includes not only firms, but their regulator, the Ministry of Finance: several of their officials have been charged with bribe-taking and other criminal offenses. The wide-scale arrest of MOF officials[6] on corruption and sleaze charges was a further blow to the Ministry, whose authority has already been undermined by Japan's epidemic of scandals emanating from the financial sector it was charged with regulating.

The MOF's setbacks are, in themselves, epoch making. The linchpin holding together the security of Japan's national convoy system was MOF hegemony over the nation's real estate market. Since Japanese banks lent according to the value of collateral—usually land—systemic credit could be wiped out by controlled inflation in land and other asset prices. The MOF, when needed, induced this inflation, aided in very large part, by its control over land-taxing policy, its control of bank lending via its "administrative guidance" policy, and its inordinate sway over monetary policy.

During recent decades, the Japanese system long had its ultimate safety valve in large, external, American-sponsored markets into which surplus production could always be dumped. This safety valve has eroded with Japan's rise to global industrial prominence. Further, the stock and property price crashes of the post-bubble period mean that the MOF can no longer engineer controlled bouts of inflation in asset prices to wipe out credit mistakes. Thus, new modalities are needed to keep Japan Inc. afloat. Thus the need for the Big Bang.

Although a variety of factors can be cited as triggering both Japan's current recession and the Big Bang reforms, falling Tokyo land prices, once thought immune to downward pressure, are at the epicenter of the mire. Land's role in the bubble and its effects on the Big Bang are dealt with in the next chapter.

[1] Harry Truman

[2] von Wolferen, Karel, The Enigma of Japanese Power, New York, Alfred A. Knopf, 1989, p. 413.

[3] All dollar figures, unless otherwise noted, are U.S. dollars.

[4] "Salaryman" will be used throughout for the Japanese term sarariman, or "salaried employee."

[5] The true amount is hard to fathom, partly because of the sheer scale of the problem and partly, as will be explained, because of Japan's quirky accountancy practices.

[6] Several MOF officials had been compromised by con men and other disreputable types with visits to sex shows and gambling joints. Several of these once-proud mandarins committed suicide quickly after their indictment on charges of taking bribes from the banks they were being paid to regulate.

The Tokyo Land and

Share Price Bubble

The Japanese refer to the 1980s as the Bubble Economy. The Bubble Economy, fueled on cheap and super-easy credit, spawned major scandals, which have had direct and lasting impacts on Japan's real economy and political fabric. Unlike similar scandals in the West, Japan's bubble scandals herald lasting changes: the fabric, the interlocking mosaic of Japan Inc., has been irreparably damaged as a consequence. The Big Bang is the MOF's response to this disaster.

The bubble's aftermath makes a sorry tale. Once-respected stockbrokers compensating favored clients for losses by defrauding their smaller clients, once-respected securities companies financing attempts by organized crime syndicates to manipulate stock prices, and once-respected bank managers issuing billions of dollars worth of certificates of deposit as fake collateral all pointed to an unholy trinity of politicians, gangsters, and financiers wallowing in sleaze, corruption, nepotism, and downright crime. This was not the picture of a developed economy, marching invincibly to world domination. This, for the most part, was gross, systematic ineptitude by bankers, financiers, regulators, and politicians. Only the gangsters seem to have played their allotted role, as societal wreckers. The story of how Japan went, in less than a decade, from financial juggernaut to financial basket case, is the story of the bubble and of this chapter.

On December 31, 1989, Japan accounted for 42% of the total capitalization of world stock markets, compared with only 15% in 1980. The markets were valued at 150% of Japan's GDP, compared with just 30% in 1980. This was a colossal rise, a colossal bubble.

When the bubble burst, the market lost $2.25 trillion, or more than three times the size of the world's then outstanding Third World debt. By 1992, the Japanese who had enjoyed la dolce vita of the bubble years had come to earth with a crash: the biggest financial crash in world history.

Japan's total stock of property was valued in 1990 at ¥2,000 trillion, or four times the value of the total stock of property in the United States. Any fall comparable to the Nikkei fall would mean a plunge in the value of the collateral held by Japanese banks and other institutions that had lent so traditionally and so recklessly against land. It would mean a crisis.

In 1993, at the height of the bubble, Tokyo land prices reached $350,000 per square meter. Since the peak of the bubble, the value of Japanese real estate has fallen by more than $5,000 billion, over 110% of Japan's GDP. This is a colossal fall, made all the more melodramatic by considering the dizzy heights those self-same prices had hit only a few years earlier.

As land prices soared during the 1980s' bubble, the Tokyo property market took on all the trappings of a traditional gold rush, Everyone, including banks and their subsidiaries, rushed to purchase any available land they could get their hands on for speculative purposes. So too did the yakuza. Once they saw the profits to be made, they started their own real estate businesses and developments, using their traditional strong-arm, bully-boy tactics to clear out recalcitrant plot-holders from lands they or respectable, affiliated companies coveted. Because financial companies continued both to lend them money and to implicitly condone their land-clearing methods, a strong, mutually beneficial, and mutually consensual base was built between the yakuza and Japanese banks and securities houses.[1] The Japanese property and financial services industries are, as this chapter explains, still paying the moral price of colluding with these tattooed thugs.

Paper stock and land profits formed the core of JFIs' reserves. It was against these volatile reserves that JFIs lent, and so, as the bubble economy blew out, so too did bank lending. These extra paper profits were funneled back into shares and property, which bloated still further their shares and property collateral and allowed them to lend still more money. Their whole credit pyramid was formed on the supposition that prices would not fall but would in fact continue to rise to keep the whole frenzy permanently profitable. It was a mania, a lending frenzy comparable to the 1920s Florida land boom, the Dutch tulip mania, or, the granddaddy of them all, the South Sea Bubble, which bankrupted England's George III, Isaac Newton, and a host of other notables.

The Japanese bubble began in the September 1985 Plaza Accord, the international agreement to drive down the dollar and so help reduce America's huge trade deficits with both Japan and Germany. Britain and France, the other players in the Accord, had comparatively minor cameo roles to play by comparison. By the time of the Louvre Accord of 1987, the dollar had collapsed, putting unprecedented pressure on the Japanese and German exporters and causing a slowdown in their export-dependent economies. As part of this accord, the Japanese, much more so than the more independent and more streetwise Germans, loosened monetary policy. They lowered the official discount rate to 2.5%, its lowest level in the postwar period. The resulting cheap credit ignited the bubble.

Japan's banks lent heavily and recklessly against both property and land. At the end of 1991, a total of ¥116 trillion had been lent directly to the property and construction sectors. City banks' outstanding loans, collateralized by land, stood at about 50% of Japan's GNP. In the boom years of 1987-88, loans collateralized by property accounted for more than half of city banks' incremental loan growth. The banks, preoccupied with their land-speculating deals, ignored their core business of prudential banking. Their speculations have come to a grinding halt with the Tokyo stock market crash, the land-price crash, and tougher capital adequacy standards for banks. The crash has brought their problems home to roost with a vengeance.

The nub of the Japanese banks' problems is that the conditions that let them boost their lendings so dramatically during the 1980s have dramatically reversed. The Japanese banks were singularly unprepared for the collapse of their bloated credit pyramid. During the bubble, almost 40% of the banks' trading profits were from stock market gains—not from their core business of banking. They had allowed their core business of prudent banking to stagnate and had, despite the admittedly mute protestations of their MOF overseers, turned themselves into stock and property speculators. This was to destroy their credibility in their core business activity in the eyes of the international community and, later, in the eyes of their domestic customer-base as well.

Japanese banks depended on their unrealized stock earnings to meet their reserve requirements under the Basel-based Bank for International Settlements (BIS), which stipulate that international banks should have capital equal to at least 8% of their risk-adjusted assets. The Japanese banks were allowed to count 45% of their unrealized stock gains toward their capital. Thus, the capital of the world's biggest banks, and therefore their ability to lend, went up and down with the short-term whims of the notoriously thin Tokyo stock market. Their ability to lend was dependent upon the degree to which the yakuza were allowed ramp up stocks, by whether the MOF was instructing insurance companies to load or offload stocks, and by a host of other abuses that have no part to play in the free, fair, and open markets to which the Big Bang aspires. Their position was, therefore, unstable and, ultimately, untenable.

The Japanese banks, whose ability to lend was dependent upon the level of the erratic Nikkei index, accounted for over 25% of the Nikkei themselves. In other words, they could lend more if they ramped up the value of their own stocks. To phrase it differently, if they could artificially inflate their own stock price, they could lend out more money, unchecked, unfettered, and, as it transpired, unwisely. Such was the system of governance that had evolved.

Because their ability to succeed could be artificially induced, these banks were ridiculously overvalued. The Industrial Bank of Japan (IBJ), for example, had a profit-earnings (PE) ratio of 100, meaning that an investor would need to receive dividends for a hundred years to recoup the initial investment in it. Affiliated companies held these absurdly overvalued shares as an insurance against being deprived of credit. And the banks, convinced that these imperfections would continue to fester, lent more and more as the Nikkei surged ever forward. A gigantic commonality of interest thus evolved. The more prices were ramped upward, the more Japan Inc.

benefited. Prudence, caution, and plain common sense were abandoned as Japan Inc. ramped up the stock and property prices to record levels.

Anywhere else, this would have been seen as the deck of cards that it was, needing only a corrective puff of wind to bring the whole edifice tumbling down. A crisis would, given this keiretsu cross-shareholding scenario, have a devastatingly quick, downward-rolling snowball effect on stock prices. A falling Nikkei would lower the value of the credit building blocks on which the entire edifice of the bubble had been built. Because the TSE had risen with hardly a break in tempo from 1945, the banks were serenely oblivious to the great risks inherent in their activities. As long as the TSE continued to rise, the banks ignored their bloated PEs and artificial BIS ratios. Believing they were earthquake-proof, they ruthlessly and, in hindsight, recklessly used the bull market to issue new shares and thereby expand their assets. Between 1987 and 1989, city banks issued some ¥6 trillion of cheap equity and equity-related finance. When the crunch came shortly afterward, only Kyowa Bank could meet the 8% BIS ratio without resorting to costly junk-bond-like subordinated financing. The speculative house of cards came crashing down. Now, a decade later, they are still picking up the pieces. Unable to fully restore the former status quo, they are instituting the Big Bang instead.

Already, the change has been epoch-making. The Japanese banks, almost in the blink of an eyelid, went from being cash-and-asset rich to being cash-and liquid-asset poor. Fazed but undaunted, they rounded up the usual suspects in their keiretsu. Affiliated life insurance companies bought subordinated loans to boost the banks' capital ratios. This withdrawal of bailout funds from the TSE sent the Nikkei lower and put their erstwhile white knights, the insurance companies, under a bankruptcy cloud themselves. The interlocking system, which had propelled Japan Inc. ever upward, now sent her into a tailspin.

The Japanese social and economic system, to reiterate, had been studiously built upon the foundation stones of a homogenous, hardworking, and well-educated workforce, a relationship-based financial system providing low-cost capital, an efficient production system based on company unions and business groups, a national concentration on incremental innovations and improvement, and strong and consistent MOF initiatives and guidance keeping the whole convoy sailing in the same direction for the same national prize of recovery and economic sustainability. All of this helped Japan achieve the foreign dollars its better-and-cheaper policy was aimed at securing. The bursting of the bubble brought much of this good work unstuck. The Big Bang is an attempt to regroup, to build anew.

Japan has fallen a great distance and the task ahead will, in its own way, be as hard as was the road facing Japan in August 1945. Japan's collateral base, for example, has, to all intents and purposes, been destroyed. Although America is 25 times bigger than Japan in terms of its physical area, Japan's Management and Coordination Agency reckoned Japan was worth ¥2,000 trillion, four times the value of the entire United States in 1990. On a micro scale, Tokyo's land boom made multimillionaires of very many of the 62% of Japanese who own their own homes. On a macro scale, in theory at least, all of Tokyo could have bought all of the United States in 1990. The Imperial Palace was worth more than California. On an even grander scale, Japanese real estate was worth over 50% the value of the entire world, meaning that, in theory at least, the Japanese could have bought the rest of the world by selling their modest, mountainy archipelago. On a more micro scale, a $100 bill would not buy the land it covered in downtown Tokyo.

Though these may be dismissed as theoretical absurdities, credit lines supplied the link between theoretical and real prices. Japanese banks lent against the value of the asset, whereas Western banks lent against the rental value. The Emperor, then, could have borrowed enough to buy California by remortgaging his palace. Though he wasn't that dumb, many of his subjects were—and dumber. They rushed in and bought more and more stocks and property in the biggest speculative frenzy of all time.

Major Japanese financial institutions went on an American trophy-hunting expedition and lost fortunes in all cases. The IBJ, Japan's premier bank, financed the Grand Hyatt Hotel farce. Mitsui Real Estate bought Exxon's building for $610 million, even though Exxon wanted only $375 million for it. Mitsui paid the extra $235 million just to get in the Guinness Book of Records. Although all of these American investments proved disastrous, nobody asked their shareholders what they thought about having the company's wealth squandered on overpriced French Impressionist paintings, American white elephants, and the like. For the entire duration of this orgy, there was no oversight or accountability, there was no bank discipline, and, as the shareholders were ignored, there was no stock market discipline either. It was a massive corporate crime committed against the Japanese people by the JFIs which the MOF ignored. It was a massive crime for which the culprits have yet to be brought to book.

Japan's current economic stagnation stems fundamentally from the subsequent post-bubble collapse in domestic property prices. Silly and all as their overseas adventures were, at least secondary markets exist in the United States and similar countries that meet global standards. The JFIs tied up even more gigantic amounts in the local market where no secondary market exists to test theoretical value. Some property prices have slumped by 80%, and as yet there is little sign of recovery. It remains a buyer's market.

The property boom was driven by the banks who lent recklessly in the late 1980s and who now have bad debts conservatively measured in hundreds of billions of dollars. The banks have become extremely reluctant to extend new credit, even to healthy businesses. Despite historically low interest rates, stagflation has cast a seemingly perennial cloud over Japan. The Big Bang is aimed at dissipating that cloud. It is a tall order.

While the Big Bang is forcing companies to reduce their dependence on the indirect financing the banks supply, smaller companies, which are not experienced in raising funds directly on the markets, have few, if any, alternatives left open to them. Though healthy, they are going bankrupt. These smaller companies are suffering most from the credit crunch. To take but one example for the moment, Daido Concrete, a leading maker of concrete piles, went bankrupt, largely as a result of the bank's refusal to lend to it.

The insistence of its banks that Daido guarantee loans to its Asian subsidiaries, coupled with the bank's failure to supply it with short-term funding, forced it into bankruptcy. Daido, like countless other companies, found that a decline in the value of its assets, triggered by the fall in property prices, has provided the self-same banks with justification for demanding an increase in bricks-and-mortar type collateral—an impossibility, given Japan's ongoing recession. The banks, which fueled the bubble, are making others pay in blood for their own mistakes.

Many of Japan's largest contractors have been allowed go bankrupt. Tada and Tokai Kogyo, among others, liquidated as a result of a combination of high debt and loan guarantees made to affiliated property developers in the late 1980s when rising property prices spurred an epidemic of ill-considered developments. Nor is an upturn in sight. Although interest rates are at historic lows, construction and property companies are reeling under the burden of the debt they acquired during the property boom of the late 1980s.

The hollowing out of Japan's construction sector is far from complete. Indeed, many of the biggest financial disasters were in this bloated, corrupt sector and, because of their sheer scale, are far from being resolved. When the bubble economy burst, seven special housing loan companies, jusen,[2] collapsed with a combined total of claims amounting to $14 bn, at least half of which was lent to Yakuza-related companies at the peak of the economic boom. These loans are all but impossible to recover. Pumping tax money into the jusen to rescue them was, in effect, to subsidize organized crime from public funds and to further undermine the credibility of Japan's financial sector.

The jusen epitomize the property-related problems the Big Bang is trying to resolve. Though accounting for less than 20% of JFI's total bad loans, the jusen characterize their crisis in miniature. They epitomize irresponsible lending, massive regulatory failures, widescale fraud, keiretsu-linked failures, and an indictment of the uncodified system that had hitherto linked lenders, owners, and parent firms with Japan's criminal fraternity into Japan's national convoy system—into Japan Inc. There were a total of eight jusen. One of these eight was based in the agricultural sector and is still afloat; the other seven sank with ignominy in 1996.

Before the jusen were set up, individual housing loans were a comparative novelty in Japan. City banks and regional banks entered the business only in the 1960s, and at the time treated housing loans as consumer loans. As Japanese consumer demand grew, JFIs established jusen as special subsidiaries to circumvent the MOF's interest rate regulations on such loans: the jusen, as nonbanks, could charge higher interest rates. Their conditions were less strict, and they also provided loans for the construction of apartments, stores, and office buildings. Working with long-term loans from their parent institutions, the jusen grew rapidly along with the expanding housing and real estate markets. When, with interest rate deregulation, the larger banks entered the market, the jusen, rashly in hindsight, entered the real estate loan market, just as the bubble economy took off. The jusen quickly transformed themselves from quasi-legal bricks-and-mortar lenders into providers of speculative capital to the yakuza and other members of the quick-buck brigade. By the time the real estate market collapsed in 1990, the jusen had turned into "special real estate lenders." By 1994, total outstanding loans of jusen were ¥13 trillion, less than ¥3 trillion of which were housing loans. In 1995, the MOF estimated that ¥7 trillion of the jusen loans, many of them yakuza-related, were irrecoverable.

The jusen were one of the biggest disasters of the bubble era—or indeed any other era for that matter. They lost at least ¥7.6 trillion altogether. That is to say, more than two out of every three of their loans went bad. Despite the fact that the MOF had its amakudari at the helm in all of these institutions, it abnegated responsibility both for the disaster and for the governancial shortfall that allowed it to happen.

Though these highly paid amakudari,[3] retired MOF officials almost to a man, were supposed to be in charge, they abnegated responsibility when the jusen problems became public knowledge. Then, following Japanese corporate etiquette, they passed the buck. The buck is still circulating. Even though many banks and thousands of small Japanese companies have gone bankrupt, no one, apparently, is to blame. No one will take responsibility. The buck keeps circulating.

The MOF's contradictory policies ensured the demise of the jusen. Shortly after they were established, the MOF allowed the banks and the Housing Loan Corporation (HLC), which they themselves run, to squeeze out the jusen. MOF policy, as much as anything else, forced the jusen toward the speculative end of the market. Caught by the ambivalent signals emanating from the MOF and with the highly paid amakudari providing no worthwhile leadership or direction, the jusen floundered.

Not that the MOF, preoccupied as they were with their singular objective, seemed to care. The HLC, under the stewardship of the MOF, expanded its own share of the market to 37% from 23%. Between the HLC and the banks, the jusen were utterly squeezed. As a result, housing fell to a mere 20% of jusen activities. The rest was gambled away or, just as often, given to gamblers and fraudsters. The end result was the same: bankruptcy and incompetence on a gargantuan scale.

The record of the jusen, left unmonitored, defies belief. They loaned out much more than the collateral underwriting the loans and they knowingly loaned out kings' ransoms to people of dubious character using false names. They loaned to politicians and criminals in equally generous and foolhardy amounts. And the media, the MOF, and the amakudari, like the three wise monkeys, saw nothing amiss.

The golfing industry typifies the building frenzy of the times. In the early 1990s, almost 1,500 golf courses were under construction in Japan. This would have doubled the amount of courses in land-starved Japan. Most of these proposals flopped and swindles abounded. Typical of these was one involving LDP power-broker Shintaro Ishihara, who coauthored with Sony Chairman Akio Morita The Japan That Can Say No. Ishihara had, apparently, some problems saying no himself. He was accused of accepting ¥30 million in illegal political contributions from Ken Mizunu, the owner of the Ibaraki golf club. It sold almost 50,000 memberships even though it promised to cap membership at fewer than 3,000 members and overcharged accordingly. This was only one of a gigantic range of golf-related frauds then raging throughout Japan. As a result of such scams, the banks belatedly recognized the dangers the jusen posed.

The MOF did not, and rejected out of hand the banks' early rescue plans which might have contained the damage. The MOF wanted to save face. And political influence. The jusen owed vast amounts to the nokyo, farmer-dominated groups that bankroll the LDP. The nokyo bank, Norinchukin, is one of the world's richest: it has assets of over $700 billion. One indication of the power of the nokyo is that the Food Agency in the Ministry of Agriculture has a 10,000-strong workforce to simply control the rice market and convince Japanese consumers that, for both spiritual and nutritional reasons, Japanese rice, although outrageously expensive, is best.

Though no objective observer could believe such arrant nonsense, the sheer size of their feather-bedding—a 10,000-strong army in one ministry alone—and the effectiveness of their rice-protection programs showed that no one, not even the seemingly omnipotent MOF, could ride roughshod over them. Because allowing the nokyo to suffer losses would weaken their own political power base with the politicians the nokyo bankroll, the MOF would not let the banks cut their losses and run. The MOF, for their own pragmatic if somewhat shortsighted reasons, instead drafted a costly $120 billion restructuring plan and made the banks implement it. Though the plan predictably bombed, the MOF followed Japanese etiquette: they have never apologized for this further massive loss they inflicted on the Japanese people. They passed the buck on to the JFIs, blaming them for their own considerable shortcomings. The JFIs, meanwhile, wallowed in their own ineptitude and mounds of bad debts.

The jusen showed the warts of Japan's financial system: opaqueness, lack of clearly defined rules, MOF-JFI collusion which warped market signals and accountability. It also showed Japan's biggest hindrance to the development of free, fair, and global markets: the MOF's irresponsible pervasiveness. The MOF, lacking expertise in an age demanding expertise and decentralized decision making, would not own up to its own shortcomings.

The MOF lost oodles of credibility as a result of these collapses. Because former MOF officials held key positions in the jusen, the MOF should have been forewarned of the problems. Instead, as Tokyo's share and property prices tumbled, the Japanese people were given the clear impression that those key positions were merely cushy sinecures, which did nothing but maintain, at considerable expense, the MOF at the center of Japanese financial life. Moreover, the MOF had not bothered to conduct even the most perfunctory investigation on the jusen since 1992. Instead, it used a major institution, the HLC, which it controlled itself, to push the jusen into improvident behavior. And it never bothered to check the consequences. This, by Western standards of governance, was an appalling oversight, one of very many the MOF made during the period. The MOF had, instead of grasping the nettle as their Anglo-American equivalents would have done, waited in the forlorn hope that a property price recovery would solve the problem to the satisfaction of all. Unlike their foreign equivalents, they had no written standards or rules to apply. Transfixed by their singular objective, they merely shuffled the deck chairs around as the massive debts of the jusen holed their mothership-banks beneath the bow. Prisoners to their own propaganda about the unique nature of Japan, they failed to see that the world had moved on. In this respect, the Big Bang is an attempt to catch up with the rest.

Although the MOF claimed blissful ignorance of its demise, Nippon Housing Loan, until 1992 considered the largest and best of the jusen, and Dai-Ichi Housing Loan were publicly traded on the TSE. Nippon Housing Loan was run by a retired MOF bureaucrat for 16 years. In total, there were 12 former MOF bureaucrats in leading jusen positions. This led observers to believe that, on the evidence, the MOF were more concerned with garnering the fruits of office than with actually putting in an honest day's work. Further scandals reinforced this widely held belief. The MOF's haughty attitude reinforced this belief.

At Juso, fraud played a major role. Juso had extended loans on land collateral with zero value, such as forests, and employees reportedly were ordered to change the pictures and the text on the loan approval forms prior to MOF audits, which never detected such blatant scams. The MOF continued to work on the old-world paradigm of gentlemen's agreements in a fast-moving era awash with rogues and gangsters.

There is also substantial evidence suggesting that Juso, Chigin-Seiho, and Sogo, the three jusen with the worst bad-loan ratios, were railroaded into providing risky loans by their financial suppliers. A substantial part of the loans their mother banks referred to them may have been aimed to support the mother bank by lending money to a troubled client so that the client could pay interest to the bank. Or, to put it another way, these loans were extended so that the bank could roll over the loan by surreptitiously throwing good money after loans already gone bad. Other risky loans were an extension of "relationship banking" triggered by the MOF guidance that stopped banks from increasing loans to the real estate sector after 1990. Banks would therefore typically request their subsidiary to take over the servicing of their bad loans, regardless of the credit-worthiness of the customer or the collateral. The yakuza and the other high credit risks didn't complain: the money, billions of yen, continued to feed their coffers. Billions more yen would go down the drain. Only the route had to change to accommodate the MOF's gentlemanly but ultimately useless regulations.

Eventually, as chapter four will explain, the well ran dry. The mother banks, with more than ¥1 trillion of public funding, had to shoulder the major portion of the bad loans. The mother banks were to write off completely their total loans to jusen of ¥3.5 trillion, even though total irrecoverable loans exceeded ¥9.9 trillion. Given Japan's creative accounting and the lax accounting standards evident in the industry, this is probably a gross understatement; all figures in this debacle are, after all, of galactic proportions. Though erring on the conservative side it does, however, indicate the degree of the bad-loan problem.

Still, there was an upside, albeit a very expensive upside. The jusen disaster taught corporate Japan that the days of free lunches were over. The tacit assumption that a main bank or the MOF itself would pick up the tab for the disasters of others floundered on the jusen debacle. Consolidation and rationalization of the agricultural cooperatives and federations, which were central to the mess, are on the cards: market forces and the crippling debt overhang are seeing to that. The larger JFIs are finding these losses big and bitter pills to swallow: many, unable to cope, have liquidated. However unpalatable this process may be it is, however belatedly, separating the viable from the nonviable institutions and therefore ushering in the Big Bang changes. The long overdue rationalization of Japan's financial institutions is being expedited as a result of these disasters.

These changes herald other, more basic ones. The jusen debacle held the warts of the MOF's regulatory system up to public scrutiny and public scorn. The degree to which the MOF's uncodified and opaque system triggered these disasters is echoed in later scandals. Indeed, the extent of the MOF's culpability is perhaps the main reason why Japan so desperately needs the Big Bang.

Deplorable and all as the MOF's role was, the jusen debacle showed that other societal changes are more urgently needed. Although, for example, Tokyo boasts some of the safest big-city streets in the world, several senior bank executives were murdered by the yakuza warning banks off collecting these jusen-estate related loans. As the Japanese might say, these murders are only the tip of the iceberg: a nether world of corruption that culminated with the spectacular arrest of 14 senior executives at Nomura Securities and Dai-ichi Kangyo Bank (DKB), whose former chairman, Kuniji Miyazaki, killed himself when his company's yakuza and sokaiya links were exposed. The businessmen were charged with making illegal payoffs and millions of dollars in illegal loans to yakuza-linked corporate racketeers, the sokaiya, to keep them from disrupting annual shareholders' meetings with sensitive information leaks.

During late 1997, all of the top four securities houses were implicated in these illicit payments. Public confidence in the financial sector plummeted and Nomura and DKB were suspended from key parts of the domestic market for several months over a plethora of sokaiya-related scandals. Yamaichi, the smallest of the Big Four[4] securities houses, faced a myriad of criminal charges and liquidated under its massive debt burden. Because Hitachi, Mitsubishi Dai Nippon Printing, and many of Japan's other leading nonfinancial companies also paid large bribes to the sokaiya, this collusion has not only caused their share prices to fall and to bring further pressure on Japan's financial houses but has also further eroded popular confidence levels in the entire system.

In an attempt to extricate themselves from this unholy mess, some Japanese banks are selling property-related loans at between 5% and 20% of face value. Foreign investors have purchased Japanese loans at 5 cents to 20 cents on the dollar, and some are

already reaping rewards. Many buyers of the bad debt have a two-
to five-year exit plan, largely because of debt-servicing regulations
that makes foreclosure on Japanese property a time-consuming
process. Currently, the servicing of an asset can be done only by the
bank that originated the loan, and hedge funds are not allowed to
set up an independent loan-servicing operation. Although this
dampens the market, signs for growth are portentous.

Foreign securities companies and investment houses have purchased over ¥2 trillion worth of Japanese bad loans on a book-value
basis between April and September 1998. The main sellers have
been the Japanese banks and life insurers who have rushed to dump
their disclosed nonperforming loans. However, as the Asian contagion spreads, the JFIs might find their remaining loans harder to
offload. Bad assets bought have been mainly uncollateralized loans
extended to bankrupt borrowers and loans whose real estate collateral was put up for court-administered auctions by the financial
institutions that extended the loans.

Although the JFIs have sold off over ¥4,000 billion in bad loans,
the market still has a long way to go. The government wants the sale
of bad loans to increase to remove ¥88,000 billion worth of problem
loans from the JFIs' books. Although the government's measures
include plans for special purposes companies for securitization,
plans to simplify the property code, and giving tax breaks to banks
selling off their bad loans, there are further problems to contend
with.

When the banks sell bad loans, they have to realize secondary
losses. Because most JFIs' bad-loan contingency accounting is predicated on the assumption that the properties are worth 70% of their
peak value and because many of them are worth closer to 10% of
their peak value, the banks are forced to realize heavy secondary
losses. Bank of Tokyo-Mitsubishi (BTM), IBJ, Fuji, Sumitomo,
Daiwa, Sanwa, and DKB, who have been prepared to divest themselves of their bad loans, have found willing buyers among the foreign community.

Several major international firms—Bankers Trust, Deutsche
Morgan, Credit Suisse, Morgan Stanley, and Goldman Sachs among
others—have been attracted to this market. Between them, they

have bought just under ¥1 trillion of real estate-backed bad loans, with a Texas-based real estate investment firm, Loanstar Opportunity Fund Corp., purchasing ¥600 billion worth of loans in a tie-up with Merrill Lynch. Goldman Sachs also picked up some ¥150 billion worth. Although sales tend to be secretive, perhaps as much as $100 billion in deals at book value have been done in recent months alone. Given the heavy-handed methods by which the properties were acquired, it is a sordid business they prefer to keep out of public sight. That said, the buyer must, as ever, be wary. Although Japanese banks deny that they have been selling yakuza-related loans to foreigners, perhaps as much as 50% of the loans have questionable backgrounds. Portfolios are offered and sometimes the yakuza-related loans are chucked in on a zero-value basis as part of a portfolio.

The yakuza are still heavily involved in the Tokyo property market, and the foreign companies now competing head-to-head with them are trying to devise means of dealing with them. Goldman Sachs, for example, has invented a yakuza put option, whereby the deal becomes null and void if a loan subsequently turns out to have yakuza links. The tricky mathematics of options aside, this may not be the simple resolution Goldman Sachs would like it to be. It still has to be tested in Japanese courts, and Japanese banks are loath to let their foreign competitors merely cherry-pick the Tokyo property market, especially now that the market seems to have bottomed out. Unless the yakuza are tamed, or unless the foreign firms find a novel way of collecting from them, problems-and more dead bodies-will undoubtedly surface later.

Although prices, comparatively speaking, are at fire-sale levels, Tokyo's land market remains illiquid, inefficient, and, if the market is to be believed, still grossly overpriced. There is no really liquid secondary market and so the banks which recklessly lent out have no yardstick to gauge the extent of their chronic losses.

Although all property markets have their peculiarities, Tokyo is particularly quirky. The three golden rules of property—location, location, and location—still pertain, but land prices and tax policies in Tokyo's 23 wards conspire to change these golden rules considerably. The prime location during the Meiji Restoration was the

Emperor's Palace. The British Government, the Court of St. James, built its opulent embassy opposite it, simply because it was, in Victoria's reign, Tokyo's prime location. Smaller powers built their embassies in less prominent positions in the same location. The United States, however, built its embassy in Akasaka, which is now a very important part of Tokyo in its own right. Other, lesser powers followed suit and, not being as rich as the Americans, chose less prominent locations in Akasaka. Obeying the three cardinal rules of property, they chose bad locations in the good location of Roppongi. And they paid accordingly.

As in the diplomatic field, so also in the business world. The central business district (CBD) of Tokyo, which earlier was concentrated around Tokyo Station and later spread to Marunouchi, has expanded greatly since the 1970s. While the Marunouchi-Otemachi district generally remains the top choice of the largest companies, the new subcenters also offer plentiful first-class office space at competitive prices. As in the diplomatic field, new subcenters have been gradually added to the definition of what comprises Tokyo's CBD: office premises in Tokyo are available in a number of districts along the circular Japan Railway Yamanote Line. The seemingly disjointed areas of West Shinjuku, Kamiyacho, Ebisu, Hamamatsucho, Omori, Shinagawa, Tennozu, the Tokyo Waterfront, and Nakano-Sakaue are now all much sought-after locations. New developments and infrastructural improvements continue to widen the perception of what is central.

Adjacent cities are also being included in the definition of what is central. Major redevelopment has been occurring at Yokohama, Japan's second largest city. It aims to ease pressure on Tokyo, only 30 kilometers away. Three government organizations have already relocated, 10 more plan to follow suit in the near future, and the projected final total is 79. They join 15 foreign government organizations that have established themselves in the city. The ongoing Minato Mirai 21 (MM21) project on 186 hectares of former shipyard land in Yokohama already includes the nation's largest building, offices, concert halls, and three hotels. A new transit line will be added by 2000 to improve access from Tokyo to this important site.

Thus, whether at the diplomatic, industrial, retail, or wholesale level, well-located property and land are central to business in Tokyo as they are elsewhere. Business people have to pay for locations in accordance with the laws of supply and demand. Because well-located premises will continue to be in high demand and short supply, they will command premium prices and premium rents. The problem is that the definition of what is a prized location has ebbed and flowed with time.

Prices have changed out of all recognition since the bubble years. Rental ranges for Tokyo top $120 per square meter for the Marunouchi-Otemachi belt.[5] Capital values of premium office space are in the $35,000-per-square-meter range, with important variations determined by locality. The Marunouchi area, for example, has plunged 77% from spring 1987 to ¥53 million per tsubo. The value of commercial real estate in Akasaka has dived even more: 83% to ¥24 million per tsubo. Japan's current stagflation means that investors cannot pay their mortgages and tenants will not come forward, even at grossly discounted prices.

As if that were not bad enough, tenancy provisions make the Japanese market quirkier still. Commercial lease terms are normally for two years. The lease often stipulates that the contract will be continued for rolling two-year periods unless or until either party invokes the standard six-month notification period for termination. Essentially, leases are ongoing and the rental conditions are renegotiated every two years. Although, de jure, either party can terminate the contract, Japanese courts have consistently held that, except in some very special circumstances, only the tenant may utilize this right. The effect is that a landlord cannot evict a tenant, but the tenant can escape from a lease at any time with six months' prior notice or by paying six months' rent as a penalty. Needless to say, in the post-bubble years, tenants have been forking up their six months' rent and skedaddling, leaving the landlords with egg on their faces and with massive problems with the stern-faced bankers who gave them the loans they can no longer service during the bubble years.

Some of Tokyo's best retail space has developed around a variety of disjointed train station hubs such as Harajuku, Ikebukuro, Shibuya, and Shinjuku. Although Aoyama and Omotesando are both increasingly popular, the CBD's world-renowned Ginza remains Tokyo's most prestigious retail area. There is a long waiting list for rentable space in the retail heartland of Ginza. Rents for well-located buildings facing the main street have already bottomed and are beginning to increase. Once retail space is secured on Chuo Avenue, businesses rarely relinquish it. Liquidity is, as a result, tighter than optimality would desire. On Namiki Avenue, a few blocks away, renowned designer brands front the street with shops and boutiques, most just biding their time till they secure a place on Chuo Avenue. Even during a recession, Ginza's high demand and consequent illiquidity means that places are hard to come by. During the bubble period, landlords asked for deposits, generally nonrefundable, of 100 and more months' rent, to secure retail space in Ginza. Deposits have now fallen to 50 months. In other areas, the average is close to 20 months, and is often less than 10 months in less-desired areas. There are, in other words, severe discontinuities in the market.

The residential market is similarly sticky and has similar discontinuities. Tokyo's prime residential neighborhood is Minato Ward. Within central Tokyo, the most popular residential areas among expatriates are known as the "three A's": Aoyama, Azabu, and Akasaka, all in Minato Ward. Three-bedroom apartments sell, post-bubble, for prices reaching $2 million. While all three areas are expensive, the most exclusive residential area of these is Azabu, home to many foreign embassies. Rents are stratospheric, $10,000 per month being common. Because employers generally pick up the tab, rents in these three neighborhoods tend to be bloated to a degree unmatched in other major cities.

More generally across Tokyo, residential starts and land prices continue to fall. Many holders of mortgages, especially those who bought in the bubble years, have negative equity in their homes. This remains a major brake on residential activity and on consumer confidence. Tokyo land prices are now so prohibitive that three-hour train commutes are becoming the norm for a growing amount of Tokyo's workforce. Thus, while population growth in Tokyo proper has been declining, populations in the surrounding prefectures of Saitama, Chiba, Kanagawa, and Ibaraki have been increasing at around 7% per annum. This process of suburbanization, which started in the 1950s, is expected to continue in line with rising land prices and the development of transportation and communication services.

Land prices are usually determined by market comparisons using land-price indices prepared by the National Land Agency, while the building price is usually determined by the market. Japanese land law regards land as an asset separate from buildings, and the term "land price" is normally used instead of "property price." Freehold is the only type of property ownership. Although there is no equivalent system of leasehold property, there is a property-holding system called land lease, the ownership of a building exclusive of land. A land lease is granted only under a provision that the building is owned by a different party from the actual landowner. Thus, land and property are separate entities that often are owned and taxed separately.

This division between land value and property value distorts Tokyo property prices even more than does Tokyo's uneven development. So too, to an extraordinary degree, do taxes. Property is heavily taxed. These taxes include the Fixed Asset Tax, City Planning Tax, National Real Property Tax, Special Land Holding Tax on owner and buyer alike, Real Property Acquisition Tax, National Registration and License Tax, Stamp Duty, Business Premises Tax on new Building, and Surtax on Sales of Land. Inheritance taxes reach 70% for any but the more modest houses and apartments.

All of these taxes vary in size, and, depending on the tax in question, are assessed on the land, the buildings, or both the land and the buildings. Depending on the specific tax in question, they are levied on one or more of the owner, the buyer, or the seller at varying rates. The surtax on sales of land tax, for example, ranges from a low of 5% on the total of capital gain of land held for more than five years to 15% for land held for less than two years. The National Real Property Acquisition Tax (Fudosan Suhotoku Zei) is levied on the buyer of land and buildings at a rate of 2% for both land and buildings. However, to this is added the National Registration and License Tax (Toroku Menkyo Zei) which is also levied on the buyer of land and buildings at a rate of 2% for land and

5% for buildings.

Because total taxes and levies can add up to 20% to the purchase price and slash an even larger amount from profit sales, land and building prices are sticky: people prefer to buy and hold on to them—and pay the exorbitant taxes involved.

Taxes also vary according to the use to which land is put. It is for this reason that prime Tokyo locations, which in London or New York would be graced with modern buildings, are uneconomical rice paddies or cabbage patches or are cluttered up by little wooden shacks. Development would bring crippling taxes with them.

The prevalence of rice paddies and drafty, uninsulated wooden shacks in prime Tokyo sites show that massive supply-side shocks are needed to make Tokyo a truly modern city. The easing of height restrictions on building and the rezoning of land are obvious ways to increase supply and reduce prices. Tokyo has very few skyscrapers for a city of its size, while more than 5% of Tokyo's land is still zoned for agriculture. There are still 90,000 acres of farmland and 56,000 acres of vacant land in the Greater Tokyo area which, in the freer markets of London or New York, would be sold for billions of dollars.

The reluctance to sell land, and the resulting lack of supply and its continuing subdivision into ever-smaller plots, makes it hard for developers to assemble land into large sites. In the case of Tokyo, it weakens the three golden rules of property. In Tokyo, the importance of location, location, and location are all overaffected by the tax system, which was geared to keep the market stable and, when needed, highly inflatable.

Tokyo, in other words, has key, local, tax-related quirks that make its property market different. Because legislation ensures that there remains a slight overabundance of aged, inferior-quality buildings, rents continue to slide downward. Only in newer, larger, and well-located buildings have post-bubble rents stabilized.

Because tax considerations overshadow low interest rate considerations, rekindling the market is extremely difficult. Despite historically low interest rates, the pace of bankruptcies is picking up among construction companies and there are an increasing number of bail-out packages extended to keep real estate companies afloat.

The banking industry has an estimated ¥92 trillion in loans to the real estate and construction companies, an amount equivalent to 20% of their total loan portfolio. They have taken very heavy losses on their property portfolios.

At present, loans are not conducive to the liquidation of real estate assets held as collateral against loans. The laws are set to change, however, as part of the Big Bang reforms. In particular, securitization measures, discussed later, are expected before 2001. The new legislation will help financial institutions divest from the bubble and help real estate and construction companies restructure their balance sheets.

While the bottom of Tokyo's office-property market may decline further, premium-grade office values are now stable. Foreign financial institutions, in particular, are bucking the trend by scrambling for prime office space in central Tokyo, affirming how they see opportunity in Japan's Big Bang. The vacancy rate for office space within Tokyo's 23 wards declined to 4.7% in 1998 from 9.6% three years earlier. But in December 1990, the rate was just 0.6%. Tenants these days are getting a bargain, at least for Tokyo. Office rents in December 1998 averaged ¥15,410 per 3.3 tsubo, down 24% from three years earlier and 40% from seven years earlier.

The Marunouchi area has resurfaced as a prized location. State-of-the art skyscrapers, such as the new East Tower of Otemachi First Square on the fringe of the Marunouchi area, are chockablock with foreign tenants. Foreign tenants in Ark Mori Building, a 37-story office building in the heart of Akasaka, make up 45% of the whole. The building houses nine foreign financial institutions. The biggest tenant is the Goldman Sachs group, which currently occupies four floors. Mori Building is scheduled to give up a portion of the sixth floor, where its head office is located, to make room for Goldman Sachs' expansion. More than 40% of the residents at Ark Towers apartment complex, behind Ark Mori Building, are non-Japanese. All of this points to a general vibrancy in those sectors directly associated with the Big Bang.

This vibrancy does not extend to the property market as a whole. It is a bifurcated market with some locales in big demand and other parts of the city still being depressed by recessionary fears.

Elsewhere, while manufacturing employment losses have stabilized, the industrial leasing market remains relatively weak. The main demand is from companies seeking coordinated countrywide logistics combined with distribution, sales, and support logistics. Because overseas visitor numbers are increasing at rates not topped since 1990, hotel building, which bottomed in 1996, is now rising again.[6] Tokyo is getting its first Disney-brand hotel, and distress sales are further revitalizing the sector. Several of Japan's largest life insurance companies are considering investing in property for the first time since the bubble burst. The 70% fall in land prices has meant that expected yields on real estate are now competitive again.

Still, despite these bullish twitches, the nature of the Tokyo market has changed forever. Though rents may have picked up in prime business and industrial locations, the problem the JFIs and others have of divesting themselves of their considerable bad holdings remains. Securitization undoubtedly offers the best chance of solving Japan's land debacle. However, before we discuss the current state of Japan's securitization industry, it is important to explain first what securitization is and to look at its evolution in its country of birth, the United States, to see how it links in to the ideas of free, fair, and global markets that underwrite the Big Bang.

Securitization is one of the financial world's latest and most important innovations. As such, it should play a key role in any successful Big Bang. Securitization involves the pooling of loans into standardized securities, which then use those loans as collateral. The transformation of these pools into standardized securities enables issuers to deal in volumes sufficiently large that they can bypass banks and other intermediaries. Because they bypass banks, these instruments are called pass-throughs.

Mortgage-backed securities (MBSs) form the backbone of the American securitization market. An MBS is either an ownership claim in a pool of mortgages or an obligation that is secured by such a pool. These claims represent securitization of mortgage loans. Mortgage lenders originate loans and then sell packages of these loans in the secondary market. Specifically, they sell their claim to the cash inflows from the mortgages as those loans are paid off. The mortgage originator continues to service the loan, collecting principal and interest payments, and passes these payments along to the purchaser of the mortgage. For this reason, these MBSs are called pass-throughs.

Suppose, for example, that a small, regional bank has ten 30-year mortgages, each with a principal value of $100,000, and they are grouped together into a million-dollar pool. If the mortgage rate is 10%, then the first month's payment for each loan would be $877.57, of which $833.33 would be interest and $44.24 would be principal repayment. The holder of the mortgage pool would receive a payment in the first month of $8,775.70, the total payments of all ten payments in the pool, less the institution's service charges, of course. In addition, if one of the mortgages happens to be paid off in any one month, the holder of the pass-through security also receives that payment of principal. In future months the pool will comprise a smaller number of loans, and the interest and principal payments will be lower. The prepaid mortgage in effect represents a partial retirement of the pass-through holder's investment.

Although pass-throughs often guarantee payment of interest and principal, they do not guarantee the rate of return. Holders of mortgage pass-throughs therefore can be severely disappointed in their returns in years when interest rates drop significantly. This is because homeowners usually have an option to prepay, or pay ahead of schedule, the remaining principal outstanding on their mortgages. These types of rebound effects exasperate the risks inherent in MBSs and similarly engineered products.

Importantly in the Japanese context, securitization improves the balance sheets of FIs by removing the securitized assets and the liabilities needed to cover them from the balance sheet and replacing them with coveted off-balance sheet flow. This could be of immense help to the JFIs in solving their bad-debt problems. Goldman Sachs bought $100 million of bad property loans from the BTM, and Merrill Lynch, Morgan Stanley, and other foreign financial institutions have set up foreign property arms to package and resell problem loans bought from troubled banks. Although Sanwa Bank has conducted a $250 million securitization of bad property-related loans and Goldman Sachs recently organized a $35 million deal with Sumitomo Bank, substantial change will be slow.

The United States is a large and reasonably open market where mortgages would be much the same from one end of the country to the other. This being so, they would be much easier to securitize than Japanese mortgages as there is not a well-developed secondary market in land or housing in Japan. Indeed, there is not even a well-developed housing insurance market for contingencies such as earthquakes. All of Japan is prone to earthquakes and, as Kobe showed, all of Japan, Tokyo included, is ill-prepared for them. This is in contrast to the United States, where San Francisco and other earthquake-prone cities take sensible steps to mitigate the damage of such acts of God. Japan, in contrast, ignores them.

Although securitization can reduce costs and certain types of risk, credit risks and other risks based on imperfect information will probably increase. Market risk, financial exposure, and liquidity risk will remain. This is especially true in opaque markets like Japan.

Still, there is intense interest in these proposed developments. Seventeen Japanese companies have combined to jointly raise ¥70 billion by issuing securities backed by corporate bonds. Although the move, which is relatively novel for Japan, reflects the growing difficulties Japanese companies have borrowing from financial institutions, it also reflects a growing differentiation between those companies that will be able to survive the Big Bang and those whose inefficiencies will guarantee their demise.

With domestic institutional investors growing increasingly risk-averse, few BB- or BBB-rated bonds are being issued at present in Japan. This scheme is therefore not only a means to raise funds but a means of differentiating between those that will be able to raise funds in the future and those that will not.

Each firm is to issue ¥3 to ¥5 billion worth of corporate bonds abroad, which will be pooled at a special-purpose company. The idea is to pool the bonds of the 17 companies and use them as collateral for three collateralized bond obligations (CBOs) to be issued through Fuji Securities Co. A-rated companies taking part in the scheme include Taisei, Mycal, and Marubeni Corp. Participating B-rated companies include Oki Electric, Akebono Brake Industry, and Suminoe.

The CBOs will be rated and differentiated accordingly. They will then, depending on their rating, be targeted at major institutional investors. This differentiation and the bundling of bonds and subsequent unbundling to specific clients typifies the change the Big Bang seeks. Several Japanese companies, most notably Nomura, have gained considerable overseas experience with products such as these.

Nomura wants to bring to Japan the securitization skills it has gleaned in overseas markets. Industrial companies wanting to spin off inefficient, noncore investments would offer opportunities for techniques pioneered in Britain by Nomura's Principal Finance group. The group has bought British assets ranging from pubs to army housing and refinanced them by securitizing their cash flows.

Nomura has, in fact, been at the forefront of recent innovations. After the 1997 success of the Bowie bond, where David Bowie raised $55 million against future royalties in a bond issue organized by Fahnestock, the American investment bank, intellectual properties are being securitized at a frenetic rate. Rod Stewart, the aging British rock singer, clinched a $16 million securitized loan from Nomura capital. The deal is backed by revenues from his music publishing catalogue. Internationally, there is an enormous market for highly rated securitization assets that have an attractive yield relative to similarly rated corporate or indeed government bonds. The Bowie bond yielded 7.9% with an average 10-year maturity, an attractive premium even compared with other securitized bonds which generally give a 10 to 15 basis-point premium over average corporate credits. However, only a small number of artists can command such cash flows as to justify an issue.

At a time of low yields on government paper, there is strong demand among investors for these innovative products. Hollywood movie studios now regularly raise loans through securitized plans, and biotechnology companies are also heavily involved. Record companies are following suit. Richard Branson's Virgin Group, for example, has teamed up with Morgan Stanley to explore such opportunities. Unlike Bowie and U2, Rod Stewart does not own his own master tapes: EMI owns them. Stewart has only his royalties to offer as security and so the issue is considerably smaller than Bowie's.

The thinness of the Stewart offering may well resonate in the wider Japanese markets. Also, Nomura's recent losses in the derivatives markets might temper their appetite for risky products in

Japan. Further, since the Japanese property market remains plagued by low volumes and falling prices, some analysts suspect that smaller, nonproperty securitizations, such as Japan Leasing Auto's $83 million worth of bonds backed up by the income stream from car rentals, will grow fastest in the short term. As the Japanese government is determined to boost the securitization industry, the success of Japan Leasing Auto's initiative, which was twice subscribed, will have wider consequences if it is replicated in less marginal economic sectors.

Dai-Ichi Kangyo Bank plans to promote sales of securitized loan credits by categorizing loans by risk level. As a first step, ¥200 billion worth of securitized short-term loans have been subdivided into several categories, as determined by Moody's ratings. The AAA group, considered the safest and accounting for 70%-80% of the loans, have been sold to Norinchukin Bank. The riskier ones carrying the lower rating are being sold to several domestic institutional investors. DKB intends to build up its expertise and securitize other loans under a similar method in the future. At the same time, the lender hopes to cooperate with regional banks and others to combine loan credits of several institutions in new financial products.

Though properties are slow to be securitized, rents are already being converted into securitized assets. However, although companies such as Sekisui guarantee the rent, the high-deposit nature of the Tokyo rental market would, to Western eyes at least, remove default risk totally. Indeed, this securitization of rents, far from ushering in a new securitized dawn, instead highlights securitization's core Japanese problem: the over-reliance on illiquid bricks-and-mortar security. The infrastructure simply isn't yet in place to handle the bigger, fleeter-of-foot risks securitization begets.

Japan, simply, does not have the legal and accounting infrastructure in place that securitization needs. In traditional bank lending, all risks are borne by the single institution giving the loan. Securitization, however, distributes that risk among a variety of participating institutions. As a result, the risk involved in a transaction might not be as transparent as with a loan. Because the resulting factionalization of the risk holders can reduce overall risk monitoring and adjustment, already pitiably weak in Japan, accounting and regulatory practices would have to be revamped to deal with these securitized transactions. Neither Japan's legal framework nor her corporate structure currently lends itself to such a system. Further, due to the dynamic process of securitization and the apparent transferability of the risk, recognition of the risks involved might not be always full and comprehensive. Illiquid markets like Japan's will find this dynamic process particularly difficult to adjust to.

Japanese securitization-linked risks would most likely be further compounded if the banks kept their poorer debts on their books and securitized their better ones. The information pool would be reduced and creditors would be less likely to help troubled debtors. This seems particularly problematic in Japan where some JFIs are palming off their yakuza-related bad loans on the more gullible of their foreign counterparts. If, as some contend, the MOF is turning a blind eye to this practice, it is the antithesis of free, fair, and global markets. It is, in fact, but a continuation of the old Japanese ways that are being consigned to the trashcan of history where they belong.

Still, Japanese corporate customs remain a major stumbling block to the successful implementation of the Big Bang. The accounting treatment of securitization will have far-reaching consequences. The open disclosure that is central to the successful implementation of securitization has not been a feature of Japanese corporate culture. Because of past controversies concerning reserve requirements, capital adequacy, and deposit insurance premiums, Japan's accounting treatment of securitization will be of particular interest to the market. This is particularly so in Japan, where the JFIs have been particularly lax in their treatment of commercial paper and where the practice of *tobashi*[7] and bicycle loans has been so prevalent.

Although these issues and their related scandals will be discussed at greater length in future chapters, for the moment it must be reiterated that securitization cannot proceed without free and fair markets, and that free and fair markets are predicated on openness, full disclosure, and accountability, and that Japan is currently sadly lacking in these latter traits.

Banks holding securitized assets will have to make explicit capital provisions for different classes of assets, based on each asset's perceived riskiness. Explicit capital provisions will need to be made for any off-balance sheet risk stemming from letters of credit, guarantees, or credit enhancements, as well as from sales or the transferring of assets with recourse by a bank or bank holding company.

Under current practice, in order to determine whether a specified group of receivables has been sold in a securitization, the inquiring party must demonstrate a connection to the transaction before being allowed access. The records, in other words, are not public. Since the records are not public, it is impossible for potential creditors and ratings companies and other third parties to assess the credit-worthiness of parties that have been active in securitization markets. This does not conform to global standards. It also increases systematic risk significantly and delimits the interest international investors might otherwise have in a Japanese securitization market.

To approach global standards, the MOF cannot remain an unwritten law unto itself. A transparent, public, and objective system of registering security interests in receivables of all sorts is required to facilitate development of a healthy receivables market. In the absence of such a system, it is impossible for independent accounting and legal professionals to provide the assurances required by international capital markets with respect to the level of required investor protection. The fact that Japan's legal and accounting standards fall well short of world global standards also has to be addressed.

The MOF's past practices would urge one to err on the side of caution before becoming ensnared in Japanese securitization markets, where ownership, taxation and other rights and duties have not been clearly mapped out. Under current Japanese law, it is difficult for investors to obtain certainty that the bankruptcy of the assignor of the receivables will not affect the rights of investors in receivables held in the securitization vehicle. This makes it almost impossible for ratings agencies and others to view these vehicles as bankruptcy-remote for purposes of assigning a rating based solely on the assessed quality of the receivables being securitized. Modifications both to the Claimable Rights Law and the Bankruptcy Law of Japan are needed in order that investors can be assured that the insolvency of the transferor of the receivables will not affect the ability of the investors to recover from the obligors of the receivables. This issue can also affect the ability of the assignor to obtain off-balance-sheet treatment for the receivables securitized. A fully transparent reporting system is needed to abort these current ambiguities.

First of all, though, Japan's quirky legal system will have to be overhauled from top to bottom. The Justice Ministry practices a crude contraception policy to limit entries to the law industry. Currently, only about two of every 100 law graduates who sit for the bar exam are allowed to pass it. As a result, Japan has one lawyer per 6,500 citizens, compared with one per 320 in the United States. Japan's ministry-sanctioned consequent shortage of lawyers and of a judicial system meeting global standards opens the door for the yakuza and other thugs to fill the vacuum.

There is a big vacuum. The Japanese people elect their Supreme Court judges in a democratic charade, but the judges, although they have symbolic powers even the United States Supreme Court might envy, lack real power. Just as in finance, the mandarins at the Justice Ministry call the shots. Consequently, less than 2% of antigovernment litigants succeed with their cases. More surprisingly still, perhaps, less than 0.01% of defendants in criminal cases are found not guilty.

Worse still, costs can, without any reason being given, be somewhat arbitrarily awarded against the plaintiffs. And, as civil and criminal cases can take over 25 years to resolve, it is difficult to challenge the dictates of the bureaucrats who, after all, draft the vaguely worded laws that they alone enforce and interpret. This does not augur well for a free, fair, and global market.

Traditionally, to reiterate, the MOF has been loath to codify its practices. A massive change of heart here would be necessary before any worthwhile securitization market could be implemented. Even with the best will in the world toward it, the fact that the MOF is venturing into uncharted regulatory waters must force us to believe that, if anything, it will err on the side of caution and delay Tokyo's having a fully functioning market.

The tax treatment of certain types of securitization transactions, particularly those involving cross-border sales of receivables, has been a constant impediment to the conclusion of these transactions. Particularly troublesome in this regard has been the possibility of the imposition of withholding tax on payments of receivables that have been transferred to or are for the benefit of off-shore parties. The risk of the imposition of withholding taxes on these transactions has been a major impediment to foreign participation in Japan's receivables securitization market.

Although these taxes are not particularly big revenue-earners for the MOF, they do typify their oft-times niggardly attitude which acts as a deterrent to would-be market participants who prefer to go to other markets that more easily meet their ideals of free, fair, and global markets. The MOF must prune these and many other minor regulations if it expects the Japanese markets to attract sufficient overseas players to make them viable.

These issues are becoming more urgent. The banking sector, which funded the bubble, is plagued with nonperforming assets. Steps to allow full-scale securitization of property assets could create a market worth billions of dollars. If Japan were to have a real estate securitization market of the same percentage of GDP as the United States, the market quickly would be worth over $100 billion, more than 20 times the current level.

On paper, the logic is certainly attractive. A key factor dragging Japan's property market down is the huge volume of property-related bad loans held by financial institutions, including Japan's banks. With the Big Bang looming, the banks need to clear those bad loans, and although the BTM and others have made some provisions for bad loans, these provisions are something of an accounting illusion. The banks have been slow to realize the losses by calling in the loans or selling the property collateral.

This is partly because it is still very difficult to find enough investors prepared to buy land at anything other than severely discounted prices. Securitization could revolutionize this state of affairs. The bank would move the property-backed loan to a special-purpose company. This company would then use the property as an asset against which it issues bonds, which would then be sold to a range of investors.

The price of those bonds would, among other things, reflect the quality of the diversified loan portfolio that is being securitized. This would have the crucial advantage of broadening the number of potential investors. Bonds and equities could then be turned into mutual fund products that could be sold to retail investors. In theory, this would make it easier for the banks to sell the loans and would lead to a more liquid market.

This has worked elsewhere, most notably in the United States, which managed to clear its bad loans from its 1980s banking crisis by securitizing them. Japanese investors have, in fact, recently shown heightened interest in American MBSs guaranteed by the Government National Mortgage Association. Japanese investors prefer the Ginnie Mae securities because of their implicit government guarantee and because they suit Japanese capital requirements. Banks holding Ginnie Mae MBSs do not have to set aside any reserve cushion, but they must keep capital equal to 20% of the value of other American-backed MBSs.

A properly functioning Japanese securitization market, governanced like its American counterpart, would therefore be of interest to these investors. It could generate the higher returns they need. It could deepen markets in the underlying contracts and therefore make them more liquid and less risky. However, the fundamental changes in Japan's corporate outlook needed to allow such markets to function will be slow in coming.

The main reason that the necessary changes will be slow in coming has to do with the Ministry of Finance and its governance system. The next chapter examines this issue.

[1] The yakuza have an ambivalent position in Japanese society. They have a quasi-legal existence, more akin to the Triads in Nationalist China than to their Italian or American counterparts.

[2] Jutaku kinyu senmon kaisha, commonly abbreviated to jusen, literally translates as "special housing finance companies."

[3] Literally, "descent from heaven."

[4] The Big Four broking houses: Nomura, Daiwa, Yamaichi, and Nikko traditionally controlled most of Japan's broking business. Because Yamaichi has now bankrupted, we also speak of the Big Three of Nomura, Daiwa, and Nikko. See Chapter 5.

[5] Rents for office premises in Japan are typically quoted in terms of yen per tsubo per month (one tsubo equals approximately 3.3 square meters or 35.8 square feet).

[6] Japan Statistics Bureau, Management and Coordination Agency, gives the relevant figures.

[7] See p. 76.

Japan's Sullied Mandarins

"Welcome to Japan. Obey the Rules."[1]

The Ministry of Finance (MOF), Japan's primary depository institution regulator, is charged with improving the performance of Japan's financial institutions (FIs) for Japan's common economic good. It does this by enacting rules, regulations, and guidelines that enhance confidence in both the system and the FIs which are part of the system, that will prevent or reduce the incidence of insolvency among FIs, that will maintain the liquidity of the FIs, and that will allow the FIs to perform their functions with due prudence at minimal cost.

There are, necessarily, trade-offs between the various regulatory goals. Reducing the possibility of insolvency, for example, would mean that FIs cannot be as liquid as they might otherwise like to be: they have to keep reserves back to meet their unforeseen contingencies discussed at length in chapters two and four. Because holding reserves for such unforeseen contingencies debars those reserves being lent out for profit, the FIs cannot operate at minimum cost. The indirect costs of compliance—auditing and the like—add further to overheads and nibble away at the hard-pressed bottom line.

The natural temptation is to minimize their reserve holdings and run the risk of not being able to stem a run. This temptation is heightened when the regulatory authorities can be cajoled into underwriting the system. Japan's FIs succumbed to such a temptation and made their financial system deviate a long way from global prudent standards.

These policy conflicts, though easy to elucidate, have caused many financial calamities both in national and international settings. The United States savings and loan (S&L) debacle, the current debt problems of the Japanese banks, and the current financial problems of Southeast Asia are all textbook examples of the conflicting goals the regulators must accommodate.

Although earlier chapters have alluded to Anglo-American governance standards, the reader should not think that their standards were delivered to them, set in stone. Rather, they are a part of an ongoing evolutionary process. British and American regulators have learned the hard way that a properly functioning system needs the proper regulatory dosage to remain healthy.

An important sine qua non for achieving this global benchmark is to have markets that are, by and large, seen to be free, fair, and global. There must, in other words, be no unduly lengthy or expensive barriers to entering or exiting the market, there must be no undue favoritism to one or more players by the regulatory authorities, and the market's standards must be comparable with those of London, New York, and the other key hubs in the global network.

If global standards are the objective, regulators must strive toward these goals. They must regulate in a way that enhances their credibility and does not expose them to unnecessary moral hazard. The too-big-to-fail fallacy is one of the gravest moral hazard problems the central banks (CBs) face. The American, Japanese, and other authorities have, at various times, said that designated big banks are too big to be allowed to fail. Though such guarantees may increase confidence in those designated banks, if they subsequently fail, they undermine the credibility of the regulatory authorities. Such guarantees also act as an indirect subsidy to the designated banks as they reduce their risk rating; it thereby allows them to operate more cheaply than their competitors.

This is not just an academic or semantic problem. The scuttling of Japan's convoy system has brought this problem to the fore. Japan long operated a too-big-to-fail policy. When it abandoned it in spring 1998, both the credibility of the Bank of Japan (BOJ)-MOF axis and the credit ratings of the JFIs they supervised plunged. Although Japan bit the proverbial bullet, the sheer scale of the problem makes it almost intractable.

Like so much else, the Japanese had a prototype on which to base this debacle. The failure of the American S&Ls, with the loss of billions of dollars, was also due to both moral hazard and regulatory failure reasons. The moral hazard problem was caused by United States federal deposit insurance guarantees to the savings institutions. Because the American authorities were guaranteeing them, in effect writing them a blank check, they engaged in high-risk policies that they would not have entertained without the blank check of a federal guarantee. Federal regulators in the United States failed to address this, the moral hazard problem of deregulation, until the damage—which ran to billions of dollars—was done.

The S&L fiasco is an example of the moral hazards that all regulators must guard against. One of these is the moral hazard of making deposit insurance available. Because the American regulators did not want its FIs to fail, they made depository insurance available; that is, they allowed the FIs to insure themselves against failure. The S&Ls abandoned considerations of prudence and engaged in the risky business practices that cost the American taxpayer billions of dollars to remedy.

The United States is not unique. Britain and Australia are further examples of countries that have had to bail out distressed banks in recent years. The regulators of those countries know that money is a coward that flees instability. Those countries pumped money into failing institutions to contain the damage a loss in credibility of their financial systems would cause. Other countries—Thailand springs to mind—have tried to do similar things but with less success.

Thailand's central bank lost any semblance of credibility when, despite its prior assurances, it was unable to act as a lender of last resort to its troubled FIs. The ensuing loss of credibility of Thailand's CB triggered the current financial crisis in Southeast Asia which has since spread to all other parts of the world. Credibility and avoiding the problems of moral hazard are, as Thailand exemplifies, very important to the maintenance of a sound financial system.

Japan now finds itself battling these self-same problems. Like the Bank of Thailand, the BOJ acted as a lender of last resort to Japanese banks after the bubble burst. It stood willing and able to lend to any designated temporarily illiquid but otherwise solvent institution. It did this to prevent the FI's illiquidity leading to a general loss of confidence in that institution or in others. It provided the necessary liquidity to see these designated JFIs through recent turbulent times. This inevitably led to the moral hazard of the too-big-to-fail dilemma, exemplified by the plethora of financial scandals which have dogged the JFIs and the BOJ which, rather rashly in retrospect, pledged to cover their debts.

The problems of the JFIs mirror the current Asian collapse, which exemplifies the problems of negative externalities and, in the case of the International Monetary Fund (IMF)'s loss of credibility, the moral hazards attendant to being a lender of last resort. Knowing that there is a lender of last resort gets the FI to engage in credit risks it might otherwise not engage in. When a lender of last resort cannot or will not meet the obligations these moral hazards give rise to, it loses credibility, the key moral asset of a CB. The recent loss of credibility of both the IMF in Asia and the BOJ in Japan will have long-term ramifications.

They are already having important, shorter-term ones. European, Japanese, and American creditors now find that their Southeast Asian clients cannot pay them. This unexpected shock to their balance sheets is a negative externality. CB credibility has evaporated in Southeast Asia, causing such negative externalities and the risk of a worldwide systematic breakdown.

If the Asian contagion spread, it would be a problem of systematic risk. Systematic risk is the risk that some depository institutions may not be able to meet the terms of their own credit agreements because of failures by other institutions to settle transactions that otherwise are not related. Clearly, if FIs in the developed world find themselves in that position, unable to meet the terms of their own credit agreements as a result of the Asian contagion, it would be an example of systematic risk.

The systematic risk in the JFI system is compounded by this regional one. Preventing such disasters is a hands-on task for the regulators. In Britain, the United States, and similarly managed countries, the regulators try to achieve their goals of maintaining well-functioning markets by periodically examining their FIs, by publishing detailed rules and standards which the FIs must meet to be allowed operate in those jurisdictions. And by having good governance!

Although the foregoing might imply that more regulation is better than less regulation, such is not the case. This is because of the conflicting goals of regulatory policy. Because FIs must, if they are to retain their domestic and international competitiveness, operate at the lowest practicable cost, the costs of complying with regulations can be stifling, both in direct pecuniary terms and in the indirect costs of the personnel assigned to meet the compliance requirements. There is, in other words, an important trade-off between the costly policy of the authorities making the FIs comply with their every rule and the moral and other hazards of not drawing up or not enforcing prudential rules.

Britain, the United States, and similar countries who meet global governance standards have found a good working balance between these conflicting poles. Their markets work reasonably well, confidence in them is high, and they are not unduly opaque or restrictive. Banks must fulfill stringent requirements in the United States, Britain, and similarly governed countries. Capital requirements, discussed later with respect to Japan, define measures of capital and establish minimum ratios of capital adequacy relative to a risk-adjusted measure of bank assets, which the banks must maintain. Regular, spot inspections are carried out to ensure the regulations are being complied with. If the banks fail to comply, they face severe penalties. The rules are written down and violators unambiguously know the risks they run.

The regulatory process in these countries is not, of course, perfect. Banks still feel fettered and try, where possible, to avoid some of the regulations that curtail their more irresponsible activities. Thus, for example, bank-holding companies were set up in the United States to allow banks to expand beyond their traditional areas without breaking the constrictions of American law. There is thus a perennial tension between the prudential urge to regulate on the one hand and the urge to let the markets take their unfettered course on the other.

Too much regulation can cause capital flight. Banks and other institutions can move their bases to avail of more lax supervisory laws. The Cayman Islands, Monaco, and similar places owe their preeminence largely to their lack of proper regulation. Still, as long as Britain, the United States, and similar major powers keep their individual and joint rules and regulations open, transparent, simple, and fair, such flight can be minimized.

Because of the conflicting pressures endemic in having properly and fairly functioning markets that are also competitive, government policy entails a difficult balancing act. For example, governments wish, other things being equal, to keep interest rates low. This serves the needs of borrowers, homeowners, and business people in particular. Cheap loans allow these people to buy their houses or to operate their businesses at a profit. Low interest rates are good for them.

They are not good for those whose funds are loaned out. If mortgage rates or business loan rates are kept artificially low, disparities between those regulated rates and other nonregulated rates tend to grow and heighten the calls for deregulation. Such has been the case in Britain, the United States, and similar countries.

Such is now the case in Japan. When Japan's interest rates are fixed and the yen is weak, capital flight, in the absence of good governance, is inevitable. This, in turn, leads to calls for a new form of regulation. Too much regulation stifles FIs and leads to calls for deregulation. Too much or too rapid deregulation leads to abuses and calls for more regulation. Such is the hydra of regulation and deregulation. Such is the dilemma Japan's mandarinate face as they try to weld an alien governance system onto their body politic.

Japan's problems are compounded by the uncodified system the MOF previously used. Nothing was set in stone and all seemed to be negotiable as long as the MOF's pliable administrative guidelines were being met. Now that the authorities are going to apply quantifiable standards, Japanese corporate culture must undergo fundamental and basic change. Even adopting quantifiable capital adequacy standards will entail basic and fundamental change.

The primary global measure of depository institution risk is its degree of capitalization under the currently prevailing capital standards. Under this scenario, riskier institutions pay higher premiums.

The Japanese authorities would like to see premiums distributed in a way slightly different from the global norm. They would like to see the newly arrived foreign companies pay more than what their relatively safer business activities would warrant.

The foreign institutions point out that the MOF's approach conflicts with global practices and that it is therefore wrong. They believe that they should get free access to Japan's financial pie. Japan's mandarinate do not believe that this is particularly fair: they believe Japan should get some sort of return, even if only nominal, if it is to hock its financial silverware away. There is, therefore, a considerable gray area between their opposing positions. On the one hand, the MOF can be seen as still favoring the JFIs at the expense of the foreigners and, on the other, the foreigners can be seen as trying to freeboot on a system they did not help to engender.

Although, in general, the CB, in consultation with the government and industry representatives, oversees the governance of the financial sector, the BOJ and the MOF share those responsibilities in Japan[2]. Although, for example, the BOJ and MOF work closely together to set fiscal and monetary policy, it is the MOF that supervises the banking system, collects taxes and customs duties, controls foreign exchange, and influences investment policy both in Japan and overseas. The Banking Bureau in the MOF oversees the activities of the banking sector, whereas the Securities Bureau regulates the brokerage industry. Banks, though subject to regulation different from those applicable to securities firms and other FIs, are allowed to enter into the securities business, but they cannot provide insurance. Thus, Japan does not permit universal banking as in Britain and Germany.

The BOJ acts as a banker to the government. The close relationship between the government and the BOJ is exemplified by the preponderance of government securities in the BOJ's balance sheet: almost 80% of its assets are Japanese government securities.

Government activity is also a major source of revenue for the BOJ, since fees are charged for issuing the government's checks and for holding its deposits of foreign currencies. Thus, the CB intermediates between the government and the private sector.

Together with the other, higher-profile branch of the government, the MOF, the BOJ closely administers the lending activities of Japanese banks both at home and abroad. Much of this control takes the form of verbal directives through the administrative guidance provided by the MOF or the window guidance used by the BOJ to control the amount of credit offered by the banks. In this, it differs from the British and American models, where the rules are much more codified. The Japanese regulatory system had engrained into it a deeper flexibility than its Anglo-American counterparts. This regulatory flexibility was its undoing.

Japanese bankers meet monthly with BOJ officials at the Second Wednesday Club at the Bankers' Association in Tokyo. Because of this active level of interaction between public and private FIs in Japan, a system of trust, as opposed to the exhaustive disclosure requirements in the United States, is used to monitor the financial condition of private FIs. The Japanese system thus gave the possibility of more operational flexibility at the expense of possibly more obfuscation and confusion in interpreting the regulatory guidelines.

This system was fine as long as it worked. Recent scandals have, however, put irreparable cracks in this system. The $1.1 billion trading loss scandal at Daiwa Bank Ltd. and the bailout of the troubled Japanese credit unions have made the MOF increase its formal oversight of private FIs: the stakes are simply too big to depend on the old gentlemen's agreements that served Japan so well in the past. There is, in other words, in the wisdom of hindsight, slightly more emphasis on Western-style governance methods and less on uncodified harmonious, Eastern-style get-togethers. This is just as well.

Japan's uncodified system has led to major accounting, auditing, and regulatory lapses, which have now come under attack from the IMF and similar institutions. It has left whole areas unmonitored and has allowed all types of shysters and criminals in to loot the till.

Japan's cozy governance system allowed a myriad of malpractices to take root. Chief of these were the *tobashi* and bicycle loans. Though tobashi literally means something that is flying, in common parlance it now refers to an accounting gimmick, where bad loans are transferred to another company, more often than not a dummy company, with the sole objective of having it temporarily disappear from the books.

The problem in Japan is that not only does the buck not stop with anyone, but that the buck keeps circulating. In accounting terms, this was achieved by means of tobashi. Tobashi was an accounting gimmick that allowed a bad loan to be converted into a good loan. If a company was owed, say, $1 million by the yakuza, which it knew it was never going to have paid, it simply loaned out that $1 million to a subsidiary. Thus, the dead loan of $1 million moved off the books and improved the company's bottom line on paper, if not in reality. Though this would have been fine if confined to a mere $1 million, billions of dollars in bad loans were recycled into good loans in this fashion. As a result, balance sheets became worse than meaningless. They became totally misleading as well.

Tobashi were used throughout the bubble for so-called bicycle loans and self-auctions, *jiko kyoraku*, which hiked up the price of property and led to today's mess. Bicycle loans were a method by which good money was thrown after bad. Again, to use our previous example, if a criminal syndicate owed $1 million, they would be given a further $1 million to repay the original $1 million. Then they would be given $2 million to repay the $2 million they owed. Then they would be given $4 million and so on. Not surprisingly, banks lost a lot of money in this way. Self-auctions were simply a means by which banks bid against themselves through dummy companies to maintain the semblance of firm prices in the markets they were involved with. They would typically set up about 20 dummy companies which would bid against each other to buy nonperforming loans from the parent bank and thereby make them appear as performing loans. Self-auctions only brought the JFIs further into the mire and kept the proverbial buck circulating not only figuratively but in actual fact as well.

Amazingly to Westerners, these accounting sleights of hand were legal practice in Japan. The MOF implicitly condoned these practices, assuming that an inflationary impetus in the Tokyo property market would make it all come right. As we now know, it all came unstuck instead.

Because the Tokyo property market is still quite flat, corporate Japan has paid a high price for condoning such low practices. As a result of such slack governance, the MOF is discredited; its officials, including Dr. Eisuke Sakakibara, Mr. Yen, have been reprimanded for compromising themselves; and a veritable galaxy of JFIs find themselves in the dock. Though Sakakibara's offense of accepting a few free meals was trivial enough, giving him and most others the lightest of slaps across their respective wrists allowed the real MOF culprits and the MOF's deeply engrained, incestuous, reactionary, and outmoded culture to escape almost unscathed.

There is something rotten at the heart of Japan's financial system. Even its most prestigious banks have been indicted for systematic abuses. The Bank of Tokyo-Mitsubishi (BTM), the world's biggest bank with nearly $650 billion in assets, and 16th-ranked Sumitomo Bank have joined this rogue's gallery, which includes most other top-drawer JFIs as well. Sumitomo was convicted of giving ¥23 billion to speculators to do a share-price ramp, the antithesis of a free market. They now stand arraigned on charges from bribing pompous MOF bureaucrats with meals served by no-pan waitresses,[3] to bribing their BOJ counterparts with golf trips and other juvenile junkets. Now that these self-same institutions are lining up at the public trough for handouts, public indignation, much to the dismay of the governing Liberal Democratic Party (LDP), is expressing itself at the ballot box. Faced with overwhelming evidence that almost all leading LDP members had their snouts in the trough as well, voters have deserted them in droves. A review of some of the spectacular failures will show why the long-suffering public feels peeved with both the system and its corrupt actors.

The first two major bank failures occurred in late 1994 when Tokyo Kyowa Credit Association and Anzen Credit were closed. Fraud was a major factor in these cases, and no white knight bank could be found in the affiliate keiretsu to take over the two banks' business. The regulatory authorities funded the establishment of a new bank to assume all assets and liabilities, and closed these two banks. Total bad loans of ¥150 billion had been accumulated by Harunori Takahashi, Tokyo Kyowa's chairman and EIE International Ltd.'s president. Through EIE, Takahashi made aggressive domestic and international real estate investments in hotels, golf courses, and office buildings. In its prime, EIE had total assets of ¥1 trillion. It also had all of the abuses of the Japanese financial system in ample abundance.

Although he only gets a few paragraphs here, Harunori Takahashi could do with a book to himself. It was he who seduced the MOF bigwigs with the no-pan waitresses. When Takahashi's empire collapsed, the MOF repaid him with over ¥685 billion of taxpayers' money. They said it was to prevent a collapse in the system. An unamused public could not see how such a gratuity to one so feckless could restore confidence in anything. They believed this bounty was more in gratitude for the low life the MOF mandarins enjoyed with him than for any residual sense of public duty they may have had. This view was reinforced when it transpired that Yoshio Nakajima, a senior MOF top official, had not only consorted with Takahashi but had taken over $1 million in bribes from him and had also undertaken several colorful joint ventures with him. Nakajima suffered a token two-month cut in pay for his profitable and nefarious side-activities. Elsewhere, in markets which are free, fair, and global, Nakajima and his fellow MOF conspirators would have been consulting high-powered defense attorneys. Japanese corporate culture, which they dominated, allowed them to escape— and prosper.

Takahashi's real estate investments were to a large extent financed by the Long-Term Credit Bank (LTCB) of Japan, which extended loans in excess of ¥380 billion to him to build a tourist empire around the Pacific Rim. Much of this money was siphoned off into more local pockets. Tokyo Kyowa, for example, had outstanding loans of about ¥13 billion to Lower House politician Toshio Yamaguchi. And LTCB ignored all basic prudential considerations as blithely and brazenly as did the jusen. It gave ¥38 billion of loans to companies controlled by the redoubtable Takahashi himself; of these, 60% exceeded the legal maximum of 20%, or ¥800 million, to nonmembers. Between 1992 and 1994, Takahashi had arranged for loans of ¥18 billion from both Tokyo Kyowa and Anzen Credit to his group of companies, although he knew that these loans were uncollectible. A strange oversight on his behalf at best. An unforgivable one on behalf of the MOF, who, though charged with ensuring that such systematic abuses did not occur, oversaw and profited by a system where they were omnipotent.

The LTCB debacle was resolved only in late 1998, more than a decade too late. The government, after an inordinately long period of decisions, reversal of decisions, and indecisions, finally decided to force through a merger with Sumitomo Bank. Though the government promised to sweeten this deal by pouring in massive amounts of public funds, in the end, its promises were not enough to push through the merger. Although the plan envisaged a large loan write-off, top management resignations, branch closures, and job cuts, these were not enough. Union Bank of Switzerland (UBS) revised its planned alliance with LTCB. It instead decided to buy out most of the cash-strapped bank's ventures. UBS previously had planned to form an asset-management joint venture with LTCB as part of their Big Bang strategy.

As both UBS and Sumitomo shied away from having the LTCB millstone tied around them, the Japanese government exercised their final option. Having no alternative and fearing the consequences of its collapse, they nationalized LTCB, the first nationalization of a Japanese bank since World War II. They therefore avoided a full-scale collapse of LTCB, which would have further eroded confidence in Japan's banking system and perhaps even shaken world markets as well. They also earmarked a further ¥60 trillion of public money to shore up the banking industry.

LTCB's shareholders were among the biggest losers of this rescue plan. Though the government will buy them out, they will be lucky to get a yen a share. Japan's taxpayers also lose, in the short-term at least. They have to pick up the tab for the bank's bad loans: at least ¥4.6 trillion of LTCB's loans are irrecoverable. Still, at least market signals are being listened to this time. It was, after all, the precipitous fall in the share price that prompted government action in the first place. This case, if handled properly, could become a template for future bankruptcies

If Japan wants to rebuild her credibility, the proper implementation of the LTCB proposals would be a good place to start. LTCB was, after all, one of the linchpins of Japan Inc.'s success. Founded in the aftermath of Japan's military defeat to provide cheap, long-term loans to industry, the bank helped lead the country's spectacular rise to economic superpower status. Dealing resolutely with such a national holy cow would send the correct message to the markets. The axe must be firmly applied. There will have to be more job cuts and a bigger return in efficiency to the taxpayer for the write-offs involved: some ¥750 billion in the case of LTCB. The sheer brazenness of this case demands no less.

Massive fraud and reckless real estate speculation, insider deals, and bribery were major factors in this case. Moreover, Japan's multilayered supervisory structure was shown to be almost criminally wanting: this shameful case alone is reason enough to dismantle the MOF. LTCB's lack of prudential oversight is also, to say the least, questionable. Unfortunately, as later examples will show, it was typical of the JFIs' bubble-related failures.

That said, the LTCB clean-up should augur well for a fundamental change in Japan's corporate culture. Public money should, in the future, be forthcoming only when the institution in question is solvent and when it has produced an acceptable restructuring plan. For credibility in the system to be restored, greater transparency and a greater degree of honesty than has hitherto been evident are essential. Fudging, the hallmark of corporate Japan, must end.

For the LTCB and similar rescue plans to succeed, vagueness must be replaced with viability. The exact size of LTCB's bad debts must be clearly spelled out and the revitalized entity that emerges from the government's rescue efforts must be publicly funded if and only if it can prove to be more viable than LTCB.

Still, the LTCB fiasco has its silver lining. Sumitomo Bank, LTCB's partner in the aborted rescue merger, played its part in auguring in the Big Bang by insisting on an independent audit of LTCB by Arthur Andersen—a stinging and unprecedented indictment of their belief in the Japanese government's own audit. Given that prior MOF and BOJ audits had found LTCB to be glowingly solvent, Sumitomo's skepticism concerning the credibility of LTCB—and, by implication, of the BOJ and MOF—seems decidedly well placed.

Sumitomo was not alone. The case had international repercussions as well. UBS AG, the megabank formed by the merger of Swiss Bank Corporation and Union Bank of Switzerland, had planned an alliance with LTCB. Sumitomo's planned merger with LTCB was, in large part, predicated on being able to tap into UBS's expertise. Because the Japanese authorities could not guarantee UBS that they would not be burdened with LTCB's debts, UBS promptly axed all reference to LTCB in their promotional literature, one indication of the low value they put on their putative partner; they later bought out the LTCB interest in the joint venture. If other foreign concerns get cold feet as well, the Big Bang, lacking the necessary expertise, will also stall.

This is a real risk. When Japan Leasing, one of LTCB's debt-laden affiliates, asked a group of private banks to write off over $1 billion in loans to it, alarm bells rang. The JFIs believe that agricultural cooperatives have secretly extended over ¥550 billion of loans to Japan Leasing and that, because these cooperatives are major bankrollers for the governing LDP, they will be supported at the expense of the banks. Whatever the truth of this, the LTCB fiasco highlights the secret web of hidden debts that bind Japan's financial institutions together. Further examples merely confirm this fact and the attendant risks to the successful implementation of the Big Bang.

Because the LTCB nationalization was quickly followed by the nationalization of Nippon Credit (NCB), one of the world's largest banks, there might be reason to believe that the Japanese government has, however belatedly, found the mettle it previously lacked. Just as with LTCB, NCB had an unsustainable bad-loan portfolio. The government ignored the managers' arguments that the standards used to judge the bank's financial state were too strict. NCB, in fact, had a total ¥3.74 trillion worth of problem loans, and suffered a capital shortage of ¥94.4 billion once the bank took necessary loan-loss provisions. They bit the bullet, promised to protect the bank's deposits, debentures, and interbank transactions, but sacked the managers and took over the bank themselves. More nationalizations are probably in the air. Yasuda Trust and Banking, Daiwa Bank, Chuo Trust and Banking, and other JFIs with credit ratings as poor as NCB's will probably have to face a similar fate. There remains much cleaning up to do yet.

The second banking institution to sink in 1995 was Cosmo Credit, Tokyo's largest credit cooperative. Out of its ¥507 billion loan portfolio, 60% were in real estate companies, more than 70%

of which are irrecoverable. The major reason for Cosmo Credit's default was rogue management by its quick-talking president, Sanpachi Taido. His goal was to turn the cooperative into a commercial bank, and to this end he expanded his business aggressively into real estate financing. All of his loans were based on bricks-and-mortar collateral, whose value came tumbling down when the bubble burst.

Although, even as early as 1993, Cosmo Credit's troubles were patently evident, it remained afloat by disguising its bad loans with more than 30 dummy companies. In so-called self-auctions, or tobashi, Cosmo Credit would sell a bad loan to an affiliated dummy company by having the dummy bid the highest price on the collateral concerned. The dummy in turn received a loan from Cosmo Credit for this purchase and for the future interest payments on the loan. On the books, a bad loan was thus transformed into an interest-earning loan. Though these pass-the-parcel self-auctions are legal practice in Japan, they are also a highly dangerous game of fake accounting, and by allowing this practice, the regulators, with the MOF in the van, clearly invited nondisclosure. Not only that, but these malpractices were so widely used that terminally ill companies could appear to be superstrong—and could get the further massive loans that a strong and vibrant company could extract from affiliates. Clearly, this was a systematic breakdown that the MOF should have addressed. Because they didn't discharge the functions assigned to them, they should be made to pay a high price for their own systematic failures

The third failure occurred on August 30, when Osaka-based Kizu Credit Cooperative was closed with irrecoverable loans estimated to be close to ¥1 trillion. Total bailout and settlement costs were estimated to exceed ¥1.5 trillion. While ¥500 billion of the settlement costs were to be covered by BOJ loans and Deposit Insurance funds, some ¥500 billion had to be furnished by large commercial banks.

Kizu was but one more variation on the old tune of criminal misgovernance. Kizu aggressively attracted new deposits by offering very high interest rates. On August 1, 1995, Kizu offered 3.5% on a 3-month deposit; this was five to six times higher than the average city bank rate of 0.6%. In order to recoup the deposit costs, Kizu had to make even riskier loans with high lending rates, 90% of which were in real estate. When the bubble burst, so too did Kizu.

It mastered three shady practices to hide its problems and to transform billions of dollars of nonperforming loans into trillions of dollars of performing ones. It used over 400 cases of self-auctions worth almost ¥100 billion to shuffle the debt around and to park it in affiliated dummy companies. It used bicycle loans or over-loans to the yakuza and other defaulting customers to allow them to reschedule their prior debt or, depending on their ethical biases, to keep the extra loans. These extra freebies topped ¥60 billion. The third mechanism, false accounting, was both the simplest, and, surprisingly enough, given the sums already mentioned, their most effective means of camouflage. The arrest of Jiro Watanabe, a former professional boxer with yakuza links, went to confirm criminal involvement as well. Some ¥38 billion deposited in his name at Kizu was withdrawn a day before the bank folded. This particular market, then, fell considerably short of being free or fair.

Kizu was not a maverick company being taken to the cleaners by the unscrupulous. It worked in tandem with its mother banks which referred its riskier loans to it. Kizu used referred deposits from its mother bank much more extensively than the law allows. Referred deposits as such are legal, but if they induce a cooperative to exceed the 20% limit, they become illegal. Further, a large portion of the referrals fell in the category of covert guided deposits, in which the referring city bank designated both the recipient of the loan as well as the interest rate. This constitutes a direct intrusion by the large bank into the business decision of the cooperative and, as it would mean that the mother bank is in fact running it, is directly contrary to Japanese law. Nevertheless, despite such blatant intrusions, Sanwa Bank denied any involvement in Kizu Credit and initially refused to support the cooperative's bailout. The MOF slept on.

Three problems led to Osaka Credit's demise. Because it was run in a one-man fashion without any semblance of checks and balances, it applied, even by Japanese standards, very lax standards to loan approvals during the bubble period. It excelled in bypass loans, intricate schemes involving affiliated nonbanks such as Osaka Mortgage to circumvent the 20% limit on loans to one customer. One of these customers was the colorful money broker, Nishiki Finance, which added its own macabre twist to events. Finally, Osaka Credit was also exposed to some of the other biggest white elephants of the bubble.

When Osaka Credit went belly-up, it had underwritten more than ¥5 billion of debt certificates issued by clients of Nishiki Finance, which provided loans based on loan bills which were simply IOUs. Nishiki would require up to 25 times the amount of the loan in bills on the gentleman's understanding—quite naive in retrospect—that Nishiki would not cash them in. Nishiki promptly cashed in an impressive total of ¥26 billion without bothering to get the due authorization. Osaka Credit, whether as knaves or as the fools they claimed to be, extended further bypass loans to Nishiki through affiliated dummy companies. Nishiki continued on its ungentlemanly way, bankrupting thousands of small Japanese businesses in the process. And no one in the MOF spotted these systematic abuses.

Tokai Bank, which took over Osaka Credit as a result of government pressure, claimed that, even though it seconded senior staff to it, it had no control over the clowns who ran Osaka Credit. This introduces the governance problem of how to define an affiliated bank, and what the legal responsibility of such a bank should be. Again, Japanese law is at fault; it does not codify this relationship, but instead leaves the MOF's gray area of administrative guidance to fill the void. Osaka Credit raises further questions of relationship banking, risk-shifting from large banks to small banks, sleaze, and collusive regulation: questions that the MOF should address, however belatedly, if the Japanese markets are to be free, fair, global, and sleaze-free.

Hyogo Bank, Japan's largest second-tier regional bank, faced two major problems when it defaulted. The first was its aggressive real estate lending during the bubble period; this included massive bicycle business loans to allow defaulting customers to reschedule their loans or, in other words, extending more credit to defaulting customers so that they could default on even bigger amounts.

Secondly, in a variation on the same old themes, its 20 affiliated nonbank financial companies had king-size bad loans of their own. As nonbanks had been supervised by MITI during the bubble years, banks and securities firms set up numerous nonbanks to circumvent MOF regulation.[4] As in the many similar cases cited here, neither the MOF, the MITI, nor the other agencies involved took any action against the firms that were exploiting their intra-mandarin division of responsibilities.

As in the other cases, Hyogo Bank's failure almost defies belief. On the day Hyogo Bank was closed, its bad loans were estimated at about ¥1.5 trillion, or 55% of its total loans. On September 1, 1995, it was revealed that Hyogo Bank's 20 affiliated nonbanks held additional bad loans of ¥1.75 trillion. The biggest lender to these 20 affiliated nonbanks was Hyogo Bank itself with ¥381 billion, or 25% of the total. Thus, depending on how you add up the numbers, Hyogo Bank managed to lose more than 100% of its loans.

Again, grave questions of regulatory oversights are raised-and not appropriately answered-by this costly farce. An audit report of May 1995 estimated Hyogo Bank's bad loans to be a mere ¥60 billion. Three months later, bad loans of ¥800 billion were revealed. In May 1995, auditors had even issued a positive earning forecast. This form of creative accounting, replicated again and again, is criminally disingenuous at best, and raises questions as to how any faith can be retained in Japanese auditors and, given their recklessness, in the Japanese system they are charged with auditing.

Whether we look at the Japanese financial system in microcosm or in macrocosm, we see the same picture of fraud, nepotism, and sheer incompetence manifest itself again and again. No matter how they cut the cards, the MOF cannot and should not be allowed to absolve themselves of their own culpability. This was a massive calamity, at the center of which stood the MOF. Until they admit that they were part of the problem, they can hardly be part of the solution.

The MOF's wholehearted acceptance of the Big Bang is a total reversal of its previous steadfast refusal to contemplate any change, no matter how minute, to its tightly regulated convoy system. The sheer size of the monetary losses the MOF's failures inflicted on

Japan have cost her, in monetary terms, much more than the Second World War did. The pain of rebuilding will be at least as great. Faced with the catastrophic results it has inflicted on the Japanese people, the MOF remains unfazed: it has yet to publicly apologize for its perfidies. It has yet to take stern action against the worst transgressors to emerge from its pampered ranks. Its whole historical culture lends it to reaction, to institute only the most minor, token, and cosmetic of changes. Anything else more substantial would upset its apple cart, by far the coziest in all of Japan. It is here at the heart of power that the biggest seismic shift, the biggest of Big Bangs, is needed. The MOF must be dissolved.

The MOF has developed into a cozy, self-perpetuating cartel of self-serving automatons. They recruit almost exclusively Tokyo University law graduates, a significant factor when we consider that to get into Todai, as the Japanese call it, one must spend years cramming irrelevant and unconnected facts and figures into one's head to pass the entrance exam. Once in, it's a four-year drinking binge, followed by a cushy sinecure, the cushiest of which is the MOF. The MOF gets these generalists, dries them out, and then molds them on the job into their obtrusive and arrogant way of doing things.

The MOF inculcates them further in its reactionary ways while they are employed there, and, in its efforts to forge feudal-style alliances, arranges weddings with influential political families for their brighter stars. Having served the MOF faithfully, the officials are then retired into their cushy numbers in a process called *amakudari*.

The term *amakudari* literally means a descent from heaven. It means, in this its most important case, that the official has now left the heavenly realm of the MOF and is taking his due reward among the less-enlightened mortals of the real world. Like Superman or any of the other comic-book heroes using an analogous system, amakudari serves both the mortals and the MOF by maintaining and developing mutually beneficial channels between them.

The reality is quite different from the theory. Postwar, it was a way of belatedly bestowing pecuniary awards on those who had faithfully served the nation. In most recent years, it merely congealed into an unseemly gravy train, where the system rewarded its own at the expense of the nation as a whole. Although the system is widespread in Japan, the MOF has the exclusive franchise on not only most of the key posts in Japan's financial services industry, but the most important ones in the entire public and private sectors as well.

The MOF officials retire early into these lucrative positions. They get their full MOF pension, as well as a hefty lump-sum payment. They are then encouraged to use their connections to secure high-paying posts outside of the MOF. If it isn't designed to breed corruption, it is certainly prone to it. The MOF directly controls some of the largest nonprivate FIs, among them the Japan Development Bank, the Export-Import Bank, and the Housing Loan Corporation. MOF retirees sit out two years in these institutions on bloated salaries and then move on to even more lucrative ones in the private sector. Each time they move their butts, they get another great golden handshake.

This will become all the more surprising when we consider in chapter five how they have wrecked the pension plans of the Japanese people as a whole. For the moment, we may merely note that the administrative guidance, which justifies their sinecures, has little basis in reality. Being generalists, there is no specific advice they can give. Often, in fact, their advice can be costly in the extreme. Japan Airlines (JAL), for example, established a world record for a foreign exchange loss in the late 1980s. The MOF amakudari they had foisted on them had told them that the dollar was going to appreciate. The Japanese and the Americans had just signed the Plaza Accord, which put the dollar into a tailspin and cost JAL billions of dollars only because, against its better judgment, it heeded the advice of its imposed advisor.

The MOF has similarly incompetent amakudari everywhere. It has its appointees in the Fair Trade Commission and the BOJ; these appointees must grapple between the job they have on hand and counteracting unrelenting and overbearing peer pressure from the MOF. The MOF also reserved the top positions in the stock exchange and the banks almost as a matter of right. Although Mitsubishi Bank has no amakudari and it refused to take any onboard when it merged with the Bank of Tokyo, it is a colossus that can, on occasion, get the better of the MOF. It is, however, almost impossible for smaller JFIs to resist their overtures and the accompanying sleaze.

Their power is so pervasive that most banks must appoint a full-time official, just to make sure that they do not anger the spoiled brats the MOF employs. The officials of the MOF have proved themselves to be formidable and unforgiving foes, and only the brave or the reckless would dare cross them. They have broken prime ministers and other politicians in the past. They have brazenly defied parliament on many others. Given their voracious record, they would have small banks and other small fry for breakfast.

Even though they have broken many of these banks, they still leach from them. Thanks to the failures of the MOF, the post-bubble history of JFIs is a litany of abuse and misgovernance. Because JFIs were overloaned, their total capital and deposits were insufficient to meet their loan demand. They borrowed the shortfall from the BOJ which made all the mistakes a lender of last resort can make. They did not insist on Western standards of global governance. The large banks the BOJ subordinated ignored the risk profile of their loans: the yakuza, colorful brokers, con men, and the dregs of Japan were all highly valued customers. Risk-insensitivity was furthered by the explicit policy of convoy regulation, gososendan shugi. Like lemmings, the convoy sailed on, confident that the MOF authorities would save them from market turbulences and from themselves.

As a result of these gigantic failings, the Japanese system of dango gyosei, or collusive regulation, became unstuck as well. Obsequious to the MOF's wishes, the more honest among them could not see that the entire convoy was going to end up high and dry. As the MOF high-fliers were so preoccupied with their no-pan waitresses and arranging their marriages and personal pension plans, their slack governance allowed the tills to be rifled. The token loss of face and loss of a month or so of pay some of the culprits have had inflicted on them does not fit the enormity of what they have done and what they have failed to do.

Besides patterns of behavior that can most charitably be explained by exploitation of situational regulation and regulatory negligence, there are those that simply constitute outright fraud.

The Japanese regulatory system ignored the possibility of widescale systematic fraud, including the Kizu's insider deals, the quaint and colorful practices of the two Tokyo cooperatives and their officers, the collusion of the mother banks, and the many individual cases of fraud which added further color to the sinking of the convoy. Muddying the traditionally dour world of banking even more is the central role the yakuza played in this massive and massively inequitable redistribution of Japan's hard-earned wealth. One titillating indicator of the role of the yakuza in the jusen affair is that none of the companies that owed money to the jusen has been shut down, even after the jusen themselves were dissolved. The rot runs deep. It permeates Japanese corporate life almost as much as the yakuza do.

Having thus dispensed with the MOF, another glimmer of hope may be mentioned. The Housing Loan Administration Corporation (HLAC), a Japanese government agency, has sued Sumitomo Bank for allegedly persuading the jusen to lend money to problem clients. The ¥5 billion suit is the first step by a government agency toward forcing some of Japan's top banks to take responsibility for their roles in the jusen debacle. Whatever the merits of this individual case, it does highlight the growing demand for accountability in Japan's shameful financial system and the move toward Western methods of dealing with the mess. Although the HLAC has a further eight banks in its sights, the allegations against Sumitomo are hardly credible—until we put them in their Japanese Alice-in-Wonderland setting. If these abuses are as widespread as the HLAC alleges, the risk of systematic breakdown is very real indeed.

Although Japan's debt problems make it more prone to systematic failure, the Japanese mandarins have, to their credit, concentrated on avoiding such a calamity. They have, however belatedly, successfully piloted Japan Inc. away from such dangers. Previously, Japan's very tight regulatory structure made such a scenario impossible. Now, with almost all of Japan's major banks technically bankrupt, the risk of systematic failure is somewhat more real. They are not out of the woods yet. The Big Bang is a search for the light.

Even after the dust from these disasters has settled, the influence of the BOJ and MOF on Japan's financial system remains pervasive.

Despite widespread dissatisfaction with its post-bubble performance, the MOF is steering Japan into the Big Bang changes. It remains firmly at the helm of Japan Inc.

This is despite the recent spate of scandals that have tarnished the reputations of Japan's financial mandarins to an unprecedented degree. When Yasuyuki Yoshizawa was arrested in March 1998, it was the first time a senior BOJ official was indicted on bribery and corruption charges in the bank's 116-year history. Most of Japan's major banks were implicated in his alleged crimes.

Though not directly implicated himself, Yasuo Matsushita resigned as governor, to be replaced by an outsider, Masaru Hayami, a former president of Nissho Iwai, one of Japan's largest trading companies. The mandarins' credibility took another nose dive. Despite the token resignation, the circus went on, almost in unbroken tempo.

This is not to suggest that the BOJ mandarins descended to ogling at no-pan waitresses. No! Overpriced golfing jaunts were their forte. Instead of concentrating on their job, or indeed, whiling away the small hours with the waitresses and their MOF clients, they accumulated 42 memberships at 39 locations in Japan's and Hong Kong's most exclusive and most expensive golf clubs. One golf club in Osaka asks corporate members to pay almost $29,000 to renew their memberships. In the case of the BOJ, each time a new head of Osaka BOJ arrived, they forked out another $29,000. Total membership fees paid by the BOJ for these 42 golf clubs reached $21 million in 1990 when golf club fees were at their peak. Though the fees have since fallen to around $6 million, the BOJ has not adequately explained to its critics why it was playing golf while Japan sank.

The BOJ doesn't believe it should explain anything. It believes that information on its golf club memberships and land holdings are being leaked to the media by the MOF via 10 aggressive young LDP Diet members in their efforts to maintain control of the Japanese governancial system. Both the MOF and BOJ are agreed that their turf wars are more important than the taxpayers finding out how they collectively squandered the hard-earned yen entrusted to them. Although, for example, the Japanese prime rate is determined by the Policy Committee of the BOJ, in reality, the head of BOJ's planning office has had to consult with the Finance Minister's secretary before deciding the rate. This, in effect, means that the MOF has had control over interest rate policy. This peeves the BOJ. It disturbs their handicaps and other symptoms of their self-importance, no doubt.

Still, there is a bright side for them. The Big Bang reforms intend to provide independence to the BOJ and consolidate monetary policy making under them, eliminating the MOF's intervention. The BOJ reform bill emerged as a result of the MOF's incompetence in the jusen cases and in the scandals that peppered Japan during and after the bubble. There is no evidence that an independent BOJ will be any more independent than the MOF. It will simply mean an intra-mandarin power realignment of no practical interest to the general public. More golf jaunts, fewer no-pan waitresses. The same puerility.

If the Big Bang project is successfully implemented, these turf wars will have to be sorted out in an adult manner. Trading at the stock market is set to increase five- to sixfold, and the life insurance market will more than double. Because the banks will be entering the stock and life insurance businesses, competition for a fixed commission base will skyrocket. However, the BOJ has power only over banks, not the stock or life insurance markets. That means that the BOJ can control only banks in implementing monetary policy. This will not fulfill the objectives of the Big Bang. Most probably, the MOF will be able to control banks, securities firms, and life insurance firms. The MOF is, if the pundits are to be believed, the odds-on favorite to win these turf tussles.

The BOJ is stepping up its inspections of those JFIs, which fall under its remit. Checks that the JFIs are complying with Japan's laws and industry regulations have been tightened. Particular care is being paid to management/internal administration, financing, markets, and back-office operations. Japanese banks are now being forced to divide loans into different categories of credit risk, depending on the likelihood of recovery. The MOF sees these inspections as an infringement of its turf and is determined to repel the BOJ.

If past form is anything to go by, the MOF should be successful. The MOF's grip on auditing is being loosened. The Financial Supervisory Agency (FSA) is recruiting a small number of certified public accountants to add a degree of expertise to its endeavors. Its initial audits have identified gross malpractices by Sanwa Bank, Industrial Bank of Japan, Sumitomo Bank, Bank of Tokyo-Mitsubishi, Dai-Ichi Kangyo Bank, Asahi Bank, Fuji Bank, Sakura Bank, Long-Term Credit Bank of Japan, Nomura Securities, Nikko Securities, Daiwa Securities, and Sakura Securities, among others.

The FSA's standards are more attuned to global standards and cover a wider range of nonperforming loans. The new rules, for example, include requirements to report problem loans much more expeditiously than previously. Although the FSA seems to be moving in the right direction, external, independently audited results are still lacking.

Still, for Japan, the FSA seems to be a marked improvement on previous norms. The government decided to recruit specialists from the private sector to improve the agency's ability to supervise and inspect the increasingly high-tech-oriented financial sector. Although most of the employees at the agency have been recruited from the MOF, the Ministry of Justice and the National Police Agency have also delegated staff—and annoyed the MOF in the process.

The FSA's CPAs are expected to direct the inspection process and examine the results of investigations. They will not be assigned to examine specific financial institutions. This accords with the MOF wish of merely separating the functions of inspection and surveillance, while maintaining overall control firmly in its grasp. Still, the creation of the agency and the involvement of other ministries has been interpreted as a diminution of their power.

Not that the MOF is particularly worried. When the dust settles after these reforms, it expects to be still firmly in control. If the reforms are not fully seen through, the MOF might even obtain auditing authority and actually expand its power. The fact that it doesn't have the required expertise is beside the point, if power, not proper management, is the objective.

Important and all as these turf wars may seem to be, they are delaying the necessary reforms. With the no-pan waitress brigade on one side and the golf caddies on the other, it more resembles a charade from a Turkish harem or the court of one of Japan's wackier shoguns than a real attempt to bring Japan's bumbling financial sector into the modern world. Governance remains a mess with the varying parties who presided over the bubble debacle bent on entrenching their power, instead of bowing out gracefully.

If Japan cannot see this, others do. The European Business Council, which represents 77 European insurance, banking, securities, and asset management companies in Japan, has asked the Japanese government to urgently reform its regulatory and governance systems ahead of the Big Bang reforms. The Europeans point out that, though the new regulatory body, the FSA, was deemed to take over the regulatory reins on June 1, 1998, it is undermanned and, in traditional MOF style, it has not made its compliance norms known. The Council, in fact, believes that the new agency would be the old, vague, regulatory wine of the MOF packaged into newer but equally vague bottles. The Europeans have a point. If a well-functioning society is predicated on a well-functioning and well-regulated financial services industry, Japanese governance has been amiss.

No matter how they cut the cards, the MOF is stuck firmly at the center of the mire. Their own incestuous culture has put them there. Their postwar success went to their collective heads. They worked as an authoritarian, arrogant mandarinate; their word, usually unwritten, was law. They held both the public and their politicians in equal contempt. When it suited them, they would change the rules and regulations governing the financial markets without redress to public hearings or public comment. MOF regulation was intrusive, obtrusive, and deliberately vague. Much as it was for the rulers of the Ottoman empire or indeed the Japanese shoguns, fear, tempered with randomness, was their favored weapon for keeping JFIs in check. Though lacking specific financial expertise, the MOF had to be informed, in great and minute detail, of all transactions and new ventures. Permission to proceed could not be taken for granted: precedent was meaningless. Nor could the time lag involved in making decisions big or small be pre-assumed. It was a system ultimately designed to inculcate fear and favoritism, not efficiency, autonomy, and individuality.

Those at the MOF, who are in charge of the Big Bang, never before particularly concerned themselves with global standards of openness and accountability. It was essentially centralized feudalism, Japan's shogun system transmogrified to the twentieth century. Unless there was untoward publicity, the MOF was largely unconcerned about the ubiquitous presence of market manipulation, fraud, investor protection, poor performance, and gross incompetence within the financial system they were charged with overseeing. Ignoring their role of ensuring that the markets functioned fairly and properly, their system fossilized, ultimately at great cost to Japan. But not, thanks to the amakudari system, to themselves.

Although long-festering, it was only during the bubble years that their many shortcomings came to the fore. Its mind on its no-pan perks, the MOF allowed the JFIs to engage in speculative and fraudulent behavior and, in the process, it ignored the interests of the small investor. It ignored, if not actively condoned, the JFI's cavorting with organized crime. Like the Gestapo, they were everywhere. And, because they were everywhere, they were all-seeing. And because they were all-seeing, they thought they were all-knowing.

Theirs was certainly not a system of global governance standards as understood in the West. Whereas the American regulatory body, the Securities and Exchange Commission (SEC), concerns itself with its core tasks of investor protection, fraud, manipulative practices, and standards of fairness, the MOF stood idly by as Japanese money managers squandered the economic well-being of Japan's pensioners, widows, and orphans through inept, irresponsible, inefficient, and often criminal behavior.

When prosecutors arrested four Dai-Ichi Kangyo Bank (DKB) officials on suspicion of illegally extending uncollateralized loans to Ryuichi Koike, the sokaiya corporate racketeer at the heart of the scandal, and indicted Nomura itself for violating the securities law by illegally compensating a firm run by Koike's younger brother, as well as two former Nomura directors for violating both securities law and the commercial code, the markets applauded. It seemed as if the rule of law was going to supersede the law of nods and winks that had led to corporate Japan's copulating with criminal Japan.

But the markets no longer applaud. To restore credibility, the guilty people, in Nomura and the other big houses, have to suffer. Having done the crime, they should be made do the time. This, after all, was not a once-off affair. Rather, it has been endemic to the system. In 1991, Nomura's top two executives, Chairman Setsuya Tabuchi and President Yoshihisa Tabuchi, were forced to resign in broadly similar circumstances. Nomura, however, was allowed retain its hammerlock on the securities business, and by 1995, the Tabuchis' ceremonial rehabilitation complete, they returned to the Nomura board.

Now, the markets find Nomura fraternizing once more with common criminals. Former Nomura president Hideo Sakamaki was arrested in Nomura's most recent spate of crime-related scandals, and prosecutors have reportedly questioned the two Tabuchis in connection with the most recent scandals. Although many major Japanese and foreign institutions, including the California Public Employees' Retirement System pension fund, have suspended business with Nomura, unless the criminals' co-conspirators in Nomura and the other major institutions are jailed, confidence and credibility will remain low.

Nomura would, in all fairness, point out that they were the MOF's fall-guys. They would point out that the conflicting signals emanating from the MOF were at least as much to blame for their shortcomings as the human frailties of some of their executives. They would also point out that the MOF's callousness was poor reward to the Nomura experts, who had previously done much of the legislative drafting work the MOF was being retained to do but had not the expertise to do. They would point out that the MOF authorities must first clean up their own act. And some others.

The authorities must, as a first priority, curb the sokaiya, the criminal racketeers who meddle in the markets and extort payments in exchange for not disrupting shareholder meetings. Japanese corporate traditions notwithstanding, such lowlife can have no part in a modern financial system. The sokaiya have no place whatsoever to play in a market purporting to be free, fair, and global.

The sokaiya have tainted the biggest and best of the JFIs. DKB provided loans totaling more than $300 million to a sokaiya group led by Ryuichi Koike, the most notorious of these criminals, for purchasing stocks from the four major Japanese securities houses. Koike and his legal advisors would first pinpoint illegal manipulations of stock prices. He and his cronies would then compile their reports and bribe or otherwise coax big favors out of the erring corporations. They would attend annual general meetings (AGMs) and dominate them with their well-researched accusations.

Although the MOF must have been well aware of this, they refused to act. Though the 1982 Japanese Commerce Law amendment specifically prohibited business corporations from paying money to sokaiya, Koike was undeterred. He attended the AGM of the financially ailing Heiwa Sogo Bank in 1986. The Heiwa's stockholders meeting was expected to be stormy because its illegal financial loans to its owner's family had become widely known. Koike dominated the meeting. Over 300 stockholders attended the Heiwa stockholder meeting. Of these, 80 were sokaiya and Koike was their ringmaster. He threatened the management with the full wrath of exposure. He spoke for over an hour, giving umpteen concrete cases of Heiwa's fraudulent mismanagement. He explained how they were in violation of Article 274 of the Commerce Law and other laws they were largely unfamiliar with. When the chairman of the stockholder meeting would try to avoid Koike's questions, his 70-strong sokaiya army would raise their noxious voices. Koike used the meeting for his own advantage. He had bigger fish to fry. He wanted to advertise himself to ensnare larger and equally corrupt concerns.

He was successful beyond his wildest dreams. His establishment of a relationship with DKB occurred almost at the same time as the Heiwa stockholder meeting. He received $300 million in loans from 1989 to 1994 from DKB, part of which was used for acquiring 300,000 shares of Nomura Securities stock, which were then manipulated upward on his behalf. Thus did organized crime pollute Japan's financial sector.

The sokaiya and other pervasive "market imperfections" cannot be weeded out overnight. A proper, legal infrastructure is needed to stamp out organized crime. To ensure that these scandals do not recur, Japan's Securities and Exchange Surveillance Commission must be given teeth. Above all, it must be given independence. It is thinly staffed and has nothing like the clout of Washington's SEC. And Japanese law, predicated on the preeminence of the convoy, treats many offenses much too lightly. Regulators recently closed Daiwa Bank's New York branch and fined it $340 million for hiding $1 billion in bond-trading losses. If committed in Japan, Daiwa's deception would have drawn a derisory fine of less than $8,500. Daiwa even talked Tokyo tax authorities into letting it claim the American fine as a loss. Japan's leniency to lawbreakers is the antithesis of good governance and global standards.

Japan's governancial system was a child of its times. Despite its myriads of shortcomings, Japan Inc.'s system worked remarkably well, simply because the MOF and its allied ministries could protect all the principal ships in the national convoy. The MOF organized Japan's banks into the notorious gososendan, or convoy system, whereby risks were spread uniformly and the pace of innovation was deliberately curbed to that of its weakest members. Thus roped together, the convoy spluttered along until the bubble wrenched it below the bow.

This convoy system was, likewise, a child of its time: Japan's postwar boom, when it appeared that stock and land prices would always rise. This perception of perennially increasing wealth gave JFIs a loyal personal and institutional customer base who didn't look for independent advice and who didn't question the recommendations or practices of the JFIs. Compensating the powerful at the expense of the weaker became accepted and tolerated practice. This Robin Hood- in-reverse governance system was fine until the bubble burst.

The Big Bang plan is partly a forward-looking set of reforms designed to put the Tokyo market back on the level of the New York and London markets, but it is also partly a backward-looking measure for clearing away the bad debts left over from the bubble years. There is a lot of cleaning to be done. When Sanyo collapsed, it was the first time in the postwar period that Japan's bankruptcy laws were employed to wind down a company; previously, MOF administrative guidance would typically force other companies to take over the bankrupt one. Although Sanyo was a start, Japan has eons to travel before it resembles the West. Codification is only the beginning.

Japan is different. Whereas American-style capitalism is the product of a long historical and cultural evolution concerning the autonomy and division of powers between judiciary and government, Japan is the product of a different historical evolution; she does not have the infrastructure of a market economy with its armies of bull-headed lawyers and accountants necessary to replace any conceivable crumbling of bureaucratic rule.

Japan has a bureaucratic mandarinate centered around the MOF. That mandarinate has done a remarkable job in building the world's second-largest economy and then steering that economy through some very troubled waters. Perhaps its sell-date is past. But until other governance modalities arise, implementing real change will be problematic.

Any radical Big Bang liberalization in governance structures could, perversely, lead to an increase in influence of the yakuza, Japan's organized criminals, who already play an all-too-pervasive role in Japanese corporate distress. Indeed, yakuza involvement in every aspect of Japan's bad-debt overhang forms what is probably the Big Bang's leading obstacle. Darkness hates the light, and as long as Japanese ways stay opaque, the yakuza, the sokaiya, and similar parasites will breed beneath the surface.

Perhaps these parasites have undermined Japan's corporate system and it will come tumbling down. The MOF is mired in an unprecedented and debilitating corruption scandal. The brokers and banks they oversee have tarnished reputations, shrinking profits, and weak finances. Fear of financial meltdown has also seen the government retreat from the rapid reform timetable implicit in the MOF's Big Bang.

Japan's governancial dearth make these fears well founded. Japan lacks acceptable accounting[5] and disclosure standards, satisfactory investor protections, and board practices designed to provide independent, accountable oversight of managers and transparency. Further, because securitization and similar reforms would force banks to realize losses in a transparent manner, bank officials would have to break with the traditional Japanese corporate group approach and accept personal culpability and concomitant personal consequences. Any reforms will have to be at least as wholesale and fundamental as those introduced under the MacArthur Occupation.

The devil, as always, is in the detail. Banks, Japan's included, must now concentrate on boosting their off-balance-sheet earnings from consultation, derivatives trading, and the like. Because off-balance-sheet banking brings certain regulatory complications, especially in today's dynamic conditions, these changes will bring problems galore to Japan. Securitization, for example, can confuse risk assessment. Although they aid risk shifting, derivatives have credit, market, and operating risks. The key regulatory issue is whether banks are hedging or speculating with them and, given their complexity, whether regulators actually understand them. The MOF, as a group, clearly do not.

Credit risk arises from the fact that derivatives change the risk of default as well as the pricing structure. Market risk arises from the liquidity and other spillover effects major derivatives losses cause. Technical risks arise from the mathematical and legal expertise needed to manage them. Operating risks of derivatives have incurred from derivatives trading. Greater proficiency in their use could lead to greater complacency, thus boosting credit and market risk. This would most likely be the scenario in Japan, unless huge changes were forthcoming.

Derivatives, in other words, represent a great step into the unknown for a market as opaque and as far from global standards as Japan's. Their introduction would compel the introduction of full transparency so that all relevant risks could be calculated. It would entail fairness, so that these prices would be factored in correctly, without undue interference from the MOF or one of its surrogates.

Such changes are unthinkable to the unaccountable. Japanese governancial systems are not conducive to taking responsibility or to letting the light of day shine through. The flurry of recent suicides of bankers and their overseers was a symptom of that: they chose death rather than take responsibility for their shortcomings. They will have to take a quantum leap before they can take the personal responsibility, accountability, and culpability inherent in a modern economy.

The same applies at company level. Japanese boards of directors, quite simply, do not encourage responsibility taking. They are typically emasculated entities. They tend to be large and unwieldy, often having dozens of members, making meaningful discussion, let alone policy implementation, difficult. They rarely rely on outside directors, preferring the appointment of in-house personnel who, for the most part, carry additional responsibilities for daily operations; as a result, much to the chagrin of their American investors in particular, boards tend to ignore shareholders' interests. They are easy meat for the sokaiya and similar predatory packs.

Japan's system is the antithesis of the West's, which, despite its faults, has many built-in checks and balances. In Japan, outside shareholders have no voice in corporate management, no representation on corporate boards, no realizable claim on either corporate assets or corporate earnings beyond a small dividend stream. Just as in the property market, without a market in which shares that represent real ownership of corporate assets can change hands, their actual worth cannot be properly ascertained. Further, because the threat of bankruptcy or takeover are both absent, large, well-connected Japanese companies have neither the will nor the incentive to modernize and rationalize.

It is not a system that engenders responsibility, accountability, and transparency. The boards tend to be remote from the day-to-day running of their concerns. Most major decisions tend, as a consequence, to be made by other top-level groups, such as meetings of managing directors. Boards tend to meet only to approve matters submitted to them as a formality, thus adding yet another bureaucratic layer to a highly bureaucratic country. Because there are no clear lines of demarcation, no one takes responsibility. No one takes the rap. The buck keeps circulating.

Japan lacks the type of efficient and advanced legal system an advanced securities market demands. Because Japan has a chronic shortage of lawyers,[6] the necessary redress through litigation to sort out defaults and collect collateral will be hard to achieve. Nor does Japan have the necessary legislation to protect credit customers. Variable insurance policies have, with the collapse of stock and property prices, brought huge losses to 1.2 million largely elderly and uninformed customers the banks solicited. Neither the courts nor Japan's pitiably low number of lawyers offer the chance of redress. Although the Ministry of Finance launched some relevant legislation in April 1997, it was not made retroactive. Because consumers are increasingly loath to be the willing subsidizers of a corrupt financial sector, their confidence must, in contradiction to Japanese traditions, be restored by giving redress at the expense of the corporate sector. Because Japan lacks the necessary legal infrastructures, rapid and widespread financial liberalization could, paradoxically, lead to greater abuses and concomitant loss in confidence.

Certainly, the imposition of global standards would go against their track record. From the beginning of this century until 1984, just 23 securities-related suits were filed against Japan's financial institutions. The Japanese judicial system is simply not geared to handle the adversarial procedures central to the British and American systems.

For years, Japan has turned a blind eye to practices that were illegal elsewhere. The foisting of warrants on retirees, the acceptance of stocks ramped by racketeers, the churning of accounts, illegally skimming profits from unit trusts, the manipulation of accounts to earn commission—all have been daily sharp practices in Japan, whose securities companies in effect systematically stole from the widows and orphans they were charged with protecting.

The under-performance of Japan's investment trusts exemplifies Tokyo's endemic rot. Before the bubble burst, when the Nikkei index rose by more than 20% per year, Japanese unit trusts on average rose by less than 10%. Such persistent under-performance cannot be explained by finance theory. Japan's small investors believe-and all the evidence supports them-that their funds were purposely, and illegally, siphoned off to compensate bigger clients. Because Japanese securities companies are not required to disclose which stocks and bonds they include in an investment trust, it is difficult to definitively prove such allegations. Still, Japan's small investors have deserted Japanese brokers in droves. Ethical considerations have driven them to the largely untainted foreign houses of Merrill Lynch, Morgan Stanley, and other Wall Street household names.

The small savers and investors, whose sweat was the down payment to Japan's postwar economic miracle, have not been adequately compensated for their patriotic toil. They have been diddled, swindled, cheated, and conned by their supposed betters. And they have been given no redress.

Under Japan's Securities and Exchange Act, deliberate misrepresentation of financial information is a criminal offense. But despite Japan's huge bad-loan problem, the MOF has never sued any bank or accountant for violation of this law. Prosecutors will not, in practice, take on cases governed by this or any law that affects the MOF's area of competence without the ministry's green light. And any institution that tries to force legal proceedings over MOF opposition opens itself to the threat of retaliation through anything from tax audits to a stringent application of the disclosure requirements to the complaining institution—which is why it never happens. Japan's law is not only not impartial: it can be downright vindictive as well.

In the end, Japan cannot turn into anything resembling an American-style market economy as long as it is governed by a bureaucracy that serves as its own legislator, its own prosecutor, its own enforcer, its own judge. Indeed, the cynics contend that the most convincing explanation for the real timing and motivation behind the Big Bang is the MOF's need for political cover and self-preservation in the face of Japan's current traumas.

The mandarins are at the core of Japan's inertia. Their sell-by date gone, they refuse to take the flak for their shortcomings. Words like "accountability" and "culpability," not to mention "humility," simply are not in their collective lexicons. As long as they continue to hang together, they will not hang separately. As long as they can keep the power Japan's lack of political leadership gives them, the longer Japan will stagnate. Because the inertia such a centralization of power begets is the antithesis of a freewheeling market, dismantling the mandarins' power will be the biggest test the Big Bang faces.

The post-bubble crisis is, ultimately, the result of the unrestrained anarchy that characterized the bubble. Throughout the high-growth period, the principal source of funds for Japanese companies was indirect financing-obtaining funds through banks. During the bubble, Japanese corporations took advantage of elevated stock prices and enthusiastically sold additional shares or issued convertible bonds or bonds with stock purchase warrants—so-called equity financing. They obtained lower-cost funds with the expectation that the stock price would continue upward. It was a veritable cash-making machine that, left unchecked, developed its own ultimately fatal momentum. The MOF were too busy counting their gains to keep their minds on their job.

The bubble, left unbridled, made this equity financing possible. Companies misused these funds. They tapped funds but did not put them to productive use. They raised more money than they needed and ended up with surplus cash, with free cash flow, which they used to speculate on stock and property prices. That was the Japanese system.

America's adversarial system, by contrast, makes free cash flow hazardous: it makes the firm a takeover target. The normal American practice is to use such funds to buy back the company's own shares or to pay dividends. If managers choose to do nothing with it, institutional investors will demand that it be redistributed as dividends. In short, there is no hoarding of funds as in Japan.

U.S. Steel exemplifies the American position. Looking upon steel as a sunset industry, they invested little in equipment renewal. As a result, they ended up with cash flow equal to the value of the depreciation taken on their facilities. When U.S. Steel's surplus cash made it a takeover target, it bought Marathon Oil. This divesting of its free cash flow ended its status as a takeover target.

Japanese firms, on the other hand, invested their free cash flows in speculative, financial assets. They should have paid it out as dividends and let the shareholders invest it as they saw fit. Japanese managers did not have the check of an organized shareholders' lobby. In the fluid conditions of the bubble, Japan lacked the checks and balances of a dynamic system. It lacked Anglo-American global standards.

This free-flow had macroeconomic consequences as well. The availability of surplus money in the economy as a whole without the possibility of reinvestment or the high liquidity of surplus funds coupled with an absence of discipline caused asset prices to soar. These assets were used as the basis to buy other assets. Thus did Japan's mandarins allow the bubble to be built, like a deck of cards, needing only a correcting gust to bring it all tumbling down.

This chapter looked at the role that the MOF and the other mandarins played in the whole sordid affair. The next chapter looks at the JFIs' role.

[1] The first sign foreigners see on arrival at Narita Airport, Tokyo.

[2] So too do MITI and local prefectures. Generally speaking, however, the MOF towers over all of the others in terms of power and influence. The MOF is, in many cases, used as shorthand for the very many groups involved in overseeing JFIs.

[3] The no-pan waitresses were a popular distraction during the bubble years. The waitresses, who wore no panties (thus their name), kept their clients' minds away from where they should have been: on their jobs.

[4] Again, too many regulatory cooks made Japan a fraudster's paradise. The quick-buck brigade merely played one group of mandarins off against another.

[5] Although Japan's accountancy practices are modeled on those of the United States, there has been a lack of public disclosure of information. Indeed, instead of addressing the banking sector's very real fundamental problems, the Japanese government is drawing up plans to change banks' accounting rules to prevent recent stock market falls triggering a crisis in the financial sector. The move has been prompted to allow banks meet the 8% capital adequacy ratio stipulated by the Bank for International Settlements. Because the proposed schema would reevaluate equity portfolios at their book value rather than at the prevailing market value, this would boost banks' capital because it would ignore the massive fall in the market prices of their assets; valuing land assets in terms of market prices rather than in terms of the initial purchase cost would create further book gains as most land was obtained decades ago.

[6] Japan, with a population of 125,000,000, has fewer than 15,500 lawyers.

Japanese Financial Institutions

"Leading Japanese financial institutions are primitive."[1]

Japanese FIs fixated themselves on emulating their manufacturing confreres and capturing market share, a highly questionable goal in many areas of lending. Any institution, as the JFIs proved, can gain market share by aggressive pricing or lending to poor credits. This type of activity does not necessarily lead to market dominance. In the case of Japan's FIs, it has led to huge market failures.

The Westerners, in contrast, concentrated on the so-called bottom line, boosting profits and shareholder value. Indeed, if we compare Japanese and American banks' profitabilities by after-tax margins, return on equity, earnings per share, dividend per share, or any other standard financial ratio, there is no real comparison to be made: vibrant Western firms appear as profitable whereas the Japanese appear as being in complete and utter financial disarray. Market share, the Japanese yardstick, merely brought them more losses, more bad loans, more flypaper to enmesh themselves in.

The discrepancies in financial ratios were caused by factors other than the JFIs' primitivisms. They have at least as much to do with the keiretsu form of organization. Because debt, rather than Tokyo's securities markets, has been the backbone of keiretsu fund raising, banks and similar financial intermediaries have played the crucial role the equity markets do elsewhere. As a consequence, debt-to-equity ratios as high as 4:1 have been common. Although debt ratios of this magnitude would be unacceptable in the West, Japan's unique corporate structure made both this system-and its subsequent day of reckoning-inevitable.

The primitive practices of JFIs were thrown into sharpest relief in their overseas operations. Their lack of focus, their outmoded hiring practices, their rotation and generalist systems, their lack of expertise, all came back to haunt them with hellish vengeance. As Honda, Sony, Toyota, and other Japanese manufacturing corporations accelerated their expansion overseas, JFIs followed to service their client base. The JFIs established their multiple beachheads in all major overseas capital bases and started raising funds in the less restrictive and less regulated overseas markets. Thus, despite having excess capital at home, Japanese companies borrowed aggressively overseas.

Japanese banks, for example, borrowed short on the Euromarkets to lend long. This is, generally speaking, the most basic of basic mistakes. Except in mortgages, where immovable bricks and mortar stand as collateral, it is usual to borrow long to lock in your funds and their costs and to lend it out for shorter terms so that interest-rate changes can be monitored. As if that were not bad enough, more often than not, they used the proceeds of the borrowings to purchase financial assets without regard for the credit risks or the fact that they were mismatched with their own liabilities. All they looked at was the yield with no regard to the higher risks that necessarily accompany higher returns. Transfixed by the higher yields their risky investments promised, they frittered away billions of dollars in losses and underperformance on their overseas adventures. Japan's overseas economic empire was emasculated by a malfunctioning financial system that has its roots in domestic overprotection and overregulation without the corrective of market accountability. JFIs, in the aggregate, were grossly incompetent in their pursuit of overseas investments, loans, joint ventures, and acquisitions. Their lack of skills and the bureaucratic red tape they wallowed in ensured their multibillion-dollar losses.

Despite their pompous claims to the contrary, JFI overseas operations were almost criminally short-term in their planning horizons. Even the most partial list of the nonachievements, nonaccomplishments, and nonperformances of the JFIs overseas make a veritable Harvard Business School case-study textbook in disaster writ large.

Such a list would include their real estate-related losses, their leveraged buy-out (LBO) loans made without even perfunctory local knowledge; their abysmal acquisition and joint venture strategies; their pathetically low or negative returns on equity in their overseas operations; their inability to transfer technology to their domestic base; their disdain for perfunctory let alone proper research; their failure to employ hedging techniques in investment or trading areas; their lack of focus and planning in establishing their overseas businesses; their failure to produce a skilled and knowledgeable personnel base to handle sophisticated business transactions; their fixation on mindless asset growth.

In true Japanese corporate fashion, they refused to acknowledge their blunders. Instead of biting the bullet, they rationalized their mistakes by adopting fairyland payback horizons of 50 or more years, by believing that their projects had some (very) long-term strategic value that only they could discern, that their competitors carried equivalent dead weight, and that, in any event, the MOF, their uncomplaining, unthinking, all-forgiving lender of last resort, would always bail them out.

The faults of Japanese society, warts and all, came home to roost with a vengeance in these foreign endeavors. The self-correcting aspects of accountability and market forces were buried in their bureaucratic, promotion-seeking preoccupations. Checks and balances were replaced with an overreliance on politically safe choices of transactions, partners, or businesses. Thinking that they were still in quirky Japan, they switched off their brains and operated only with prestige partners or prestige projects. They got smitten by these glamorous and overpriced white elephants on the assumptions that, as in Japan, market forces and plain common sense would not rule and that, their tour of duty done, they would be promoted to a cushy Tokyo desk job where they could sleep away their remaining decades to retirement.

The JFIs overseas were not only not profitable: they were criminally profligate. They followed their herd instinct from one fashionable financial disaster to another. Ultimately, they were universally regarded as an intellectually despised source of cheap, commodity money. The JFIs overseas were the antithesis of the Japanese manufacturing sector. Of the many factors that help explain the overseas success of Japan's manufacturers and the abject failure of its JFIs, chief among them must be the cosseted position from which the JFIs emanated, debarred, by MOF dictate, from domestic competition. Manufacturers, on the other hand, had to develop superior products and pricing strategies or die. The JFIs became cheap providers of capital. The manufacturers added value.

The poor results of Japanese real estate investment in the United States are a testament to their unprofessional and arrogant behavior which led them to believe that they could conquer regional, highly specialized markets with their primitive and parochial approach. Cash-rich and brain-dead, they became the dumping ground for well-packaged but overpriced white elephants. They and the white elephants they had so rashly acquired became the laughingstock of the financial world.

Japanese investors poured some $45 billion into Hawaii and California from 1985 to 1995 and accumulated losses close to $25 billion. Some of the biggest deals were among the worst. The $840 million purchase of the prestigious Pebble Beach Golf Course in California with a $540 million loss was only the most conspicuous disaster of the Japanese indulging themselves in their favorite fad: buying overpriced American golf courses. Like their other fads, they picked up overpriced golf courses with no regard to their value, their expected returns, their potential for growth, or the like. All that mattered was the made-in-America nameplate.

Their most extravagant, and arguably most insane Hawaiian venture was the Grand Hyatt Wailea Resort and Spa on Maui, which has been accurately described as the most luxurious hotel ever built. The 800-bedroom hotel cost $600 million to build. It would need to charge at least $750 a room and to have a 75% occupancy rate to have any chance of breaking even. Because this is an impossibility in a holiday resort, they have been forced to offer their rooms at substantial losses. Further, because its opulence will entice customers away from other Hawaiian hotels and thereby weaken other Japanese investments as well, it typifies the lack of planning that went into this squandering of Japan's assets.

The Asian crisis has sealed the grim fate of these ill-conceived adventures. Hawaiian hotel occupancy rates have fallen every month since May 1997 and no major upturn seems in sight. Not even massive price reductions during Japan's Golden Week[2] have stemmed the decline-and the losses of those Japanese who overinvested in Hawaii. The Grand Hyatt investment was, in fact, typical of their spendthrift ways when both the convoy system and common sense were thrown overboard in the safari to acquire white elephants and other Pyrrhic trophies.

Implicit in their analysis was an ever-growing economy, large hidden reserves, and an ultimate safety net in the lender of last resort-the government. All would stay as it was. Or so they believed.

Credit research and other banking fundamentals were ignored as blithely at home as they were abroad. IBJ, the JFIs' flagship, lent $2 billion to Ms. Nui Onoue, the toad-worshipping owner of a small Osaka restaurant, popular with the Yamaguchi-gumi, Japan's largest organized crime syndicate. IBJ lost over $500 million to her. They claimed that she duped them. If she did, no doubt many others did as well. However, the IBJ's refusal to take responsibility for being duped by a yakuza-loving, sushi-serving granny is, perhaps, the most unsettling aspect of that sordid affair. Large financial institutions are supposed to be professional and granny-proof.[3] If they are not, confidence in them is, clearly, misplaced.

Any confidence in JFIs at the time of Ms. Onoue's moment of glory would have been misplaced. Still, IBJ had plenty of confidence in her. They were her chief source of credit. She, in turn, was not only their largest individual shareholder but she had major stakes in Sumitomo Bank, Toshiba, and a host of other Japanese blue-chips. In the process, she briefly became one of the 20 richest people in the world, even though she lived in the sleaziest part of town where she also operated a sleazy restaurant business, her only apparent source of income. Despite her colorful toad idols and sake-sipping gangster clientele, IBJ had so much confidence in her that they allowed her to take out her collateral from their vaults so that she could reuse it to raise more funds. They had so much confidence in her that they conspired in allowing her to reuse, on four different occasions, collateral she had lodged with them. Their confidence blinded them to the fact that collateral is meant to be locked securely away, not lent out on a revolving basis to the person who lodged it. IBJ's confidence was undented by Ms. Onoue's membership in the Mikkyo, an esoteric Buddhist cult, which conducted midnight rituals in her tacky sushi joint. When we consider that the colorful Ms Onoue was eventually arrested in 1991 for trying to pass off as collateral ¥340 billion of fake certificates of deposit (CDs), IBJ's oversights, indiscretions, and culpability can be seen in their proper light.

Not that IBJ was alone. Fuji Bank, to take another example, issued over ¥260 billion of false CDs which were used as collateral to buy 400,000 shares in Fasuke, a sock-making company whose shares were ramped and cornered on a regular basis. The fake CDs later disappeared from Fuji's vaults, indicating a degree of complicity by Fuji's high command in the crime. Fuji's problem was that it had tried to match Sumitomo's aggressiveness but its staff, spoiled Tokyo University graduate brats in the main, were not up to the job. Fuji Bank was not alone. Tokai Bank and Kyowa Bank admitted to using fake collateral as well in an ill-thought-out scheme to bypass constricting regulations. Their employees were encouraged to take such shortcuts so that their favored clients could use the fake collateral to borrow from their affiliates. These criminal and duplicitous acts were, not to overstate the point, the antithesis of free, fair, and global markets.

It was, as the previous chapter explained, the criminal tango between Harunori Takahashi and LTCB that held the naivete of such schemes up to the full ridicule of the light of day. Although the LTCB eventually walked away from him, they continued to indirectly finance him through the Tokyo Kyowa Credit Cooperative and the Anzen Credit Cooperative. He loaned himself and his companies ¥37.6 billion, roughly the same amount the LTCB had lodged with these two institutions. The MOF, to their credit, did outlaw such abuses-but only after the credit unions collapsed. The MOF had intended to bail out Takahashi's front companies with public funds until the revelation that Takahashi himself had been directly responsible for some 60% of the loans caused such an uproar that the MOF had to back down.

Sumitomo went a step further into the mire. Its chairman

allowed a gangster, Suemitsu Ito, to be appointed to the board of Itoman, a prominent trading company. The gangster then fleeced the company and Sumitomo to an extent that even the hapless Takahashi might have envied. Not that Ito was an isolated case. Susumu Ishii, the boss of bosses of the Tokyo-based Inagawa-kai, Japan's second-largest crime syndicate, was helped to ramp stocks in Tokyu Corporation. Nomura and Nikko are alleged to have financed him and to have ramped the stocks on his behalf. Whatever the truth about that, they blatantly financed him both directly and through their affiliates to the tune of about $100 million. They did not even use middlemen to dissipate the resulting stench of criminality but dealt directly with him themselves. Although stock manipulation cannot be proven as such, the shares did rise very rapidly once he bought in. The MOF, in fact, accused Nomura in front of a Diet hearing of deliberately ramping the stock.

Nomura's contrary views are interesting. They feel they were scapegoated by the MOF who sent them contradictory orders to pay and not pay compensation. They point out that the MOF had instructed the Big Four[4] to support the market after the 1987 Black Monday crash and that the practices they now stand accused of were part and parcel of that process. Although, for example, it was legal to pay compensation in Japan, to promise to do so was illegal and, in such a semantic-ridden world of nods and winks, Nomura could not see where it had especially erred. In the quirky world of Japanese finance, guaranteeing clients' capital was an accepted practice to win and maintain market share—even though stock markets are supposed to be risky and gains are won to offset the risks of capital loss. Nomura's dilemma came to light only when the tax man leaked the story. Nomura, honorably enough in Japan's quirky world, tried to claim the illegal reimbursements as legitimate business expenses.

Compensation was done by buying back warrants at inflated prices or by paying much more than market value for government bonds. The yakuza were not the only favored clients. Others included the MOF-controlled Pension Welfare Public Corporation and the police and teachers' unions. When Nomura drew attention to the MOF's culpability in the affair, the MOF retaliated by banning

Nomura from a range of activities: proof, if proof were still needed, that the MOF remains the major obstacle to the establishment of free, fair, and global markets.

JFIs have major structural weaknesses that make such recurrences likely. Although they have great placement power, they have shown no ability to manage money professionally. Their vested interests, together with those of the MOF, mitigate against reform. Weaknesses are deeply imbedded into their structures and into their collective psyches. Market forces are all but nonexistent. The JFIs, although large, are prisoners to the xenophobic, inward-focused system that spawned them.

The Japanese educational system's emphasis on national identity and cohesion, detail, small-group loyalty, self-sacrifice, peer pressure, and a hierarchical command structure may suit the manufacturing sector's needs to produce specific items to order. The more fluid needs of the financial sector, in terms of direct communication, spontaneity, objective research and evaluation, conceptualization, and abstractive thought are not traits encouraged either within the educational system or, indeed, within the JFIs themselves. Sheer size and the raw power that comes with size were their favored tools even when such power was as costly and self-defeating as it so patently was in so many of the cases mentioned here.

These systematic failings were due to the changed nature of the world's capital markets, Japan's included. The postwar strengths of the JFIs were based on MOF patronage, postwar bullish stock and real estate markets, the savings of individual Japanese, the cash generated by Japan's manufacturing sector, the keiretsu cross-shareholding arrangements, and a compliant, nonconfrontational press and society. All of these advantages have now evaporated.

Although Japan's banks were required to maintain non-interest-bearing demand deposits with the BOJ, these reserve requirements were very low compared with those in other countries. Because this enabled Japan's banks to operate with low interest margins, market share was won not by product innovation but by an underpricing strategy that ultimately bankrupted them. Furthermore, because the schedule of reserve requirements subsidized small banks at the expense of large banks, the sector was, in the aggregate, inefficient.

The end result was that the banks failed to meet international prudential and profitability standards and were penalized accordingly. A bank's capital is a significant expense and a crucial reserve against bad debts. Because Japan's banks were allowed to maintain significantly lower capital adequacy ratios than their foreign competitors, they had the advantage of a very cheap cost of funds which allowed them to capture significant market share overseas, while their domestic market was rigidly protected.

When, in 1989, depository institution regulators from the United States, Western Europe, and Japan gathered in Basel, Switzerland, to announce the mutual adoption of risk-based capital requirements, they recognized that many depository institutions barely met the new standards and that a few large institutions would fail to meet the new requirements. To reach the new standards, banks would have to reform. None more so than the Japanese banks which, in 1990, were rated as having the ten largest banks by market capitalization or by market share in the world.

They are unlikely to ever again reach such lofty heights. Although the Japanese banks must now increase their capital adequacy ratios to conform to international capital adequacy standards, they are grossly overexposed to both the depressed Nikkei index and the depressed Japanese property market.[5] International banking authorities have, in consequence, expressed concern that, in the event of an international crisis such as that now pertaining in Southeast Asia, the global banking system could be undermined by the insufficient capital reserves of Japan's banks.

Because of the MOF's lax supervisory standards, the true extent of the Japanese banks' bad loans problem is difficult to quantify. It is, however, at least $1 trillion, over 25% of Japan's GDP. If we accept this figure, a total bailout would cost in the region of $400 billion if the Japanese government followed past practices and refused to allow the weakest banks to go bankrupt. The MOF's own figures put the total credit exposures of the Japanese banks at ¥624,864 billion. It states that ¥548,156 billion of this figure is in safe, performing loans; that a further ¥65,289 billion in loans needs careful monitoring; and that only ¥8,724 billion is in serious doubt and that a mere ¥2,695 billion is dead. These are undoubtedly optimistic figures, especially as the MOF admits that the figures are the banks' own estimates and that each bank's standard of classification on doubtful loans' exposures varies significantly among themselves. The MOF is, in other words, saying that, in the light of previous experiences, these figures have to be treated with the utmost caution.

Even if we accept a figure of bad debts for the entire Japanese banking sector of ¥2,000 trillion, this would be the largest percentage of nonperforming loans a sector had to carry in world history. It would be at least four times that of the American S&Ls. If we accept unrecoverable bad debts to stand at ¥55 trillion and when we compare that with their collective equity holdings of ¥40 trillion, we see that the bubble has left the entire Japanese banking system technically bankrupt.

The nub of the Japanese banks' problems is that the conditions that let them boost their lending so dramatically during the 1980s have now reversed. Their credit pyramid has collapsed and their accounting methods have become totally discredited. Japanese banks had almost unlimited discretion in presenting their accounts. Nonperforming loans didn't have to be disguised for one very good reason: they didn't have to be shown at all. They could continue to report income from a troubled loan for up to a year after they stopped receiving any income from it. And that's before their accounting chicanery came into play.

This chicanery proved poor protection against the foreign investors and rating agencies who could see through such parlor tricks. Because their cold calculations continue to make them skeptical on the Japanese financial sector, the JFIs must pay a much higher premium to borrow than might otherwise have been the case. Someone must take the blame for this.

And again, the MOF must take its lion's share of the blame. Its banking bureau does not monitor banks' capital adequacy ratios to see how they can cope with bad loans. Nor has it codified rigorous prudential standards for the entire banking industry. The banks must ask for permission to adjust their capital adequacy ratios on a case-by-case basis. The banks are the biggest taxpayers in Japan, and loan reserves can be deducted against tax only if permission is specifically granted. Traditionally, the tax authorities have allowed deductions for reserves against truly bad credits, where the borrower is bankrupt. As long as the faintest hope remains that the debt might be repaid, the banks cannot write it off without the MOF's specific permission. The MOF's rules, in other words, encourage the banks to use deliberately misleading accounts. They make the price of observing global standards too high.

They make it even higher for some than for others. The trust banks exemplify. Although Japanese trust banks are supposed to specialize in the trust business, they were much more heavily involved in property speculation. At the peak of the bubble, more than 50% of their total loans of ¥55 trillion were property-backed, almost 40% of which were to the nonbank sector. Because the trust bank is not the legal owner of these loans and is therefore legally constrained from selling them, they cannot transfer these bad loans to their related subsidiary companies—even though most of their property loans are in their trust accounts. In Japan's quirky world, this put them at a disadvantage. They could not cheat as much as their competitors who had enjoyed greater leeway to hide their bad loans.

The MOF says only 45 banks consider themselves operationally active compared to 80 in 1997. The government injected ¥1,800 billion into the capital base of Japan's top 21 banks in March 1998. Almost half of Japan's top banks applied for an injection of these public funds to strengthen their capital bases. They did this on the instructions of their government which, in a typical, logic-defying, face-saving, cosmetic exercise, did not want the scheme to be associated in the public mind with failing banks only—unaware that the public would have to be stone blind, deaf, and living on a remote island not to realize that Japan's banks are grappling with serious problems.

Bank of Tokyo-Mitsubishi (BTM) has no such delusions. It is raising the capitalization of Tokyo-Mitsubishi Securities Co. and its 13 other group brokerages by a total of ¥100 billion in preparation for deregulation of the sector in October 1999. Tokyo-Mitsubishi Securities, the largest brokerage subsidiary of any domestic bank, has total working capital of ¥55 billion including reserves. They intend to double that amount. Its pretax profit of ¥5 billion in fiscal

1997 was higher than any other bank affiliates and was a credible fourth in the entire industry overall. It has also increased the capitalization of its New York and London subsidiaries

Because Japan's problems run deeper than BTM, they will need much larger infusions to solve it. With over $1 trillion on loan, Japan is the world's largest international lender. Although Japan's exposure to third-world debt is second in magnitude to that of the United States and is particularly high in the depressed Southeast Asian region, Japanese banks have established reserves for only a minuscule portion of their loans to these high-risk countries. The possibility of a systematic breakdown in the Japanese financial system is, as a consequence, much higher than it might otherwise be.

Japan is establishing a new bridge bank to take on the business of any bank that fails. It will be backed with public money and will guarantee deposit security and ensure that credit lines are secure. The idea of a bridge bank is borrowed from the American experience where such a bank was used to sell off those failed S&L-related institutions for which buyers could be found. The rest were allowed go bankrupt. Shareholders lost heavily in all of these.

Japan, while borrowing the name, does not intend to borrow the experience. There is, as yet, not much of a secondary market for such glorified nameplates in Japan. Although it may succeed in averting a collapse in the orderly flow of financial services, it is not sufficient as a framework for motivating banks to expand their lending, though such is precisely what is needed to cut the vicious cycle of the credit crunch and revitalize the Japanese economy. For the Japanese economy to overcome the difficulties it faces, it must go beyond merely dealing with bad debts. Mechanisms must be put in place within the financial services industry that will enable sound banks, acting under principles of self-responsibility and self-governance, to replenish their capital and expand their lending. Japan will also need a new bank regulatory system better suited to global standards to replace the outmoded convoy-style regulation of the past.

JFIs must move away from bricks-and-mortar-only collateral and put weightings on managerial and technological know-how, essential features in modern business, as NASDAQ's success amply illustrates.

Japanese banks must engage in thorough disclosure of their asset quality, but Japanese society must also be willing to accept that lending rates in the future must reflect risks.

Still, the JFIs have taken some interesting initiatives. The credit union industry, for example, is rapidly consolidating as they merge or are taken over by banks or other financial institutions. There is clearly not enough room for all of them in the fast-approaching Big Bang world.

Nor is there room for the army of workers the industry currently employs. Banks are busily installing ATMs and are transferring eligible staff from their failing branches to their product/service development departments. Sanwa Bank, for example, has almost 750 unmanned branches, more than twice the number of its full-service branches. Fuji Bank has 600 such branches, against 340 staffed branches. Sakura Bank and BTM, both the result of large-scale mergers, are closing branches at particularly rapid rates. Sakura Bank cut 16% of its staffed branches over the past five years, while BTM closed 10%.

Further closures should follow. IBM Japan Ltd., for example, has built a mobile ATM in cooperation with Suruga Bank. Mounted on a truck equipped with a generator and telecommunications equipment, the device will relay banking transactions via satellite. Sugura Bank is deploying the mobile ATM along several routes in Kanagawa Prefecture. Although mobile ATMs are quite popular in the United States, they have yet to appear in Japan, where few car parks offer ready power sources or telecom facilities. Because the system built by IBM Japan can operate independently, it should give Suruga a competitive edge. Other banks have expressed an interest in acquiring the machines, which are quite secure and retail for about ¥100 million.

NEC and Sumitomo Bank, meanwhile, have jointly developed computer equipment that significantly reduces paperwork and costs in retail banking. The terminal can automatically scan transaction slips, transfer the data to the bank's main computer, and verify personal seals. Sumitomo plans to spend ¥15 billion over the next two years to install 4,000 of them at about 300 branches across the nation with the loss of 700 jobs. NEC hopes to sell 40,000 terminals in the first round of consolidations.

Sumitomo has many more sackings in the cards. They have recently introduced differentiated wage scales for their employees with the objective of attracting specialists. Derivative and currency traders, fund managers, and similar experts will be given incentive bonuses in addition to their annual salaries which will be determined by their market value. The bank hopes the revised packages will allow them to poach the specialists they need from their domestic and foreign competitors. The other two new salary scales for career-track employees are also performance-based and will help to change the whole ethic of the bank. These systems will also be employed by a securities company Sumitomo and Daiwa Securities have jointly formed

Some of the smaller, regional banks are trying to stay abreast of this wave of rationalization. Hokuetsu Bank, a regional bank based in Niigata Prefecture, wants to link its ATMs with the post office ATM network. Linking up with the post office network would provide account holders access to the postal savings' 600 ATMs in the prefecture, almost double Hokuetsu's number. It hopes the move will help it survive tough competition in the wake of the Big Bang's reforms. The bank has long been demanding that the post office should complement the private sector as a savings option, rather than competing for deposits in small areas where there is not enough custom for both the public and private sectors.

Other JFIs are also busily headhunting. Bank of Yokohama has affiliated with Fidelity Investments Japan Ltd., Morgan Stanley Asset and Investment Trust Management Co., and the investment advisory affiliates of Merrill Lynch and Co. and Schroder Investment Trust Management Ltd. as well as several domestic investment trust firms to exploit the deregulated over-the-counter sales of investment trust products. Bank of Yokohama will sell the products, which they are jointly developing with their partners, who will also train their staff. Bank of Yokohama has also joint projects afoot with the investment trust arms of Nomura Securities Co. and Nikko Securities Co.

Sumitomo Bank and Daiwa Securities, meanwhile, have established a joint venture focusing on investment banking. This new firm will, inter alia, take over Daiwa's corporate business and Sumitomo's securities operations. They have set up another company to handle derivatives business and another as an investment advisory outfit to develop financial instruments, such as investment trusts. Because all of these particular ventures represent another sign that the MOF will also not insist on maintaining firewalls between the bank and the joint venture, they mean that one-stop shopping may be near to realization. Japanese regulators had previously debarred banks or their subsidiaries entering the brokerage business. The sole exception to this was Cosmo Securities, which was acquired by Daiwa Bank under an MOF-brokered rescue package.

Still, the JFIs seem determined to change all of this. Fifty-three financial institutions and companies have set up a joint venture to develop even more financial-related products. The venture, The Smart Banking Consortium, will provide information on its Internet homepage on six kinds of financial products, including foreign currency deposits, commodity funds, and foreign bonds. It also plans to develop new products by combining services such as individual asset management support and travel packages. The consortium includes Sumitomo Bank, Bank of Yokohama, Suruga Bank, several of Tokyo's leading credit associations, Credit Saison, IBM Japan Ltd., NEC, and Goldman Sachs.

Many new products are already coming on to the market. Japanese brokers are offering euro-denominated money-market funds to avail of the growing demand for investment vehicles denominated in foreign currencies. The funds, which are technically investment trusts, will invest in short-term, low-risk securities denominated in Euros. They aim to offer annual yields ranging from 3% to 5%. Nikko Securities' fund will be managed by the brokerage's British asset-management arm. An affiliate of Industrial Bank of Japan (IBJ) will manage similar funds offered by New Japan and Okasan. Similar dollar-denominated funds have already proved quite popular and profitable for the brokers.

Zenshinren Bank is selling investment trusts to individual customers at 55 of its affiliated banks; the majority of Japan's smaller banks should join the scheme by 2000. City banks are also preparing to enter the investment trust market on their own, thus making competition even more intense.

Although many domestic securities houses are boosting investment trust operations, most are currently concentrating on foreign trust funds since a ban on trust-fund sales on bank premises was revoked. Nomura, meanwhile, has initiated interbank foreign exchange trading in Tokyo to cater to the increasing demand from customers for foreign-currency-denominated bonds and investment trusts. Nomura recently became the first nonbank company to deal foreign exchange in Tokyo. Revisions to the Foreign Exchange and Foreign Trade Control Law made the move possible. Monthly turnover is expected to reach ¥10 trillion, putting Nomura on a par with the major city banks.

Sumitomo Bank, meanwhile, became the first Japanese bank to sell commodity funds denominated in a foreign currency. The dollar-based investment vehicles for wealthy individuals are being sold at Sumitomo branches nationwide. Foreign concerns, including Merrill Lynch and Amro Bank NV of the Netherlands (ABN) have been retained to guarantee a minimum return by investing in risk-free financial products. Although Sumitomo plans to make the commodity funds one of its main offerings in its line of high-return foreign currency products for high-worth clients, their allies have their own plans. Merrill Lynch hopes to use Sumitomo to expand its Japanese sales channels in Japan, while ABN wishes to market more financial products in the retail market.

So too do other JFIs. More than 5% of the population have savings of $500,000 or more. Although an impressive 600,000 of these are high-net-worth individuals, Japanese private banking is in its infancy.[6] Japan's Long-Term Credit Bank and Swiss Bank Corporation recently signed a deal aimed at establishing a series of joint ventures, including a private banking group.[7] The private banking arms of Citibank and Goldman Sachs are all building up their Japanese operations.

The Big Bang will help this labor-intensive sector, especially middle-aged executives eager to avoid Japan's punitive inheritance taxes.[8] Because Japan's trust banks, the obvious vehicles to supply these services, do not have the required skills, further joint ventures and mergers with foreign concerns are inevitable. The foreign companies are, in fact, already making incredible inroads into what, for them, is virgin territory. Foreign-capitalized investment trust management companies now control more than 10% of managed assets in Japan. The managed asset balance of 19 foreign firms exceeds ¥4.2 trillion, more than double the amount of previous years.

The city banks are also addressing their bad-debt overhang. They set up IBA Investment in the Caymans as a shell company to take over some of the Japanese banks loans to the less-developed nations. The banks sold $6 billion of Mexican loans to IBA at deep discounts and subsequently took tax deductions from the resulting losses. They have placed most debt from Peru, Ecuador, and Costa Rica on a nonaccrual basis.

Sumitomo Bank launched a $1 billion securities issue in the United States to boost its capital base and shield it from currency risk. The issue was made via an American subsidiary in the form of dollar-denominated perpetual preferred shares targeted at international investors. The move is somewhat innovative because, though other banks and insurance companies have issued preferential shares before, none has done it in dollars in this way. The group plans to back those securities with U.S. Treasury Bonds, part of which will probably be purchased with the proceeds of the capital raised.

Since the preferred securities will not be converted into shares, the issuance will not dilute the bank's return on equity. Sumitomo further argues that the scheme would shield it from currency risk. Though the bank has no capital in dollars, it holds dollar liabilities, meaning its capital adequacy ratio is eroded if the dollar strengthens against the yen. Thus, this largely cosmetic exercise may well come unstuck if the yen plummets.

Sumitomo may, in all probability, have to pay a rate of interest of over 10%—equivalent to junk-bond rubbish-status. It is much higher than Japanese banks have formerly paid and is indicative of their lowered status. And, more ominously, Sumitomo is considered one of the healthier Japanese banks.

Sumitomo is doing the deal because perpetual preferred shares can be counted on as part of the bank's tier-one capital, which counts toward its capital requirements under international guidelines. Accounting necessities are making it engage in these high-tech, high-risk gimmicks.

All of these reforms, though useful and important, merely nibble at the edges. The big JFIs are hurting. BTM is now the third-largest bank in the world with a capitalization of $60 billion. Though linked to the best keiretsu in the country, it is also saddled with massive bad debts. Overall Japanese exposure to the Asian collapse is, according to the Bank for International Settlements, some $280 billion. Both BTM and Sanwa Bank have much of this exposure. They wrote off over $10 billion of property-related bad loans between them in 1997. In BTM's case, the scale of the write-off (over $6 billion) shows some belated resolve to deal with ailing financial affiliates, whose bad debt does not have to be included in official figures. If such bad debts were included for all Japanese banks, the $140 billion in nonperforming loans at Japan's top 20 banks would more than double to at least $300 billion. In addition, Nippon Credit Bank, the long-term credit bank that was forced to conduct an emergency recapitalization in 1997, still holds over $10 billion of bad loans.

BTM's write-offs resulted in the group's risk-adjusted capital ratio falling to 8.49%, close to the 8% international minimum. However, because BTM is the leading financial institution in Japan's biggest corporate grouping, it is well poised to recoup its losses. The bank is also among the least exposed to the property market.

Sanyo, on the other hand, typifies the problems other banks will have in surviving the Big Bang. It expanded at the peak of the boom, when the TSE had a turnover of 1.5 billion shares a day. Later, when turnover slumped to around 300 million trades a day, its negative cash flow, small asset base, and large liabilities relative to the size of its business made its position nonviable in the Big Bang era. Sanyo became the first broker since World War II to go bankrupt. When, as a consequence, it defaulted on its loans, creditors tightened their policies toward other vulnerable companies. This unprecedented reappraisal of default risk helped trigger the ongoing lack of confidence in Japan's vulnerable finance sector. The first casualty was Japan's tenth-largest bank, Tagugin, which collapsed following a run on it.

Kyoto Kyoei, a regional Japanese bank, closed in October 1997 after admitting it was insolvent. The bank's operations were taken over by Kofuku, an Osaka-based regional bank, and its losses were covered by funds from Japan's banking industry insurance scheme. Kyoto Kyoei had a total capital base of $108 million. It had $220 million in nonperforming loans, leaving it with over $110 million of losses.

The government used the Deposit Insurance Corporation, a government-backed fund that levies money from bank deposits, to cover the losses where, previously, they would have forced the stronger banks to bail out their weaker competitors. Although the fund should have over $20 billion when it is fully operational, it is questionable if it will have sufficient funds to cover the largescale bank failures that seem increasingly likely.

Compounding these problems, Japanese banks have made woeful strategic blunders. In the 1980s, to take but one example, Japanese companies issued billions of dollars worth of bonds that were convertible into stock at a specified price. The assumption was that because stock prices would rise, bondholders would want to convert their bonds into stock to capture the profits. In that event, the issuers of bonds would never have to pay debt service to redeem the bonds themselves. With stock prices now reaching record lows, an agonizing squeeze on borrowers is expected as they scramble to find funds to pay debts that they thought would never fall due. Disasters, in other words, on top of disasters.

Because Japan's banks have held stocks as part of their reserves and have relied on their stock holdings for collateralized lending, the Nikkei's slide has also impeded the growth of credit in a time of record low-interest rates. Lower interest rates, when financial institutions are preoccupied with internal restructuring, is not boosting credit for business expansion. Japan's ongoing stagflation compounds these problems and inhibits corrective action.

Nor does the pain end there. The life companies have traditionally provided large subordinated loans—over ¥100 billion in toto—to related banks and brokers. Life assurers have also lent to several groups, including Sanyo Securities and Hokkaido Takushoku, both of which recently failed. Most life groups believed that Japanese banking laws would ensure that these subordinated loans would be repaid. However, when Hanwa Bank, a small region-al group, collapsed in 1997, the insured groups received only about 60% of their loans. It is doubtful if they will be repaid that much on future failures.

Japanese life assurance companies,[9] poorer and wiser, have warned government officials that they may not extend further loans to the country's weaker banks. This could deal a new blow to Japan's weaker banks, which have relied on unsubordinated loans from life assurance groups to expand their capital base.

A refusal by the life groups to extend new loans could dent the banks' attempts to boost their capital bases, thus encouraging the government to use even more public funds, with attendant moral hazards, to recapitalize the banks.

Though less spectacular than the JFIs, the ordinary Japanese saver is hurting as well. Popular textbooks painted the typical Japanese housewife, Mrs. Watanabe they called her, as the Belgian dentist of the Orient. The Belgian dentist owes his high financial visibility to the financial windfalls his compatriots' penchant for tooth-decaying chocolates bequeathed him. Being an astute fellow, the Belgian dentist was able to put these windfalls to good use both at home and abroad. The Belgian dentist thus came to typify the medium-sized private investor, who was not averse to taking on some financial risk in the expectation of a hefty reward. In this, he was juxtaposed with the widows and orphans, those fallen on strait-ened times, who could not afford to take on any risk at all.

That was a typically false comparison. Mrs. Watanabe, in reality, was an Oriental widow and orphan, whose true situation was blurred by Japan's phenomenal postwar bull run. The rise of the Tokyo mar-ket was breathtaking in the postwar years. In 1949, when American Occupation troops abandoned the old Tokyo Stock Exchange Building-they had been using it as a dance hall-Japan's economy was still in ruins. But over the next 40 years, the market-weighted index of stocks soared to 200 times its 1949 level. (By comparison, the Standard and Poor's index, the basket of 500 major American stocks, grew a mere 20-fold.) But the spectacular 1990 burst of the stock market and property bubble brought trading-and Mrs. Watanabe's much-depleted portfolio-down to earth with a thud.

During the boom years, the soaring Nikkei obscured the fact that the Japanese stock market is hopelessly old-fashioned. Japan is still far from having its equivalent of a NASDAQ, the all-electronic American stock exchange. Many brokerage houses are highly automated, but transactions often involve mountains of paperwork. Investors had to present themselves in person within three days of a financial transaction being done in order to put their seal on certificates and documents. These obstacles cannot be cured by the thunderclap of a Big Bang.

Japan's cosseted financial markets lack well-diversified investment outlets for the more than $100 trillion of financial assets Mrs. Watanabe and her fellow citizens hold. Only 7% of these assets are in stocks and 3% are in mutual funds, while over 55% are held in bank deposits. This contrasts with the situation in the United States, where only 16% are held in banks, and almost 27% are in stocks, 10% are in mutual funds, and 11% are in bonds. Mrs. Watanabe and other Japanese individuals are holding an enormous reservoir of capital—the equivalent of $10 trillion—but because they have lost faith in the securities market, some 93% of this money is deliberately withheld from equity markets. Given past abuses and the general ignorance Mrs. Watanabe has of opportunities beyond the land of the rising sun, it is not at all clear that the range of new investment vehicles being offered will be successful.

Meanwhile, Japanese corporations have flooded the equities market with new issues. The overly liquid market means that stock prices are destined to be depressed for years to come. This is hardly going to encourage Mrs. Watanabe or anyone else to invest heavily in it.

Hopes for a recovery of the equities market have been hindered by the proliferation of foreign-currency bonds, discussed above, many aimed at attracting the funds of gullible private investors. In many cases, it seems that these bonds are being issued by the very same companies whose salesmen foisted risky equities and warrants on more than a quarter of a million gullible pensioners. These companies are now encouraging small investors to put their money into "dual currency" bonds, highly illiquid instruments that carry severe downside risks. There are no worthwhile legal impediments in their way.

Whatever about Mrs. Watanabe, there is even less reason for her younger and poorer sisters to expose themselves to the Nikkei. Although Mrs. Watanabe may hold a considerable portfolio of shares, her younger sisters are deterred from entering the equities markets by the prohibitively high price of quality stocks. For example, the minimum investment in shares of supermarket chain Ito-Yokado is more than $60,000. Such prices are not geared for the average middle-class investor who generally forms the backbone of such funds. Lately, Daiwa Securities has introduced minifunds that can be opened for as little as $900. But lowering the cost of entering the equities market may not be enough to restore confidence to an industry that has treated its clients much too shabbily in the past.

Mrs. Watanabe simply did not figure in the brokers' calculations when times were good. Mrs. Watanabe and other typical owners of investment trusts are typically in their 50s and 60s, whereas their American counterparts tend to be at least 10 to 20 years younger. The Japanese mutual funds industry simply does not cater to this lower age-cohort. Given their abysmal records, this is probably as well. Although the poor performance of these mutual funds have weakened overall market indices, the general lack of confidence also reveals itself in the structural weakness of the Japanese stock market. As share prices slip, banks' latent capital gains on their portfolios shrink and their losses grow, weakening their financial position and making their own share prices fall; this has turned into a downward spiral.

There was simply no room for Mrs. Watanabe and her sisters. More than two-thirds of stocks on the Tokyo Stock Exchange are held in an interlocking fashion by firms in the same keiretsu, the interlocking corporate entities that control over 70% of Japanese business and finances. Because these keiretsu generally do not sell the shares they own, Japan is not as liquid as London or New York, and is therefore less suited to either raising finance or attracting Japan's equivalent of the Belgian dentists. Unless these keiretsu are broken up, the TSE will continue to be a thin market, unsuited for the equity-raising roles New York and London perform.[10] It will remain prone to excessive bouts of volatility, making it an improper vehicle for long-term investment by Mrs. Watanabe and others.

The Big Bang reforms mean that financial failures, once a comparative rarity, are now commonplace, with over a dozen major ones occurring between December 1994 and January 1998. Some of the larger ones have been in the securities industry.

Japan's Big Three brokerages are posting dismal results in recent quarters as depressed share turnover and deregulated commissions squeeze profits. Industry leader Nomura Securities saw its profits fall 58% to ¥15 billion in early 1998. Second-ranked Daiwa Securities posted a fall of 85% to ¥2.5 billion. Nikko Securities saw losses balloon to ¥7.5 billion, making pundits speculate on whether it will join Yamaichi as a footnote of Japanese corporate history. Unless the Big Bang is a rude awakening, it will, on these figures, be a death knell.

The Big Bang is certainly sounding the knell for Japan's lesser brokers. Liberalization of commissions on stock transactions exceeding ¥50 million and the lifting of restrictions on foreign exchange to allow investors greater flexibility in placing money abroad were among the program's first initiatives. Both combined to hurt the brokerages.

Although low trading volumes and liberalized commissions were the main reasons for these pathetic results, all of these companies have cash-flow problems as well. They have to further prune their cost structures.

Penalties imposed by the MOF for involvement in a payoff scandal dogged Daiwa through 1998 and similar punishments against Nikko also weighed on their results. The Big Three saw their combined share of the Tokyo Stock Exchange turnover slip amid the increasingly competitive environment caused by the Big Bang changes and drops in business in the wake of the scandals.

The Big Three claimed 21.6% of all trading on the TSE during 1998 as measured by the value of shares, down from 23.8% a year earlier. The slide came even though one of them, Yamaichi Securities, folded in the meantime, leaving more business for everyone else. Only Nomura was able to improve, lifting its share of TSE traffic to 10% from 6%.

In the wake of the rapidly changing environment, Nomura and Nikko are aggressively forging alliances, the scale of which will see the start of a fundamental realignment of the industry. IBJ and

Nomura plan to establish a 50-50 joint venture in Britain to focus on derivatives and proprietary trading of equities. Based in London, the venture will not be subject to Japanese regulations, but will instead operate under the more liberal British rules. And in June 1998, Nikko announced a broad tie-up with American-based Travelers Group, which owns Salomon Smith Barney. The two companies will operate a trading and research joint venture in Japan. Travelers will also take a 25% equity stake in Nikko. Daiwa has yet to seek a partnership.

Nomura, Japan's biggest securities house, is, despite current turbulences, financially rock-solid. As recently as 1987, Nomura was not only the most profitable company in Japan but the most profitable financial institution in the world. Although the MOF at the time shielded Japanese brokers from credit and market risk-they did not have to commit their own capital to making markets in Japanese equities—Nomura remains a force to be reckoned with. Nomura has the money, the will, the know-how, and the hunger to survive and thrive. It has huge assets and at least six times the required minimum capital adequacy ratio. Its financial depth will keep it vibrant for many years. Nomura, in fact, claims that the arrival of foreign competition has consolidated both its earnings and its profit, that it has picked up much of Yamaichi Securities' business, and that the market share it lost to Merrill Lynch and Morgan Stanley was low-margin-trading business.

The Japanese houses are trying hard to be at the cutting edge of things. They are, for example, offering shares and futures trading on the Internet and claim this service is steadily gaining popularity among individual investors, with 19 brokerages and investment trusts now offering such services in Japan. Daiwa Securities, which pioneered cyberspace share-trading in Japan, now has some 14,000 accounts and claims its business is growing at a rate of more than 1,000 new accounts a month. Though Nomura Securities, by contrast, has only 7,000 cyber-accounts, they claim that demand for their products should show a sharp increase in the months ahead.

Merrill Lynch, nonetheless, seems happy with its increasing market share. They have plans for a Japanese nationwide retail broking network. The group hired about 2,000 former employees of

Yamaichi and thereby tripled the number of their employees in Japan. They are aiming to capture a large share of Japan's $10,000 billion personal savings market. The company will compete head to head with Japan's remaining Big Three brokers-Nomura, Daiwa, and Nikko.

Given that Daiwa and Nikko have their own considerable problems, Merrill Lynch should do quite well. Daiwa was so tainted by the recent epidemic of financial scandals that the Ministry of Posts and Telecommunications suspended business ties with the group. The Australian government also suspended Daiwa Australia as one of the lead managers of Telstra's float. As Telstra's float was one of the world's biggest in 1997, Australia was not prepared to risk the erosion of confidence that Daiwa's involvement might bring. Although Daiwa's president, chairman, and five other senior executives resigned in an effort to contain the loss in public credibility, they were, in accordance with Japanese practices, retained as advisors. The Aussies were not impressed.

While the recent failures of major Japanese institutions were probably accelerated to some degree by rumors and media reports, the key point is that they were brought about through the working of market forces. The MOF and BOJ were unable to control the situation. This is in sharp contrast to what happened about 30 years ago, when Yamaichi had an earlier crisis. Kakuei Tanaka, the minister of finance at the time, arranged for a then-unprecedented emergency infusion of funds from the central bank, enabling the troubled brokerage to survive. The recent collapses, in other words, ironically show that Japan's financial system is finally inching toward the market mechanism and that the age of overprotection by MOF is ending. Furthermore, the unwillingness of Fuji Bank to rescue Yamaichi, its client and a member of the same corporate group, marks the demise of the main bank system.

The road to Yamaichi's ruin began in August 1997 when Ogawa Securities, a small Osaka-based group, became the first brokerage to close in Japan in 17 years, with almost $18 million of debts. In Japan's largest-ever corporate failure, Yamaichi, Japan's fourth-largest securities house, closed its doors in late November 1997 with liabilities of $28 billion after more than 100 years of trading.[11]

Coupled with its weak business base, Yamaichi saw its core clients desert it in the wake of a series of scandals linking its president and other top-ranking officials involving payoffs to the yakuza. An inspection by the Securities Exchange and Surveillance Commission found that Yamaichi had more than $200 billion off-the-book debts, including those from tobashi, the illegal practice in which securities firms shuffle losing investments of corporate customers through a series of accounts to hide the losses from investors.

Both Hokkaido Takushoku and Yamaichi made the initial announcements of their problems in press conferences held late at night over the weekend, while domestic markets were closed. The timing was arranged to blunt the impact of the news on market participants and avoid a precipitate collapse of confidence in other related institutions. But Tokuyo City Bank, a smaller player headquartered in Sendai, Miyagi Prefecture, announced during regular market hours on Wednesday, November 26, 1997, that it would sell off its operations.

Although there were no extreme developments, during the course of the day financial stocks plunged as rumors of further troubles whirled through the market. A number of major and medium-sized institutions, such as Daiwa Securities, the Long-Term Credit Bank of Japan, Keiyo Bank, Ashikaga Bank, and Hiroshima Bank, hastily called press conferences to dampen fears of their imminent demise. It took an extraordinary joint statement by the finance minister and central bank governor to calm the markets.

In the meantime, short selling in the form of margin transactions by foreign brokerages and speculators had exacerbated the pressure on stock prices. In fact, the danger of systemic risk was high. The presence of this sort of factor should be taken as another sign that, though Japan's financial system is entering the age of the market, it will remain fragile until the MOF straitjacket is removed and it can find its own level and place in the global economy.

Theory posits the various types of risks extant in the financial worlds. Much of this risk is quantified into quasi-mathematical models. When, as in the recent crisis in Thailand, the risk is of a non-quantifiable nature, it is marginalized as being of tertiary importance.

Such events, though originally marginal, do impact on the center. When, for example, Yamaichi Securities wound up on November 24, 1997, the Thai crisis impacted into the epicenter of world finance. The Japanese, who thought they could help solve the Thai crisis, now found themselves in danger of total collapse from it. Yamaichi's collapse, coupled with other unprecedented collapses in the Japanese financial world, asked the unaskable: could Japan, the world's second-largest economy, follow Thailand, South Korea, and Indonesia and implode?

The Asian contagion conspired with Japanese-specific events to seal the fate of Yamaichi and some smaller players as well. When Sanyo Securities collapsed, the government could not induce any other financial house to take it over, and so a new factor entered the Japanese body politic. Sanyo, being bankrupt, would default on its debt. This was unprecedented in Japan and had not been anticipated by international creditors, who immediately cut credit to other vulnerable Japanese companies.

Tagugin, Japan's tenth-largest bank, suffered a run on it—government too-big-to-fail assurances that the top 20 banks would be protected notwithstanding. Tagugin went to the short-term money markets to raise cash, its traditional lenders cut credit, and, at the 11th hour, the government persuaded North Pacific Bank, a regional group, to take it over.

Yamaichi was grouped in along with the other vulnerable companies. Its share price plummeted to ¥57, one-tenth of the January 1997 value, Moody's downgraded their debt to junk-bond status and, as a consequence, the international community lost confidence in it. Fuji Bank, Yamaichi's traditional ally, refused to bail it out and the government's unwillingness to assume Yamaichi's ¥260 billion losses ensured its liquidation.

Yamaichi's collapse and the refusal of both the government and the Fuji-led Fuyo corporate family to rescue it had a swift impact on the markets. The share price of Japan's other banks and brokers plunged, credit lines were cut, overnight rates shot up. The Japan "premium"—the cost Japanese banks had to pay to borrow money compared with American counterparts—doubled. This reflects the financial world's decline in confidence in Japan. Though Japan's banks are among the world's biggest, and though they are in the world's largest creditor nation, they are being charged a risk premium when they borrow money internationally. Previously, the MOF's guarantees had effectively underwritten them. Now that that has been removed, the premium has soared. Clearly, beneath the pomp, there is still much to be done to achieve the holy grail of free, fair, and global markets.

Yamaichi's collapse was due as much to the purging of its senior management by the MOF and the public prosecutor as to anything else. And following right on the heels of the bankruptcy of second-tier Sanyo Securities, Yamaichi's demise brings on with a vengeance the much heralded consolidation of an industry already facing the end of fixed commissions by the year 2000; an industry in which Japan's Big Four traditionally handled over one-third of all transactions, while 228 small firms employing some 60,000 people split the rest.

When, as with Yamaichi, JFIs have bankrupted, the liabilities of failed companies have nearly always vastly exceeded disclosed figures. Bad loans at Sanyo Securities turned out to be ¥220 billion against the ¥80 billion previously admitted, following the discovery of 14 affiliated companies not listed in the accounts. Similarly, it was the admission by Yamaichi of ¥264 billion worth of losses on hidden off-balance-sheet tobashi-style deals that ultimately sealed its fate. Yet, there had been two prior government inspections at Yamaichi, neither of which had uncovered such misdeeds, even though, as in the LTCB case, pointed rumors had been circulating through the industry for at least the previous six years.

Japan's poor disclosure rules compound the problems of market thinness. Although, for example, Yamaichi was rumored to have tobashi losses long before they were officially acknowledged, the government blamed share-price falls in Yamaichi, Yasuda Trust, and other ailing companies on planted rumors, instead of on the fact that the volatility of thin markets breed rumors.

Many more brokers should fail as the Big Bang unfurls. The brokers most at risk are groups with unhealthy capital bases, weakened by poor profits caused in part by low volumes on the TSE. Five of the second-tier brokers have had six years of consecutive losses.

Recent heavy falls in share prices have highlighted those most vulnerable. They include New Japan Securities, Kankaku Securities, Okasan Securities, Yamatane Securities, Cosmo Securities, Tokyo Securities, National Securities, and Dai-Ichi Securities.

Critical to their future will be the position taken by their affiliated banks. Even though Fuji Bank was Yamaichi's biggest shareholder, it effectively abandoned it. By contrast, IBJ has indicated that it intends to support its affiliated brokers, New Japan and Wako. IBJ said that it would extend new subordinated loans to New Japan. DKB indicated it would support Kankaku. The question is whether the markets can or should believe this. There are, after all, too many cases recorded in this tome of JFIs telling what amount to barefaced lies.

The surviving Japanese brokers have lost much of their market share as a consequence of these scandals. Japan's largest 20 foreign brokers now have a combined share of almost 30% of the Tokyo Stock Exchange, a percentage share unthinkable even two years ago.

The foreigners are also acquiring business that would have been unthinkable until recently. Nichiei, one of Japan's largest nonbank finance companies, recently sold at least $470 million worth of shares to American and European investors in the largest international offering ever made by a Japanese company. Nichiei decided to target international investors alone and not issue in Japanese markets at all. The rare move by a Japanese company reflects the advances that foreign investment banks are making in Japan: the Nichiei offering, which was lead-managed by Union Bank of Switzerland, was the first Japanese equity offering to have been managed by a non-Japanese group. Again, this would have been unthinkable until very recently. The vast placement power of the Japanese securities houses is, in other words, being gradually supplanted by ethical considerations. Chapter five will explore these issues more in the important pensions and insurance industries.

[1] The Economist, Japanese Finance Survey, December 8, 1990, p. 3.

[2] Golden Week, which lasts from April 29 to May 5, is one of the peak holiday seasons in the Japanese calendar.

[3] Ms. Onoue was in fact an aged spinster at the time. However, as "spinster" has become a pejorative word, I prefer the use of "granny" to symbolize IBJ's ineptitude. That said, IBJ should have been spinster-proof as well.

[4] The Big Four broking houses of Nomura, Daiwa, Yamaichi, and Nikko traditionally controlled most of Japan's broking business. Because Yamaichi has now bankrupted, we also speak of the Big Three of Nomura, Daiwa, and Nikko.

[5] Japanese banks are allowed to count some 45% of the value of their unrealized gains as "capital" for the BIS ratio, the standard measure of financial viability. Thus, their recent $20 billion fall in unrealized gains from this source, when coupled with their property losses, lowers the BIS ratio considerably.

[6] This is almost two-thirds the equivalent American number and is larger than the combined equivalent numbers for Germany and France.

[7] Subsequent chapters discuss the consequences of LTCB's nationalization on this important deal.

[8] Inheritance tax rates top 70% on estates worth over $15,000,000.

[9] Although the terms "insurance" and "assurance" are often used interchangeably in the United States, there is a difference between the two. Assurance companies tend to concentrate on paying sums on certain events such as death. Insurance companies, in contrast, tend to concentrate on uncertain events such as accidents and other randomly occurring but potentially financially crippling events.

[10] The Tokyo market is so thin that the Ministry of Finance believes that planted rumors can drive the market. During the turmoil of late 1997, the MOF instructed the Securities and Exchange Surveillance Commission, the financial watchdog, to probe whether banks' and brokers' shares were affected by market players placing rumors. The loss in investor confidence from the government trying to control ephemeral rumors is typical of thin markets.

[11] Hokkaido Takushoku, a leading bank, and Sanyo Securities, the seventh-largest broker, also closed within the same month.

Land of the Rising Liabilities

Japanese life tables make depressing reading. Japan's population of some 126 million is growing at a miserable rate of 0.25% annually. Japan has both the highest life expectancy in the world and the most rapidly aging population in world history. Japan already has the second-oldest population in the Organization for Economic Cooperation and Development (OECD); falling fertility rates and rising mortality rates guarantee that by 2025 Japan will have the world's oldest OECD population. The dependency ratio could then hit 56%, putting an almost intolerable strain on the working taxpayer.

In 1990, for every 100 working-age Japanese adults, there were 31 retirees. By 2025-far too soon for even a sudden and improbable rise in the birthrate to make any discernible difference-that number will rise to 61, a ratio worse than that of any other major industrialized country except Germany, and far above the anticipated 49 in the United States.

During the postwar baby boom, there were 2.7 million births annually in Japan. Today, the figure is less than 1.2 million. In 1950, Japanese women gave birth to an average of 3.65 babies. It stabilized at just over 2.1 until 1975, when it sank to 1.91. It has been falling ever since and is now less than 1.42. Today, the average Japanese woman has only 1.4 children, compared with the American equivalent of 2.1 While there will be three workers per retiree in America in 2010, there will be almost a one-to-one match in Japan. Among industrial countries, only Germany and Italy currently have lower rates than Japan. The shrinking of the younger population will make the growing taxation and social security burden that much heavier. Thus, although Germany, Italy, the Netherlands, and Japan face the most apocalyptic demographic trends among developed nations, Japan is well behind in terms of funded pension systems.

Japan has a demographic and social welfare nightmare. The old-age dependency ratio, i.e., the number of people over 65 as a percentage of those of working age (15-65), will rise from 22% at present to 47% by the year 2030.[1] Proper provisions have not been made to fund the graying of Japan. Because public pension liabilities are over 110% of GDP and Japan's specific birth rate of 1.46 is significantly lower than the 2.1 needed to maintain the current population, meeting rising future pension contingencies will curtail expenditures elsewhere.

The share of those 65 and over reached 7% of the population in 1970. It exceeded 14% just 24 years later, in 1994. Most Western countries took at least 50 years to see the share double from 7% to 14%; in the case of Sweden, it took 120 years. The number of elderly people will continue growing by an average of at least 600,000 a year through 2025. That means there will be more than 36 million elderly Japanese in 25 years' time. Amazingly, to Western observers at least, the MOF has not made any worthwhile provisions for these changes.

Pensions—36 million pensions—must be paid to these folk. And because elderly people need greater medical care than younger people, their growing numbers mean higher medical bills for the nation as a whole. Under the present health insurance system, patients do not pay the entire bill. Most of the costs are paid with taxes and health insurance premiums. If the number of younger people who pay the taxes and premiums were also rising, the problem could be addressed with a larger probability of success. But like other industrial countries, Japan has a declining birthrate. Hers is falling faster than any other country's. Japan, the Japanese have decided, is just too expensive a place to have and raise children in.

Japan's shrinking workforce, her rapidly expanding aged population, and the JFIs' pathetic returns will put relentless pressure on her pension-funding system and on her workers. The number of beneficiaries is fast approaching the number of contributors. So far, the government's stop-gap measures have included raising the retirement age from 60 to 65 and increasing the contribution rate for employee pension insurance from 14% to 16.5% of monthly salaries, with plans to raise it to 29.6% by 2025-nearly double the current rate in other words.

To deal with the looming crisis, Japanese policymakers are tinkering with their system, embroidering onto its cuffs the semblance of reforms. Employee and employer contributions to pension schemes will double from 15% to 30% of earnings by 2020. Starting in 2000, the retirement age will be raised from 60 to 65. Benefits will be indexed to "net" earnings-after payment of social security taxes. This tinkering is, to use a cliche, much too little and much too late. Quite bluntly, not enough is being done.

Japan's pension system is not geared to even begin to cope with the looming crisis. The Japanese authorities, phlegmatic as ever, believe the nation's high savings rate will, as if by magic, solve this dilemma. Although the Japanese government is not panicking, the OECD is. It believes that rising Japanese pension expenditures will result in a budget deficit-to-GDP ratio of almost 20% by 2030, much higher than the nearly 13% projected for Italy, the world's next worst case.

Because of the time lags in changing people's expectations, the Japanese government has to get cracking on this problem immediately. That being so, the starting point has to be the separation of medical and pension benefits, which are kept together so that the MOF can siphon off funds into its pet projects. Such separations were completed decades ago in the West. Such a separation in Japan would bring in the thorny question of investment returns which, even by Japan's abysmal standards, have been dire. Combining the two simply allows the medical benefits part to be used as a fig leaf to cover up the fact that pension contributions are not being used to boost pension funds but are being used instead for short-term political expediencies.

Returns will most likely fall even further. Increases in Japanese social security pension expenditures plus larger health-care payments also related to aging populations—and the growing cost of debt servicing—will lead to enormous increases in net public debt levels in the early decades of the next century. According to OECD projections, Japanese net public debt will grow more than 12-fold, from 25% of GDP in 2000 to 315% in 2030. Though starting from a lower base, Japanese net debt will be more than three times its American, German, or French equivalents-and, lest we forget, three times Japan's GDP. This will inject huge intergenerational and other tensions into the fabric of Japanese society.

Pensions and insurance take the lion's share of Japanese social security spending. Slightly more than half of the total amount spent on social security in Japan goes to public pensions. A further 40% is spent on the public health insurance system. The remaining 10% provides the balance of social security services, including care for the elderly, welfare for the disabled and children, and unemployment insurance. Japanese social security spending is a growing black hole, which gives little comparative returns to those forced to pay into it.

The Japanese public pay 16% of their income to keep their social security system going. The burden of taxes and social security on the Japanese people exceeds 37% of their income-16% for social security and 21% for other public services. Therefore, individuals and enterprises have 63% of their income at their disposal. The government says that social security expenses, which are now 16% of national income, will rise to 30% by 2025. When combined with spending for other public services, the total burden will be equivalent to 60%. If the burden rises to 60%, individuals and companies will be able to spend only 40% of their income. If this happens, the private sector will lose its vitality. If the private sector loses its vitality, it will negate fiscal policy as a tool of boosting the economy. A deflated, aging economy with increasing demands on the public bourse is a doomsday scenario.

Even if social security payments increase, they would not be a heavy burden were the economy to grow in tandem with it. For instance, a 6% growth in social security spending could be easily offset if national income also were to grow by 6%. Japan, alas, will be lucky to achieve growth rates of 2% over the coming decades. Japan's growing fiscal deficit of more than ¥450 trillion between national and local governments also has to paid from taxes. Thus, even as the dependency ratio increases and the number of taxpayers decreases, overall taxes will have to increase. It is a doomsday scenario.

Although fiscal tightening, cutting overall social security spending, retrenching government workers and the like would put a dent in this figure, some fields of services will have to be expanded. For example, more money must be spent to care for elderly people who are bedridden or senile.

This is particularly problematic in Japan, whose already high bedridden population of 1,200,000 is expected to reach 2,300,000 by 2025. This problem could be alleviated if the Japanese government could somehow rejuvenate its growing legions of old folk. When we consider that Japanese patients tend to stay in hospitals much longer than their European or American equivalents, this seems unlikely. The average Japanese hospital stay is a 35-day marathon as against the more pragmatic 11-day average in the West. Nursing expenditures constitute 11% of social security expenses other than pensions or medical costs. Though this small share was sufficient in the past, it is now too little to service the growing number of elderly people needing care: about one in every ten elderly people. Many new nursing homes will need to be built to care for this growing voting lobby, and more health workers will have to be trained to look after the elderly people who choose to remain at home. This will need further taxes.

As the cost of caring for elderly people increases, the financial burden on the public at large will also increase. Therefore, social security expenses in other areas will have to be lowered. And the cuts will have to come from both pensions and medical expenses.

Japan is thinking about privatizing the Japanese pension system, which would indirectly mean putting public money into private stocks. The MOF currently prohibits investing public money in private stocks. Instead, it is continuing its past policies of using pension funds to fund the economy and to fund targeted industrial sectors at the expense of retirees, current and future.

The MOF manage the Nenpuku, the Pension Welfare Service Corporation Fund, on behalf of the Ministry of Health and Welfare (MHW). It had cumulative losses of ¥700 billion in 1995. Not an impressive record but one these buffoons, secure in their own retirement packages, can live with. The MHW does not want to live with it. They have objected to public pension funds being used by the MOF to prop up the stock market. It wants these funds to be handled as they are in Britain and the United States, in the interests of the policyholders, not in the national interest as determined by the MOF. The MHW's views conflict with several leading members of the ruling Liberal Democratic Party who still continue to urge using public pension funds to prop up stock prices for bank solvency reasons. They also conflict with the MOF's Trust Fund Bureau, which uses most of the monies for the government's loan and investment program.

Indeed, before moving on to the Fiscal Investment and Loan Program (FILP), now is probably a good time to summarize some of the main ways the MOF has damaged the industry. The MOF, through the funds it controlled, pumped public funds into the market at its peak and cajoled the insurance companies to throw their funds in as well. It pumped in national pension funds, national insurance funds, and funds from the postal life insurance system. All in all, the MOF squandered as much as $15 trillion in public sector funds in this way. These funds should have been prudently invested, not punted, without consultation or accountability, on the market by MOF generalists in such a cavalier fashion. Mrs. Watanabe and the other Japanese savers could have bought in stocks either directly or through a mutual fund, if such was their desire. They certainly didn't need the MOF to squander it away for them.

The MOF also colluded with the JFIs in hiding their losses. It gave life insurance companies a special exemption from declaring losses on foreign exchange; it pardoned regional banks from disclosing bad debts; trust banks were allowed flexibility in reporting defaulting borrowers.

The ¥350 trillion FILP, the Zaito, is, in fact, the MOF's greatest source of revenue and, despite the considerable competition, it should be their greatest source of shame. The FILP employs postal savings and public pension insurance premiums to fund a potpourri of policy objectives, including social and economic development and public welfare improvements. Return on investment does not figure: a nominal return, camouflaged in quasi-patriotic MOF gob-bledygook, is paid instead.

Although the FILP differs from government borrowing through bonds in that the future repayment comes not from tax revenues but from fund repayments by the enterprises that receive the funding, it smacks of just another fund-raising dodge of no direct benefit to those who have their funds hijacked in this way.

Although the MOF admits that the FILP is, in essence, a means to implement fiscal policies with financial instruments, they see it as being fair and reasonable. Although it may be so with respect to the 57% of the total commandeered from postal savings accounts, it is decidedly unfair to the 31% commandeered from pension funds. FILP also borrows and invests these commandeered funds in low-risk, pitiably low-return investments, such as Japanese government bonds, loan trusts, financial institution deposits, and Shiteitan, funds that are drawn from the Postal Life Insurance Corporation and managed by designated advisors.[2] None of these gives any prospect of providing positive real returns: they can barely manage positive nominal returns after all. Though safe, they are the sorriest of investments. Though they may aid the lofty intentions of the MOF, their meager returns do not serve the interests of the pensioners who own the press-ganged funds. They are fleecing future taxpayers to pay for the MOF's multitudinous mistakes.

Pensions are, in short, currently another tax-levying mechanism. Although contributions are hefty, investment performance is paltry. So too is governance. Short-term benefits and long-term benefits are combined with an eclectic bunch of payments to TB suf-ferers, newlyweds, and the like. The result is that Japanese pensions are mismanaged, misgoverned, underperforming, and underfunded. Because Japan's life assurers cannot even meet the guaranteed returns they promised, foreign-managed funds are thriving.

The issue of equity in pensions has to be addressed. This is most obvious in the case of foreign workers who are denied their pension rights. Payments are capped at a maximum of three months' salary for those who have worked in Japan for less than twenty-five years: the government pockets the remainder-and, to add further insult, taxes the three months' payback as well. The extra contributions—

8.25% of 23 years' salary from both employer and employee—go into the government's coffers, to be used as the government sees fit. The government justifies this inequity by saying that, as most foreigners stay for three years or less in Japan, those who stay for longer than three years should be penalized in the national interest. When Western countries are making their pension systems internationally portable and concentrating on defined benefits, foreigners in Japan cannot even get their contributions refunded.

The Japanese themselves are also shabbily treated. The aging population, coupled with misguided governance directives, has left many corporate pension funds seriously underfunded. Though the proportion of private-sector workers covered by corporate schemes is similar to Britain and the United States, their assets are only a seventh of the size. Even worse, many small employee-pension schemes have collapsed in recent years. These include a pension scheme run by the National Rice Dealers Association. Significantly, this was the first such industry association to fold.

Their plan was typical in its lack of strategic planning. Like most others, it could succeed only when the Japanese markets were increasing. The scheme started in 1978 by offering two different forms of pension plans. One was a normal defined contribution plan where the member paid a defined monthly contribution. The other scheme was a relay scheme whereby a pair of rice dealers, usually a father-and-son combination, would make joint contributions. The older partner would get a lump sum on retirement and hand his membership over to a younger member.

The scheme worked well when membership was rising and Japanese investment instruments were yielding high returns. But deregulation has pushed many rice dealers out of business and investment returns have slumped because of the sluggish Tokyo market. To cope with shortfalls, the organizers asked retired members to return part of their money. This weird demand unsurprisingly provoked panic and fury

This problem is not confined to these companies. The pension schemes of the 25 Japanese companies that file American returns are all underfunded by 40% and more. Perversely, these underfunded companies would be strong by Japanese standards. Indeed, Japanese life companies have seen business fall as clients become increasingly uneasy about entrusting their funds to incompetent companies. Toho Mutual Life, for example, has seen its corporate pension business fall by over 60%.

When Tokyo Jitsugyo Kosei Nenkin Kikin, a corporate pension fund comprising 850 retailers and wholesalers, recently sued Kokusai Asset Management Co. for compensation of ¥2.8 billion, it was the first time a Japanese-based corporate pension fund sued for losses stemming from derivatives. They alleged that Kokusai Asset Management, part of the Kokusai Securities Co. group, invested mainly in Euroyen bonds involving high-risk derivatives, which significantly reduced their principal.

Many similar lawsuits might follow. Rates of return have been pathetic because of a falling market, primitive techniques, and a reluctance to sell underperforming shares in keiretsu-related companies. Self-serving government regulations further help to ensure their pitiful performance. The longstanding 5-3-3-2 rule, for example, meant that more than 50% of the portfolio had to be invested in principal-secured assets, less than 30% in securities, less than 30% in foreign assets, and 20% in real estate. Not surprisingly, with negligible interest rates, a collapsing yen, and falling stock and property markets, recent performances have been somewhat less than brilliant.

Despite its obvious need for the biggest of big bangs, the insurance business will stay protected until 2001, two years after banks and securities houses are fully deregulated. This is unfortunate as insurance deregulation is vital to handle the inevitable bankruptcies that are becoming ever more commonplace as the Big Bang gathers momentum.

In the insurance industry, only products approved by the MOF can be handled, and prices are essentially determined by two rating organizations. This hampers the emergence of the necessary new, efficient products and competitive spin-offs such innovations would bring. Because Japan's insurance advisory panels have shown little interest in getting input from foreign insurers, these bottlenecks will continue to exist and frustrate the rapid implementation of core changes on which the success of the Big Bang hinges.

Until recently, corporate pension funds in Japan were managed by only the life insurance companies and the trust banks. These were generally selected not by their performance but by their traditional ties, centered around the keiretsu business families. This pattern has now come under strain. Now, investment advisers (IAs) are being belatedly allowed to handle substantial blocks of public pension funds.

This is forcing, however belatedly, important structural change onto a most reluctant host. There was a partial relaxation of restrictions in 1995 which allowed the Pension Welfare Service Public Corporation (Nenpuku) and a broader range of Employee Pension Funds (EPFs) and Mutual Aid Associations (MAAs) to hire investment advisors. Returns were boosted as a result. The remaining regulations, which prevent or limit the ability of any type of investor to hire investment advisors, provide no benefit to the investor and are inconsistent with the objective of improving the return on the nation's pool of savings. In addition, public fund investors such as Camp and Yucca should be able to hire investment advisors in a straightforward manner rather than using unnecessarily complex means such as the offshore limited partnerships they are currently using.

The MOF generalists would have to have a complete change of heart and temperament before these and other necessary changes could be implemented. Modern pension and insurance fund management is a highly skilled, specialized vocation. Because it is unlikely that the MOF can acquire the necessary skills to understand let alone to regulate the industry in the near future, they should loosen their vise on the industry before it is too late.

Japanese pension funds' current rate of return is now well below their 5.5% target. Firms chasing market share, not return on equity, led to this and the ensuing catastrophic cash flow and profitability problems. Again, the foreign firms are benefiting from this mess. Nenpuko, Japan's large public sector fund manager, is now handing over 50% of its new business to foreign fund managers. Foreign groups now control over a third of this market. Most of Sony's pension funds are managed by Schroders and other foreign concerns. The larger firms are seeing the writing on the wall. They'd be blind not to.

Because they know perfectly well that taxes cannot possibly rise high enough to finance their retirement from public spending, Mrs. Watanabe and her friends, though less powerful, are becoming equally clearsighted. They intend to rely on their own savings. But because returns to savers are so dismally low, they can only guarantee their retirement by ratcheting up their savings even more-in other words, by cutting their spending. This creates a vicious circle of ever weaker domestic demand which delimits the efficacy of fiscal remedies to Japan's current problems.

The MHW is equally aware of these funding problems. Although social security insurance contributions, when split between individuals and their employers, total 34.3% of gross income, Japan's declining birth rate, increasing life expectancy, and continually falling interest rates are conspiring to create a growing shortfall. Given its multitudinous constraints, the MHW will have no viable option but to cut benefits even further. And Mrs. Watanabe will have to ratchet up her savings even more.

Thus, though the Japanese must necessarily remain compulsive savers, they are being severely shortchanged. The pool of personal financial assets in the United States is only 70% greater than Japan's, yet the American mutual fund industry is 1,000% larger than the investment industry in Japan. Japan's burdensome regulations and business practices, rather than the state of the markets, are responsible for this. As in other countries, major corporations that can afford to implement group insurance plans will thrive but the medium- and small-size corporations will have their economic woes compounded by increased contribution demands.

Japan's quirky system belongs to another era. The requirement that when assets are taken out of trust they must be converted into cash hinders the efficient management of pension assets. Current Japanese trust law requires that the trust bank liquidate the portfolio and return cash to the pension fund. This needlessly creates two sets of transaction costs.

This is only one example of the many binds that constrict the industry. Japan's investment trust industry is stagnating when its overseas counterparts are booming. For this industry to grow, the public's faith that these funds are managed fairly and efficiently must be restored. To achieve this, annual independent audits should be introduced to introduce openness, intra-keiretsu dealings should be curtailed to remove conflicts of interest; withholding taxes should be based on the individual investor's actual gains and losses, not on the average trust cost currently being used; and the MOF's approval or disapproval of new funds should be based only upon published laws or regulations, not on the MOF's euphemistically named administrative guidance.

Though this is obviously a tall order, it signifies the degree of change necessary to rescue Japan. This raises the question as to whether Japan's assurance and insurance companies are up to the job. The short answer is no.

Japan's mutual life assurers are the hidden factor in the current financial turbulence. The plummeting stock market has wiped out equity reserves at many Japanese financial companies. As leading shareholders in and lenders to most financial institutions, life assurers have also lost fortunes as those firms' prices fell. Their mutual status means only that their problems are less visible than those of the listed banks and brokers. Their vast investments, particularly in the financial sector, give them huge power

Japan is, in fact, the world's largest insurance market. Japanese premium insurance income was $640 billion in 1995, of which life assurance accounted for 82%. Japanese insurance companies are the biggest investors in the Nikkei. They own some 15% of it, compared with less than 10% for the commercial banks, the next biggest holders. They have been active overseas investors as well, accounting for over 60% of Japan's massive outflows during the 1990s. They have been the biggest losers in the current stock and property price rout.

Japan's total pension assets were valued at ¥200 trillion in 1994, a pool of money almost twice as large as the comparable collection of funds in the ten major European countries. Japan has ¥126 trillion in public pension monies. Trust banks and life insurers manage a further ¥68 trillion in pension funds, mostly from the corporate sector. Less than 1% of Japan's pension money is managed by investment advisory companies. Over half are controlled by MOF's Trust Fund Bureau. The rest are split between trust banks and life insurance companies.

Shielded from competition, their returns have been universally pathetic. The MOF's Trust Fund Bureau pays a negligible rate of return—close to the yield on government bonds, the lowest in world history. Traditionally, 15 insurance companies and trust banks essentially rigged prices between them. Much of their business was keiretsu-referred. Expertise and competence did not figure at all. Having set an agreed cash return of say 8%, they would then manufacture this return. Because assets are carried at book value, they could revalue their assets as it suited them.

In the end, it didn't suit the policyholders. Life insurers got over ¥2.5 trillion of pension funds to manage in 1991. They had about 40% of this business and won more market share from the trust banks who were their main competitors. They pooled their pension fund assets in their general accounts with their life insurance and other policies. Then, with the MOF's approval, they smoothed out their returns in the lean years by taking profits on shares that were bought a long time ago. Thus, long-standing owners of life insurance policies were made to subsidize new pension fund clients.

Trust funds by contrast cannot pool their managed pension funds in with other funds. Nor do they have the same depth of unrealized gains. When the insurance companies boosted their returns, the pension companies quite naturally switched to the insurance companies whose returns of 8% to 9% were much superior to the 1% the trust banks offered.

During the bubble period, their single-premium endowment policies, particularly their five-year lump-sum savings, proved extremely popular. They guaranteed well over 6% against the 3% the banks were offering. As a result they averaged over 20% annual growth during the 1980s. They are now experiencing net negative cash flow for the first time since 1945.

Since 1945, Japan's life insurance industry easily met its obligations on a cash flow basis thanks to regular annual double-digit asset growth. The money flowing into their general accounts in the form of premium and interest received has always been comfortably greater than the money paid out. The life insurance companies believed they could pay out the holders of single-premium endowment policies with the surpluses built up over the years on their conventional term-life insurance policies and pension funds, which are pooled together in their general accounts.

Life insurance companies set up special tokkin accounts to gamble on short-term stock fluctuations. These did well until the Nikkei plunged. To revive the ailing stock market, the MOF allowed the insurance companies to put over 5% of their total assets into tokkin. The tokkin allowed the life insurance companies to convert capital gains into income free of tax and so pay policyholders out of the proceeds. Because Japanese law says that life insurance companies can pay policyholders only from income, not from capital gains, this was a useful trade-off for the insurance companies, who naturally thought that they could quickly recoup their losses when the Nikkei bounced back. Far from bouncing back, the Nikkei has continued to slide. Once it reaches 12,500, all their capital gains will be wiped out.

Life insurance companies also got into high-yielding overseas investments. The insurance companies accounted for some 60% of Japan's capital outflow during the 1990s into United States bonds, property, and related areas. They ignored the risk of loss: they had a huge portfolio of unrealized capital gains from the shares they held in their general accounts. They figured that any currency loss could be offset by domestic stock and property gains.

How wrong they were. From 1985 to 1995, JFIs lost over $500 billion in foreign exchange. The life insurance companies lost most of this. Their negative spreads and consequent losses grew as the MOF kept interest rates down to help the banks. They couldn't even meet their guaranteed yields. Although the Pension Fund Association, representing millions of workers, objected to this, the MOF pontificated that, regardless of past promises, the life insurance industry would have to renege on its commitments. No one was held to account for this blatant shortchanging of Japan's workforce.

Despite their mammoth losses, 15 of Japan's 16 major life insurance companies claim that their solvency margin is above the crucial 200% level. The solvency margin is an indicator of a life insurer's financial strength. When it falls far below 200%, financial authorities can order the insurer to restructure its operations. Toho

Mutual Life Insurance was the sole exception, recently posting a solvency margin of 154.3%. Seven leading life insurers recorded margins of more than 400%. Chiyoda Mutual Life Insurance and some midsize companies claimed margins of around 300%. Daido Mutual Life Insurance claimed a margin in excess of 1000%.

Although these figures are most likely colored by Japan's lax accountancy standards, some facts are irrefutable. Their assets are relatively illiquid property and nonperforming Japanese shares. Their liabilities, endowment policies and the like, are easy to surrender. Therefore, their dubious ratios notwithstanding, they have underlying difficulties they must address.

Their own considerable difficulties may, paradoxically, possibly be a major catalyst for change: the refusal of a group of nine life assurers to roll over subordinated loans to Sanyo made its capital fall below acceptable levels and it had to file for bankruptcy when no government help was forthcoming.

The unprecedented failure in April 1997 of Nissan Mutual, a medium-size life assurer, sent a shock wave through the insurance sector and weakened the confidence of policyholders in all Japanese firms. Policy cancellation rates have since been running at record levels and as the insurers have few reserves—after years of paying out higher returns to policyholders than they were getting on their own investments—they have had to sell assets to refund the policies. This has further undermined the weak Japanese stock market. The collapse of Nissan Mutual has also forced the insurers to rethink their investment strategies and lending exposures.

Neither actuarial calculations nor other professional yardsticks have been at the core of Japanese insurance companies. Their problems are due in large part to the traditional habits of cementing business ties with shareholdings. Insurers bought shares in client companies to ensure a steady flow of business. But when the companies hit their bubble-related difficulties, the insurers were the first to be drained for more funds. Demand for easy loans escalated, leaving insurance companies deciding if and when to say no to further outlays, and thus to endanger their existing exposure.

The insurers' keiretsu-related problems are compounded by a profound tactical bind: they cannot abandon too many stricken affiliated companies too quickly as that would usher in a torrent of bankruptcies, with consequent pessimistic ramifications.

Japan's leading life assurers have, in fact, dangerously high amounts of problem loans. Yasuda Mutual, part of the Fuyo group, which includes the struggling Yasuda Trust Bank[3] and which has links with the collapsed Yamaichi Securities, has seen problem loans increase by 62% in 1997. Nippon Life, the market leader, has seen a 55% increase to over $1 billion. Nippon Life has, in fact, decided to curb subordinated lending to Japanese banks and brokers because of a perceived growing credit risk. This more rigorous approach to credit risk was triggered by concern that loans would not be repaid if more Japanese banks or brokers failed.

The combined value of individual life insurance products for the seven largest insurers decreased in fiscal 1997, for the first time since 1945. The prolonged low-interest policy has hurt them hard. While it helps banks offset their bad loans, the negative spread between promised yield for policyholders and actual investment return continues to squeeze the insurers.

The assurers are suffering from lower premium income and policy cancellations, as well as the long-standing problem of fixed yields to policyholders being higher than yields available on Japanese stocks and bonds. They are paying out much more than they have coming in.

As the dust of recent disasters settles, there are signs of growing differentiation between the stronger companies and the weaker ones. Even though the whole industry has suffered, consumer policy cancellations have been much higher at the weaker ones. Further bank and brokerage collapses will further accelerate this process of differentiation. It will be a radically transformed industry that will emerge at the far side of the Big Bang.

As in the rest of the financial sector, Japanese insurance companies owe their preeminence in large part to the exclusive franchise the MOF gave them. They benefited from the MOF's restrictive licensing regime that kept out competition. Now the Big Bang is posed to put them in head-to-head competition with foreign concerns.

In trying to pick up the pieces of the Japanese insurance industry and reshape them for the challenges ahead, the MOF is up to its old tricks. The Japanese government is proposing a Payment Guarantee System as a replacement for their current policyholder protection fund. In Britain, the United States, and similar countries, insurance companies contribute to a designated fund. The broad purpose of such policyholder protection or guarantee funds is the maintenance of confidence in the insurance industry in the face of unforeseen and unforeseeable contingencies. Companies contribute in proportion to the riskiness of the business they are involved in: those in riskier areas contribute proportionately more and are not cross-subsidized by those in less-risky sectors.

Although the Japan Securities Dealers Association and similar organizations support these cross-subsidization proposals, opposition to them is strident and vocal. Some 23 Japanese securities companies have set up their own investor-protection fund, and a consortium of 37 foreign brokerages have begun preparations to establish a similar fund of their own. These moves anticipate the introduction of the MOF-brokered Investor Protection Fund, which would be financed by the brokerage groups, and which would be the securities industry's version of the banking industry's Deposit Insurance Corporation. More importantly for our purposes, these unilateral moves show the deep distrust of the government sector so evidently widespread in the JFIs and their foreign equivalents.

If Japan wishes to adopt Anglo-American global standards, then, clearly, the payment guarantee system should be preceded by clear measures that allow and encourage the sound and responsible financial management of insurance companies: this, in itself, would be a major change from the past. In order to assure stronger companies that the creation of a guarantee fund will not create undue cross-subsidization type costs for their policyholders, the payment guarantee system should be accompanied by appropriate measures to promote global-standard business practices industry-wide.

Critical attributes of a regulatory structure that promote such global standard business practices in Japan include variations on the same old theme: transparent and publicly available financial reports; well-defined minimum solvency standards with an early-warning system to promote levels of capitalization appropriate to risks; and the ability to freely design and price new products.

This is at variance with the current keiretsu-style system where allegiance to one's own convoy supersedes solvency standards, contingencies, early warning systems, and other norms of prudence, where the guaranteed business and market share the keiretsu guarantees obviate the need to design and properly price new products, and where the ubiquitous MOF underwrites the stability of the system. Clearly, there is a long way to go.

If Anglo-American global standards are to be adopted, it is imperative that guarantee assessments do not inhibit the growth of energetic new companies or the better-managed older firms. In other words, one can have competition, managed or otherwise, or one can have an MOF-dominated industry: one cannot have both.

If the proposed payment guarantee system is overly burdensome, it will discourage new entrants and innovators bringing their new products, services, and efficiencies to customers. In other words, if the market is to be free, fair, and global, the foreign insurance companies and other new entrants must be allowed to bring their new products and pricing mechanisms to the market in a free, fair, and expeditious way without the MOF causing undue delays to allow favored companies to replicate their innovations.

Because MOF intervention could, by such stalling tactics, prop up inefficient competitors and products, it would postpone the industry restructuring that is central to a successful Big Bang. To achieve real reform of the insurance industry, several steps, all of which involve an MOF volte-face, are necessary.

Real differentiation in product design is needed. Currently, the MOF ensures that prices are uniform in the nonlife insurance through the rating organizations and in life assurance through a tightly controlled approval process. The MOF's commitment to deregulate the primary sectors will not be met if the rating organizations are merely replaced by MOF-directed uniform prices. If market forces are to rule, the MOF must allow the more innovative foreign and domestic companies to capture market share with better-priced and better-designed products. They cannot hope to maintain their current exclusive franchise system and have meaningful market competition as well. Because exclusivity and market competition are the antithesis of each other, the MOF will only compound current problems unless it accepts the need to allow the players to bring their differently designed and packaged products to the market.

American critics of the MOF's lethargy are in something of a bind over this. Their insistence on a deregulation timetable has made them oppose Japan's plans to liberalize the lucrative third sector of specialty finance which the foreigners dominate. The third sector, which occupies a fuzzy area between primary life and non-life insurance categories in Japan, features products such as cancer, senile dementia, and nursing insurance. The restrictions which stop the Japanese companies operating in these areas were originally introduced when foreign companies began developing such products in the 1970s, when the Japanese had little if any interest in them. However, today's aging society has made these niche markets very lucrative. The Americans are trying to use their dominance in this market as a bargaining lever to make the Japanese open up the primary market.

Real differentiation in distribution is needed. If the global standard of universal banking is to prevail in Japan, the banks must be allowed to distribute all insurance products they see fit to distribute. Currently, the banks are limited to distributing two insurance products only, both of which are allowed to come only from subsidiary or related insurance companies. Because foreign insurers, from whom most innovation can be expected to come, do not have their own keiretsu networks, they must rely on alternative sales channels. Though allowing the banks to distribute the products of the foreign firms would lessen the market share of the larger Japanese companies, it would also open up the market to competitive forces, thereby benefiting all viable companies, both domestic and foreign. The longer the MOF delays opening up newer distributional channels, the longer the Big Bang's positive effects will be delayed.

Still, the Big Bang is creating its own momentum here as it is elsewhere. The Lawson convenience store network, which handles some 5.7 million customers daily, is now cooperating with Tokio Marine and Fire Insurance and other domestic and foreign life insurance firms to sell policies and other financial products at its 6,800 strategically placed convenience stores. The deal heralds more tie-ups between Japan's vast networks of convenience stores and those foreign financial institutions which, though eager to expand their Japanese business, have hitherto had too few retail outlets for their products. The Lawson and other chains are the perfect vehicle to break the cartel the JFIs have previously enjoyed.

Although the Japanese firms have declared themselves unperturbed to date by these innovations, they might become less phlegmatic in the future as the novel forces of price competition begin to bite. The foreign companies' aggressive marketeering strategies have, for example, netted ¥1.3 billion ($9 million) in car insurance premiums to American Home Assurance Co. and 400 million yen to Zurich Insurance Co.

The nonlife sector has been one of Japan's most tightly regulated industries, essentially a legalized cartel of 33 highly profitable companies. The United States, by contrast, has more than 3,000 nonlife insurers. Big Bang might very well upset this cozy apple cart. Until recently, for example, the Automobile Insurance Rating Organization of Japan set rates, which all insurers adopted. Now, price differentiation and American Home's and Zurich's aggressive marketing are changing the playing field-and attracting new players. Axa-UPA, France's largest insurance group, is preparing to expand into the Japanese nonlife insurance. Direct Line of Britain, the world's largest mail-order auto insurance company, is also poised to jump into the market. Things will no longer be as comfortable as they once were.

Real access to all insurance markets should be allowed. The MOF, in accordance with the keiretsu-based franchise system, has allowed domestic nonlife companies to perpetuate a profitable haven in the large commercial market, safe from competition with the new nonlife subsidiaries of life companies. Such major market distortions must be corrected if the MOF wishes the Japanese insurance industry to move into the modern age, let alone toward Anglo-American global standards.

These distortions damage the consumer as well. Under the Anglo-American system, large companies would simultaneously deal with many insurance companies, picking and choosing between them, in accordance with their particular needs and cost-pricing constraints. Under the keiretsu system, clients have the keiretsu-franchised insurance company foisted upon them, whether or not that company or that company's products and prices are appropriate for each and every one of their needs. If the Japanese government wishes to have a market meeting global standards, it should create a fiduciary obligation for employers to choose only the most appropriate products for their employees irrespective of keiretsu affiliations. Although this will loosen the keiretsu grip in the insurance industry in the short run, in the long run a healthier Japan will emerge.

Full disclosure of real financial strength is needed. Proper global standards for capitalization and surplus requirements, solvency margin requirements, early warning systems, and payment guarantee systems are needed. The tobashi system, shuffling bad debts between keiretsu-affiliated companies, and massaging solvency, subordinated loans, and other key liquidity margin and accountancy ratios to obscure the real financials of some of the weakest insurance companies are the antithesis of global disclosure standards. To create incentives for policyholders to select financially safe companies which avoid unnecessarily risky practices, a cap should be put on the guarantee to policyholders' benefits in the case of insolvency. This would be a great and intelligent leap forward the MOF is simply not prepared to sanction.

Despite the MOF's foot-dragging, the power of the market has its own momentum. GE Capital, the American group, is doing a joint venture with Toho Mutual, the life assurer. The $250 million company will have the largest capitalization of any listed life assurance company. Meiji Life Insurance Co., the oldest and the fourth-largest life insurer, is counting on its sound financial strength and its new alliance with Dresdner Bank to position itself to thrive in the fully deregulated market of 2001. Sony Life Insurance, a unit of Sony Corp., is gearing up to sell insurance in the Philippines in what marks a groundbreaking foray into Asia for a relatively new company. The life insurer aims to launch Philippine sales operations, with a staff of around 30 targeting wealthy clients in that country. The local unit will be capitalized at roughly ¥1.5 billion, with Sony and

Sony Philippine also holding stakes. So far, only Japan's largest life insurer, Nippon Life Insurance, has managed to establish a beachhead in a neighboring Asian market.

Big changes are also happening on the domestic front. With the number of new life insurance contracts declining and cancellations of existing contracts rising, Japanese companies cannot sustain their huge sales forces. Nippon Life Insurance has reduced its sales personnel from 74,000 to 64,000. Nonsales employees are also being retrenched.

Sales agencies are being drastically reduced at an astounding rate: over 30,000 a year. Japan currently has over half a million such agencies, much too many for the cutthroat competitive field that lies ahead. With the sole exception of Dowa Fire & Marine Insurance Company, all of Japan's 14 listed nonlife insurers have been laying off large numbers of workers. Dai-Tokyo Fire & Marine Insurance Company, for example, have eliminated more than 10,000, or 20%, of their total amount of agencies. Commissions are also being revised as the industry streamlines as part of the Big Bang. Yasuda Fire & Marine plans to give agencies that sell more policies higher payments than the rest. Although this would be considered mundane elsewhere, it is novel in Japan and augurs a greater professionalism.

Japanese housewives formed the backbone of the JFIs' sales staff. Their intensive networking was one of the main reasons Japan had the highest percentage of life insurance policyholders in the world. Just as in the banking sector, bulk and size was all-important. Now that the Big Bang is forcing change, these armies have to go. However, Daido Mutual Life Insurance and other, smaller, more innovative life insurers are actually increasing their sales staff to meet the demand their market-focused products have brought. Other nonlife insurance companies are now selling disaster-insurance policies tailored to the needs of individual customers. Current premiums can be cut by not having total coverage. Exempting typhoons, for example, would cut the premium by 10%.

The Big Bang is set to increase competition and players here too. The banks, for example, will be allowed to sell investment trusts directly to the public in schemes analogous to the pension plans

American banks operate. Foreign financial institutions with an edge in asset management and product development will gain market share.

The MOF and the Financial Supervisory Agency plan to sharply ease requirements to begin investment trust operations to stimulate the market by allowing nonfinancial firms to enter the sector. To begin an investment trust under the revised rules, companies must have capital of at least ¥100 million, a prospect to maintain net assets worth ¥100 million for three years after starting operations, a prospect to secure an annual profit in three years, and personnel with knowledge and experience in securities management. Formerly, companies that were not securities houses or overseas management firms had to have investment advisory firms as parent companies to set up investment trust firms. These parent companies were required to have a working balance of at least ¥300 billion. As a result of these constrictions, nonfinancial companies were virtually prevented from starting investment trusts.

Currently, Japan has some 54 investment trust companies. Of these, 13 are affiliated with securities houses and 24 are affiliates of foreign-owned firms while four are affiliated with life insurance companies and 13 are affiliates of banks. Bigger shakeouts should happen here as well.

Mitsui Trust & Banking's alliance with Prudential Insurance Co. of America reflects an ongoing trend of tie-ups between Japanese and foreign financial institutions seeking to capitalize on new opportunities in the Japanese market for investment trusts. Mitsui's merging its existing sales network with Prudential's global strength in asset management is a move designed to retain market share in Japan's ¥1.2-quadrillion pool.

As in the case of the Mitsui-Prudential collaboration, foreign financial institutions bring expertise in asset management and product development, while Japanese firms offer domestic sales networks for marketing investment trusts. Although IBJ and Nomura still dominate the industry, they now have formidable competition in Schroders, JP Morgan, Baring Asset Management, and Jardine Fleming. AIG and GE Capital are also expanding. AIG bought Nissan Mutual and GE Capital bought Toho Mutual. Although the foreigners, to revert to the sumo analogy used earlier, are the new players on the block, they do not feel hidebound by Japan's quirky etiquette. They are, here as elsewhere, the biggest harbingers of change.

The locals are well aware of these changing conditions. Japan's leading nonlife insurance companies have been strengthening group investment advisory units, aiming to move into pension fund and investment trust services as these markets grow. With the ban on sales of investment trusts by nonlife insurers gone, subsidiaries of Tokio Marine and Fire Insurance Co. and Yasuda Fire & Marine Insurance Co. have obtained government approval to enter the business. Yasuda Fire & Marine Global Asset Management Co. began selling investment trusts in July through a securities arm. Meanwhile, Sumitomo Bank and Daiwa Securities also have a joint venture afoot in the area.

This may not be enough. Japan's city banks want to directly enter the market. With the walls separating different financial services crumbling, the nation's nine city banks are looking to expand fullscale into new areas of business. Since 1993, eight city banks have established beachheads in the trust-banking field through subsidiaries. Daiwa Bank has been permitted for historical reasons to conduct trust-banking operations directly.

Until now, the city banks have called only for an easing of the rules separating operations of the parent bank and trust subsidiaries and a broadening of the range of permitted trust business. The need to cut the overheads in maintaining separate subsidiaries, computer systems, and personnel are now driving them to be given direct entry.

They are also eyeing the securitization market. They want to use their superior credit ratings to guarantee asset-backed securities that banks and companies issue with loan credits as collateral. This would allow companies to procure funds at lower interest rates with guarantees by nonlife insurance companies replacing guarantees by major banks, whose credit rates have fallen as the size of their bad loan problems become plain.

Tokio Marine & Fire Insurance has tied up with Financial Security Assurance of the United States to guarantee asset-backed securities. Tokio Marine finds companies wishing to issue such securities and it examines the loan credit to be securitized. The American firm markets the products to financial institutions and companies managing assets in the euro-markets. Yasuda Fire & Marine Insurance Co. guarantees issuance of bonds by Japanese companies in the euro-market via its London unit. Yasuda Fire has already guaranteed redemption of $300 million worth of asset-backed commercial paper, the sale of which will be managed by Fuji Bank's British securities subsidiary. Sumitomo Marine & Fire Insurance has guaranteed payment of principal and interest for ¥2 billion worth of asset-backed securities issued by SB Leasing with its lease credit as collateral. The nonlife insurer is also in charge of sales to investors. The interest rate for asset-backed securities with a three-month maturity period is set at 0.7%.

Yasuda Trust & Banking has tied up with Goldman Sachs to develop dollar-denominated money trusts for individual investors. Goldman Sachs manages the funds on behalf of Yasuda Trust's clients, with the principal guaranteed in dollars by Chase Manhattan Bank. About 20% to 30% of the fund is invested in foreign stock markets and is managed by Goldman Sachs Asset Management, with the rest being allocated to time deposits at foreign banks and other financial instruments for stable returns. The minimum investment in the five-year trusts is ¥500,000.

Other Japanese companies are trying to mitigate their own limitations. Nippon Fire & Marine Insurance, for example, is withdrawing from the investment advisory business. It has already surrendered the license of an affiliate to act as an advisor for discretionary investing. When it saw its funds under management slide from ¥40 billion in 1990 to about ¥25 billion in 1998, it decided to abandon its investment advisory affiliate and concentrate instead on its core business. This is despite the fact that Yasuda Fire & Marine Insurance and other nonlife firms are preparing to sell investment trusts through affiliates.

Yasuda Mutual Life Insurance, Mitsui Mutual Life Insurance, and several other major life insurers are considering transforming themselves into publicly traded companies to meet these challenges. Switching to a stock company structure will enable them to raise funds on the market, form capital ties with foreign firms, and establish holding companies.

Mutual companies are currently the norm in the life insurance industry. Although this makes the policyholders the company owners and entitles them to receive insurance payments and dividends based on premiums, mutual companies cannot raise funds by issuing shares, and must rely on premium income and subordinated loans. Although the ban on insurance firms publicly listing was lifted in 1996, the necessary procedures remain cumbersome and the rules are unclear.

Although the insurance companies have been less at fault than the banks, they clearly still have a long way to go. So too do the Japanese markets. The next chapter looks at the bond market, the most important of these.

[1] The dependency ratio must also take into account babies born into the future geriatric state. They must also be supported from the ravished public funds.

[2] The Shiteitan structure allows certain designated investment advisors to manage Japanese public pension funds. The poor performance of these funds has strengthened calls for the deregulation of this structure.

[3] Standard and Poor's downgraded Yasuda Trust Bank to junk-bond, noninvestment status in November 1997. This prompted a flood of customer withdrawals and a share-price plunge. Moody's rates a further four life assurers as high-risk. Moody's has radically downgraded Toho Mutual Life and Tokyo Mutual. Its downgrading helped to doom both LTCB and Nippon Credit Bank and it remains highly skeptical of Mitsui Trust, Yasuda Trust, and Chuo Trust among others. If Nippon and Chuo were further downgraded, they too would have junk-bond status. Moody's downgrading of Yamaichi to junk-bond status helped trigger its demise. Investors' reaction to Yasuda's changed status shows that Japanese credit rating is, albeit belatedly, conforming to Western norms. The Japanese MOF continuing to foolishly accuse international investors and credit rating agencies of being overly pessimistic on Japan is not.

The Japanese Bond Market

The Japanese bond market is the second-largest fixed income market in the world-second only to the U.S. Treasuries market. There is over ¥220 trillion of outstanding Japanese government bonds (JGBs). This amount is close behind the United States' $250 trillion and well ahead of third-place Italy's comparatively modest $900 billion.

Japan is currently raising some 25% of her total revenue through bond issuances; this is much higher than the 12%–15% range that typifies the United States and Germany. Japan's budget deficit is over 6% of GDP, up markedly from previous years. Although critics have warned that Japan's outstanding bond debt is getting too high to service, the Japanese government intends to borrow even more to pay its way through its ongoing crises.

This might not be as easy to do as they think. JGBs are no longer the attraction they once were. As recently as 1990, they gave a respectable yield of over 8%. Since then, the yen has plummeted, oil prices have deflated, government debt has doubled to over 100% of GDP, the private sector's debt is more than 200% of GDP, and recent financial packages have increased the money supply in circulation by over $600 million. The result is that Japanese bonds now give the lowest yields in recorded history—lower even than Genoa in the seventeenth century. Not only are they no longer so attractive; they are downright unattractive.

Though unattractive, they are quirky. Being quirky and being Japanese, they are under the thumb of the MOF and so have latent attractions for the favored few. There are four broad types of JGBs that cater to this large and quirky market. There are short-term treasury bills, first introduced in February 1986 with maturities up to one year and patterned, in a manner, after their American equivalents; medium-term bonds, both with and without coupons, with maturities of two, three, and four years, which are usually issued monthly; long-term 10-year, coupon-bearing, noncallable bonds, usually issued monthly; and superlong, 20-year coupon-bearing, noncallable bonds, issued three times a year.

Over 95% of all JGBs are sold in registered (book-entry) form and are cleared over an electronic payment system operated by the Bank of Japan. The remainder are bearer bonds. Because bearer bonds are less liquid than registered bonds, they carry a 5-basis-point liquidity risk premium in yield. Settlement takes place every fifth day, on the 5th, 10th, 15th, 25th, and last calendar day of each month. This noncontinuous settlement procedure produces a lag between the value date, the date on which the security is priced, and the settlement date, the date on which the transaction is cleared. Trades are settled on the settlement date that falls approximately two weeks after the value date. This period can last as long as 15 days and leads to considerable unnecessary speculation within the period. This is but one of the many quirks that make up the second-largest bond market in the world.

Although the market works through one single designated underwriting syndicate, consisting of 788 approved FIs, the majority of all JGBs are issued by public auction. After consulting with the syndicate, the MOF sets the issue size and the coupon rate for all JGB issues. The syndicate must purchase any JGBs that remain unsold after the auction. In this, Japan is typical of other markets.

However, in many other core areas it is atypical. Secondary market trading is illiquid in all issues except the benchmark bond. More than 90% of all trading is in the benchmark bond. The benchmark bond is a liquid bond issue, usually, though not always, the most recent issue, chosen by the big Japanese securities houses for their common characteristics: a coupon that is near the prevailing market rate, a large outstanding amount of at least ¥1.5 trillion, a wide distribution and a remaining maturity as close to 10 years as possible.

Because benchmark bonds are, by definition, bigger and more acceptable than others, they are more liquid and less risky. Because they are less risky, their yield is obviously lower than the non-benchmark issues. Not only is this much higher than in other countries, but it often jumps to 100 basis points or more. This huge differential is because, though the JGB market is the second-biggest in the world, it remains a thin market, hostage to the vagaries of the MOF as much as to market forces.

Another characteristic of the JGB market that diverges from other financial market practices is the reverse coupon effect. When two JGBs have the same maturity, the one with the higher coupon will generally carry a lower yield (and therefore a higher price) than the JGB with the lower coupon. This is unusual. Since higher-coupon bonds have greater reinvestment risk exposure, they should offer a higher risk-adjusted yield than equivalent lower coupon bonds. This seems irrational.

However, it also seems quintessentially Japanese. Japanese regulations foster a perverse demand for current income as the Japanese insurance companies illustrate. They are not allowed to pay their policyholders dividends that exceed their receipts of dividends and interest income. By investing in high-coupon JGBs, the insurance companies can circumvent these regulatory restrictions on their payout policies, so as to compete with other Japanese and non-Japanese FIs which offer more realistic returns. This leads to a clientele effect in JGBs and other non-Japanese bond markets in which Japanese FIs prefer to invest in high-coupon as opposed to lower-coupon issues. They pervert the market—and unnecessarily skew and complicate the pricing of these bonds.

The Japanese government bond market is burdened by a host of unnecessary and costly regulations. Wartime measures, designed to cement the MOF's control by licensing certain bond market investors-primarily domestic banks and insurance companies—and imposing withholding tax on coupon payments to everybody else, continue to prevent the emergence of a unified bond market. Since the efficiency of the JGB market directly affects the cost at which the government is able to access funds, reform of the JGB market is of immediate interest to every Japanese taxpayer-and to the ubiquitous MOF.

The existence of the securities transfer tax, for example, is a significant impediment to all transactions in securities and significantly impedes the revitalization of Japan's securities markets. The dramatic negative impact of this tax is nowhere more evident than in the market for JGBs for all maturities where the bid/offer spreads are very narrow. The higher tax imposed on transactions between onshore and offshore investors also distorts and encourages more dealing in the offshore market.

As if that weren't bad enough, even the core products are badly designed. The five-year JGB futures contract, for example, was initiated in 1997. However, there is no new issue of five-year fixed-income JGBs in the Japanese market. Since the only JGBs are 10-year JGBs which have a small issue size and are illiquid because they are often held by domestic individuals as well as institutional investors, the trading volume of the five-year JGB futures contract has been only nominal since the commencement of its trading in February 1997.

This MOF maneuver seems self-defeating. The simple fact at the root of their problems is that they cannot serve two masters. They cannot, on the one hand, advocate free, fair, and open markets and, on the other, continue to load the markets in favor of their allies. One is the antithesis of the other.

One would have thought that a sine qua non for achieving the Big Bang's objectives of fostering a free, fair, and global market would be that government bonds would be at the very least sovereign, not beholden to any vested interest. Such, alas, is not the case. The absence of JGB cash products is due to political pressure from Japanese financial institutions that are currently franchised to issue five-year fixed-income securities. To avoid conflict with the five-year products of these institutions, the MOF does not issue five-year fixed-income JGBs. As a result, the Japanese JGB market lacks a five-year benchmark issue. This shortsighted favoritism is inconsistent with the level playing field philosophy behind the Big Bang reforms or, indeed, with plain common sense for that matter. The fact that it increases the Japanese government's cost of borrowing does not seem to faze the MOF generalists.

Still, the Big Bang reforms are biting. The government plans to further liberalize the government's short-term securities market to make it more transparent and attractive to foreign investors. They intend to introduce open, competitive auctions for their financing bills (FBs), their two-month government securities. These financing bills are used by the MOF to raise funds for such things as foreign exchange market intervention or to fill temporary budget gaps.

Although these plans are, in large part, a response to American pressure, they are also the logical consequence of previous liberalizations. The ¥14,000 billion treasury bill market already has been substantially liberalized. Prices are set twice weekly through competitive auctions. Non-Japanese concerns hold about two-thirds of all of these bills. However, because the financial bill interest rate is only very marginally below the official discount rate, private buyers are not interested in them. Because the BOJ is legally compelled to buy any unsold FBs, they hold almost all of the bills currently extant. Clearly, there is much room for improvement here.

So much could be done here if the MOF were to use the least bit of common sense. If the Japanese government issued five-year fixed-income JGBs to create a benchmark for mid-term fixed income securities, it would kick-start trading in the five-year JGB futures contract. Furthermore, it would also increase the liquidity of the JGB market and allow the Japanese government to finance at a significantly cheaper cost, something the MOF should be concerned about.

Although five-year zero-coupon JGBs exist, they are subject to 18% withholding tax which is added on to the issue price. Accordingly, the five-year zero coupon JGB serves as a tax-advantaged savings vehicle for high-tax-bracket individual investors but not for portfolio investments of institutional investors. By effectively acting as a tax on syndicate participants, this does not help the JGB market. Because they cannot purchase the shorter-term JGB bills and because of the tax quirks, individual investors tend to dominate these medium-term bond markets and, since they tend to buy and hold, the medium-term market is quite illiquid.[1] Because this does not serve the interests of the government, they would be advised to issue five-year fixed-income JGBs and reform the five-year zero coupon bonds at the same time in a mini-bang. The current thin, tax-driven market ultimately serves no one's interests.

Their product choice lags far behind Western markets. Strips, separate trading of registered interest and principal of securities, are now a key feature of European and American markets. These instruments unbundle the interest and principal parts of an instrument and sell them to different clienteles. Thus, for example, a three-year bond, with coupons being paid half-yearly, would be unbundled into seven zero-coupon bonds. The principal would be a three-year zero-coupon bond. The six coupon payments would be zero-coupon bonds with maturities ranging from six months to three years. Such stripping has increased the liquidity of British and American bonds: they are one of their major innovations of the last decades. They increase the products available, from one to seven in the above example. Increasing the choice increases the customer base. Increasing the customer base lowers the average cost. Lowering the average cost increases the customer base still further. That is the essence of a Big Bang. That is the logical way Britain went about her Big Bang.

The Japanese way, quirky as ever, is different. No strippable JGB has ever been issued in the Japanese market. This lack of an active JGB market has needlessly increased borrowing costs for the Japanese government.

And things get quirkier. Japanese government bonds continue to be issued with a call provision, which is extraordinary for a sovereign issuer in the world's second-largest economy. Such call provision permits the Japanese government to require early redemption of these obligations. This option to refinance if interest rates fell would make sense for a cash-strapped country such as Mali, Malawi, Benin, Burkina Faso, or Rwanda. But Japan?

Because investors will naturally demand compensation for the risk of being subjected to a call, bonds that are subject to call provisions quite naturally generally trade at significantly higher yields than bonds without such provisions. Quite unnaturally, the call feature of JGBs has persisted despite the fact that the Japanese government has never exercised the early-redemption option, and domestic market participants do not therefore expect them to exercise an early redemption in the future.

Because the domestic market participants understand that the call option is unlikely ever to be exercised, they trade JGBs among themselves at prices comparable to the price at which they would be traded if the call provision did not exist. However, because foreign investors remain dubious that the call might be exercised, they usually avoid the quirky JGB market entirely. This reduces participation and inflates the cost to the government of Japan of borrowing in their own capital markets. Surely, this MOF policy is self-defeating.

Oddly enough, however, lowering their own cost of borrowing does not seem to be a top priority. The BOJ has been using the bond market to subsidize Japan's major financial institutions. It has been buying back bonds at high rates from banks that have been making extraordinary profits out of the deals. If this is simply a bank-subsidization ruse, it is a very devious way for the Japanese government to use public money to fund the banks' bad-loan problems. The BOJ has bought back bonds from the banks, allowing the banks to make trading profits of around ¥800 billion a year in recent years. Because the BOJ has been buying up bonds at precisely the wrong time to buy them, the banks have made profits of over 100% on their investments. Although these profits are gigantic, they will cover less than 4% of the banks bad loans. Rigging the market in favor of pauperized banks does not help to make the markets free, fair, and global.

The BOJ has also helped the banks refinance by forcing down short-term interest rates. Although this has slashed the banks' cost of funds to almost zero, they have not passed on the savings to their borrowers. Further, not all interest rates have fallen by the same proportion. Because overnight interest rates have declined much more rapidly than ten-year interest rates, the banks have been able to play this yield spread to good advantage. This difference not only boosts the margins the banks can make on their lending; but, because banks have a higher concentration of shorter-term liabilities and a higher proportion of longer-term assets, the banks' overall financial position has improved markedly at the expense of others—thanks to the BOJ. Bully again for the banks. Bad news for those aspiring to free, fair, and global markets.

Still, some improvements have been made. Securities companies are now able to utilize registered government bonds, which account for the major portion of outstanding government bonds, as collateral for bond financing. The revised system allows government bonds held by securities companies to be transferred to the BOJ, which then issues substitute certificates that are eligible for use as collateral for bond financing. In this way, registered government bonds can be quickly converted into collateral, and this system has been very convenient for securities companies. More changes along these lines are needed.

Any current discussion on the Japanese and bonds would have to mention the massive hordes of United States government bonds the Japanese hold. Japan's central bank and private investors hold 10% of all outstanding U.S. Treasury bills, notes, and bonds—some $320 billion in all. Theoretically, the Japanese could solve some of their domestic problems by selling these bonds and repatriating their funds. Although this has been much talked about, and Dr. Sakakibara, among others, has rashly threatened to do it, it remains unlikely for a variety of reasons. The main reason they won't sell their U.S. bonds is because the yield on 10-year U.S. Treasury bonds is more than four percentage points higher than that on equivalent Japanese securities. Rather than sell Treasuries, Japanese institutions would be more likely to borrow against them. The BOJ, in fact, already has a swap line with the Federal Reserve allowing it to do just that. This raises the intriguing possibility that the BOJ might also offer yen loans to banks, with Treasuries as collateral. Borrowing against Treasuries could keep Japanese banks, brokers, and insurers liquid. That would allow them to honor commitments they have made around the world. It would also mean accepting that American bonds are vastly superior to their Japanese equivalents.

Still, if the American bonds are so superior to their Japanese equivalents, how can the Japanese authorities hope to create a world-class market in their bonds? The short answer is they can't, and the sad thing is that they think they can. They tried before to create an artificial market and failed.

The Japanese equivalent of International Banking Facilities (IBFs) is the Japanese off-shore market (JOM). Eurodollar lending was boosted by the introduction of IBFs in the United States. These are subsidiaries of American banks that engage only in international banking business. The inauguration of IBFs enabled American branches of multinational corporations to conduct their Euromarket activities without leaving the United States. Although the Japanese copied the concept, they could not replicate the market. Japan's tight regulatory environment has condemned JOMs to a very limited usefulness. Tokyo has, unsurprisingly, not become a major Euromarket center in this area either.

The Shogun market was an MOF-controlled 1980s market for foreign-currency-denominated bonds issued by a foreign entity in the Japanese market. It failed for a variety of important reasons, chief of which included the lack of a well-performing secondary market, the lack of an adequate clearing system, the inability to short bonds, and the unwillingness of brokers to maintain a secondary market in an artificially created and maintained market. Japanese brokers, like their confreres elsewhere, were concerned with selling securities, not making artificial markets. The essential difference between the Shogun markets and the Euromarkets they tried to supplant were that the latter were liquid, properly regulated well-functioning markets with good clearinghouses. The MOF thought they could simply coax, cajole, bribe, and bully the JFIs to make markets that, by definition, cannot be created by a mandarin's handclap but must, on the contrary, evolve of their own volition.

The highly stylized, dysfunctional Shogun security was an example of the Japanese emphasizing form over substance. They ignored the dynamics of the market and made a plastic bond that no one wanted: the Shogun bond resembled a public bond but behaved like a private placement. The Shogun market was a study in structural weakness as exhibited by the MOF and the JFIs and in its misinterpretation by those foreigners who thought it was a real market created by an osmotic Big Bang. The MOF still believed that it could replicate a free, fair, and global market as easily as Toyota could replicate an American car part.

Perhaps, it is said, corporate bonds could take up the trading slack. Though corporate bonds currently amount to a comparatively modest $400 billion, that market should, despite Japan's many anomalies, flourish in the years ahead. Japan's recent financial crisis is forcing corporate Japan to seek fresh financing outside their traditional banking partners. Total straight corporate bond issuance is at record levels, over ¥1 billion a month. This reflects a longer trend, where larger Japanese companies are deserting their traditional banking partners to use capital markets for their funding in recent years. The Big Bang should accelerate this trend and allow foreign companies a greater share of underwriting.

Japan's corporate bond market is getting larger almost by the day, reflecting a growing shift by corporate Japan to the capital markets and away from bank borrowing as a means of raising funds. Annual issuances are now around ¥10,000 billion per annum, a dramatic increase on former times. The growing use of capital markets by Japanese companies corresponds with the continued decrease in bank lending to companies, which is falling by about ¥2,000 billion a quarter. As the Big Bang bites, companies are finding it easier to diversify their sources of funding; some of the more cumbersome procedures which previously stymied corporate bond issuances are gone and the poor performance of Japan's equity markets are making bonds a more attractive alternative.

However, the growing success of the Japanese corporate bond market is leading to its own problems. The smaller, weaker companies are being squeezed out. Okura Trading Company, Mita Office Equipment, and many other medium-sized firms have gone bankrupt. Personal bankruptcies in Japan are at record highs and are increasing at unprecedented rates, reflecting the underlying societal changes the Big Bang is bringing.

Although Japan badly needs a fully functioning corporate bond market, it has a long way to go before it can have even the semblance of a free, fair, and global corporate bond market. For a start, Japan would require a credible system of ratings, a system that any ordinary investor could rely upon. For it to properly function, outside investors would have to have good and cheap access to relevant information via the services of reputable rating agencies. The problem is that the major accredited rating agencies in Japan—those that make the bonds officially purchasable by Japanese companies—are directly or indirectly under the control of the ubiquitous MOF. For a fully functioning bond market to work, there must be fully independent rating agencies, as well as a completely independent and adequately staffed accounting profession. As long as the MOF stays all-pervasive, Japan cannot have a fully functioning corporate market as understood in the West.

Japan might instead end up with no market at all. Listed Japanese companies are expanding dealings with foreign banks to secure new sources of credit and to exploit their financial expertise. Toshiba secured long-term loans totaling ¥25.25 billion from a consortium of American and European banks. The firm had never before tapped foreign banks for funding for capital investments. Mitsubishi Electric borrowed ¥7.5 billion in short-term loans from France's Banque Paribas. The firm had previously no outstanding short-term loans from foreign lenders. Misawa Homes took out ¥3 billion in short-term loans from Germany's Westdeutsche Landesbank. Oji Paper borrowed some ¥25 billion from foreign banks to see how their skills in asset securitization and derivatives would help operations. As a result, foreign lending is now 10% of their firm's short-term loans.

Orix Corp.'s short-term loans from Westdeutsche Landesbank, Credit Lyonnais, and two other foreign banks rose to a combined ¥32.4 billion. Dainippon Ink & Chemicals Inc., which took out ¥5 billion in short-term loans from Italian and Singaporean banks, has also securitized loans with the help of Citibank. This enables them to avoid the Japan premium. Toyo Kanetsu KK, a major maker of liquefied natural-gas tanks, entrusted stock worth a book value of ¥7.3 billion to a European trust bank and received ¥4 billion in a custody-guarantee deposit.

Even more dramatically, Matsushita Electric Industrial has set up a financial base in Malaysia in order to build a system to manage group company funds on a global basis. The major consumer electronics maker has already set up financial subsidiaries in Japan, the United States, Britain, and Singapore, and a financial base in Hong Kong. The six financial bases will net trading settlements within each area and settle transactions between bases. Under the new system, group companies with surplus funds can extend loans to financial bases. These funds will be used to make loans to other subsidiaries, reducing interest payments within the group.

This massive loss of business is a consequence of the underdeveloped state of the Japanese bond market. Because the MOF decreed that long-term banks were to be at the center of postwar reconstruction, the corporate bond market is grossly underdeveloped. Even worse, it is inefficient. Every domestic bond issue, for example, must have a commission bank, which acts both as consultant to the issuer and as a trustee for the investors. The commission bank earns a fee for this compulsory service. Since banks can look at every deal before it comes to market, they have traditionally kept the best credits for themselves by lending out the money directly. This system gives banks control of the corporate bond market, even though securities houses actually launch the issues and do the underwriting. Because only firms with an A credit rating can issue bonds, over two-thirds of firms listed in Tokyo are debarred from using the market. The process is also tediously slow, three months or longer being normal. To reach global standards, the banks' protected role would have to immediately go. So would the monopoly of the bigger broker houses in underwriting and pricing new issues. Such monopolies are incompatible with competitive markets.

The MOF must now reform to make the domestic financial market a more attractive investment market. It must, above all, reform the short-term financial market and make the market mechanism work fully. The quality of Japan's short-term financial products needs radical improvement. CD transactions in Japan are much too formalized, paper-obsessed, and inconvenient. Although the commercial paper market has been deregulated, Japan's cumbersome inefficiencies delimit their efficacy. Because CDs are legally interpreted as promissory notes, they attract stamp duties and other bureaucratic irritants. A centralized clearinghouse is needed for such paper to replace the current direct delivery system. Again, there is a lot of groundwork to be done before the Big Bang is a reality.

Still, Japan is going to have its Big Bang and the fallout will be more noticeable in the bond markets than elsewhere. The centerpiece of the securities market reform is the liberalization of brokerage commissions: total fee liberalization is set for the end of 1999. However, the market is glutted with players and major rationalization is needed. Four of the nation's six brokers of call money-short-term money-have established or plan to establish securities subsidiaries even though the bond brokerage business is steadily shrinking. Margins are already wafer-thin and the entry of call-money brokers' subsidiaries could hurt aggregate profitability in a shrinking market where bonds are the lowest yielding ever recorded in world history.

Mitsui Marine and Fire Insurance, Japan's third-largest nonlife insurer, also hopes to enter the industry. With at least four foreign-exchange brokers extending their businesses to securities brokerages, competition will heighten and transaction fees will fall to unsustainable levels. The result will be further redundancies and bankruptcies in a country with negligible previous experience of such traumatic events.

Some city banks have started direct dealing in the money market, bypassing the money brokers altogether. They aim to reduce risks for settlement of large amounts of money and to cut costs. Sumitomo Bank and Sanwa Bank have started direct trading of call money, used to adjust cash positions, with other financial institutions, including regional banks, trust banks, and foreign banks. Sanwa already has agreement with about 20 institutions. Bank of Tokyo-Mitsubishi started direct dealing in the interbank deposit market with other major banks from the end of July 1998. The bank raises one-month loans. The size of the market exceeds ¥1 trillion. City banks raise around several trillion yen daily through overnight uncollateralized call loans. With interest rates at record lows, banks are becoming increasingly conscious of the 0.02% commission paid to money brokers. The days of these middlemen seem limited.

On a related topic, Japan's five regional bourses in Kyoto, Fukuoka, Sapporo, Hiroshima, and Niigata, which collectively account for just over 1% of stock trading volume in Japan, will have their problems compounded by deregulation. The over-the-counter stock-market, which gives regional companies direct access to the nationwide pool of investor money, will essentially deny them their traditional functions. They will most likely be subsumed into the larger Tokyo and Osaka markets.

This huge and unwieldy JGB market shows that the MOF's past policies are, once again, coming home to roost. The MOF granted the JFIs a franchise and protection. In return, the MOF demanded obedience, homage, and the hiring of retired officials.[2] It was centralized feudalism in modern garb. Alas, this is not the closed, controlled Japan of the Edo era. It is the modern globalized world where there are too many players running after too few opportunities.

Japan's iniquitous and highly quirky tax system is also a major stumbling block to producing the free, fair, and global markets the Big Bang aspires to. Under current regulations, foreign holders of Japanese government bonds are not exempt from Japanese withholding tax on their coupon payments. Not only is this against current OECD norms, but forcing the financial intermediaries to certify the nonresident status of beneficial holders of these securities is outmoded and inconsistent with the internationalization of Japan's financial markets. Because these requirements impose an expensive and unrealistic due diligence burden on financial institutions, they do not even help achieve the MOF's stated revenue or market objectives.

Nonresidents have to pay an 18% withholding tax on interest gained from discounted securities such as short-term government bills. Tax-exempt corporations, such as foreign private financial institutions, are refunded this tax when they redeem their investments. Foreign central banks and other governmental institutions are refunded the tax when they purchase their investments. Although these lessen tax burdens on foreign institutions, tax refunding procedures are, like so many things falling under the MOF's ambit, so complicated and convoluted that foreign investors are reluctant to purchase the discounted securities in the first place. They take their custom elsewhere.

Deregulation has at least unified the Euroyen and domestic yen markets. Previously, Euroyen issues could not be placed with Japanese investors for 90 days after launch. The Euromarkets are now within range of Japanese domestic investors which have been traditionally slow to buy foreign-currency bonds. The development of the Euroyen market for Japanese issuers is, in fact, one of Japan's best deregulation successes to date. It could, as the next chapter discusses, form the basis for an Asia-wide market.

[1] This preference is consistent with the preferred habitat theory (PHT) which combines two other interest rate theories, the seg-

mented markets theory with the expectations theory. It recognizes that bonds with different maturities are not perfect substitutes yet are sufficiently substitutable that their yields must be related to each other. The PHT predicts that even if short-term yields are expected to remain the same, the existence of a term premium will cause it to slope upwards. If short-term yields are expected to rise, then the yield's curve will steepen. If short-term yields are expected to fall, then the yield curve will tend to become shallower or even inverted.

[2] The form of golden parachuting called amakudari, "descent from heaven." See Chapter 3.

The Asian Contagion

As we look at Asia's economic mess, it is funny to recall that only a few years ago, the IMF and similar bodies were holding Indonesia, Malaysia, and Thailand up as models of fiscal rectitude for the West to follow. Now, as the Asian contagion wobbles the world, they are more muted in their praises of the Asian miracle. Today we see the entire economies of Asian nations wobble on the verge of total fiscal collapse, and domino effects being felt throughout Asia, the former Soviet Union, Latin America, and the developed markets of Western Europe and North America as well. The crisis has dented both profits and confidence worldwide. This sorry sight is all the remarkable when we consider that less than two years ago, the World Bank was lauding the Asian miracle, and the Asians, with former Prime Minister Nakasone and other prominent Japanese spokesmen to the fore, were lecturing the world on how their economies and societies should be run.

Before the Asian financial crisis developed, it was almost an economic article of faith that their economies would maintain rapid growth ad infinitum. Malaysia, for example, had factored in growth rates of at least 7% until 2020 even though the quality of its growth had been deteriorating for almost a decade. Malaysia suffered a chronic shortage of labor, which meant that wage increases outstripped productivity gains. The government compensated by boosting investment in increasingly grandiose and economically questionable projects. Giant irrigation and building projects sucked in billions of investment dollars and led to a massive current account deficit—even as exports stalled. All of these signs were there long before their bubbles burst.

The roots of the problem lie in the role the United States has played in Asian affairs since the Second World War. When faced with the Communist victory in China, the United States brought Japan firmly into its own fold. As part of this process, it set the yen's value at 360 to the dollar in 1949. That exchange rate was maintained until 1971, when the United States abandoned the gold standard of $35 to the ounce. The yen then appreciated against the dollar, until the 1985 Plaza Accord, signed by the United States, Britain, France, West Germany, and Japan on September 22, 1985, at the Plaza Hotel in New York City. The meeting agreed on a coordinated push to devalue the dollar, to stabilize currencies generally, and to overcome trade-related imbalances.

The Japanese, more so than the others, agreed to stimulate their domestic economies to help solve America's chronic trade deficit. This allowed the United States to export more goods to them without having to suffer the political fallout of dampening their own booming domestic economy. The Japanese, in return for loosening their protectionist policies, believed they would play a more prominent role in global economic affairs. Like Ronald Reagan, who believed that a strong dollar signified a strong America, Premier Yasuhiro Nakasone believed that a strong yen signified a strong Japan. Like Reagan, he hadn't read too many books on economics— or on anything else for that matter.

When, in the early 1990s, the United States artificially depressed its interest rates to enable American banks to repair their balance sheets following the 1990-91 recession, the Southeast Asian countries, whose rates were pegged to the dollar, had to follow suit. When Asian interest rates fell as low as 6%, well below the perceived rates of return on capital to be had in their fast-growing tiger economies, capital flooded into the area, resulting in huge balance-of-payments surpluses at the prevailing fixed exchange rates.

Singapore wisely fended off the inflows by letting its currency strengthen; it also kept money and credit growth under firm control. Hong Kong kept its exchange rate fixed to the dollar and prepared to suffer the monetary consequences. These two were almost unique in that, unlike Japan and the other unleashed tigers, their authorities enforced sound banking practices. Singapore emerged with a stronger exchange rate, negligible inflation, and a modest asset bubble. In Hong Kong, inflation and the asset bubble were greater, but the fixed rate remained intact. Neither Singapore nor Hong Kong suffered a banking crisis.

In Thailand, Malaysia, the Philippines, and Indonesia, however, the policy responses were quite different. These countries wanted to have their cake and eat it too—pegging their currencies to the U.S. dollar while welcoming the inflow of capital. Both liquidity and credit ballooned. Their central banks played the foreign exchange markets to peg exchange rates to the dollar; they also started issuing central-bank debt in the domestic money markets to borrow back the additional liquidity they had so rashly created. By allowing excessive rates of growth of money and credit, their central banks fostered strong economic growth which was good, but rising real exchange rates and large current-account deficits, which would be totally unfinanceable once the torrents of foreign money slowed or stopped.

Just as in Japan, monetary policy fueled the Asian bubbles. Southeast Asia's excessive money and credit growth was channeled into real estate and infrastructure investments, despite signs of overbuilding so extravagant that portfolio managers began to joke that the national bird of Thailand was a building crane.

Japan had also a more direct role in fueling the Asian bubbles. Although Japanese economic management has largely been determined by the yen-dollar rate, the current East Asian crisis shows that the yen-dollar rate is not the concern only of Japan. Asia's boom was also, in part, triggered by the post-Plaza soaring yen. The yen's post-accord rapid rise seriously undermined the international competitiveness of many Japanese products. Japanese manufacturers moved offshore in droves in their quest for lower-cost production bases to service both the Japanese and other markets. Their cash inflows fueled the Thai, Malaysian, Indonesian, Chinese, and other bubbles.

These Japanese industries had astounded the world by maintaining their competitiveness as the yen defied gravity. As the yen went from 360 to the dollar to 79 to the dollar, the Japanese manufacturing companies, in acts of engineering genius, could maintain

their competitive edge. Their successes were all the more remarkable as they had been made to get their supplies from very inefficient Japanese suppliers, who, by and large, just acted as further
MOF-sanctioned parasites on them. However, when the yen broke
80 to the dollar, they had no choice but to relocate. Even they could
not indefinitely defy gravity.

The torrent of Japanese cash flooding into the area just acted as
oil on troubled waters. The area had been financially unstable since
China and Vietnam devalued their currencies by over 60% in the
1990s. The simultaneous depreciation of the yen by almost 50% put
pressure on the external competitiveness of the rest of Asia, eroding
external trade positions and causing trade deficits. Problems first
surfaced in Thailand, where foreign investment was pouring in,
attracted by its cheap and uncomplaining labor force and, of course,
its world-renowned pagodas and brothels. Bangkok enjoyed its own
property and stock market bubble, which was largely financed by
money borrowed in dollars. Because Thailand's central bank had
pegged the country's currency to the dollar, all seemed well and risk-
free. Because Thailand's central bank stood ready as a large, unthinking, and uncomplaining lender of last resort, foreign investors
poured into Bangkok's buoyant markets. When sentiment changed
in 1997, Thailand devalued the baht—after spending $7 billion in
reserves on the spot-currency market and committing an extra hidden amount of $23 billion to the forward market. Although
Thailand became the first of the dominoes to fall, the effects spilled
over to the rest of the region within days.

On July 2, 1997, Thailand's central bank abandoned the pegging of the baht in favor of a managed float. This started a chain of
devaluations across Southeast Asian countries as they devalued to
remain competitive with Thailand. As the competitiveness of the
Asian tigers fell, China, in particular, conquered export markets,
leaving countries no option but to devalue to remain competitive.
The problem for Thailand, which no longer had the confidence of
investors, was that it could no longer rely on foreign investment to
finance current account deficits. Fast running out of foreign reserves,
the Thai government finally sought help from the IMF. That help
was approved on August 20, 1997.

After the attack on the Thai baht, the Malaysian ringgit started to depreciate. The authorities held firm; they decided not to raise interest rates. Both the ringgit and the Malaysian stock market fell through the floor. The Malaysian government scaled back—abandoned, one could almost say—several of its multibillion-dollar construction projects.

The Indonesian rupiah was the next domino to tumble. Since 1970 the Indonesian economy had been one of the fastest growing among developing countries, with real GDP growth averaging 7% annually. Despite widespread corruption and nepotism, the Indonesians were the darlings of the IMF. Or at least they had been. The scale of Suharto's nepotism and crony capitalism made the world's most populous Muslim state one of the world's most unstable.

The chill winds next hit Taiwan. Its currency depreciated. This made the Hong Kong share market plummet. Though other Asian countries had abandoned their pegs to the appreciating U.S. dollar, Hong Kong strove as valiantly as Don Quixote to defend its fixed exchange rate regime.

The falling New Taiwan dollar also contributed to the depreciation of the won, the currency of Taiwan's closest competitor, South Korea, which had expanded rather a trifle too rapidly in the post-Plaza period. Government funds were put into a small number of interrelated baskets: the chaebol, or large conglomerates, which, in many ways, are the Korean equivalents of Japan's keiretsu.

Like the other countries, South Korea had local factors hastening her demise. In her case, it was the 1993 presidential victory of the populist, Kim Young-sam. In an effort to boost growth during a mild recession, he encouraged Korea's chaebol to invest heavily in new factories and other capital goods. The chaebol, always heavily geared, ended up with massive debts and excess production capacity. When the collapse of computer chip prices and the depreciating yen destroyed their export markets, a number of cash-strapped firms, including the large conglomerates of Hambo Steel, Jinro, Dianong, New Core Group, and Kia Motors, went bankrupt. Short-term foreign borrowing by industrial groups and banks rose rapidly as they struggled to service their long-term debts. Foreign loans were particularly attractive to the chaebol, since they carried lower interest rates than domestic issues, which reflected a capital shortage that resulted from Korea's closed financial markets.

However, as the won collapsed, so did they. Hanbo Steel collapsed in January 1997 under $6 billion of foreign debts. Hanbo, a prime example of South Korea's crony capitalism, collapsed as a result of Kim's authority collapsing. Other chaebol followed, including Sammi Steel, Korea's largest specialty steelmaker, and Kia Motors, Korea's third-largest specialty steelmaker and Jinro, Korea's largest alcohol maker. International credit agencies downgraded ratings for banks with heavy exposure to troubled chaebol. Korea's banks faced Japanese-style liquidity problems; several went bankrupt. Confidence waned, monetary policy failed, and, faced with excessive external short-term debts exceeding $100 billion, Korea found herself unable to service her debt. Korea's debt was accordingly downgraded, and, prodded by the collapse of the Hong Kong stock market and other Asian turbulences, capital fled Korea.

Soon, all the currencies in the Asia-Pacific region came under attack. These currency attacks revealed the fragility, if not the sheer artificiality, of the financial system underpinning their growth. Companies that had borrowed heavily in U.S. dollars found themselves unable to repay their debts. As in Japan, these debts had generally been underestimated. As the firms failed to repay their dollar debts, their banks faced a cash crisis. This led to a credit crunch, which then crippled their economies. They moved from haughty tigers to international begging-boys faster than anyone could imagine.

Asia's problems, then, both mirror and compound Japan's. High economic growth masked underlying problems until their bubbles burst. Banks lent excessive amounts of money to risky clients. Assumptions about continued high growth meant that banks did not monitor the quality of their loan portfolios adequately and their quality consequently collapsed. This became a major problem when their bubbles burst.

Most Asian countries had either fixed or semifixed exchange rates against the floating U.S. dollar. Many companies and banks had unhedged exchange-rate exposure as they took advantage of domestic and international interest-rate differentials. When their currencies bombed, their external liabilities, most of which were short-term, became impossible to service.

Bank supervisory standards were even worse than Japan's. Like those in Japan, lax accountancy systems and accountancy conjuring tricks hid the true extent of their problems. And as in Japan, the social cost of the crisis is high. Unemployment has tripled in both Korea and Japan; they have risen even more alarmingly in Southeast Asia. Immigrants are being deported en masse, causing further micro and macro tensions in the region. Higher prices for basic imported foodstuffs have hit the poorest hardest.

As a result of the crisis, the OECD has continually revised downward its projections for world growth, especially as Japan's economy is now contracting at a rate of 5% per year. Though Western economic growth is still positive, the financial markets have been rattled by the crisis. Central banks—mindful of the international effects of their actions—have been more reluctant to raise interest rates than they might have been.

Though Japan's fall from grace has not been as dramatic as her neighbors', she has lost much face. The United States government has had to repeatedly intervene to prop up the yen which is no longer in demand. Far from helping to solve the Asian contagion, Japan is now an integral part of it.

Many Asian countries had hoped that they would be able to buy their way out of the crisis, with revenues from exporting their natural and other resources. Although their competitive bouts of devaluation should have made their products more competitive, the economic downturn has caused the reverse to happen. Demand for their commodities has fallen and the resulting oversupply of their export goods has caused their prices to nosedive still further. The resulting scramble to maintain export earnings as prices tumble has fanned the crisis out into even more countries.

Most, if not all, of China's banks are insolvent, with nonperforming assets estimated at around 25% of total assets. Indonesia owes approximately $80 billion in private offshore debt. Because of the high level of nonperforming assets and Indonesia's deteriorated economic conditions, all Indonesian banks are technically insolvent.

The country's currency, like its economy and banking system, is in a shambles. When the IMF came to the rescue of Indonesia, its erstwhile darling, it lost most of its remaining credibility as a result.

Malaysia, in its considerable wisdom, decided to forgo assistance from the IMF. Malaysia instead announced a string of tough austerity packages to stop the hemorrhage. Federal government spending was slashed; lending to costly property projects, low-cost housing, and other public projects halted; new stock market listings, rights issues, and corporate restructurings were capped. Though nearby Singapore has managed to fare comparably well, no real upturn can be expected there until the general area improves.

The days of the boasters are gone. Thailand is swallowing the IMF's medicine. So, too, is Korea, until recently the world's tenth-largest economy. High interest rates and declining employment will keep her quiescent for some time. South Korea, interestingly enough, intends to sell its two most indebted commercial banks to foreign investors. The two banks, Korea First Bank and Seoul Bank, were hurt by bad debts totaling more than $4 billion after a series of major conglomerates collapsed. The government has already injected $1.5 billion into Korea First Bank and $1.2 billion into Seoul Bank to write off approximately 56% of its problem loans. After it writes off another huge slab, it will sell them off.

Although all major international financial regulators failed to spot the overexposure of Western banks to the crisis, and that many Asian companies had taken on much larger loans than they could ultimately afford, the IMF has come in for some well-deserved criticism. The IMF acting as a lender of last resort to Suharto's corrupt Indonesian regime raised the moral hazard problem of IMF intervention. Suharto, knowing that the IMF would come to the rescue, rifled the national till. Having allowed it to happen, the IMF now sees its credibility in tatters.

IMF critics have pointed out that as long as the IMF stands ready and willing to bail them out, such corrupt regimes will never reform. Other commentators accuse the IMF's tough prescription of accentuating the current panic. Still others stress the tremendous yen-dollar fluctuations described earlier as the root of the problem. They say that those fluctuations, coupled with fundamental changes in the global economy, put undue pressure on those smaller tigers and their currencies. Yet another school of thought criticizes their style of managed capitalism which looked so successful a few years ago. This school believes that further liberalization of the financial sector coupled with full transparency is the only long-term solution to their problems.

Although these viewpoints are further explored in Chapter 8, suffice to say here that Japan must decide where it stands. If the yen plunges in value, not only the Asian tigers but the Chinese will be forced to devalue as well. Although European and American consumers would benefit by having these cheaper goods, international tensions would resurface. The Japanese government can choose between its natural inclination to put purely domestic considerations first and keep the yen depressed, or it can try to have a firmer yen and drag Asia out of the doldrums.

Japan's Big Bang, then, has wider repercussions. Unless Japan initiates a major coordinated approach, the situation might well deteriorate further. Vietnam's clueless cadres face their biggest dilemma since the collapse of their Soviet paymasters. Faced with a stagnating economy, plunging foreign investment, and peasant unrest, they will be left further behind when the others eventually reform. Vietnam has so far managed to privatize fewer than 20 of its 6,000 state-owned firms. Most are overstaffed, undercapitalized, and bankrupt. Those enterprises were propped up for years with soft loans from Vietnamese banks that now can't be repaid. Because most of its trade is intraregional, it cannot hope to pull itself out of its morass until the other tigers get moving again.

Fueling the anxiety are the outbreak of rioting and the virtual breakdown of the economy in Indonesia. Although the Indonesian economy is relatively modest in size, the country's population of 204 million is the world's fourth-largest; chaos there threatens its neighbors because its 13,000 islands straddle sea lanes vital to Asian commerce. Moreover, the looting and violence, which accompany the crisis, have provided a shocking reminder of the wrenching social adjustment facing the region's other ailing economies. Myanmar, Vietnam, and the former Soviet Union come to mind.

A collapse in the Russian economy would pose even more disturbing problems for the Clinton administration than the Asian crisis, since Moscow is a nuclear power. The IMF, which has been pumping billions of dollars into that vast, anarchic land, is at a loss what to do but mumble its cure-all panacea.

Perhaps even more so than Japan's MOF, the IMF has a case to answer. The International Monetary Fund and World Bank (collectively the Bretton Woods institutions) were established in 1945, 15 years and one world war after the world spiraled into depression. The IMF was established to act as a central bank for central banks—a lender of last resort-and to codify the rules of international finance.

The IMF are the archetype dismal economists, blithely adjusting their monetary knobs, ignoring the rampant kleptocracy, nepotism, and crony capitalism in Suharto's Indonesia and its other model states (and ignoring in the process how far their kleptocracies deviate from global standards) and all the time whining for more money from the American Congress and its other patrons. The IMF's unoriginal cure-all panacea of tighter monetary policies, higher taxes, and lower government spending savage the middle class and the poor and do not contain the contagion.

Japan is an integral part of this wider malaise. There are, in fact, many common threads linking these crises with Japan's. Inefficient banking systems allowed excessive credit to build up, creating bubbles that caused untold damage as they burst. Although Japan was allowed to ignore her bubble-related problems for more than eight years, the markets did not allow the weaker economies to wait so long. Just as in Japan, the fault lies not so much with the banks that went for construction and other short-horizon profit ventures but with their governments for mismanaging their countries' finances and national development. It was this lack of proper direction that led to extremes in speculative lending practices which in turn led to inflation in asset values.

Malaysia, Hong Kong, and Singapore fared much better than Thailand, Indonesia, and Korea because they adhere much closer to global standards. Their rule of law, their disclosure requirements, their systems for conflict resolution, their auditing practices, their treatment of minority shareholders, and their other forms of governance much more resemble those of the West than do those in the worst-affected trio. In today's globalized world, countries that do not adhere to those standards will be much more prone to capital flight when turbulence occurs. The crisis has also undermined the idea, most notably in Indonesia, that authoritarian governments can be tolerated if they raise living standards. Whatever about the past, transparency and authoritarianism will seldom go together in the future. Japan should learn from this and iron out the many quirks in her own system.

Like Japan, all the worst offenders lack the political will and the credibility it gives. In the final analysis, political leadership is needed to rescue the region. Part of that leadership involves having a successful debt market to recycle the debt. A well-developed local currency bond market would help. An intermediate swap market should be developed to lessen the currency risk that permeates the area. However, just as in Japan, the epicenter of the crisis is the banking sectors' bad loans and their general inefficiency and bad governance. Just as if the MOF were controlling the entire area, the longer-standing deterrents have not been removed. These fundamental blocks to the establishment of a free, fair, and global market include settlement problems, withholding taxes that eat into yields, and illiquid currency and interest-rate swap markets, which traditionally supported the fixed-income markets. Current cross-currency swap markets are too illiquid simply because too many of the local currencies are illiquid. Nevertheless, the potential exists for a world-class market.

Japan should also be the linchpin of any such market. Asia needs a deep, liquid, and mature debt market that can transform Asian savings into powerful liquidity. The IMF and World Bank have also called for such a market. Asian companies, Japan's excluded, have about $650 billion issued in bonds when domestic and foreign currency bonds are aggregated. Given that Asia's huge savings pool has been inefficiently utilized, most notably in Indonesia, where it went into funding a national car company controlled by Suharto's family, there is clearly room for improvement. And for a financial center to handle that market.

If Japan does not show leadership, others will. Singapore, for example, has instituted its own big bang to surpass Hong Kong and beat off its rivals. McKinsey has been retained to study how they can make their financial sector more competitive and more in line with market standards. Singapore has its eyes on the big prize such a market offers. Singapore intends to allow foreign concerns to invest in Singapore Telecom; PSA Corporation, which runs the world's second-busiest port; and other blue-chip companies. They will also be allowed to buy seats in the Singapore Stock Exchange. Members are being allowed increasing access to the Central Provident Fund, the body charged with managing $47 billion in members' pension funds. As members are being allowed to invest their entitlements overseas, greater opportunities will be created for the non-Singaporean funds operating there. If Japan wishes to stay ahead of Singapore, it had best expedite its own Big Bang.

Whatever about Tokyo, most other centers are sitting on their thumbs. Hong Kong has established a Hong Kong dollar yield curve. The government there has now issued exchange fund bills (Treasuries) with a maturity of up to 10 years. Although Hong Kong is not big enough to create a substantial bond market, if they can dovetail some of the Chinese financing requirements to restructure China's 370,000 state-owned industries, that would sufficiently boost demand by supplying the necessary critical mass.

Hong Kong's establishment of a mortgage corporation and the planned creation of a compulsory pension scheme are partly motivated by the desire to create long-term supply and demand for long-term securities. The Hong Kong Mortgage Corporation will take mortgages out of the banking system and issue securitized bonds against them and, they hope, thereby jump-start a mortgage-backed bond market. The proposed 1998 launch of the Mandatory Provident Fund, a mandatory pension scheme in Hong Kong, could create substantial demand for fixed-income securities.

The Hong Kong Monetary Authority (HKMA) is hoping to launch a regional clearing and settlement system through a series of bilateral agreements with countries that have achieved acceptable depository, clearing, and settlement systems. Most of the requirements for a regional market are in place. There is a big pool of savings, and demand for capital for corporate restructuring, for housing, and for infrastructure finance. The World Bank estimates that the latter demand alone will require over $8,000 billion up to 2004—much more than the banking system could provide. Therefore, given Hong Kong's global standards and the role it plays in China's strategic thinking, it would have to be a serious contender for any such center.

Asians have invested their savings outside the region, while funds tend to come back in the form of foreign direct investment and portfolio investments, thus creating a maturity mismatch with concomitant liquidity risks in many East Asian economies. While East Asia has more than $600 billion in foreign exchange reserve and the region has five of the six largest foreign exchange reserve holders, those funds are invested overseas in long-term bonds and come back in short-term instruments. Asia's foreign reserves have funded the fiscal deficits of the G7 nations, and the banking systems of the G7 nations have funded Asian development.

It is a cruel irony that Asia's past thriftiness now impedes her recovery. Although Asia's bid to develop a regional bond market had in the past been slowed by the lack of government debt in the region, the Asians' high propensity to save, thin liquidity, and poor infrastructure, it now finds its credit-worthiness in doubt. The lack of a vibrant bond market forced Asian companies to accrue U.S. dollar debt and invest in illiquid assets such as real estate. Because of this historical overhang, the short-term prospects for an Asian bond market are dim. If Japan can successfully implement her Big Bang, she just might be the center of an Asian bond market, which could stand on an equal footing with its European and American counterparts.

Asia presents the Japanese markets with a golden opportunity. Asian bond markets are fragmented and hampered by a lack of transparency, supportive tax regimes, and efficient clearing and settlement systems. There needs to be a proper sovereign yield curve—that is, a government benchmark against which corporate bonds can be priced. This is not well established at the moment because Asian governments had tended to run budget surpluses and therefore have had little time or need to launch debt programs. The region needs to build up a larger pool of pension funds so that there will be a larger demand for long-term assets to match longer-term pension liabilities. Asian companies will have to change their attitudes to bonds. So far, they have been averse to long-term debt. Companies have relied on internal cash flow and equity, followed by bank debt, and use long-term debt financing only as a last resort. They have also been anxious to minimize funding costs, rather than ensure that they build up a debt portfolio to match their investment needs. The result was a proliferation of short-term debt issuance and therefore much more exposure to the recent rises in short-term interest rates.

Bond markets need reliable sources of information, especially credit ratings. Japan apart, Asia has no established regional credit-rating agencies-and even Japan's are poor. Although Western credit-rating agencies have local offices, their ratings of Asian bonds carry less authority as do their rating of comparable European and American bonds which, having more liquid markets, trade at narrower spreads.

Because they lack modern credit-rating systems, banks are favoring the bigger, more credit-worthy borrowers and are being increasingly hesitant to lend to the rest, bricks-and-mortar collateral notwithstanding. Because they still lack basic credit-rating skills, they may still misprice their loans. Perhaps, then, it is just as well that they do not have the necessary reserves to take further unanticipated losses or, should the opportunity arise, to expand. Asia is probably better off without them.

Still, the tigers will remain hungry for more cash. East Asia's demand for fresh capital to clear up bad loans is allowing Western institutions to make unprecedented inroads. American concerns with their Wall Street windfalls are very active in the Asian M&A market. The influence this change of ownership will have on Japan's Big Bang is discussed further in the next and final chapter.

What Is To Be Done?

Chapter 7 put Japan's Big Bang into its international setting. To fully appreciate its relevance and to gauge its probability of success, it is now important to see it in the context of Japan's historical evolution. Japan's evolution has been punctuated by three major external shocks. These shocks, the three Ps, are the arrival of the Portuguese and the guns they brought with them to Japan, Commodore Perry and his Black Ships, and the Plaza Accord.

The 1543 Portuguese arrival ushered in a big bang of its own. In less than 30 years, Japanese-made guns, copied from Portuguese prototypes, were being produced in vast quantities. As well as being exported, they allowed samurai overlord Nobunaga Oda to begin the big bang of his era, the unification of Japan.

Nobunaga was the type of charismatic leader Japan currently needs. He did not balk at the hard decisions. On the contrary, he happily bit the bullet and removed the major obstacles to his reforms. His 1571 torching of the monasteries at Hieizan and the wholesale slaughter of the tens of thousands of Buddhist monks encamped there showed that he was prepared to pay any cost and carry any burden to modernize Japan. Nobunaga's liberalized economic policies of rakuichi and rakuza built Japan a solid economic base. Rakuichi opened Japan's internal markets; rakuza abolished merchants' unions and other market-impeding cartels.

His firm, if somewhat ruthless, leadership and foresight propelled Japan forward. Whereas Nobunaga's actions preempted events, the Big Bang reforms are belated, occurring as they do more than a decade after their American and Europe prototypes. Japan now finds herself playing catch-up, trying to emulate the reforms Britain and the United States implemented almost 20 years ago. Japan's leaders must learn from Nobunaga and bite the bullet.

Other parallels exist between Nobunaga's reforms and the current ones. Brilliant and all as Nobunaga was, fear of the new and of the unknown followed his reforms. Specifically, the fear of European influence and ideas turned Japan into an isolated, largely self-contained mandarin-ruled universe. Similar fears by today's mandarins are prolonging Japan's recession and making the ordinary Japanese citizen suffer unduly. Because the old ways cannot be reconstituted, the sooner change happens, the better

Although Japan can learn from her past, the post-Nobunaga period of sinecured security cannot be replicated. That Tokugawa Peace which followed Japan's self-imposed isolation gave shape to the present-day social order in Japan. It marked the emergence of bureaucratic control of the political system. Since then, Japan's history has been the history of mandarin rule, broken only by the other two sudden and unforeseen changes enunciated above. Indeed, Japan's mandarins regard these shocks as bothersome anomalies of no real consequence to their eternal and almost divine mission of steering Japan to its destiny.

The MOF, the bete noire of this tome, actually goes much further back than the Tokugawa period in its tawdry quest for legitimacy. They trace their lineage back to the Taika Reforms of A.D. 645, when a systematic form of tax collection was introduced. They actually rather pompously refer to themselves as the Okurasho, in remembrance of the great storehouse ministry founded in A.D. 678. Better still, because the Okura was an integral part of the temple network of that time, they not only lay claim to an unbroken 1,300-year history, and to principles of national duty that are not constricted by MacArthur's constitution. They actually see themselves as the guardians of the nation's purses and, odder still, of the nation's soul. God's soulless paymasters, if you will.

Japan has this major hurdle to overcome. It has a self-perpetuating clique of Tokyo University graduates in the MOF holding the levers of power. And that clique has been slave to an antiquated system which has its organizational roots in the distant past-even before France was born and almost a millennium before France's Sun King strutted across the European stage. Because the MOF was almost totally untouched by the MacArthur purges, that fossilized system has continued up to the present day. It actually consolidated its postwar power and helped bring about Japan's current dilemma. Like the Buddhist monks of Nobunaga's era, they are an obstacle to progress.

Given their pervasiveness, it is little wonder that, when he visited Japan in 1994, Bill Clinton singled out the MOF and the Ministry of International Trade and Industry (MITI) as Japan's major nontrade barriers. Although MITI has received much more coverage in trade wars than the more powerful MOF, the MOF is, in fact, the real barrier to trade and to Japan's Big Bang. This is because MITI, by and large, generally does its job. The MOF, by contrast, has merely bumbled through.

Although the wholesale incineration of the MOF's personnel may not be necessary, for the Big Bang to be effective, the MOF will have to largely surrender its control mechanisms. Interest rates must be market- not MOF-set. They must fully surrender their control over the banking and foreign exchange systems. Strategic financing institutions, such as the Japan Development Bank and the Export-Import Bank of Japan, must become fully independent, answerable only to the Diet, not to faceless MOF bureaucrats. Finally, the MOF must surrender its key power over the national budget. Being naturally ultraconservative, the MOF had always insisted on a balanced budget. They actually applauded the bubble, simply because it meant that as taxes rolled in, bonds did not have to be issued. True to form, they absolved themselves from the ensuing calamities.

Absolution is not enough. They must realize that the centralization of power which they so epitomized is redundant in today's information age. The sheer scale of the MOF's interventionist style was centralized planning at its very worst. Not content with allocating the national funds, it insisted on deciding how they would be spent. Because of its ignorance of the Japanese microeconomy, obvious priorities were ignored and idiotic quotas were met elsewhere. Like a mad bull, it plunged into the markets it controlled without knowing anything about their mechanisms or without thinking through the consequences of their actions. Its meddling in the futures markets skewed the market and allowed Morgan Stanley and Salomon's to make huge, riskless profits at the expense of the Japanese trust companies. The MOF must realize these, the consequences of their own shortcomings. Just as in Nobunaga's time, firm leadership and direction are needed. If the MOF cannot give it, they must be disempowered.

The second major P-factor external shock Japan's mandarins survived was Commodore Matthew C. Perry's 1853 gunboat diplomacy which forced the Tokugawa shogunate to open its ports to trade and therefore to Western influence. Seeing that Perry had them hopelessly outgunned, Japan, on the surface, came quickly to terms with the new situation in what has become known as the Meiji Restoration. One of the reasons for Japan's subsequent emergence onto the world stage was that the Meiji period threw up good leaders with an intense consciousness of the national interest, a sense of mission, and the will to use the power they had. Like Nobunaga, they focused on modernizing Japan and ignored their critics.

They were great visionaries, great leaders who all sprang from the samurai class. They were all relatively young, capable, proven leaders of their own locale and highly educated in specialized skills with a keen sense of national duty and a high degree of common sense. Among other things, they pensioned off the obsolete samurai (shortchanging them in current fashion) and brought in thousands of foreign experts to modernize Japan in all imaginable fields, something unimaginable to the MOF's dour generalists.

Still, one unredeeming consequence of the Meiji Restoration was that it allowed Japan's bureaucracy to consolidate its power. Their bank-centered financial system was, after all, modeled on Germany's. Bismarck himself had specifically advised Japan's leaders to depend on domestically raised capital. Around 1880, when Matsutaka became finance minister, he followed the Iron Chancellor's advice and put Japan's banks and postal savings system at the center of her push to modernization. The Ministry of Finance handled the deposits section of the National Treasury from the postal savings system and similar sources. They have been at the center of Japan's finances ever since to a degree unmatched in the West.

Nor did the Second World War change this. Because postwar reconstruction was financed domestically as well, capital and stock markets were underutilized and the mandarins remained in charge. Under the American Occupation, political reform was abandoned after the Maoists grabbed power in China. Japan, politically leaderless, was handed back over to the mandarins who, like the Catholic Pontiff, strategically think in millennia, not in the microseconds the modern world demands.

Their financial arsenal was continually boosted by the postal savings system which, with around ¥250,000 billion in deposits, has now begun to be unprofitable because it is still being forced to give its funds to the MOF to put into the Fiscal Investment and Loan Program (FILP) and similar underperforming programs. Although the MOF has promised to run these funds itself, this seems to be based on reasons of control, not on reasons of financial prudence which would demand, as a minimum, that the MOF be kept firmly away from the national till and that some form of future cost accounting be introduced to ensure that the MOF meddling does not bankrupt future generations.

The abundance of leadership at the time of the Meiji Restoration is in great contrast to the foot-dragging that characterizes the MOF's approach to today's challenges. If Japan needs a Big Bang anywhere, it is at the core of the MOF, which has controlled every aspect of the finance industry, from the building of new branches to the establishment of deposit interest rates. Though generalists lacking the required expertise, the MOF, like an all-knowing foreman managing a widget factory, gave detailed guidance on all financial actions from the largest macrostrategic ones to the tiniest, inconsequential one. The MOF presumed, wrongly as it has patently transpired, that the Japanese financial markets would stay as small, as inconsequential, and as manageable as they were in August 1945. Because markets are increasingly global, complex, and diverse, MOF generalists are so much excess baggage.

Japan's recent experiences have been compared to Japan's depression following World War I when the country's economy boomed. Kobe's 1995 earthquake, the Tokyo sarin nerve gas attack, and the meltdown of the JFIs have their echoes in the 1920s recession, Tokyo's massive 1923 earthquake, and the Showa Financial Panic of 1927, which took its name from the imperial reign era that started the previous year. Certainly, the challenges facing Japan are at least as great now as they were then. The political landscape has, however, changed. Foreign adventurism, for example, can no longer solve Japan's internal contradictions. Only political reform and bureaucratic sackings can. The Big Bang then must herald changes as fundamental as the Meiji Restoration did. Fundamental policy questions concerning the future direction of Japan must be raised and answered.

The third P-factor was the Plaza Accord, which led to a high yen, further market liberalization, and expanded domestic consumption. The Plaza Accord's aftermath has undermined Japan's twin pillars of bureaucratic control and industrial self-reliance. The challenge facing Japan since the Plaza Accord is how to fashion coexistence with the global capitalism that has shaken the Japanese bureaucratic and economic system at its roots.

The bubble's problems were accentuated not only by Plaza's fallout but also by the BOJ's lack of independence to deal with that fallout. Raising interest rates would have been interpreted by the Americans as being against the spirit of both the Plaza and Louvre Accords. MOF preclearance would have been needed, in any event: the MOF's much wider remit delayed the formulation of a common bubble-pricing strategy.

The BOJ, in fact, does not use monetary policy as such. One reason is the lack of intermediate targets: national inflation indices, for example, do not include share prices and, because they use a lagged rental index, they only approximate land prices. Because land prices fell outside of the BOJ's remit, its monetary policy response could not, in any event, be finely crafted enough to prick the bubble. Further, both exporters and those profiting from the bubble formed a powerful lobby against pricking the bubble. Lack of leadership did the rest.

The task now confronting Japan is how to make the Big Bang successful. It is easy to spew out shibboleths on what Japan should do. Spouting about free, fair, and global markets, deregulation, letting the market rule, and other neo-Thatcherite cliches is not enough. Although the government should follow the Thatcherite road and privatize Japan Railways, NTT, Japan Tobacco, and its other cash cows, it must launch even more fundamental change. It must remove the mandarins' power base and the nepotism and corruption it spawns.

Even that is not enough. Japan needs a strategic plan to address the strategic choices facing it. Most fundamentally, Japan needs a firm and decisive leadership who can think strategically and who can foster Japan's many advantages for the greater good. Japan's new electoral system might be especially efficacious in this respect. The shift to single-seat constituencies might make Japan's elected officials more accountable. It might even take them out of the pockets of the construction companies and racketeers who finance their campaigns. Even that would not be enough. Just as under Meiji, so also is a new, tried and proven type of leader needed. Japan's successful companies should have a more direct say in the running of the nation, and the mandarins should be consigned to a less-exalted role more fitting their limited abilities.

Japanese companies such as Sony, Toyota, Kyocera, Hitachi, Honda, and Komatsu are world leaders. They are second to none. Toyota and Honda can make better and cheaper cars than their competitors. Intel relies on Japanese ceramic and silicon wafer technology. The Japanese make most laptop computers and almost all of the screens, which are their most expensive component. The Japanese excel in game software as well as embedded software for elevators, cars, consumer electronics, and office equipment. Japanese companies, in fact, dominate the global market in laser-jet printers, fax machines, video cameras, and many other high-value-added consumer goods. They control a large variety of key components in jointly produced goods. High-tech batteries for cellular phones and computers, the precision machines the Koreans and others use for producing semiconductors, and the key pieces of scanning equipment all carry the made-in-Japan logo. Anywhere else, the people responsible for these successes would have a large say in how the nation was run. Petty mandarins impeding progress would not be tolerated.

Deregulation might let more Japanese firms attain their true potential. Perhaps deregulation will allow the better of Japan's small-er companies to emulate its higher-profile giants. Germany's postwar successes were, after all, built not on the giants but on the small to medium-sized enterprises. If the Big Bang allows Japan's smaller companies access to world financial markets and to deregulated Japanese markets, they might well fill the vacuum and revitalize Japan.

This has certainly been the case in Britain, which is again boom-ing. Britain's system of centralized cabinet power, checked by par-liament and independent media, is, in large part, responsible for this resurgence. Britain has traditionally also had a keen sense of inter-national political propriety. She is now a senior partner of the EU and should benefit even further as Europe continues to integrate.

Japan, by contrast, finds itself at the edge of an unstable region, ravaged by the Asian contagion and by the political instability North Korea and China engender. Instead of tackling these prob-lems, as Britain would, Japan stands impotent. She is seen as a GATT freebooter, who won't honor United Nations military and other commitments, but who thinks she can absolve herself, as in the Gulf crisis, by writing out (in U.S. dollars) derisory checks instead. Although she gets to sit on the U.N. Security Council, so too do Nicaragua, Canada, and El Salvador. She is just not seen as a respon-sible member of the international community, either regionally or globally. Being a pygmy, Japan must be satisfied with a pygmy's lot.

Not so Britain. Whereas Tokyo has fallen to fourth place, behind New York and Boston, London is now the world's largest equity investment center. London's market capitalization is now big-ger than Tokyo's. The London Stock Exchange has now merged with its biggest European rival, Deutsche Boerse, laying the founda-tion for a single European stock market. The City of London will thereby solidify its position as the world's premier international cen-ter serving global markets. London, with almost 19% of cross-bor-der bank lending, is the world's largest single market for interna-tional banking business. There are now around 550 banks from near-ly 80 countries based in London. There are more American banks in London than in New York, while the City is home to more Japanese banks than anywhere outside Japan. Foreign banks constitute over

50% of all banks in the British finance sector. There are also 200 representative and other offices of foreign banks, further indicating the wide representation of foreign banks in the City. London is the world's largest foreign exchange market, accounting for $1,200 billion in global daily turnover. The dollar and deutsche mark are more heavily traded in London than in Germany or the United States. London also dominates the Eurobond market. When the euro replaces the franc and mark, and the obligations to issue paper in those currencies in France and Germany, the City's bond market share should further increase.

A variety of pertinent factors contribute to London's ongoing successes. These factors include the depth of its financial markets, the quality of its telecommunications, London's tradition as a financial center, and an appropriate regulatory regime. Monetary policy is tight, the Bank of England is credible, its regulatory structures are being continually finessed, and compliance costs are being monitored. This all ensures stability, price competitiveness, and overall efficiency.

Japan's problems have already been spelled out in some detail. Perhaps, to emulate Britain, she needs a fourth P to galvanize her forward. Many Japanese now believe that the only way to create change in Japan is through gaiatsu— foreign pressure. Foreign pressure will continue and will permeate all levels of Japanese society. Daimler, for example, is buying Nissan's diesel truck division. This will put it at the heart of Japanese industry. Nissan belongs to the struggling Fuyo group, the keiretsu behind troubled banks of Fuji Bank and Yasuda Trust that allowed Yamaichi to go belly up. In tobashi fashion, many of Nissan's dealership affiliates have big liabilities of their own.

So too has Fuji. Moody's has downgraded Fuji Bank's long-term debt rating and financial strength ratings to near junk-bond levels. This will not only also raise the cost of funding for Fuji, Japan's fifth-biggest commercial bank and the world's 10th largest, but it will also put its entire future in jeopardy. Fuji is the ninth major Japanese bank that Moody's rates at or around junk-bond status. These downgraded Japanese banks, including Sakura Bank and Daiwa Bank, are seen as being unable to resolve their loan-quality problems anytime soon without outside help.

Fuji claims to be profitable, to be making about ¥300 billion a year. It also claims that its international capital adequacy ratio is at 9.4%, significantly above the minimum 8% required by the Bank for International Settlements. Given the litany of creative accounting this book has catalogued in Yamaichi as well as in the broader Japanese financial community, this claim cannot be taken seriously.

The markets are not very impressed. Fuji's share price is so low that if it cannot merge or effect massive structural changes, it is doomed. Further, the three-month yen—the rate at which banks are prepared to lend to each other within the London market—is now much higher for Fuji Bank and Sakura Bank than for Bank of Tokyo-Mitsubishi (BTM) and other well-rated Japanese banks. Previously, the Japan premium, the extra fund raising cost for Japanese banks in euro interbank markets, did not vary greatly, particularly among major city banks, because the market was unable to differentiate the credit risk of each bank. However, the market has since then reassessed the credit risk of individual banks, rather than looking at the sector as a whole. Because Moody's ratings played such a crucial role in the Long-Term Credit Bank (LTCB)'s demise, this augurs well for the Big Bang's success.

LTCB, which, for so long, played fairy godmother to the infamous Mr. Takahashi, has now not only floundered but irretrievably sunk. Despite the government protestations that LTCB was solvent and despite massive taxpayers' subsidies, it folded in Japan's largest post-World War II bankruptcy. It even eclipsed the failure of Crown Leasing Corp., which folded in April 1997 with ¥1.3 trillion in debts. LTCB's management, instead of issuing writs against journalists and market analysts honestly commenting on its unseemly mess, should have addressed the mess which they themselves begat.

Japan Leasing, Japan's second-largest leasing company, collapsed two days after the government stopped subsidizing LTCB, Japan's 10th-largest bank and Japan Leasing's de facto parent. Japan Leasing had total liabilities of ¥2.4 trillion. Two other affiliates of LTCB are almost certain to share the fate of Japan Leasing.

So, of course, are many others. Japan's banks are struggling under the weight of ¥87.5 trillion in bad loans, and, with many close to failure, this is widely regarded as the largest crisis now facing the world economy. At the center of that crisis stood the LTCB, which had pleaded for public money to keep itself afloat until it effected a rescue merger—a takeover, effectively—with Sumitomo.

LTCB found humility too late in the day. Having broken so many banking rules in bankrupting itself (and others), the bank's belated promise to bail out three affiliates by writing off ¥520 billion in loans extended to them cut no ice with the government. LTCB was instead nationalized with the government making a forced purchase of its shares at a low price with the option to resell them in the future. This act-and the subsequent nationalizing of Nippon Credit-showed that the government was prepared to follow through on its promise to nationalize failed or failing banks by making a forced purchase of all of their common shares regardless of any shareholder protest. Again, this is portentous for the Big Bang.

As LTCB was being nationalized, 11 other major banks announced vast hidden losses on securities holdings-a major source of concern for their already shaky balance sheets. Fuji Bank disclosed the biggest loss of ¥580.5 billion, and Sakura Bank declared ¥498.5 billion losses.

The survivors have had to abandon their received culture. Sumitomo Trust's planned alliance with LTCB undermined investors' confidence in Sumitomo. Fearing a further decline in market credibility, Sumitomo Trust instead joined Sumitomo Bank's alliance with Daiwa Securities. This seems part of a more general strategy of strengthening alliances within traditional business groups, forming partial partnerships with foreign financial institutions through joint ventures, or, in the case of Tokai and Asahi, finding fresh domestic partners because they don't belong to any industrial group. It is also the beginning of an overdue rationalization of the industry.

The lack of alliances is one of Industrial Bank of Japan (IBJ)'s major problems. It, in fact, was the first to seek help from the $520 billion bank bailout fund which the government created with taxpayers' money. Prior to that, the banks had seemed reluctant to apply for the funds available, because of the tough conditions attached to the money. Other major Japanese banks are waiting to see what conditions the government attaches to the IBJ's loan before they apply. Because such conditions might include implementing and admitting to past perfidies, they have been slow to follow the IBJ's lead. Asahi and Tokai, for example, are seeking mutual survival by focusing jointly on their traditional strength in services for smaller enterprises and retail clients.

This might be just a choice of hanging together or hanging separately. Their merger plans include consolidating operations and branches in and outside Japan, boosting their equity stake in each other, and cooperating in new financial services and products, such as private banking, investment trusts, and derivatives and forming a holding company, which will also call for participation from other financial institutions. First, however, they must solve a more immediate problem before their true genius can shine in all its splendor. They must completely dispose of their massive bad loans.

If they can do this, the combination of Asahi and Tokai would be a formidably large force in the domestic retail banking market. Tokai is Japan's seventh-largest commercial bank in assets and has an extensive retail network in central Japan. Asahi, Japan's eighth-largest commercial bank, has a branch network particularly strong in the eastern area of Japan, including Tokyo. They would, in other words, complement each other in terms of strategic location.

Their assets would total ¥61.2 trillion, putting them second only to those of BTM among Japanese commercial banks. The combined force would rank first in several categories of core domestic services, such as outstanding loans to smaller enterprises, outstanding loans to individuals, outstanding deposits by retail clients, and the number of pension accounts they handle.

However, before they could shine, they would have to deal with Japan's core problem. Asahi has about ¥1 trillion in bad loans and Tokai has a further ¥1.22 trillion in bad loans. Because neither bank is thinking of applying for public funds to help write off its bad loans, the markets are interested to see how they intend to clear them.

LTCB's death throes raise some interesting and pertinent questions. Its proposed alliance with UBS incorporated three joint ventures, in asset management, investment banking, and private banking. It also included a 1% cross-shareholding—the first between a

Japanese and non-Japanese bank. Other foreign banks quickly followed suit. In perhaps the most significant of these moves, Travelers, the American financial services group, took a 25% stake in Nikko Securities. More generally, although these moves were designed to give Western institutions rapid access to Japanese markets, they also raise the quandary as to how they can manage any liability their Japanese partners beget them.

The government's reaction to LTCB's demise is of more note. LTCB was not a weak bank in the narrow sense. It was quite innovative but remained heavily exposed to the nonperforming construction sector. Still, this was enough to make Moody's downgrade its subordinated debt to junk-bond status.

In today's turbulent times, Moody's will probably be demoting other JFIs as well. Despite the huge losses overseas hedge funds have suffered from the Russian and Asian financial crises, many new instruments investing in these foreign funds are being launched in Japan. The new instruments are mostly "funds of funds," which invest in several different types of hedge funds to reduce risk. Many of them guarantee principal.

Super Hedge Fund released by Daiwa Securities and managed by Deutsche Bank has gathered in more than ¥20 billion. Though people can invest as little as $1,000, principal is not secured. New Japan Securities' products do guarantee principal in U.S. dollars. Given that the net assets of Daiwa Securities' Super Hedge Fund and the fund futures of Nikko Securities both plunged by about 10% after being released onto the market, it is not at all clear if these companies have the required expertise to successfully face the challenges the Big Bang will unfold.

In the case of Daiwa, the net assets have already dropped below the level of total initial investments. If the poor showings of hedge funds continue, assets will continue to dip further. If investors cancel their funds under such circumstances, they will lose part of the principal—and further erode confidence in the Big Bang in the process.

The mechanism of management discontinuation is also adopted by most funds securing principals. However, since assets are moved to deposits, worthwhile yields cannot be expected with the currently low interest rates. There will also be exchange risk when the dollar-term principal is converted to yen. Again, it is not at all clear that the required expertise is there to deal with these contingencies.

Even Nomura seems to be in trouble in this regard. Its much-vaunted financial engineering division brought it huge losses in 1998. Nomura had to inject $380 million of equity capital and $150 million of subordinated debt into Nomura Holding America Inc. to help offset pretax losses of about $700 million.

Nomura has been at the forefront of the securitization business on both sides of the Atlantic. This does not look encouraging for the British end of Nomura, which has been buying up everything from pubs to defense land and betting shops, downsizing the management, and then securitizing the assets. As well as paying for its exposure to the securitization market, Nomura also appears to have lost heavily in emerging markets, including $125 million in Russia.

Moody's cut Nomura Securities' long-term and short-term debt ratings, citing its financial difficulties. Nomura's long-term debt rating was reduced to A3 from A1 and its short-term debt rating to Prime-2 from Prime-1. The credit rating agency also put the brokerage's new A3 long-term rating under review for possible downgrade. Moody's cut the financial strength rating of Nomura Bank International Plc to D from D+.

If Nomura is the least bit wobbly, other Japanese institutions' viability must be extremely doubtful. No doubt the crass, competitive winds of the international marketplace will winnow them out. The divisiveness, rationalizations, traumas, and redundancies that ensue will, in the end, be good for Japan.

This differentiation between the strong and the weak, the viable and the nonviable is the beginning of the Big Bang. Although it will spell the end for some of the outmoded keiretsu, it will open a door of opportunity for other companies and conglomerates, both domestic and foreign. It will, therefore, despite the odds, help secure the future for Japan.

Brave New World

Since the War, Japan has thrived by selling cars, camcorders, and cameras to the world and by using the foreign exchange these products earned to buy oil, food, and other vital necessities. This strategy has proved beneficial to Japan: much more so than the military adventurism that characterized its foreign policy from 1930 to 1945. Japan's postwar leaders made good strategic decisions that have continued to benefit the entire Japanese people down to the present day.

Japan must now make new but equally important strategic decisions. Japan faces a new international environment requiring a different strategy to ensure national survival and advancement. The world is glutted with cars, camcorders, and cameras, Japan's traditional exports. Though new products are needed to replace the old export earners, these products must be of a different nature if they are to recapture lost markets. Japan must develop and export services, financial services in particular. Japan needs to successfully implement the Big Bang to remain competitive in financial services, one of the keys to success in the new millennium. Although information technology, telecommunications, and other future-oriented industries will continue to grow in importance, unless Japan gets her financial reforms through, she will be in no position to avail of the opportunities these other industries offer.

This new millennium presents Japan with new and diverse challenges. Two large blocs, NAFTA and the EU, stand poised to dominate the financial and commercial worlds. The United States which, since the Second World War, has been forced to be both the policeman and economic dynamo of the Free World, will benefit when Europe assumes its fair share of the costs of maintaining global stability. It has taken two world wars, several long-lasting recessions, and many brave political leaders to achieve it. But it has been achieved. Europe is at peace and her peace will enrich the world.

America can be pleased with Europe. Together, they will be able to fulfill the high expectations of their 600 million citizens. Although they will have their differences on all conceivable trade-related issues, they share a common vision for the future. Pettier squabbles will not get in the way of that.

Across the Pacific, it is a different story. Two great nations vie for the political and economic respect they believe their vast populations warrant. They feel that the international order has short-changed them. They are making their grievances felt throughout Asia and, from Asia, throughout the world. Their vast armies and unhealed grievances threaten the international order the emerging European and American-brokered stability would otherwise augur.

Those two countries are India and China. The collapse of the Soviet Empire has caused a power void at the heart of Asia. The key strategic question is how that void will be filled. The Europeans have, however belatedly, devised a peaceful division of labor among themselves. Germany, in essence, makes the machinery, France takes care of the politics, and Britain takes care of the money. Germany, France, and Britain, for so many centuries at odds with one another, have learned, however belatedly, to benefit by living in peace.

Japan should coax Asia into replicating this strategy. She must convince Asia's other great powers, China in particular, that EU-style cooperation is the best path to future prosperity. This will take a major diplomatic effort by Japan and her allies. They must convince China that, even though she lies at the center of East Asia, she cannot dominate Asia, no more than Germany can dominate Europe. China's massive food and energy needs force her to engage with the world. China must acquire her necessities either by force or by trade. A vibrant Asia will allow China to secure her needs through trade. A depressed Asia might well mean that China's bellicose saber rattling degenerates into further adventurism in the South

China Sea and beyond.

Japan cannot say that she was not warned of China's potential to wreak havoc. Napoleon famously warned that one day China would wake and threaten the world. That day has not yet dawned. Maybe it will never dawn. Maybe America's superior military technology will convince her that she cannot win an arms race. If America's military and economic muscle were reinforced by Japan's economic strength, then China would not be so belligerent. She would see the benefits of constructive involvement and cooperation.

The EU offers Asia a model of competitive cooperation among a small number of medium-ranking states of near-equality and a slightly larger number of satellite ministates. The EU model is a working reality that the mid-European states are eager to join. It is a model that pragmatic Asian politicians, the Japanese ones in particular, should be able to emulate.

The Asians can copy the EU model if they obey a few ground rules. The labor must be equitably and intelligently spread around to avoid charges of neocapitalism, exploitation, and the rest. Specialization must occur and, in the process, many oversheltered industries will have to die. Most critically for our purposes, one country must act as premier banker to the rest. That country must be Japan. Japan, like Britain, has the political stability that such a center demands. She has the financial resources, almost infinitely vaster than Britain's. All she needs is the expertise, which Britain has in abundance. Once she acquires the know-how, she is the preeminent candidate to assume the financial leadership of Asia. The world needs Japan to anchor Asia. Once Japan financially anchors the region, the other pieces might well fall into place quickly. The new millennium might then bring the same peace and prosperity to Asia that the EU has brought to Europe. The proverbial swords might then more easily be turned into tractors, cars, cameras, camcorders, and the other capital and consumer goods Japan excels at making.

A hard-working Asia, bankrolled by Japan, would be a worthy complement to NAFTA and the EU. It would open up all sorts of vistas, centered on the idea of hope, which is at the heart of economic progress. It would mean the amelioration of the region's poverty, which currently stalks China, India, Indonesia, and Japan's other great neighbors. It would mean a community of Asian nations, working in harmony, not being stuck in the old groove of trying to gain at one another's expense. It would ultimately mean that Asia would take its rightful place as the lodestar of the new millennium.

The alternative to this idyll is a return to the great game scenario of the nineteenth century where India, China, Russia, the United States, and the other regional powers become locked into an ultimately self-destructing game for regional hegemony. Such a scenario would entail the permanent deployment of the U.S. 7th Fleet in the East China Sea. It would mean the continued militarization of Korea; it would mean continued nuclear war tensions between Pakistan and India. It would entail a permanent diversion of Asia's hard-won dollars into arms buying and other wasteful expenditures. It is a scenario that ultimately benefits nobody.

On the micro level, it would mean an escalation of the violence that accompanied the fall of Suharto in Indonesia. The mobs, goaded by political opportunists, would again run wild, venting their spleen on that nation's ethnic and religious minorities. Such attacks can have a snowball attack. India, Pakistan, Malaysia, and Indonesia have all witnessed such violence on massive scales. The longer Asia stays in recession, the higher is the probability of a return to mass slaughter and the extremist brand of politics that accompanies it. Japan, alone among the Asian powers, has it in her power to halt that slide into the abyss.

Japan literally holds the key to Asia's success in her national purse. Hong Kong and Singapore, Japan's two most obvious competitors for regional supremacy, simply do not have the critical financial and logistical mass a major world financial center demands. Japan alone has the necessary wherewithal to assume this leadership position. Only she can drag Asia out of its economic and financial morass. And she can do that only if the Big Bang is successful.

Simply put, if the Big Bang succeeds, Asia will not only recover but will regain the phenomenal growth rates and accompanying peace of recent years as well. Conversely, if the Big Bang fails, regional tensions will continue to fester, instability will continue to haunt the continent, and all of Asia will lose. Asia's recovery will not, in other words, happen until Japan' Big Bang is successfully implemented.

Japan is faced with a dilemma. Having resolutely refused to don the mantle of international leadership since 1945, she now finds herself being forced to assume the leadership position her economic prowess demands. This is an opportunity that most major powers have literally killed for. Japan is being offered not a poisoned chalice but an economic Holy Grail: the chance to be master of her own destiny for the foreseeable future. The cost being demanded is small: she is being asked only to be politically mature and politically responsible. It is a small price being asked for a big prize, the prize of being Asia's economic lodestar for the coming decades.

Japan must first of all push through these reforms. She must bankroll Asia by adopting global standards, not by the shoddy standards and practices of the past. This calls for the kind of resolute leadership that Japan has hitherto lacked. The risks attendant to this leadership would be short-term in nature. Just as at the time of the Meiji Restoration, she has many friends in Europe and America prepared to help her. Japan should continue to listen and continue to reform. The Meiji leaders knew the consequences of both success and failure. They were prepared to learn, to reform, to start anew, and, most importantly, to take nothing for granted

Japan cannot take for granted the prize of being Asia's financial center as theirs by right. Other contenders hover in the wings. Singapore and Hong Kong are putting up credible challenges of their own and might well win out by default. Simply put, unless the Big Bang reforms are resolutely adopted in spirit as well as in the letter of the law, Japan will lose this golden opportunity to revitalize herself and Asia as well. Singapore and Hong Kong will fill the breach. Japan cannot afford to stall. She must push the entire package of reforms through as speedily as she can.

To succeed, she needs courage. Japan needs the political leadership and political self-confidence necessary for constructive engagement in Asia. Japan must stake her claim and resolutely push forward with the reforms necessary to make that claim a reality. Only when the Big Bang is successfully implemented can her financial houses emulate the earlier experiences of Toyota, Sony, and Honda. Only then can the Japanese financial institutions command the same international respect that the other major Japanese brand names do.

Only then can Japan earn the extra revenue she will need in the years ahead. If she delays the reforms, she will find herself as obsolete as her financial system now is. Given the growing demands on Japan's shrinking national purse, that is a doomsday scenario.

Japan must bite the bullet and push through the Big Bang reforms as thoroughly as she pushed through other epoch-making changes in the past. As she assumes economic leadership in Asia, she must also change the nature of her currency. She must internationalize the yen and put it on a par with the euro and the dollar. The yen must become as significant in the Asian region as the dollar and the euro are in theirs. For this to happen, Japan must be constructively engaged in Asia. She must forge stronger alliances with the other key regional players and copy the EU experience. Japan must push through her own reforms and get other regional players to follow suit. Japan must have the vision, foresight, and perseverance to overcome the old enmities and jealousies her neighbors harbor against her. She must also impress on them the need to push through with their own reforms.

Japan is at a crossroads. She is being asked either to resolutely reform or to face the consequences of remaining glued to outmoded ways. The nationalization of LTCB and similar financial dodos has shown that the government is choosing, however guardedly, the path of reform. They are being wise and prudent. Because they are opening a window to future opportunity, they are allowing future leaders to build on a sound basis.

They are, of course, only building on the prudent strategic choices of their predecessors, who chose the path of constructive competition in 1945. Japan owes much of her postwar success to her alliance with the United States. The successful implementation of the Big Bang will allow that relationship to continue to flower to the benefit of both. American FIs have a lot to teach their Japanese counterparts, who are becoming increasingly eager learners. Some of them, like Nomura Securities, could teach the Americans a thing or two themselves. Where Nomura is pioneering, other JFIs will follow. The result will be a smaller number of JFIs, organized along American lines and able to compete for the high-value-added business that is currently the forte of the Americans. The laggards are being weeded out and Nomura and the other viable entities will find their natural place in the international financial system. The Japanese can, once again, thank American competition for that.

They can also thank the Americans for the free and easy access to their markets. America remains the biggest and freest market in the world and the JFIs, once they are properly restructured in accordance with the Big Bang reforms, will once more enjoy the profits America offers. This will help to reverse the considerable advantage America currently enjoys in exporting her banking and other financial services to Japan.

Although this will lead to some trade squabbles, these will be of no real consequence. America, with her many and varied worldwide interests, needs a successful Big Bang to allow her own business interests to proceed smoothly to their natural levels. Though angry words might be exchanged from time to time, dollars will also be exchanged. The difference this time is, though the bucks will continue to circulate in Japan, they will do so to the benefit of all. Japan's people will continue to benefit from the American link.

So too will America. A stable and vibrant nation on the far side of the Pacific, engaging in healthy competition, operating by the common sense rules that underwrite both global standards and the Big Bang reforms, will be good for America and the world-view America represents. It will mean that American FIs will have to continually strive to retain their competitive edge against the reconstituted JFIs. It will mean that American foreign policy makers can sleep some way easier at night, knowing that Japan is playing her proper role in Asia. It will, in short, mean a better world. Japan must make not only the next move but many, many more moves after that. Revitalizing Japan, overcoming her present inertia is, after all, what the Big Bang blueprint is all about.

ABOUT THE AUTHOR

Declan Hayes is Professor of International Business at Tokyo's
Sophia University, where he lectures in the undergraduate and
postgraduate Business and Economics programs. He has previously
worked in Australia, Ireland, and Mexico during their financial
upheavals, and has written extensively on the economic changes in
the economies of those countries. He holds a Ph.D. from
Australia's Trobe University and M.A. and M.Litt. degrees from
Trinity College, Dublin.